F*CKBOYS

A DARK REVENGE ROMANCE

HEIDI STARK

Copyright © 2024 by Heidi Stark.

All rights reserved.

No part of this publication may be reproduced, distributed, or transmitted in any form or by any means, including photocopying, recording, or other electronic or mechanical methods, without the prior written permission of the publisher, except for brief excerpts for review purposes, or as permitted by U.S. copyright law. For permission requests, contact heidi@heidistarkauthor.com.

The story, all names, characters, and incidents portrayed in this production are fictitious. No identification with actual persons (living or deceased), places, buildings or products is intended or should be inferred.

Contents

Author's Note

F^{*ckboys} contains several themes that might be triggering for some readers:

- graphic violence including torture and mutilation

- graphic sex scenes

- mentions of childhood bullying

- suicidal ideation

- mention of sexual assault, including flashbacks

- unfaithfulness/cheating (allegations, none between the two main characters)

Reader discretion is strongly advised.

This book *does* contain a guaranteed happily ever after.

Sign up for the latest on new releases, promotions and other important updates at https://subscribepage.io/heidistarkauthor.

Join me on social media:

Facebook: @heidistarkauthor

Instagram: @heiditstarkauthor

TikTok: @heidistark_author

Goodreads: https://www.goodreads.com/author/show/22799159.Heidi_Stark

Bookbub: https://www.bookbub.com/authors/heidi-stark

Heidi Stark's Book Group: https://www.facebook.com/groups/heidistarksbookgroup/

For everyone who dreams of something bigger and/or better.
Even if that thing is a dick.
If you can't find what you're seeking in real life, may it always be available in book form.

And to anyone who has ever thought they wanted revenge, only to channel that energy into something way better. I see you.

"Vengeance is in my heart, death in my hand, blood and revenge are hammering in my head."

-William Shakespeare

"The best revenge is massive success."

-Frank Sinatra

Prologue

The vast event space pulsates with people but I immediately spot him. Even through the bustling crowd, he's hard to miss with his meticulously styled dark hair and his icy blue eyes that seem to sear into my soul. He's well-dressed as usual, too. Always making sure he has the latest pair of sneakers and designer jeans, and fitted T-shirts that cling to his muscular figure in all the right places. Only the best for him. Even I have to admit he looks good.

He's engaging, and his ability to make people feel like they're the only person in the room is second to none. But he's the only person who he treats so well. His outward persona is merely a façade, a mask carefully curated for the outside world, because within, he's a predator, a connoisseur of suffering. Everyone else is second-class according to him. Especially women. In fact, in his eyes, women are just vessels to satiate his hunger, to be discarded without a second thought.

While I slipped in discreetly in order to observe him from afar, I hope he notices me while I'm here. Not that he knows me yet, but he will very soon. In fact, I yearn for him to feel my presence. After all, I'm going to make him pay for what he's done. I've known many men like him, and I know the person he's hurt most recently. She's a human, not just a statistic, and his actions damn near destroyed her. He's going to feel more pain than most humans could bear, and I'm going to make it last, because he deserves it for what he's done. Though we are strangers now, he will soon know me intimately. I am the harbinger of retribution, and he will pay for the agony he's inflicted.

There aren't many people who generate this kind of hate in a stranger, but he's managed to invoke mine.

I don't just want to destroy his mind and body, I want to destroy his soul, and every trace that he ever existed.

In fact, I think I'm going to save him for second to last.

Because there's only one person I hate more.

Chapter 1

FALLON

Fuckboys.

We might not all know them by that name, but nearly all of us have almost certainly met at least one in our lifetimes.

The dictionary's definition of a fuckboy is a 'weak or contemptible man' or 'a man who has many casual sexual partners'.

In my view, there's nothing wrong with the second definition here, as long as everyone knows what they're getting into. I prefer to go with the internet's top offerings—'a guy who lies to girls so he can pull as much as possible', 'the male version of a thot', or even better, 'a low value male who is only good for hookups.'

After all, this is where the traditional dictionary gets it wrong. Because the entire premise of the fuckboy lifestyle is based on deceit and a one-sided understanding of relationship dynamics. Some might say 'Don't hate the player, hate the game', but it's my prerogative to despise both.

In the open, I run workshops designed to help people identify and free themselves from toxic fuckboy behavior. But underground, in the shadows, I run a very different operation. That's why I've made it my life's mission to exact revenge on the worst offenders. You see, I operate a clandestine business where I help the people who have been most wronged by these contemptible individuals who are mostly, but not always, men. You see, I seek revenge on behalf of others. I hunt them down and systematically ruin them. Just like they did to their victims.

This service isn't intended for your run-of-the-mill narcissistic loser who has purposely inflicted a certain amount of hurt feelings. No, this is for the ones who methodically destroy the self-esteem of the women they're with to the point they're forever changed. And sometimes it goes much further than that. I may not be able to pick up all the pieces, but I'll damn well try. I'm a firm believer that the punishment needs to fit the crime. An eye for an eye type of thing. No need to go overboard.

Some might believe that we should let karma take the wheel, and eventually the fuckboy will get their just desserts. But that's not guaranteed or timely, and sometimes the universe needs a little, or very large, nudge. That's why I do what I do.

I take my place at the sleek steel podium I selected to convey that my company means serious business. It gleams under the bright overhead lights that illuminate the intimate lecture theater in my office building.

The crowd murmurs with eager anticipation at what I'm about to say, many of them already sitting with pens poised above spiral notebooks. A few even have laptops open ready to type what I say verbatim. I'm certain most of them are going to hang onto every word so I know I need to be precise with my language.

Tiered seating ensures all attendees have a clear view of the projector screen, whiteboard, and of course the speaker, which is currently me. It's a far cry from when I used to run these sessions in the cramped living room at my tiny old apartment. It's taken me time and tenacity to work my way up to this point, and I'm proud of what I've achieved.

My childhood best friend and current assistant, Mia, smiles and nods with encouragement as she hands me the microphone.

"Hello everyone," I beam at the crowd. "Thank you so much for coming to today's bootcamp. I can assure you it's going to be an informative and enlightening session.

Many of you will find our time together challenging because of the information we'll be covering. At some points, you may find yourself feeling frustrated or angry or hurt. Perhaps even a little sheepish or ashamed. But that's no reflection on you, and these emotions are completely understandable.

You are merely going through the cycle of grief associated with freeing yourself from the conditions that have been holding you back."

I glance around the hushed room, making eye contact with as many people as I can to convey the seriousness of my words.

"Now to begin with, let's ground ourselves. Why are we here today?"

All eyes are fixed on me. There is no texting, no whispered small talk between attendees. This isn't like a college lecture theater where people are phoning it in and showing up just to get their attendance checked off. Everyone wants to know what I have to say on this topic. And they're paying for it, too. This course isn't cheap.

I press my lips together as I nod at the eager crowd. "We're here to break down the profile of a fuckboy. The myths, the legends, the ways they treat us. And how we can free ourselves from our current situations. How we can heal as quickly and as thoroughly as possible, and most importantly, how we can prevent ourselves from ever getting into this type of dilemma again."

I take a moment to pause and let my words sink in.

"Now, we've all had our own interactions with one of them, and that's why we're here, right?"

People nod and murmurs of affirmation are heard around the room.

"I can't hear you. We've all had our own interactions with at least one fuckboy. Am I right?"

Someone calls out 'you can say that again!' And another yells 'Lying cheating asshole!'

I smile and let out a small laugh that creates a husky effect in the microphone.

"That's the spirit. Well, welcome to my course. I'm so glad all of you have made the decision to be here today. I can promise you, it's going to change your life like it has for the many thousands who have passed through these doors before you. Now, are you ready to be transformed?"

The room erupts with applause. The crowd nods and smiles and there's the odd 'hell yeah!' and 'let's go!'

I scan the room again, navigating my way to the front of the podium.

"To begin with, what do we know about fuckboys? First of all, they're not a one-size-fits-all, cookie cutter model. They span a wide range of backgrounds. However..." I punctuate the air with my finger, "they share a number of key traits which enable us to spot them a mile away. If..." I pause for effect, "we know what we're looking for."

I gaze down at the floor. "Unfortunately, more often than not, this tends to happen in hindsight. But today, we're going to bring these commonalities to light so we can be proactive when we see these signs."

I click my remote, and bullet points appear on the oversized projector screen that illuminates the wall to my left.

"Fuckboys first and foremost are pretenders. Illusionists. Many of them will go so far as to embellish key aspects of their lives. For many, the first deception will be about their career. When claiming a career, they will often gravitate toward occupations involving what they believe to be impressive job titles associated with significant income. Think engineers, medical students, businessmen.

Where do they hang out? They're often, but not always, found at the gym or at least talking about it. But you could just as easily find them in your local cafe or bookstore pretending to be the artistic, sensitive type, or at a club or bar with their friends.

What do they look like? Now, this is a trickier one. They're typically, but not always, very physically attractive. However, in some cases, they may not be physically attractive at all, but instead they're exceptionally charismatic and confident. A big dick syndrome, if you will. In any case, they're almost guaranteed to be prettier on the outside than the inside.

As I mentioned before, fuckboys come from all shapes and sizes and backgrounds. This extends to intelligence. They span all intelligence levels, although from TV it would be easy to assume they're usually dumb as a box of rocks. This simply isn't true. The less intelligent ones are just easier to pick out."

The audience nods and murmurs in agreement, and I catch a few people glance at each other with knowing looks.

"Let's talk about their behavior now. They're of course prone to lying and cheating. They're quick to block you on social media, and ghosting is one of their special skills. If social media trickery was a subject in school, your average fuckboy would have a Ph.D.

Now, some people ask me, are fuckboys just sex-positive people who are open about having many partners?" I shake my head vehemently. "The answer is no, absolutely not. This is not ethical non-monogamy. This is not polyandry or polygamy. This is lying-to-your-face, narcissistic bullshit where one person is manipulated and deceived so the other person can get whatever gratification they are seeking. This is not sexual empowerment or freedom. It is a complete and total power imbalance designed to destabilize and destroy the innocent party."

A dark-haired woman in the third row raises her hand. I gesture toward her. "You have a question? Welcome! Introduce yourself with your name and why you're here, and then please go ahead with your question."

"Thank you! Hi everyone, I'm Cindy." She smiles nervously and waves around the room, but then her smile turns into a frown and she looks at the floor. "I'm here because I just found out my boyfriend of two years has been cheating on me with countless other women throughout our entire relationship. He recently told me he wants to end things, but he keeps popping back up and I keep letting him back in. I know I need to get out of it but I don't know how."

The crowd murmurs with sympathy and several people shake their heads. This seems to spur Cindy on and she returns her gaze to me. "Why do they engage in these behaviors? What's their motivation? How could he hurt me like this and not just be honest from the start about what he wanted, and why would he choose now to break things off? I guess that's my main question, why now?"

"An excellent question, Cindy," I nod, smiling at her in a gesture of empathy. "First of all, I'm sorry you've had to endure that, but thankfully you're here and we're here to help. To answer your main question, typically a fuckboy will end things for one of two reasons. The first is that he will often ghost once he gets what he wants. This can range from a one-night stand or general sexual gratification to full-blown financial exploitation, gold-digging, theft and even extortion. So while for many, an interaction with a fuckboy might only last a matter of hours or days, it sounds like you're one of the not so lucky people who's secured yourself a long-hauler."

Cindy puts her face in her palm and shakes her head, her cheeks reddening under the sympathetic gazes of her fellow attendees.

"Whatever you've been able to provide for the last two years has been enough for him to keep stringing you along—be it financial support, emotional security—hell, even sex even when he's also getting it from somewhere else."

I write 'GHOSTING' in large capital letters on the whiteboard with a dark blue marker. By the embarrassed look on Cindy's face, I'm almost certain she's been covering some loser's living expenses and providing whatever emotional support he's been lacking elsewhere in his life for the past two years.

"And the second reason may be that he believes you're close to blowing his cover. That you're onto him. No matter how slick he thinks he is, a fuckboy's ultimate fear is of being caught in his lies before he gets to be the one to run. So the fact you've discovered his cheating and have either confronted him about it, or he can sense you are about to, is enough to make him run."

I add 'BLOWN COVER' to the whiteboard. "Does that answer your question?"

Cindy nods with enthusiasm. "Yes, yes it does. Thank you!" She takes a seat once again.

I glance back over the crowd. "Okay, so what are some of the other common behaviors we see in these individuals? Let's go over a few common attributes."

On cue, Mia pulls up the next slide in the presentation featuring a series of bullet points outlining the most common fuckboy behaviors.

"They often claim they're not into what they like to call the 'relationship bullshit,' which is a way of avoiding any type of commitment that's not on their terms. You might find yourself constantly having to text them first because they claim they 'forgot'. Or maybe they are excellent at remembering to text you something like 'hi' or 'what you doing' first thing in the morning every day—often a simple 'wyd' because it's faster than typing the whole thing out—and they're mass sending it to their roster of women. And then you hear zip zilch nada from them until the following morning when you receive basically the same message again."

Some bitter laughs ring out around the room.

"It sounds like that hit a little close to home for some of you?" I quirk an eyebrow and see several people nod as well as a few wry grins. "Again, no judgment here! We've all been there."

A couple of audience members look palpably relieved, their shoulders lifting at the realization they're not alone.

"Fuckboys will say the same lines to multiple girls at the same time, making each and every one of them feel like they're their one and only special person.

Some of them are particularly confusing. They will accuse you of clinginess at the slightest sign of interest from you in anything more than casual sex, but will come running if they think you've moved on."

I see several nods in the crowd. A couple of women turn to each other and shake their heads, and I can tell my words are resonating. I nod to Mia and she clicks to the next slide which features the logos of several of the most popular dating apps, resulting in nods of recognition from the crowd.

"They'll play games on dating apps just to boost their egos. Whether they act on anything or not is up to the individual and the specific circumstances, but there's a high chance that regardless of their relationship status their profiles will remain active on these platforms. This ensures they have a backup and a steady supply of victims who are easily accessible to them at all times. If and when they do decide to ghost you. Which they will almost certainly do at some point when it benefits them."

Mia flashes the next slide with logos of messaging apps known for providing temporary communications that automatically delete after a short period of time.

"Some of them will insist on only speaking with you through Snapchat or other similar apps so their communication with you isn't permanent and doesn't show up on their phone bill. This particularly applies to the married ones, but we'll get to that. The older fuckboys will try to insist on using something called Kik.

Regardless of what they choose to use, they're quick to delete or clear messages so they don't leave a trace.

But it's a free country, right?" I shrug and purse my lips. "Nobody can force someone to become emotionally invested in a casual relationship. So why do we care if they don't want to get serious?"

A new slide flashes up, this one featuring a series of images of emotionally distraught people.

"These are not victimless crimes, of course, or none of us would be here. So who are the victims? These men aren't just screwing over single women. They can also be in serious relationships including marriage. Their behavior can become worse with age and is often accentuated by a mid-life crisis. And like I said, this is a non-judgmental environment... except of course when it comes to the fuckboys themselves... you see, side chicks can get fucked over, too."

I see a couple of shocked faces in the crowd, as well as a few nods.

"Hmm, what else...". I look over at Mia. She clicks to the next slide and I glance up at the large projector screen.

"Ah, yes. Perhaps the most important part of all. What are the impacts of a fuckboy? Why is this an issue? There's an enormous range, here, depending on the specific variety that snares you in their trap. At the mildest, their behavior can lead to hurt feelings and a sense that you've wasted time getting to know them and engaging in whatever your relationship consists of while it lasted. It can be mildly embarrassing and you can pick yourself up and move on quite quickly. But it can also extend to degradation and humiliation... the unwanted kind," I wink at the crowd resulting in a few snickers, "depression, financial ruin, drug or alcohol addiction." My tone grows hushed. "Even suicide."

A few people gasp.

"This is serious stuff, folks. Which is why we run these sessions. To help you to identify your own situation and get out of it as quickly as possible before it escalates, and to prevent it from ever happening again."

While the audience remains very engaged in my presentation, I sense the energy in the room could benefit from some curated audience interaction.

"What did your fuckboy do to you, Katherine, if you don't mind sharing with the group?" I point at an attractive woman in her late twenties who is sitting in the third row of the audience. Mia walks over and hands her the microphone.

Katherine's hand is shaking but her voice is clear as she describes her situation. "He… he cheated on me repeatedly and got me fired from my job when I broke up with him."

I shake my head and frown. "I'm so sorry that happened to you, Katherine. And how did that make you feel? If you could share with the group it would be very helpful."

Katherine looks down at the ground, obviously close to tears.

"His behavior was pretty awful, right?" I prompt her. "Come on. Share with the group."

She sniffs and nods. "I was devastated and I still am. Nobody will hire me in my industry after the rumors he spread. He sent letters to my work, and even showed up in person a couple of times."

"And maybe you felt a bit ashamed that you fell for it?" I glance at her, an eyebrow lifted.

She nods again. "I feel like an idiot for putting myself in that position. He acted badly and then punished me for it afterwards."

Sympathetic glances and murmurs of support pour in Katherine's direction.

"Now, you're a catch, Katherine." I turn to face the class. "You see, Katherine here is a very smart woman. Graduated magna cum laude from an Ivy League school and later received her MBA from a top-tier business school. Was on a great career trajectory and was on track to be one of the most successful businesspeople in her industry. Hardly anything to sniff at. She's obviously gorgeous, and I can tell you from personal experience she's also funny and kind." I pause and shake my head.

"But here she is, sniffling in front of us because some waste of space, who probably has only a sixteenth of her IQ or potential, displayed classic fuckboy tendencies, and she fell for them. And then he got vindictive when he realized the gig was up. His cover was blown. My reason for sharing all of Katherine's accolades isn't to blow smoke up her ass or even to alleviate her tears. No, it's to show you that even the best and brightest among us have the potential to fall for this shit, and often do."

I always find someone like Katherine and get their permission to showcase their story early on in the program. It helps the other audience members to let their guards down and get over the shameful, embarrassed feelings that prevent them from truly addressing their own situations. The thought of losing a job or worse is often enough to spur some kind of action, or at least recognition that change is needed.

"So how do we avoid these men?" I look at the crowd, my expression inquisitive. "Some would say the best way to avoid attracting a fuckboy is to stay off the dating apps and enter the dating pool otherwise known as the friend zone. After all, isn't that where we keep the people who we have the most trust in? At least, that's what I thought. And I was very wrong. But that's a story for another day...".

The rest of the day's seminar goes off without a hitch. Thanks to Mia, all the materials are in perfect order. My delivery is strong and, after the course material is completed, several attendees approach to thank me and share how they're going to put my advice into practice.

"Another session done. You crushed it," smiles Mia as she helps me to pick up the last of the course materials in the lecture theater. "We've already had five referrals and two sign-ups for the advanced course. At this rate we're going to need a bigger lecture theater!"

I smile, but it turns into a frown as the alarm on my phone goes off reminding me of my obligations for the evening. "If only family dinners went as smoothly as these sessions."

I switch off the light as we walk out of the theater together and head back toward the main office area.

"Oh yeah, that's tonight," nods Mia. "I was going to see if you wanted to grab a drink down the street. No problem, though. We'll do that another time. Hi to your family and good luck." She gives me a knowing look.

"Thank you," I reply. "I have a feeling I'm going to need it."

Chapter 2

FALLON

"Well, look who we have here. I was waiting for you to come crawling back." My father, Colton Dempsey, runs a hand through his meticulously coiffed salt-and-pepper hair. His navy blue suit is like a uniform, crisp and perfectly molded to his imposing figure. He's even wearing a pocket square which I'm sure my stepmother picked out for him. He's a handsome man who exudes confidence whether he's negotiating in the boardroom, playing golf at the country club or relaxing in his own palatial estate. He's also especially demanding in any setting.

"Dad, there's no need to be dramatic." I roll my eyes. "It's only been a month. You know I always come to dinner when I can, and I was just particularly busy with work." Not necessarily true. I've been avoiding coming around here until I couldn't put it off any longer. These dinners don't always leave me feeling great.

My stepmother, Zara, sniffs with disdain, as if she's miffed that I didn't take part in the family's weekly dinners. But if she's honest with herself, and if she removes the mask she puts on for my father's benefit, she's really thrilled that I haven't been able to make it. After all, that enables her to be the center of attention around my father and my four older brothers, all of whom she's far more enamored with than me. The fact we're around the same age probably doesn't help.

It's gross, the way she acts toward my brothers. She gets all giggly and tries to impress them with her latest recipes. It's almost like flirting, although I'm not sure that she would ever truly try to go there with any of them if the opportunity arose. Besides, they aren't that stupid, and I think they see right through her good stepmother act. They just have the common sense to play along in order to stay in my father's good graces. Whereas I'm not that restrained.

"Well, you know we have a weekly family dinner, Fallon," he says, his voice stern and disapproving. "We all have things going on in our lives, and your brothers manage to make it, rain or shine. If they're in the middle of a huge merger or acquisition, they don't use that as an excuse not to attend even though they could be dealing with many millions of dollars." His voice oozes with condescension as he continues. "Yet you are running this... dating website or whatever it is, and the slightest excuse has you skipping out on us for an entire month."

There it is. I'm my father's greatest shame. He's so dismissive of what I'm doing with my life. He had such high hopes for me after helping me to attend a prestigious business school to complete my MBA, and here I am running what he refers to as some kind of 'cute small dating business'. He has no idea of the impact I make, let alone the things I do behind the scenes, and I resent him for it.

"Dad," I sigh. "I've told you before, it's not a dating website. I help women, and occasionally others, who are trying to get out of bad situations. I empower them to make meaningful changes in their lives."

An annoying and familiar voice interjects from the sidelines. "Yeah right, Fal. You are a platform where bitter shrews can complain about fuckboys. Isn't that what they're called?" The youngest of my brothers, Lincoln, smirks, and I have the urge to smack the look right off his face. He takes great pleasure in teasing me, especially when it reinforces my dad's belief that I'm the 'worst' child. Lincoln, or Link for short, is the closest thing to a black sheep out of my four older brothers and he's committed to ensuring he doesn't drop into the place I currently hold.

"Yeah, well you sell unhealthy food to people," I scoff. "How many arteries have you clogged this year, Link?"

He rolls his eyes. "Oh come on, Fallon. You know we're committed to a national healthy eating program endorsed by the best and brightest, so get off your high horse."

Link runs a trendy national burger chain that's recently partnered with a well-known Olympic medalist and an award-winning musician. Sales have been off the charts despite the irony that neither of these celebrities have probably ever enjoyed a burger in their life. They're as hypocritical as Link is and he knows it. Still, for whatever reason my dad is vocally proud of his business, unlike mine.

"Let's agree to disagree," I sniff. "And my clients are not bitter shrews. They're vibrant, dynamic people who deserve love and happiness."

Link rolls his eyes.

"Can you two please knock it off?" Cheston speaks up, always the one trying to diffuse the animosity that inevitably sparks between me and Lincoln whenever we're in the same room. As the oldest brother, he's always played a role in placating the group. He's starting to look so much like dad it's uncanny, with his distinguished gray hair and the way his eyes crinkle at the corners when he smiles.

"Since when has Fallon ever known how to play nice?" Fenton, as usual, jumps to Link's defense. They're the closest in age, barely a year apart, and for whatever reason they always have each other's backs. Especially when it has something to do with me. To be honest, I'm envious of the close bond between them. As the only girl, I've always felt a bit jealous of the closeness between the guys, but especially with these two.

They even look so similar that people frequently mistake them for twins, although Fenton's hair is more of a sandy blond compared to Lincoln's own dark brown hair. They both have the same piercing green eyes and one dimple only. Lincoln's is on the left and Fenton's is on the right, making them some kind of mirror image of each other.

But when it comes down to personalities and our father's perception of what we've each achieved in our life, I'm definitely the one who is 'opposite.' The outcast, the maverick, the intruder in my own family. We have many family secrets, but this is not one of them.

"I do want to talk to you about the upcoming charity event in Palm Falls, Fallon," says my father. "I expect you will be attending to network on behalf of the company."

I sigh. Even though I've shied away from working for the family corporation on a day-to-day basis, my father likes to leverage me by having me attend events, especially ones that take place in the town where I grew up. He thinks there's an advantage in me being a 'girl' and going along to events like this and promoting the family name. It makes me uncomfortable, but I do it out of a sense of familial obligation, and the fact my father pays for my condo as well as providing me with loans for my growing business.

"Dad," I sigh, "I really would prefer not to go."

"Why? Are you afraid of seeing all your ex boyfriends?" Link tosses his head back in glee, eliciting a snort from Fenton.

"I have one ex-boyfriend from when I was at high school who might be there, Link." I narrow my eyes at him. "And I would have no problem being in the same room as Aksel King."

"Everyone knows that's a lie, Fal. You can see it all over your face."

"Whatever did happen to that guy, anyway?" Bronson speaks up for the first time. He's been oddly preoccupied tonight, rarely speaking, although he does have a tendency to try and stay out of our sibling drama as much as possible. Still, when he has to pick a side he usually goes with the other guys.

Here I am, surrounded by family, and as usual, I'm feeling alone. I glance at my stepmother, even though there's no hope that she'll side with me. She avoids eye contact, busying herself with an ornate napkin ring. So much for female solidarity.

"Come on, Fallon. This is important." My dad presses his lips into a thin line, one of the ways he conveys seriousness. "It's crucial to our bottom line that we are selected for the Eternity Development Project. Our acquisition of Stephenson Industries is resulting in some skepticism from the local council. We're seen as creating a bit of monopoly with this acquisition, and having you generate some goodwill would go a long way toward humanizing our operations and making it seem lower-risk to the local community." He pauses. "And besides, it would give you the opportunity to build up your client base in Palm Falls. I've been looking at your metrics recently, and you're not expanding at the rate we'd anticipated when I agreed to give you the loan."

I feel my cheeks redden at his mention of my company's performance. It's bad enough that he keeps track of my day-to-day earnings, but it's embarrassing when he recites the metrics in front of my brothers who are all involved in much more profitable pursuits. None of them seem to understand that growing a business takes reinvestment. And obviously there's an entire set of operations I can't share with them.

"That's not good, Fallon," Link pipes in, eager to jump on this new piece of information, with a condescending tone that mirrors my father's. "You know most small businesses fail within the first year or so. If you're already trending down, it sounds like you'll be scurrying back to Dempsey Industries before you can even say 'fuckboy'." He smirks.

His words sting and my skin crawls with indignation. "Very clever, Link. Good one." I roll my eyes. "But I'll have you know the business is growing far in excess of my expectations. I don't know what your financial advisors imagined as a reasonable ROI, Dad, but I think we're doing quite well. Our programs are regularly selling out and we're building quite a reputation."

On paper, I know the business looks like it's failing compared to his high financial expectations, but it's not just about the money for me. Neither my father nor my brothers are privy to the darker side of what I do. And if they were, they would never understand.

I sigh, eager to change the subject. "Fine, I'll go to this stupid gala. Although I really think you're overstating the benefits." I glance at my most annoying brother. "Pass the mashed potatoes, please, Link. With a side of shut the fuck up."

Chapter 3

FALLON

The opulent ballroom of the prestigious Palm Falls Grand Plaza Hotel is the perfect venue for tonight's black-tie charity gala, the only one in Palm Falls fancy enough to draw this group of attendees except for maybe the local country club.

The air is alive with the clinking of crystal champagne glasses and the murmur of conversations among Palm Falls' elite. Elaborate, sparkling chandeliers cast a soft glow on the polished marble floors, and the walls are adorned with modern art, creating an atmosphere of sophistication and elegance. Palm Falls may be a smaller town, but there's a lot of old money here and certainly enough pretentiousness to go around. I take a deep breath, the scent of expensive perfume and anticipation filling my lungs.

I move gracefully through the crowd, my sleek, form-fitting teal gown complementing my fiery red hair which cascades down my back in soft waves. The subtle click of my heels against the marble floor is drowned out by the ambient music and lively chatter, and I almost kick myself for wearing what must be the world's most uncomfortable pair of heels.

My heart thuds in my chest like a caged bird, but I keep my composure, refusing to let anyone see my vulnerability. He, of all people, doesn't need to know how I'm feeling inside. In addition to attending the event out of familial obligation, I have another reason for being here tonight. This is the perfect place, the perfect moment, to put my plan into action.

My piercing green eyes survey the room until they lock onto a figure that stands out amidst the sea of suits and gowns—Aksel King. Damn him. Even after all these years, his mere presence sends a shiver down my spine. Tall, imposing, and with an air of quiet power about him, Aksel looks every bit the part of the merciless businessman he's now rumored to be. He immediately notices me, his eyes locking onto mine, eliciting a shiver down my spine.

Even though I knew he was going to be here, his presence at the gala hits me like a tidal wave, drowning me in memories I'd rather forget. It's been several years since we've seen each other, with him working all over the globe and on the other side of the country for most of that time.

He stands across the room, whiskey tumbler in hand, exuding the same suave arrogance that once consumed my thoughts day and night. For a fleeting moment, I'm transported back to our high school and early college days—moments of passion and betrayal, and the ruthless competition that has defined us and always will.

The sparks of attraction that linger between us are now mingled with the embers of old rivalries and betrayals, creating an atmosphere charged with electricity. I can feel the curious glances from those around us, recognizing the potential collision of two powerful forces that haven't seen each other in some time.

"Fallon Dempsey," Aksel says, approaching me with a faint smirk playing on his lips.

"Hello, Aksel King," I say coolly as I approach him, my voice steady despite the turmoil within me.

"Didn't expect to see you here." His slate gray eyes appraise my body.

"Nor did I expect to see you, Aksel," I reply, lying because I knew he would be, struggling to maintain my composure. Those damned dimples still haunt me, even after all these years.

"Fallon," he replies, his voice low and smooth as silk, sending another involuntary shiver down my spine. "You look stunning."

"Thank you, but flattery will get you nowhere tonight," I retort, refusing to let him charm me like he has so many times before. I study his face, noting the faint lines that time has etched around his eyes and mouth, adding a touch of maturity to his once-youthful features.

"That's a shame," Aksel says with a hint of a smile, his eyes twinkling with mischief. "I was hoping we could put the past behind us and start anew... have a little reset, if you will..."

"Really?" I raise an eyebrow, not quite ready to let my guard down. "Or are you just trying to get information on the Eternity Development Project?"

His smile fades slightly, replaced by a more serious expression. "We're both here for the same reason, aren't we?"

The Eternity Development Project is all my father and brothers could talk about the other night when they weren't taking digs at my career choices. Everyone wants to get their hands on contracts for the multi-billion dollar reinvigoration of the second biggest city in the state. The biggest decision-makers for the project just happen to be residents of Palm Falls, and the wife of the head of the Project, Tony Farelli, runs all of the town's most prestigious events, including this one.

I clear my throat. "I'm here for business, King." His name rolls off my tongue like a curse.

"Likewise, Dempsey," he replies coolly. Despite his words, I can't help but notice how his eyes roam over me, lingering on the curves of my dress, and I hate that it excites me. He's not worth it. Not anymore.

"Your family's influence reaches far," I comment, trying to sound disinterested.

He chuckles darkly. "Everyone wants what we have." He takes a sip of his drink, his lips grazing the rim of the glass before he sets it down on the counter. "Your father sent you, I take it? You're here to butter up Farelli?" We may not have seen each other in years, but he knows me well enough to know I wouldn't attend an event like this by choice.

I nod once, keeping my mask in place. "And you as well?"

He takes another sip of whiskey from his etched crystal tumbler, and I can't help but check out his profile, his strong jaw and the way his eyebrows knit together when he's deep in concentration. The sight is so familiar, it hurts. "My family supports many causes."

"I doubt that," I say, my voice steady even as my insides churn. "Your grandmother's reputation precedes her. I'm sure every cause the Kings support is quite strategic."

His eyes rove over my body again. "The same could be said about your family."

Our gazes lock for a moment too long, sparks flying between us. The air sizzles with tension as we both remember our intense attraction. A slow burn builds between us, threatening to consume the entire room. I force myself to break the eye contact first.

"I suppose we could both benefit from being part of the Project," I concede in an attempt to divert the conversation to more comfortable territory. "It could be a good opportunity for a partnership. We're not in direct competition with our respective family businesses, and there's enough funding to support both of us being involved provided we push out some of the other players." I pause and narrow my eyes. "But don't think for a second that I've forgotten what happened between us. You may say you've changed, Aksel King, but I'm still the same Fallon Dempsey who swore she'd make you pay for your betrayal."

He holds my gaze, his own eyes darkening with a mixture of regret and something else—desire? I can't be sure. But as much as I hate to admit it, part of me wants to believe that he has changed, and that we could find a way to work together again. But I can't let my resolve falter just because he looks so damn handsome in his suit.

"Let's focus on the task at hand," I suggest, forcing myself to push aside my conflicting emotions. I glance over at Tony Farelli and Aksel follows my gaze with his own. "After all, there's only so much funding to go around, and both of our families have a lot at stake. We have to push out some of the smaller fish." I gesture at the couple who have Tony cornered. "The Barnstones are already over there trying to grease the wheels."

"Agreed, I noticed that too," he nods, scowling at the pair. "Let's grab a drink and then rescue Tony," his tone is all business once again as we start making our way over to the bustling bar area. And for tonight, at least, that will have to be enough.

At the bar, we stand shoulder to shoulder, our bodies almost brushing against each other unintentionally. His cologne—a mixture of woodsy spice and leather—wafts around me, making my pulse race. Memories of passionate nights flood back, despite my better judgment. I gulp down the whiskey in my glass, champagne no longer sufficing, hoping it will help me focus on work rather than my emotions about Aksel.

The room is loud with the combined cacophony of muffled conversations, clinking glasses, and the low murmur of background music. The smell of rich food fills my nostrils as waitstaff hurry by, balancing trays of canapés and champagne flutes. I try to focus on everything, anything else, to distract me from the gorgeous man standing next to me.

"Before we go see Tony, I have to ask you something, Fallon. Do you remember that night on the rooftop?" he asks, his voice low and sultry.

"Of course I do," I snap, my hands balling into fists, furious that the memory elicited by his words cause heat to generate in my core. "But that was a lifetime ago, Aksel. We're different people now."

"Are we, Fallon? Are we really so different?" His gaze bores into me, challenging my resolve.

I bite my lip, cursing myself for allowing him to get under my skin. This isn't just about our past. It's about ambition, power, and revenge. It's a game we both know how to play, and I can't afford to let my guard down.

"Fine," I spit, eyes narrowing. "Let's see who comes out on top this time, Aksel."

"Ah, you do remember," he winks. "Looking forward to it, Fallon." His smirk grows as he raises his whiskey glass, clinking it against mine with a wicked glint in his eye.

And just like that, the game is on. Just like it always has been.

Chapter 4

FALLON

Overwhelmed by emotion and in deep need to recenter myself before approaching Tony, I excuse myself and walk to the ladies' room. I dab cold water on my face and gaze at my reflection. *Get it together*, I think to myself as I touch up my eyeliner and lipstick. *Your family is counting on you.*

I've barely been gone a few minutes, but as I make my way back out into the main ballroom I immediately see them across the room. Aksel stands with Carissa Owens, her hand resting on his arm as she laughs at something he said. She looks stunning as usual with her wavy blonde hair twisted into an elegant updo, gentle tendrils cascading softly around her perfectly contoured face. Her gown clings to her curves, and her sparkling silver heels showcase her shapely calves.

Of course she'd be at this event, never one to shy away from an opportunity to see and be seen. And if she had any idea Aksel was going to be here she'd be like a moth to a flame. She certainly didn't waste any time, practically jumping on him the second I left the room.

My nails dig into my palms, drawing blood. Does he think I've forgotten how he chose her over me, allowing her to drive an unfixable wedge between us? How he humiliated and discarded me without a second thought?

They don't see the storm brewing, but it's coming. After all these years, the reckoning has arrived. This is no longer just business, it's personal. It's not only my clients that I look out for.

Aksel glances up, pinning me with an unreadable look. I straighten, smoothing my expression into indifference. Let him wonder and guess. Let him squirm the way I did. Victory will taste so much sweeter when he realizes too late that he's been outplayed by the girl he once betrayed.

The game isn't over yet, but it will be. And I will emerge the winner.

Aksel strides toward me, Carissa clinging to his arm. I turn away, scanning the room for potential allies and dismissing him from my thoughts. He doesn't deserve my attention.

"Fallon." His voice is rough, edged with an emotion I can't identify.

I face him, arching a brow. "What is it?"

"We need to talk." His gaze darts to Carissa. "Privately."

"I have nothing to say to you."

"Please." There's a hint of desperation in that single word. "Five minutes. That's all I ask."

I consider refusing but curiosity wins out, plus him ditching Carissa for me will give me a sense of satisfaction. What does he want now, after all these years?

I nod curtly. "Five minutes. No more."

Carissa sniffs and wrenches her hand away from Aksel's arm. She scans the room, her gaze quickly finding the bar, and she slinks in that direction.

He leads me to a secluded alcove, tension radiating from him in waves. I fold my arms, waiting. The clock is ticking.

"Listen, I made a mistake," he says. "Choosing my family's company over you is the second biggest regret of my life. Listening to her," he gestures over his shoulder toward Carissa, "is the first."

My lips twist. Is this meant to be an apology? It's too little, too late. "Time's almost up. And if you really felt that way, it seems a little strange that you'd be spending all night with her, laughing at her jokes and letting her hands roam all over you."

"Fallon, please. I never stopped caring for you." He reaches for my hand and I jerk away. "We can start over. Together we can do what we promised and finally be free of our families' control."

"And why would I trust you now?" I sneer, my eyes flitting in Carissa's direction. "You betrayed me once. You'll do it again. It's like a joke to you. She's even floating around ready to destroy us all over again."

"I won't. I swear on my life, I'm done letting others control me." His eyes meet mine, burning with passion. "We always dreamed of building our own empire. This is our chance. Say you'll give me another chance, and it will be just like old times. You and me against the world."

The words ignite bittersweet memories that assault me without warning. Once upon a time, I might have agreed. Once upon a time, Aksel had my heart. But not anymore.

His words transport me to our senior year. We're lounging in Aksel's room, papers strewn across the floor as we plot our next move while completing an assignment. His fingers trail up my arm, leaving goosebumps in their wake.

"Your father will never see it coming," he murmurs against my neck. "By the time he figures out our plan, it'll be too late."

A shiver runs down my spine at his touch and words. This is our world: secrets, forbidden romance, and outmaneuvering our powerful families. Vowing to distance ourselves from our family businesses and to alter the courses of our destinies.

"We're going to rule the city one day, Fallon." His eyes gleam with ambition and something else I'm afraid to name. "Together, no one can stand in our way."

The memory fades, bitterness flooding my senses. Together. What a joke. Within months, Aksel betrayed me, among other things siding with his family to secure a position in their rapidly expanding company. While Aksel climbed the corporate ladder, I was left behind sticking to what we had promised. I felt like a pawn that had been played in a game I didn't know I was part of.

I slam back into the present, rage simmering beneath my skin.

"Time's up," I say coldly. "Get out of my sight."

Aksel's face crumples, but he has no one to blame but himself. The time for fairy tale endings is over. Now, there will be only vengeance.

The gala swirls around me as Aksel disappears, defeated, into the crowd. My heart pounds with equal parts fury and satisfaction. I've won this round, but the game is far from over.

A bony hand touches my shoulder, and I whirl to find Carissa standing behind me. Her smile is sympathetic, but her eyes gleam with triumph. She knows how much Aksel's betrayal cut me, and now she thinks his failure here gives her an opening.

She's wrong.

"Fallon, darling, are you alright?" Her nails dig into my skin as she gives my shoulder a squeeze, and I flinch at her touch. "I saw Aksel bothering you. You know you can always talk to me."

I shrug off her hand. "I'm fine, Carissa. Go find another target for your fake concern."

Her eyes flash. She drops the pretense, her smile twisting into a sneer. "You Dempseys always were too arrogant for your own good, even if your brothers are all pretty hot. Did you really think you could win Aksel from under me?" She leans close, her breath hot against my ear. "You'll always be second best, Fallon. To me, to your family, to Aksel. You're a joke, and everyone here knows it. I'll make sure Tony Farelli knows it too." She glances over at the executive and gives him a small wave, which he reciprocates.

Rage boils in my veins. Carissa has always looked down on me, has always thought I wasn't good enough. She ruined my relationship with Aksel so many years ago, and now she thinks she'll sabotage my family company.

I meet her gaze with a chilling smile. "The joke's on you, Carissa. You have no idea who you're dealing with."

Her eyes widen at my tone. Before she can reply, I turn on my heel and stride away, leaving her spluttering behind me. Let her believe she's ruffled me with her threats. Soon enough, she'll learn the truth.

The Dempseys always get revenge

I scan the room and spot Aksel leaning against a marble column, whiskey glass in hand as he talks with the influential man who is the reason why my father insisted I be here this evening. My chest tightens at the sight of his smile, and the way he casually touches Farelli's arm. I know those gestures, those subtle power plays. He's working his charm, and judging by the man's laughter, it's having the desired effect.

Fear and fury war inside me. If Aksel wins this man over and I don't, it'll just reinforce my status as the family let-down and it'll be yet another time where Aksel bested me at something. I can't let that happen. I walk up to them, interrupting their conversation with a bright smile.

"Mr. Farelli, there you are! I hope I'm not disturbing you." I extend a hand, ignoring Aksel's gaze burning into me. "Fallon Dempsey. My father speaks highly of you."

Tony Farelli's eyes light up in recognition. The Farellis and Dempseys go back generations. I play on that connection now, watching Aksel from the corner of my eye. His jaw clenches, and satisfaction uncurls inside me. I'm not going to make this easy for him. His family might have deep ties to influential people, but so do mine.

"Fallon, what a lovely surprise!" He clasps my hand warmly. "Call me Tony! Your father was just telling me about your new business venture. Restaurants, was it?"

I laugh, keeping my tone light. "You must have me confused with my brother. I run a personal empowerment and development service. We help our clients to achieve their goals and take ownership of their lives." I can't quite bring myself to tell this man my business is based on the annihilation of fuckboys, so I use the broad generalized explanation that nobody really understands. "But I do remain heavily invested in Dempsey Enterprises, of course."

"How admirable." His brows rise in interest. "We should discuss the Eternity Development Project further. You can tell your father I'll be in touch."

Success flickers inside me, but I mask it behind a graceful smile. "I'm sure he'll be delighted. Thank you."

Farelli nods and steers the conversation to lighter topics. I chime in occasionally but keep watch on Aksel from the corner of my eye. His jaw stays clenched, and he keeps throwing me narrow-eyed glances. I stare back, a challenge in my gaze.

You didn't win yet, Aksel. The game has only just begun. Just because I'm not a member of the boy's club doesn't mean I can't use my own charms to get what I want.

The lingering tension in the air is electric, charged with the collision of our worlds.

Farelli excuses himself and we go our separate ways. As I grab an hors d'oeuvre from the tray of a passing server, I feel Aksel's gaze burning into me from across the room, dark and inscrutable. But I know him well enough to recognize the sharp edge of calculation beneath his aloof facade. He's watching, waiting for my next move in this intricate game we play.

Always ten steps ahead. Always in control.

The memory of calloused hands and whispered promises flares, and I grit my teeth against the unwanted flash of heat. Aksel does not get to have this effect on me anymore. He lost that right a long time ago.

I turn away, scanning the room for new alliances to forge and weaknesses to exploit. My father expects results, and while the conversation seemed to go well with Tony Farelli there are no guarantees that will be enough. I can't fail again, or Dad might withdraw his financial support from my business completely. It's always an overhanging threat. But failure has never been an option. Not when I have so much to prove.

My fingers curl around the stem of a champagne flute as I approach a cluster of executives that I recognize, a calculated smile curving my lips. While Tony Farelli was the main target of this evening's networking, my father asked me to approach these men too if I saw them at the event. Like with any business, rubbing elbows with the right people at events like these tends to open doors that wouldn't otherwise exist. "Gentlemen, it's wonderful to see you this evening. I'm Fallon Dempsey of Dempsey Enterprises."

Their appreciative gazes sweep over me, and I incline my head, playing the role I was born to inhabit but have railed against since I was a teenager. Poised. Polished. Aloof. The consummate businesswoman. It irks me to have to do it but I'm a damn good actress.

If the men glimpse the shadows beneath the facade, they don't show it. But then, men often see what they want to see.

"The contributions of each of your companies will be invaluable to the innovation and success of Dempsey Enterprises." I meet each of their eyes, a nonverbal promise of the prosperity to come. "Our corporation looks forward to a bright future together with you."

Murmurs of agreement and flattery follow, and I bask in the glow of their enthusiasm, even as my gaze drifts to Aksel again. A challenge glints in his eyes, the silent dare that has always spurred me to greater heights, to beat him at his own game.

The familiar rush of competition stirs in my veins, awakening an old hunger. Victory over Aksel would be the ultimate prize. And this is one game I fully intend to win.

"A dance?" Aksel suddenly appears at my side and takes firm hold of my elbow. "I seem to remember you're quite a fan of this song."

The men smile at his sudden arrival, and I can tell by the looks on their faces they assume we're a couple. If only they knew. I grit my teeth, maintaining my polite smile, determined not to let him win by showing the men how I really feel and causing a scene.

"Let's just get this over with," I mutter as I head towards the dance floor where couples sway to the music.

But when Aksel steps closer, his body brushing against mine, I can't help but feel a jolt of awareness flash through me.

I try to ignore how his proximity affects me, keeping my expression neutral even as my pulse quickens. His hand finds my waist and I'm instantly transported back to another time, another dance.

"You really do look beautiful tonight, my Fallon-y," he murmurs, his breath hot against my ear.

I clench my jaw, willing myself not to react to the nickname he knows I detest or the way the closeness of his body is making me feel. "Don't."

His fingers tighten almost imperceptibly on my hip. "Come on, Fallon. We've never been very good at staying away from each other."

The truth of his words hits me like a punch to the gut. Our attraction has always defied logic, consumed common sense. "That was a long time ago," I say tightly.

He spins me out and then pulls me back in, our bodies pressed together. "Doesn't feel that way to me."

His eyes burn into mine and I see desire swirling in their depths. My breath catches. No, I can't let him affect me this way again.

I try to extract myself from his embrace but he holds me close. "We're not done here yet, love."

"Let me go, Aksel," I hiss, hating the way my body thrills at his touch even as my mind rebels. "And don't you ever use the word love around me."

His fingers trail down my bare back. "I never could get enough of you," he rasps before crushing his lips to mine.

"Aksel, stop! What are you doing?" I pull away, shocked by his brazen kiss in front of the entire room. I glance around but thankfully everyone seems to be absorbed with their own dancing or conversation.

Except for Carissa, that is. I see her watching us from across the room, her eyes narrowed. We lock eyes and she turns on her heel and scurries off.

Although I didn't intend on it, I seem to have reignited not one but two enemies in one night. I just didn't expect one of them to kiss me.

A wave of emotion rushes over me. "I can't do this," I push Aksel away and hurry off the dance floor. My family obligation has been fulfilled, and at this point this is some kind of torturous extra credit I don't want or need. I'm out of here.

Chapter 5

FALLON

My gown trails behind me like a whisper of regret as I step into the empty elevator. I press the button for my floor, my fingertips trembling against the cool metal, my heart racing in tandem with the ding of each level.

The doors slide open, and I walk through the quiet hallway, each step echoing off the marble floors. My penthouse suite is a sanctuary of peace, a stark contrast to the chaos I left behind. I kick off my heels, letting out a sigh of relief as my bare feet sink into the plush rug in my living room. I pause at the window, staring out at the city lights twinkling below, a stark reminder of how differently our lives have turned out. He's had everything I ever wanted while I was left standing there, and although my dad affords me this residence, I know it's not really mine.

I pour a glass of whiskey and plop onto the couch, yanking my hair into a messy updo. I take a glug from the glass and the amber liquid burns down my throat, soothing the anger that still simmers within. I remember the way he touched me, the way he looked at me—as if I was something precious. A pang of longing hits my chest before I can stop it, but I push it down, reminding myself of what he really is—a liar and a cheat. And dangerous for me. The memories of him are like fragments of a broken mirror, each piece cutting deeper than the last.

I crawl into bed, pulling the silk sheets up to my chin. The scent of his cologne lingers on me, and I scrunch my nose, trying to push it away. I stare up at the ceiling, my mind racing with the events of the night. My heart beats wildly in my chest as I recall our dance, the heat between us almost enough to make me forget why I was there in the first place. But I won't forget and I can't forget.

I roll onto my side, the cool sheets against my naked skin, and close my eyes. His voice echoes in my ears, taunting me with promises of forever. Laughter bubbles up from my throat. Forever? More like a few hours.

A tear slips down my cheek, and I brush it aside, disgusted with myself for letting him make me feel these feelings. I hate that he still has such a hold on my emotions, even after all these years.

I clench my fists tightly under the covers, steeling myself for the revenge about to come. He crushed my heart all those years ago and I'm going to do the same to him, just like I'd do for any of my clients in the same situation.

The city lights twinkle and sway below, distracting me from my thoughts. The air conditioning kicks on, a cold blast of air washing over my skin. I hate how it feels, the way the memory of tonight's kiss and the ones that came before it make my head spin. I take a deep breath, trying to forget him.

Chapter 6

FALLON

The sunlight filters through the blinds and casts slatted shadows across my desk, a jarring reminder of the outside world. I'm grateful for the seclusion my office offers—a place where I can truly let down my guard. The minimalist décor and soft glow of ambient lighting provide a calming atmosphere, but they do little to soothe the storm brewing within me.

"Fallon," Mia's voice is gentle, her concern evident as she sits across from me and hands me a mug of the steaming coffee she knows I need to get through the day. Her soft features and dark curls frame her freckled face in a picture of kindness. "Tell me what happened last night."

Taking a deep breath, I recount the events of the gala, my voice wavering as I detail the unexpected dance with Aksel, Carissa's insults and threats, and the relentless pressure from my father's towering expectations. "I—I don't know how to make sense of it all, Mia. It's like all the memories from the past came crashing back at once, and I can't help but blame Aksel for some of the things that happened after he broke my heart. Last night just ripped everything back open again. And *she* was even there, to make matters worse. It felt like history was on repeat."

Mia listens intently, her expression a mix of sympathy and understanding. I watch as she grips the edge of her chair, leaning forward slightly. The air in the room seems charged with the weight of my revelations.

"Fallon, you can't hold onto resentment forever," she says softly, her words laced with empathy. "You need to find a way to move past what happened between you and Aksel. Holding onto all this anger won't change the past and it's only going to cause you pain. I'm sorry that last night brought up lots of feelings for you, which is understandable because it's been so long since you've seen him, but it also means you haven't healed after all this time."

"I know," I admit, my voice barely a whisper as I rub my temples, feeling the headache building. "But every time I think I've moved on, something happens to remind me of the pain he caused."

My phone buzzes, interrupting our conversation. Glancing at the screen, I see a new message from Aksel. My pulse quickens. I want to ignore it, to continue burying the emotions his presence stirs, but I can't help myself.

"It's him." I sigh.

"Fallon," Mia prompts, her eyes softening as she studies my face. "What does he say?"

I hesitate, my fingers hovering over the screen. The walls I've built around my heart feel fragile, ready to crumble at the slightest touch of Aksel's words. But I can't let him in again. I can't risk giving him the power to break me once more. I unlock my phone and preemptively flinch as I open his message.

Aksel: Fallon. I'm so sorry that I upset you. I don't really understand what I did. Will you just please talk to me? I mainly just want to make sure you're okay. I do care about you, despite what you clearly think. A.

"He's trying to understand," I say, my voicefdesefedd clipped as I force myself to maintain a semblance of composure. "But he can't. He doesn't know what he did to me."

"Maybe you should tell him," Mia suggests, hesitating as if testing the waters. "You don't have to forgive him, but it might help you both find some closure."

"Maybe," I concede, the word tasting bitter on my tongue. But I'm not ready to share that part of my past with him. Not yet. For now, I'll keep those memories locked away, where they belong—and hope that one day, I'll be strong enough to confront them head-on. Besides, there's only going to be one way for me to achieve real closure. Revenge.

The door clicks shut behind Mia as I'm left enveloped in the silence of my office, the sleek, minimalist space now feeling cold and stark. My heart races, and I can hardly catch my breath, each inhalation a reminder of everything that has led to me feeling such hatred for

Aksel.

I pace the room, the sound of my combat boots against the polished concrete floor echoing through the stillness. The blister that formed from the heels I wore last night serve as a reminder of why I was wearing such painful shoes. The memories of Aksel—his touch, his warm gaze, the whispered promises we once shared—are both bitter and sweet, lingering in the air like a haunting melody. But instead of offering solace, they only serve to remind me of the darkness that followed.

"Damn him," I mutter under my breath, clenching my fists as I recall how my life spiraled out of control after he broke my heart. In my desperate attempt to forget him, I'd fallen in with the wrong crowd, seeking solace in the numbing embrace of alcohol and drugs. One night, when I was most vulnerable, a group of guys from my school took advantage of me, leaving me broken and bruised in more ways than one. That was only the start of a series of abusive relationships that followed, each layering on trauma that I haven't yet begun to process.

The thud of bass reverberates against the walls of the dingy flat on the outskirts of the city's main party area. The space is unfamiliar, and I barely remember how I got here. The plan was to have a few drinks at home, then go to the club for some dancing. To get our minds off the idiot guys we normally hang out with. At some point, I must have gotten separated from my friends. I look around the room at the five men who flank me on the couch and surrounding armchairs. They're my new friends, now.

They offered to take me home with them, said there would be good music and more drinks. A couple of them are particularly good-looking, and one of them seemed interested in me. It feels nice, having this attention. And there's no Carissa in sight, trying to steal any of my new friends from me. Plus, these guys seem more mature. They're older, wiser, more confident.

"Drink up," says one of the guys, thrusting a plastic cup in my direction. I glance at the contents but can't quite figure them out. I quirk an eyebrow at the man. "It's my special cocktail. I made it especially for you. You're our guest. Drink up!" I shrug. It's not like I have anywhere else to be. Taking a sip, I flinch at the sharp taste and the slightly effervescent tingle I feel on my tongue. I gulp and press my lips together. "Delicious," I say, nodding, eager to please the man who took the time to make me a special drink.

"That's my girl," he says, approvingly. His teeth begin to morph in front of me, growing sharper, as my mind grows fuzzy at the corners. He starts to say something else, but it sounds like a warped groan, and everything fades to black.

I come to, gasping for air and feeling the unmistakable grip of a hand wrapped around my throat. "Can't... breathe!" I manage to rasp as I attempt to flail my arms and legs around me. But quickly, I realize that each of my limbs are being held firmly, too.

"Shut the fuck up, slut! We're giving you what you were asking for. We're taking what's ours." The pain hits me like a knife searing me from within, threatening to rip my insides out. "You may as well have been walking around that club naked, looking like that," one growls as he pulls his cock out of his pants.

I can't keep track of the rough hands, the cold voices, directing me and yelling at each other.

And then they're inside me. Pounding away. I can't move. I can't breathe. I try to cry out but a hand presses against my mouth so tightly I'm helpless.

My body feels numb. My mind feels numb.

I float away to safety...

I'm dirty, sticky, and I have the overwhelming urge to be clean.

I sit under the shower, water running over my back. Grabbing a loofah from the caddy, I lather it with soap and begin to scrub myself. Dirt runs from me, ridding me of the soil that clung to my skin when they smashed me into the ground. I'm washing away every hint of body fluid I can find as well. Unfortunately, there's quite a bit of that.

My skin grows red and begins to bleed in several areas as I continue to grate the harsh material against my tender, swollen skin.

They treated me like a vessel for their warped needs. In their flat, and out into the garden. By some miracle, one of them had the sense to drive me home and discard me on my front doorstep. Otherwise, I'm pretty sure they would have left me for dead.

There's no way I can tell my parents. They'd never understand. They'd judge me, tell me I should have been at home studying. That I should be more like my brothers. Anyway, Mom and Dad have both seemed preoccupied lately. Something's going on between them, I can feel it. So I'm the least of their worries.

And you can forget calling the cops. I've watched enough episodes of true crime shows to know how that tends to work out. Me too my ass.

I guess this is just destiny for someone like me. I wasn't good enough for Aksel, so I found people more on my level. And look where it got me. Look where he got me.

I'm worthless. He broke me, and now so did they.

"Fuck them all," I snarl, slamming my fist against the cool glass windowpane causing it to rattle and reverberate violently in its frame. While I did end up telling my parents who in turn called the cops, the justice system failed me, those vile monsters walking away without so much as a slap on the wrist. To this day, I can't shake the feeling that it's Aksel who is the root cause of my trauma, and I resent him deeply for it.

If he'd been faithful and trusting of me, and if he'd truly loved me, life would have turned out much closer to how I'd planned it. How we'd planned it together. But now his life is set and wrapped up in a pretty little bow, whereas I'm struggling and beholden to my family. Sure, I'm not struggling day-to-day, but it would take me refusing one task from my father for everything to be taken away in a flash.

My phone buzzes on the desk, its vibrations cutting through the haze of my thoughts. I glance at the screen, my heart catching in my throat as I see Aksel's name again. It feels like some cruel joke, his message arriving just as I relive my darkest moments. With trembling hands, I pick up the phone, forcing myself to read his words.

Aksel: Fallon, please stop ignoring me. I know things between us aren't easy, but I want to understand. I want to help us both move forward. Please just agree to speak with me. That's all I ask.

"Move forward?" I scoff, my grip on the phone tightening. The audacity of him, thinking he can just waltz back into my life and mend what's been shattered beyond repair. But beneath the anger, if I'm honest there's a flicker of something else—a raw, unbidden longing for the connection we once shared. I don't know why I still crave his very being like this. It's something primal and it disgusts me. Maybe I'm just a sucker for punishment. Trauma bonded to the person who first betrayed me.

"Fallon," I whisper to myself, "don't let him in." The walls I've built around my heart are fragile, and if I allow Aksel any closer, they'll crumble to dust and my heart will be completely vulnerable. I've developed a strong shell around myself, but that's because the heart that lies underneath has been shattered and barely holds together anymore. Yet, as much as I try to deny it, the pull towards him is undeniable.

I relent, typing out a terse response.

Me: Fine. We can talk. But don't expect me to bare my soul to you, Aksel. That part of me died a long time ago, back in high school. Just like your frosted tips.

As I send the message, my stomach churns with a mix of anticipation and dread. I know that by letting Aksel back into my life, I risk giving him the power to break me all over again. It caused me enough angst to have to be in the same room with him at last night's event. And yet, despite the turmoil raging within me, I can't help but hope that this time, things will be different.

I get an immediate reply:

Aksel: Okay. You name the time and place that works best for you.

I put my phone down. My brain is too scattered to come up with a concrete plan to meet with him. Maybe if I don't reply immediately he'll be distracted by something or someone else. Although, from his persistence, I know that's just wishful thinking on my part.

My thoughts drift towards my family, and the strings that tie me to them like marionette wires. I can't escape the pressure that comes from being Colton Dempsey's daughter, a trophy he parades around at corporate events. The weight of expectation is a constant shadow, darkening my life. I thought by forging my own path with this business I'd be able to escape some of the family expectations, but if anything it's only served to put me under further scrutiny in a futile competition with my brothers that I could never win.

"Fallon," my father's voice rings in my ears, "remember who you are and what you represent." His words feel like chains, binding me to his ambitions and desires. I never asked for this life, but with the financial support he provides for my business, I feel shackled by obligation. I purposely avoided joining his firm but I may as well wear its logo on me permanently. Besides, everyone knows I'm a Dempsey. There's no escaping this.

"Damn it," I mutter under my breath, frustration simmering beneath the surface.

Clenching my fists, I force myself to focus on Aksel, trying to make sense of our most recent interaction. It's not just me battling demons, there's something haunting him too. I saw it in his eyes, the way they darkened with unspoken pain when he thought no one was looking. I wonder what's happened to him in the years since we were last in contact, and why his energy seems heavier somehow, despite him living the good life with a silver spoon in his mouth.

"Hey, Fallon?" Mia's voice breaks through my reverie. "You okay?" I hadn't even noticed her slip back into my office while I was deep in thought about the two men who have left indelible impressions on nearly every aspect of my life.

"Fine," I say, trying to sound casual while my heart throbs with a cacophony of emotions. "Just thinking."

"About?" She presses, concern etched on her face. "You still worried about Aksel?"

"No, not everything is about Aksel," I hiss. I instantly realize I'm being snippy with her when she's just being a concerned friend. She tends to bear the brunt of my emotions and I should really stop taking things out on her. "Family," I admit, the word leaving a bitter taste in my mouth.

"Ah, your father," she says, understanding dawning in her eyes. "He's...complicated." Having grown up spending countless hours at each other's houses, she has more insight into him than most people. Not that he was home very often, always on business trips and no doubt shacking up with Zara the homewrecker and who knows who else. But she got to see a side to him that most people don't. His version of a family man, and his impossible expectations of his one and only daughter.

"Complicated? More like controlling and oppressive." My laughter is hollow, devoid of any humor. "He's got me trapped, Mia. I'm drowning here."

"Fallon, don't let him define you. You're stronger than that," she encourages, reaching out to squeeze my hand.

"Am I?" I question, doubts swirling like storm clouds in my mind. "Sometimes it feels like I'm just a pawn in his game, and my only purpose is to serve him and the family name[."

"Hey," she says firmly, "you're so much more than that. You've built your own life, your own business. Don't let him take that away from you. And I do really think he loves you deeply, but he has a hard time knowing how to show it."

"Thanks, Mia," I murmur, grateful for her unwavering support and unique insight. But as I stare at the walls of my office, I can't help but wonder if I'll ever truly be free. She gives my shoulder a squeeze and heads back out the door.

Aksel's past seems to haunt him too, I remind myself, the thought simultaneously comforting and painful. It's a strange comfort knowing he seems to be fighting his own battles too, even though privilege seems to be oozing from his every pore, but it also highlights the distance between us.

"Maybe," I whisper to the empty room, "we're both just broken beyond repair." And as I sit alone, the pieces of my shattered heart scattered around me, I can't help but wonder if Aksel and I will ever find a way to mend what's been irreparably torn apart, or if I'll ever feel like a whole person again.

My fingers drum absently against the cold glass surface of my desk as I sit in the quiet, dimly lit office. The afterglow of Mia's support lingers in the air, but with it comes an uncomfortable realization creeping into my thoughts.

"Shit," I mutter under my breath. Lately, Mia and I have spent all our time together trapped within these walls, discussing work or brooding over my vendetta against various scumbags. She deserves better than this, she's not just a colleague, but a true friend who's been there for me through thick and thin. Lately, I've been doing a lot of complaining and haven't been giving her much positivity in return.

I push myself up from my desk and pop my head into the open space where her desk is located. As usual, she's busy working. I think she'd work all night sometimes if I didn't send her home. She hears me approaching and turns to face me, and as usual of late her tone is tinged with worry. "Is everything alright? Did I forget something?"

"Actually, I was thinking that we should make plans to go out tonight," I say, surprising myself with the suggestion. "We haven't spent any time together outside of work lately, and I think we both could use a break. I know I've been leaning on you a lot and the least I could do is buy you a drink."

"Really?" Mia's eyes widen with surprise, but then she grins, nodding in agreement. I feel even guiltier seeing how happy such a small gesture made her. I've really been a shitty friend to her lately, proven by the mere fact I suggested a spontaneous girls night out had her perking up like an attention-starved puppy. "You know what? You're right. We do need to have some fun. Let's do it!"

"Great," I reply, a genuine smile forming on my lips. "It's settled, then. We'll go out tonight and forget about all this drama, even if it's just for a little while." A night out with my best friend actually does sound refreshing, and like the distraction I so desperately need.

"Sounds perfect," Mia agrees before turning back to her desk to wrap up her work for the day.

As I sit alone once more in my office, the pang of guilt continues to tighten in my chest. Mia has always been there for me, offering unwavering support and understanding. And what have I given her in return? Stressful conversations and late nights at the office. She deserves so much more.

"Tonight," I vow to myself, "I'll make it up to her. I'll show her how much I truly value our friendship."

But even as I say the words, I can't shake the heaviness that continues to press down on my heart. Aksel's message still lingers like a ghost, haunting me with its carefully chosen words and hidden meanings. Can I ever truly escape him? Or will he always remain an indelible part of my life—a dark shadow cast over everything I do? I'm going to try to delay our inevitable meeting for as long as possible.

For now, though, I push these thoughts aside. Tonight isn't about Aksel or my father or any of the other demons that plague me. Tonight is about Mia and celebrating the bond we share beyond these walls.

"Let's make tonight count," I whisper, steeling myself for the evening ahead. As I rise from my chair and switch off the ambient lighting, I allow the darkness to envelop me, if only for a moment. But when I step into the hallway, it's with renewed determination, ready to face whatever challenges lie ahead.

"Tonight," I think again, "is for friendships and fun."

Chapter 7

FALLON

The bass of the music thumps through my chest as I step into the trendy Scorch nightclub with Mia by my side. Mia has been mentioning wanting to check it out for a while after it was featured in several reviews of hot new local nightspots. It's a sexy space with dim lighting and a DJ spinning tunes from a turntable high up to one side of the bustling dance floor. The atmosphere is electric, charged with an energy that's almost palpable. Scantily clad women and men in tightly fitted outfits gyrate to the rhythm of the music in a seductive game of flirtation. While there's no official dress code, there's a silent understanding that nobody will be let in unless they're dressed to the nines. The air hangs thick with a heady mix of sweat, perfume and expensive cologne. The sensory overload is a welcome distraction from the unending thoughts of Aksel and our dangerous game of cat and mouse, as well as the heartwrenching plights of my clients.

"Come on, Fallon! Let's go get some drinks!" Mia shouts over the pounding music, her eyes wide and alive with excitement. She grabs my hand and pulls me toward the bar, weaving through the crowd with practiced ease. We're both dressed for the occasion, Mia in a sparkly tube top and matching skirt, and me in my teal tank top and black short shorts. Having learned my lesson the other night, instead of blister-inducing heels I've opted for my signature black combat boots. Much more practical, and useful for kicking ass if need be.

"Sure thing," I grin, feeling the adrenaline coursing through my veins. "You look gorgeous by the way!"

I'm ready to lose myself in the night, to forget about the darkness that has taken hold of me lately.

We reach the bar and order our drinks, the bartender sliding them to us with a flirtatious wink that makes Mia giggle like a giddy schoolgirl. I take a sip of my cocktail, the bittersweet taste dancing on my tongue like a warning, a reminder that tonight is only temporary. But for now, I'll savor it.

"Let's dance!" Mia urges, tugging me toward the throng of bodies writhing to the music. I laugh, allowing her to lead me onto the dance floor. It's a crush of people all there for only a few possible reasons: to lose themselves in the music and distract themselves from the not-so-pleasant aspects of their lives, to find someone to take home for the night, or maybe both. Either way, it's a welcome escape and there's comfort in the commonality of why we're all here.

As we dance, I feel the gaze of men around us, appraising and hungry. For once, I don't shy away. Instead, I embrace it, locking eyes with each one, daring them to come closer. I flirt shamelessly, reveling in the power it gives me, even if it's just for tonight.

A particularly sexy guy with ruggedly good looks approaches me, his jawline sharp and defined, every angle of his face seemingly chiseled from stone. His tanned skin glows softly under the strobing dance floor lights, his broad shoulders and chiseled chest emphasized by his tight-fitting T-shirt. He wraps his large hands around my waist and I lean back against him, letting his hips grind against me and his stubble graze against the small of my neck, his intoxicating cologne emphasizing his sheer masculinity. He whispers something into my ear, perhaps asking for my number or offering a drink and I just smile as he weaves his way back out of the crowd.

"Nice one, Fallon, you're on fire tonight!" Mia shouts into my ear, her body moving fluidly to the beat. "Keep this up, and we'll have every guy in here begging for our attention."

"Maybe that's what I need," I think to myself, a wicked smile playing on my lips. A distraction from Aksel, from the thought of our tangled, twisted connection. But my mental image of him still lingers, a shadow lurking in the back of my mind. I continue to dance and flirt with the men around us, enjoying the feeling of their eyes on me, their desire for me fueling my own inner fire.

The night continues, a blur of music, laughter, and carnal energy. I feel alive in a way I haven't in so long, untethered from the burden of my past and the weight of my perpetual quest for revenge. But even in this momentary escape surrounded by hot men, I can't help but think about him. Aksel. The man who has become both my nemesis and my obsession. Every feature on a man that could potentially remind me of him, does, and I keep thinking I see him in the crowd, but of course he's not here.

"Are you okay?" Mia shouts over the music at one point, concern etched on her face as she catches my distant gaze. Guilt immediately hits me as once again I see how closely attuned her mood is to my own. And I have certainly been a Captain Bring-Down lately.

"Oh I'm fine," I lie, forcing a smile. "Just need another drink. I say we do shots!"

"Okay," she says, not entirely convinced I'm alright but willing to let it go for now. "Shots it is!"

We head back to the bar where the bartender once again greets us with a flirtatious grin and a wink. His actions are cheesy, but he's a decent-looking guy. Mia clearly thinks so too, leaning over the bar to order us each a shot of blanco tequila with a lime wedge, and exposing more of her cleavage to the attractive man. "Those are on the house," the bartender beams at Mia. We cheers, lifting our glasses high in the air. "To a well overdue girls' night!"

As the night wears on, I continue to flirt and dance, fully embracing the freedom it offers. I know that this is only an interlude, a brief respite from the darkness that awaits me. But for now, I'll take it. For tonight, I am Fallon Dempsey—fierce, unapologetic, and unafraid haver of fun. And I'm determined to make this a good night for Mia. She deserves at least a few hours of my time to let go and enjoy the more carefree friend she's used to.

A couple of shots later and I've had my fill for the evening. My brain feels fuzzy, which was pleasant at first, but I keep thinking of Aksel and the alcohol has only made things worse. As the people around me drink more, they're just getting grabbier and it's starting to get on my nerves as my personal space is increasingly being encroached on by strangers. These days, I prefer to be the one doing the grabbing. It's been fun to get out of the house, but I'm ready to return to the sanctuary of my condo.

"Fallon, come on! Don't be a buzzkill," Mia pleads as I announce my intention to leave the club. The bass thumps through my body, making my bones tremble with the beat. She often gets like this when we go out, wanting us to be some of the last to leave. I usually don't mind, but I'm getting tired and my negative feelings are making me feel guilty.

"Sorry, but I can't afford a hangover tomorrow," I reply, shouting over the music. "You're welcome to stay, though. Just make sure you get home safe." My mind is already racing with plans for tomorrow, and I know I need to be sharp.

"Ugh, fine," Mia huffs, scanning the crowd before her eyes land on the tall, muscular man with smoldering good looks who's already approached her several times before. He's got the brain capacity of a goldfish, but tonight, she doesn't seem to care. "I guess he'll do."

"Be careful," I warn, grabbing her arm and locking eyes with her for emphasis. "And text me when you get home."

"Whatever, mom," she rolls her eyes but nods in agreement.

As Mia saunters toward her conquest, I make my way through the throng of dancing bodies. I can feel their heat, their sweat, and their lust pressing against me, suffocating me. I push through, ignoring the leering eyes and suggestive comments thrown my way.

The cold air outside the club hits me like a slap to the face, bringing clarity and relief. I close my eyes, taking deep breaths of the crisp night air mixed with the overpowering stench of cigarette smoke from the clubgoers who are done with dancing but aren't quite ready to go home yet. My thoughts drift back to Aksel, that infuriating man who has infiltrated every corner of my life like the smoke that permeates the otherwise pure air.

"Damn him," I mutter under my breath, summoning an Uber to take me home. Luckily, it arrives within minutes, and given the hour it's a straight shot to my condo.

The door to my condo shuts behind me with a soft click, the quiet sanctuary of home providing instant relief. I head straight for the kitchen, filling a tall glass with water before padding into the bedroom. My eyes linger on the bedside table, where I place the glass within easy reach. A small smile tugs at the corner of my lips. Some might call it adulting, but I say it's present Fallon looking after future Fallon. I almost don't recognize myself.

"Who am I even?" I mumble to the empty room, shaking my head at my newfound sense of responsibility.

An hour or so later, my phone buzzes in my pocket, and I pull it out to see Mia's text.

Mia: Home safe. Have fun being boring xo

She's clearly teasing. I snort and roll my eyes, typing back a quick response:

Me: Glad you made it. Have fun doing whatever or whoever. Sleep well xo

I change into my pajamas, the soft fabric caressing my skin like a gentle embrace. In this moment of solitude, my thoughts can't help but drift back to Aksel. That infuriating man who has infiltrated every corner of my life, even when he's not physically present.

"Ugh," I groan, massaging my temples. "Not tonight, Fallon. You need sleep."

I crawl into bed, pulling the covers up to my chin. The cool sheets feel like heaven against my overheated skin. I close my eyes, willing my racing thoughts to quiet down.

"Sleep," I command myself, taking deep breaths. "You can plot your revenge tomorrow."

Slowly, my body begins to relax, sinking into the mattress. The tension from the club, from the lingering presence of Aksel, starts to ebb away. I drift off to sleep to the sounds of some deep sleep-inducing ASMR, a rare peaceful slumber enveloping me like a protective and much-needed cloak.

When morning comes, I awaken feeling refreshed and focused, a welcome change from the usual haze of exhaustion that has recently plagued me. I glance at the barely touched glass of water on my bedside table and smile to myself.

"Thanks, past Fallon," I murmur before swinging my legs over the side of the bed and preparing for the day ahead. I'm full of good intentions, aiming to have a productive day where I can truly help my clients.

"Watch out, fuckboys," I whisper under my breath as I slip on my shoes, determination surging through my veins. "I'm coming for you."

And with that silent promise, I step into the world, ready to tackle whatever challenges lie in wait.

Mia's text message pops up on my phone screen as I hop into my car:

Mia: Club again tonight?

I hesitate for a moment before typing my response. When that girl gets on a roll she really gets on a roll. I'm pleased that she wants to spend more time with me outside of work, but I just don't have it in me to go out two nights in a row. There's way too much work to be done tomorrow.

Me: Sorry, Mia. I need some me time tonight. Have fun without me. Let's maybe go to that new wine bar later in the week though!

Mia: Boo! But okay, you do you, babe. See you at work xo.

Her reply is almost immediate, and I can picture her pouting face.

With Mia mostly off my conscience, I have a productive day of work where we're both so busy we barely interact. I'm mainly occupied preparing course content for an upcoming program. In the afternoon, I have a few consultation meetings with potential vendors for an innovative personal empowerment framework that critics have been very positive about in its early stages.

Before I know it, it's dark outside. As usual, I'm one of the last to leave the office and I listen to one of my favorite podcasts on the short drive home.

I pad over to my kitchen, the sanctuary where I find solace from the outside world including the demons that haunt me. "Let's see what we have here..." I mutter, rummaging through the fridge. My fingers wrap around an array of fresh ingredients, and my mind races with the potential dishes I could create.

"Ah, perfect," I say aloud, settling on a coq au vin recipe with a double-baked soufflé accompaniment that have been passed down through generations in my family. Both recipes are complicated and time-consuming, requiring intense concentration to make each item just right, but the challenge is exactly what I need to keep my mind occupied.

At first, the rhythmic cadence of chopping vegetables and stirring sauces grants me much-needed respite from thoughts of Aksel and revenge. Tonight, I'll lose myself in the art of cooking and forget the world beyond these walls.

As I chop and sauté, the memories of my past dance behind my eyes like ghosts, never far from the surface. I shake them away, focusing on the task at hand. My determination to drown out the painful echoes fuels my every movement, each knife stroke and seasoning adding another layer of armor against the darkness.

"Shit," I curse under my breath as I accidentally nick my finger with the knife while chopping carrots. Sucking on the small wound, I taste the metallic tang of blood mingling with the bitterness of unfulfilled revenge. In this moment, it feels fitting.

"Focus, Fallon," I remind myself, returning to chopping. The pain subsides as I continue slicing vegetables, losing myself in the repetitive motion. The familiar dance of sautéing, simmering, and stirring initially shields me from the relentless pressures of my mission and the haunting memories of my past.

But as muscle memory takes over, my mind eventually strays, and I can't help but think about why I chose this path, growing my own company and rejecting full immersion into the family business. It was never just about the money or power; it was about preserving a piece of myself, maintaining my autonomy in both my career and personal life. I refuse to be swallowed up by the darkness that surrounds me, and cooking offers an escape, a balm for wounds that are yet to heal.

I pour myself a glass of rich red wine, watching as the liquid swirls and settles. There's something comforting about it, the deep color reminiscent of the blood that courses through our veins—a reminder that we're alive, fighting, and surviving.

"Here's to you, Fallon," I murmur, raising the glass in a mock-toast to myself. The sound of my own voice ripples through the quiet condo, shattering the stillness for a moment.

Taking a slow, mindful sip, I let the velvety warmth of the wine coat my tongue and throat, savoring its bold flavor. I acknowledge that cooking isn't just a skill—it's a refuge, an escape from the chaos that surrounds me. As the simmering dish on the stove crackles with anticipation, I can't help but think of the unresolved tension between Aksel and me. No matter how hard I try to fight it, we're like two volatile ingredients waiting to collide, creating an explosion of heat and passion.

The scent of garlic and shallots sautéing in butter invades my senses, luring me further into the culinary trance I've created for myself. Each chop of my knife against the wooden cutting board is methodical, precise—a distraction from the tangled web of emotions threatening to consume me.

"Fuck going out tonight," I mutter, pouring a generous amount of white wine into the pan. The sizzling sound drowns out Mia's voice lingering in my mind, trying to persuade me to join her at the club. "I'm so glad I decided to stay in instead."

As the fragrant steam wraps around me like a comforting embrace, I lose myself in the rhythm of cooking. My condo, bathed in soft light from the setting sun, becomes a haven where I can momentarily escape the chaos that has become my life. The gentle hum of the stove and the clinking of utensils orchestrate a soothing melody, allowing me to forget—if only for a moment—the vengeance I so desperately crave.

I taste-test regularly as I go. "Bon appétit," I murmur, taking a bite of the exquisite gruyère and époisses cheeses used in the soufflé recipe, followed by a bite of the crispy bacon ready to crumble on top of the coq au vin. The flavors meld together seamlessly and dance on my tongue.

"Ugh, too much again," I sigh, eyeing the overflowing pot on the stove. It's become a habit of mine—making way more food than necessary. Cooking for one kind of sucks. But I know what I'll do with the leftovers: freeze them and take some to work for Grave. He pretends to loathe my "pretentious" cooking, but I've caught him savoring every bite before. It's one of our unspoken rituals, and it brings a rare smile to my face.

"Looks good," I whisper to no one in particular, admiring the rich sauce that has come together in the pan.

"Are you talking to yourself again?" Mia's voice echoes in my head, teasingly. "Crazy cat lady without the cats."

"Shut up," I snap back, even though I know she's not here. "Can't a girl enjoy her own company?"

But as the silence of my apartment settles around me, the weight of loneliness presses down on my chest. I swallow hard, pushing it back, refusing to let it overtake me. I've handled being single and fiercely independent for years. No time for weakness now.

"God, I'm good," I muse to myself as the dish nears completion. The tantalizing aroma of bacon, wine-marinated poultry, fresh citrus and pungent French and Swiss cheeses fills the kitchen, a testament to my little-known culinary prowess.

"Too bad no one else will ever get to taste this the way it's meant to be," I think bitterly, my mind automatically defaulting to Aksel as the primary target. "He doesn't deserve it anyway." I think about Grave feasting on the many Tupperware-filled containers I'll be taking into work for him, and it makes me feel slightly better.

I begin plating the dish with precision and care, each element meticulously arranged for maximum visual appeal. It's an emerging masterpiece that deserves to be admired and I snap a couple of pictures for Instagram. If I don't have anyone special to share it with in person, I may as well demonstrate my plating skills to my social media following. I even set the table for one, adding a candle and a single black rose in a gesture of self-care.

Maybe I'll even have a bubble bath after this and snuggle under my blanket with a good book. And yet, as I look over at the table, another pang of loneliness strikes me. I shake off the feeling, reminding myself that solitude is a small price to pay for the revenge I seek.

"Alright," I say aloud, determination steeling my voice. "Almost time to eat. Just a couple more steps to go."

I finish the glass of wine in one bold gulp, savoring its warmth as it spreads through my body, igniting a spark of determination.

The beeping of my phone startles me from my thoughts, and I realize I've been standing still, lost in my emotions.

Mia: Fallon, are you okay?

Me: Uh, yeah, lol. Just got a little carried away with my cooking.

Mia: Alright, just checking on you.

Her text pings back immediately, and I let out a shaky breath. It's like she's here even though she lives across town.

I pour myself another glass of wine. The vibrant red liquid swirls around as if reflecting my own turbulent emotions. Taking a sip, I close my eyes and focus on the flavors that dance on my tongue, allowing them to anchor me in the present moment.

My phone vibrates again, breaking my reverie. Glancing at the screen, I see another message from Mia.

Mia: Hey, I'm about to head out but just wanted to remind you that you're stronger than you think. You've got this. Love you xo

A small smile tugs at my lips as I read her words. It's comforting to know that, despite the chaos and turmoil that surround me, there are people who care for and support me. Even if the path ahead is fraught with danger, I'm not alone.

I feel a surge of gratitude for her unwavering friendship.

Me: Thanks, Mia. Love you too xo

Chapter 8

FALLON

About to put the very final touches on my meal before sitting down to eat, the sudden buzzing of the intercom startles me, disrupting my thoughts. Who could be calling at this hour? Reluctantly, I press the button to check who it is. Mia's clearly texting me from across town so she's not here, and it's not like my family to drop in unannounced.

"Fallon, it's Aksel. Can I come up?" His voice sounds hesitant, yet hopeful.

Ugh, of course it's Aksel. I finally get my mind off him and am about to enjoy my meal, and here he is, ruining it. The man who used to make my heart race, but now twisted it with pain and bitterness. Why would he be here now, though? Warily, I buzz him in, a mix of curiosity and apprehension swirling within me.

I hear a soft knock at the door, and as I open it, there he stands: Aksel, with his piercing gray eyes, filled with uncertainty and hope. He's dressed casually in designer jeans and a fitted shirt which accentuates his toned body. God, he looks good.

"Hey," he says, rubbing the back of his neck. "I messaged you, but didn't get a response. Thought I'd take a shot and just show up."

My phone lies forgotten on the counter where I placed it after responding to Mia. I must have missed his message while finishing up the meal. As much as I want to be angry with him for showing up unannounced, I can't ignore how attractive he looks or how my heart races at his presence.

"Come in," I say reluctantly, stepping aside to let him pass. As he walks by, I catch a whiff of his aftershave—a scent that's strangely familiar, like something from our shared past.

As he enters my apartment, I find myself torn between conflicting emotions. Part of me wants to slam the door in his face, to protect the fragile peace I've built. But another part...that part longs for the connection we once had, yearning to know if it can still be found amidst the ashes of our past.

I lead Aksel into my carefully curated space, my sanctuary. The aroma of the French dish I've been preparing fills the air, and as he breathes it in, his eyes widen with surprise.

"Wow," he murmurs appreciatively. "That smells amazing. You made this, or did you order in?"

"It was all me," I shrug, feeling a spark of heat making its way onto my cheeks.

He lets out a low whistle as he admires the contents of the pot bubbling away on the stove, as well as my artistically plated meal. "I didn't know you could cook like this."

"Neither did I," I admit with a small smile, unable to resist the lighthearted banter that comes so easily between us. "I've come a long way from high school, huh? Remember when I set that kitchen on fire in home economics?"

Aksel laughs, the sound warm and familiar, and for a moment, it's as if the years of heartache and distance have never existed. "How could I forget? You were so mortified."

"Hey, it wasn't entirely my fault," I protest, crossing my arms defensively. "That stove was ancient."

"Sure, Fallon. Blame the under-funding of the school system for your culinary inadequacies. Whatever helps you sleep at night."

My cheeks burn, but not just from embarrassment. The easy back-and-forth we slip into is both comforting and disconcerting. I can't help but feel drawn to him, even after everything that's happened.

As we share laughter over memories, Aksel reaches into his pocket and pulls out something small and flat—a Polaroid photograph. He hands it to me, and my breath catches as I recognize the scene: Aksel and me as teenagers, grinning widely, his arm around me.

"I found this at my place the other day," he says, watching my reaction closely. "Thought you might want to see it."

The photo is a relic from a seemingly distant past, a time when things were simpler, and we were inseparable. A mix of pleasure and conflict washes over me as I realize he kept the photo all these years.

"Thank you," I murmur quietly, tracing the edge of the picture with my thumb. "It's nice to remember the good times."

"Is that all they are now?" Aksel asks, his voice low and intense. "Just memories?"

The question hangs in the air between us, heavy with unspoken words and unresolved feelings. And though I want to answer him, to tell him that there's still a chance for us, I can't find the courage. Or maybe I have the courage to know he'll ultimately hurt me, so instead I should protect myself by pushing him away before he gets a chance.

Instead, I just smile sadly and say, "A lot has happened since then, Aksel. It was a different time."

Aksel

I can tell the photo has thrown Fallon. She was clearly surprised I kept it all this time. I was somewhat surprised myself, finding it in the drawer where I keep scant personal mementos from years ago. Sensing the delicate nature of the moment, I reach into my pocket and pull out a small velvet pouch. "I brought you something else, too," I say, trying to maintain eye contact as I hand it to her.

She looks so gorgeous today, casually dressed in the comfort of her condo. Her joggers and tank top are a departure from her usual more edgy style. Her hair is thrown into a messy bun and she's wearing minimal makeup. There's a glow about her, and I can't help but sense that cooking has energized her.

Fallon looks at me with surprise, her eyes cautiously flicking between the pouch and my face, searching for any hidden meaning behind my gesture. She hesitates for just a heartbeat before taking it from me, her fingers brushing against mine in the process. The brief touch sends an unexpected jolt through me, but I keep my expression neutral, waiting for her reaction.

As she opens the pouch, her eyes widen when she sees the amethyst crystal inside. "Aksel, this is... I don't know what to say."

"Say you like it," I reply softly, the tension in the room palpable. "It's a symbol of peace. I remembered you used to collect crystals back in high school."

"Wow, I can't believe you remembered that," Fallon murmurs, her voice full of wonder as she runs her fingers over the rough surface of the crystal. The fact that I've remembered such a small detail seems to have an effect on her—her eyes glisten with unshed tears, and

I can see her wrestling with conflicting emotions.

The exchange becomes slightly awkward as I worry about the impact of both the photograph and the gift. I'm not sure if it's too much, if I'm pushing her too hard by bringing up our past. But the truth is, I want her to remember the good times, the connection we once had, even if it's painful.

"Thank you, Aksel," she finally whispers, cradling the crystal in her palm. "This means more than you know."

I nod, my heart pounding in my chest as I gauge her reaction. I need her to know that despite everything that has happened between us, there is still a part of me that cares for her deeply.

"Fallon," I begin, my voice steady despite the uncertainty swirling inside me. "I know this is all... complicated. We have a past, and it's not something we can just forget about or ignore. But maybe, if we can face it together, we can find a way to move forward."

She looks at me, her eyes searching mine, as if she's trying to determine if she can trust me—if she can trust herself. We both know that navigating this delicate dance of accepting the past while facing the uncertainties of the present won't be easy. But as I stand before her, offering her a symbol of peace and reconciliation, I can only hope that she'll take a chance on what could be between us once more.

She takes a deep breath, as if convincing herself of what to say next. "Well, I guess you might as well stay for dinner," she shrugs. "I made enough to feed at least five people. I'll take some into work tomorrow for Grave and Mia, but there's still way too much."

There's his name. Grave. I wondered when he'd come up in conversation. If only she knew how he came to be her trusted business associate. There's no way I can bring it up to her now, or she'd probably never speak with me again. Instead, I nod as if I'm following along like anyone else would. If I stand any chance of reconciling with Fallon, I need to focus only on her tonight.

"Sure, that sounds wonderful," I say. "Let's eat."

As we sit down to enjoy the meal, the energy in the room shifts. The flickering candlelight casts a soft glow on Fallon's face, and I can't help but be reminded of the times we spent together in the past. The laughter and shared memories that filled our earlier conversation still linger in the air, warming my chest with a sense of familiarity. At the same time, the reason I'm drawn to her is more than the comfort of having known her for all her life. There's something about her present self that has me almost hypnotized.

"Wow, Fallon," I say as I take a bite of the dish she prepared. "This is incredible. You really have come a long way since those high school cooking disasters."

"Thanks," she replies with a shy smile. "I had to learn eventually, right? A particularly useful cooking course in the south of France, a Christmas present from Dad and my brothers, really helped me to get the basics down, and I went from there."

We continue eating, the silence between us broken by occasional bursts of laughter and reminiscing. It's surprising how easily we slip back into the rhythm of our old friendship, yet an underlying tension remains. It feels like we're dancing on the edge of a precipice, one wrong step away from falling back into the chasm of emotions that once consumed us.

As the wine flows, our conversation becomes both more relaxed and more charged. At one point, we both reach for the bottle simultaneously, and our hands brush against each other once more. The contact sends a spark of electricity through me, making me acutely aware of how close we're sitting.

"Sorry," I mutter, quickly pulling my hand back.

"No problem," she replies, her voice barely audible over the sound of my own heartbeat.

The moment lingers between us, heavy and fraught with possibility. The undeniable attraction between us simmers beneath the surface, threatening to boil over at any moment. We continue our dance around the subject, both physically drawn to one another but also emotionally guarded.

As the meal comes to an end, I can't shake the feeling that something monumental is about to happen. The embers of connection, fueled by shared laughter, surprises, and symbolic gifts, illuminate the shadows of our past. The anticipation is palpable, and I know I need to make the first move and open up to her.

"Can I..." I trail off, unsure of how to broach the subject. "Can I ask you something?"

"Of course," she replies, her eyes searching mine for any hint of what's to come.

"Are we making a mistake by trying to reconnect?" I ask, barely able to get the words out. "Or is there still something worth fighting for between us?"

Fallon takes a deep breath, seeming to consider the question carefully. "Honestly, Aksel, I don't know. But maybe... maybe it's worth finding out."

The vulnerability in her voice tugs at my heart, reminding me of the girl I once knew.

The girl I fell in love with and could never let go. I'm acutely aware that the uncertainty of our future hangs in the balance, a lingering sense of anticipation keeping us both on edge.

Fallon clears the plates, leaving us each with a full glass of luscious red wine that's flowed freely throughout the evening. I wasn't anticipating being invited in for a meal, and am grateful the initially frosty reception morphed its way into something far more welcoming.

The apartment is cast in a soft glow, the remnants of our dinner creating an ambiance that echoes with unspoken words. I stand by the living room window, watching Fallon as she swirls the wine in her glass, her eyes lost in the dance of the city lights outside.

The air is heavy with the weight of our shared history, an uncharted territory we find ourselves navigating once again. My fingers twitch at my sides, a silent battle waged within as I'm torn between closing the distance and giving in to the desire that simmers between us, and holding back to protect us both from the inevitable complexities ahead.

As Fallon turns to the balcony, I'm drawn to her silhouette against the cityscape. The cool night air caresses my face as I follow her, the distance between us filled with the unspoken tension that has lingered for years.

I contemplate the intimacy of the evening, the laughter, the shared stories, and the undeniable chemistry that has sparked between us once more. I can't help but notice how beautiful she is, her wavy red hair framing soft features that hold a hint of the girl I once knew. And in this moment, I realize I've never stopped thinking she's the most gorgeous woman I've ever seen.

The temptation to bridge the gap between us, to let my fingers entwine in her hair and my lips claim hers, pulls at me with a force that threatens to unravel my restraint. I take a step forward, the ghost of a kiss hovering in the space between us, a question left unanswered.

Will we find our way back to each other, navigating the landmines of our past to build a future from the ashes of what once was? Or will the shadows that lurk in the corners of my mind, echoes of secrets not yet unveiled, threaten to extinguish the flickering light between us before it has a chance to burn bright once more? I still don't know the full extent of what I did to earn the bitterness and wrath she's clearly harbored toward me all these years, and I'm not sure whether she'll ever truly share it with me.

Only time will tell. For now, I move to stand beside her, our hands resting on the balcony railing, fingers almost touching. It's a tentative connection, a fragile exploration of what might still linger in the spaces between then and now.

After a comfortable silence, Fallon turns to me, her gaze searching my face as if looking for answers I'm not sure I have. "Why are you really here, Aksel?"

Her question hangs in the air between us, as potent as the unspoken desire that lingers with each fleeting touch and longing look. I hesitate, warring with the truth and the lies that have kept me bound for far too long.

"I don't know," I admit. "I just...I couldn't stay away anymore. After seeing you at the gala I just... needed to reach out. Especially after the way we left things the other night."

"Even after everything that's happened?" The waver in her voice reveals the cracks in her composure. Cracks I'm all too familiar with. Cracks I helped create.

Guilt rises inside me, a bitter taste I can't escape. "Fallon, I'm so sorry for the pain I've caused you." My hand closes over hers, the warmth of her skin chasing away the chill that has lingered inside me for years. "I don't know exactly what happened since we broke up, but I know that I hurt you and you deserved so much better."

A sad smile curves her lips, an unnamed emotion flashing across her face and disappearing as quickly as it came. "We were just kids, Aksel. We didn't know any better."

"Maybe not," I concede. "But I should have fought for you. I should have chosen you, instead of..." My voice trails off, unwilling to speak the name that has haunted us both.

"Instead of what?" Fallon searches my eyes, as if sensing there are still secrets I have yet to reveal. Secrets that might threaten the fragile bond we've begun to forge once more.

I swallow against the tightness in my throat, wondering if now is the time to finally unveil the truth. To let the light in so that the darkness of our past can no longer keep us bound. But as I open my mouth, the words refuse to come.

Some truths are better left unsaid. At least for now.

Fallon turns away, her gaze once again drifting to the city lights beyond. I can see the wheels turning in her head, questions forming that she's afraid to ask. Questions I'm afraid to answer. She doesn't know the dark experiences I've had that come with being deeply entrenched in a family company with strong mafia ties. She doesn't know the trauma I faced after she crushed my heart and blamed me. She's endured pain and so have I.

The silence stretches between us, fragile and laced with secrets. I grasp for something, anything, to chase away the ghosts that linger.

"Do you remember that time we snuck out to watch the sunrise on the beach?" I ask, a wistful smile curving my lips at the memory. "We were so tired we ended up falling asleep right there in the sand."

A soft laugh escapes Fallon, her eyes meeting mine once more. The shadows seem to lift from her expression, warmth replacing the cool distance that had settled upon her features. "I remember waking up with sand in places sand should never be. But it was worth it to see the sky light up like that. To share that moment with you."

Her words wrap around my heart, squeezing tight. Moments we once shared, now tinged with bittersweet nostalgia for a love that might have been.

"We shared so many good moments together." I reach out, tucking a stray lock of hair behind her ear. She initially flinches and then allows her body to relax. My knuckles brush against the softness of her cheek, a featherlight touch that ignites sparks inside me. "Before everything fell apart."

Fallon closes her eyes, leaning into my touch. The simple gesture speaks of a bone-deep longing, an aching familiarity that time and distance have failed to dull.

I know I should pull away. Know that we're treading dangerous ground, awakening a past that's best left buried. But the warmth of her skin against mine is an addiction I don't want to break.

An addiction that threatens to consume me whole.

Chapter 9

FALLON

The door clicks shut behind Aksel, leaving only the ghost of his presence in the air. I stand rooted to the spot, the words he left unspoken echoing through my mind. Promises unfinished, emotions undeciphered. The tenderness we shared tonight has cracked open a door I was certain I'd sealed shut forever.

After I finish cleaning the kitchen, I return to the living room where the remnants of Aksel's presence cling to the air like a ghost, refusing to be ignored. My lungs fill with the lingering scent of our shared dinner, each breath stirring up spices and memories I'd hoped were long buried. My heart races as I wander through the dimly lit apartment, my fingertips grazing over the surfaces Aksel touched less than an hour before.

I can't shake the feeling that tonight was an unexpected journey through time, each shared smile and story a cruel reminder of the connection we once had. As I replay the moments in my mind, I dissect every glance, every shared laugh, and every unspoken word. Aksel's eyes, a canvas of emotions, flicker in my memory, haunting me with their intensity. His choice of gifts were a pleasant yet disconcerting surprise, a sign that the past is not fully just a memory for him either.

"Dammit, Fallon," I curse under my breath. "You're supposed to hate him."

But it's not that simple, is it? The past refuses to stay hidden, clawing its way back into my life with every stolen moment between us. My chest tightens as I remember the warmth of his laughter, the sincerity in his gaze when he spoke of our shared history.

"Remember what he did," I tell myself, but the voice inside my head sounds weak, almost pleading.

The wine in my glass catches the light, casting a crimson shadow on the tablecloth. I can't help but think of how it mirrors the swirl of emotions inside me—a turbulent mix of longing, doubt, and the bittersweet taste of revenge. I take a deep breath and raise the wine to my lips, savoring its warmth as it slides down my throat.

"Here's to us," I whisper, my voice barely audible over the hum of the city outside. "To whatever this is, and whatever it may become."

As I make my way to the balcony, the cool night air embraces me like an old friend, bringing with it a sense of clarity that has been absent for far too long. The city lights dance across my face, casting a gentle glow on my features as I gaze out at the familiar skyline.

I can almost hear Aksel's voice in my ear, his deep, melodic tone urging me to take the leap and rediscover the love we once shared. But my heart still bears the scars of our past, and I can't shake the feeling that what we had was simply too volatile, too destructive to ever truly be called love. After all, nobody who loves you should cause you so much pain.

And yet, here I am, lost in the memories of our laughter and the vulnerability we allowed each other to see. It's a dangerous game we're playing, one that threatens to tear open old wounds and leave us both bleeding anew. But the allure of Aksel King, the man who once held my heart in his hands, is impossible to resist.

"Damn you, Aksel," I murmur into the night, my voice carried away by the breeze. "Why did you have to come back? Why couldn't you leave well enough alone and just let me continue to hate you?"

As I lean against the railing, my thoughts swirling like the wine in my glass, I know that there's no turning back now. Our past refuses to be forgotten, and whether it leads to healing or further heartache, I cannot deny the pull of the connection that still binds us together.

"Get a grip, Fallon," I chastise myself, trying to regain control over my thoughts. "Just because he's back doesn't mean anything has changed."

But even as I say the words, I know they're a lie. Tonight's dinner was an unexpected journey through time, each shared smile and story a reminder of what we once were. And now, those feelings are resurfacing within me, calling everything into question.

The city lights continue to twinkle like distant stars, watching over me as I close my eyes and take a deep breath, ready to face whatever challenges lie ahead.

Chapter 10

FALLON

The buzzing of my phone disrupts the silence in my condo, as I stare at the screen. It's Aksel's name that flashes across it, sending a whirlwind of emotions through me. My finger hesitates above the screen before opening the message. Concise and laced with an air of vulnerability, the invitation to meet him for coffee catches me off guard.

Aksel: It was so good to see you the other day. Thanks again for dinner. You're an amazing chef! Meet me tomorrow, 3 p.m. at The Roasted Bean?

His words pull me back into memories of our shared history. The Roasted Bean was our place, once upon a time, when we ventured into the city on dates. I bite my lip, feeling conflicted, but ultimately, I type out a response.

Fallon: Okay. See you there.

I take a deep breath, knowing that I need to keep this meeting a secret from Mia. She's been my ever-loyal confidante and wouldn't approve of my rendezvous with Aksel after the way he hurt me. But something deep inside me yearns for resolution, so many things unsaid the other evening, and I can't help but follow that instinct.

Feeling apprehensive, I push open the door to the coffee shop, the familiar chime of the bell overhead announcing my entrance. The aroma of freshly ground beans fills the air, wrapping around me like a comforting embrace, but it does little to ease the tension that coils in my chest.

The weight of my decision to keep this meeting a secret from Mia presses down on me like the heavy, humid air outside. I've never hidden anything from her before, and the guilt gnaws at the edges of my conscience. But I can't bear the thought of what she might say if she found out about Aksel's invitation, and how she might remind me of all the reasons we shouldn't be in each other's lives.

The quaint coffee shop nestled in the heart of the city feels like stepping back in time. Its warm, dimly lit interior creates an intimate setting, a stark contrast to the storm of emotions brewing within me.

As my eyes scan the room, searching for Aksel's face among the others, my heart races as I wonder whether he feels the same sense of unease as I do. I'm not sure either of us is ready to face the truths that lie beneath the surface of our past.

"Fallon," a voice calls out, and I turn to see him standing by our old corner table. The sight of him sends a shiver down my spine, a mixture of excitement and dread. This time he's wearing a business suit that hugs his hard body perfectly, a stark contrast from the signature leather jacket he constantly wore in high school. It turns out he looks equally hot in either attire. I walk over, each step echoing our past encounters in this very place.

"Hey," I manage to say, my voice barely above a whisper.

"Hi Fallon," he replies softly, his eyes searching mine with a mix of remorse and determination.

"Sit, please," he gestures to the seat across from him. I comply, my hands shaking slightly as I pull out the chair and lower myself into it. Aksel's gaze never leaves my face, and I struggle to keep my emotions under control.

"Thanks for coming," he says quietly.

"Yep," I nod, my voice wavering with the intensity of my feelings. "Here we are."

"Here we are," he echoes with a nod, his fingers tapping nervously on the table.

"Can I get you anything?" he asks, his gaze steady on mine.

"A double espresso with a side of seltzer," I reply, my throat tight with unspoken words.

"Okay." He signals the waiter and places the order, then turns his attention back to me. "Fallon, I want you to know that I didn't ask you here to hurt you by dredging up the past. I just... the other night, dinner, was just so amazing and I—I needed to see you again."

"Needed?" The word feels sharp on my tongue, and I can't help but bristle at the implication that he has any claim on me after all this time. But he has a point. The other night was pretty amazing, if unexpected.

"Please, let me explain." His voice is soft, almost pleading, and I feel the smallest flicker of hope ignite in my chest. Maybe, just maybe, there's a chance for us to mend the rift that's kept us apart for so many years. Still, I'm not going to give in that easily.

"Fine," I say, folding my arms across my chest. "Talk."

Aksel takes a deep breath, his eyes fixed on mine as he begins to lay bare the emotions that have haunted him since our last encounter. And as I listen to his words, a part of me wonders if we're both dancing on the edge of a precipice, teetering between the possibility of forgiveness and the inevitability of heartbreak.

"Fallon," he begins, his voice rough with emotion. "I owe you an explanation."

A bitter laugh escapes me, even as the ache in my chest threatens to overwhelm me. "You think?" I retort, unable to keep the venom from my words. "An explanation would have been nice, oh, I don't know—ten or so years ago?"

"Fair enough," he concedes, his expression a mix of remorse and determination. "But I'm here now, and I want to make things right."

The weight of our shared history hangs heavy in the air, suffocating me with the ghosts of memories long buried. My secret omission about this meeting from Mia weighs on me, adding to the angst that coils around my heart like a vice.

"Fine," I snap, my voice trembling despite myself. "Let's hear it."

Aksel takes a deep breath, his fingers continuing to drum nervously on the table. As our coffees arrive, the bitter scent mingling with the heady aroma of fresh grounds, I can't help but feel that they're a fitting metaphor for what's about to unfold between us—the promise of potential resolutions laced with the sting of truths long suppressed.

"First, I want you to know how sorry I am," Aksel begins, and I can hear the sincerity in his voice, even as my walls remain firmly in place. Then again growing up in a family like his you need to learn to be a pretty good actor. "I never meant to hurt you, Fallon. That's the last thing I ever wanted."

"Really?" I challenge, crossing my arms defensively. "Because it sure as hell didn't seem that way at the time."

"Believe me, I know how it looked," he admits, his gaze never leaving mine. "But there's so much more to the story than you know. So many things I couldn't tell you back then—things I wish I could have."

"Like what?" My pulse races, a torrent of emotions surging through me as I brace myself for the revelations he's about to share. In this charged atmosphere, my heart and mind wage war with one another, torn between the desire for closure and the fear of the pain it might bring.

Aksel hesitates, clearly struggling with where to begin. And as he delves into the complexities of our past, I find myself hanging on every word, desperate for answers yet dreading them all the same. His slate grey eyes hold mine with an intensity that sends shivers down my spine—a potent mix of vulnerability and resolve, as if he's prepared to bare his soul for me to see.

"Fallon, I need you to understand how much I've changed," Aksel says, his voice low and steady, betraying the gravity of his words. "I was young, stupid, and selfish back then. But I've grown, and I want to make amends for what I did to you."

My skepticism claws at my insides, gnawing at the flicker of hope that threatens to ignite within me. My fingers tap rhythmically against the small ceramic espresso cup, a silent drumbeat marking the tempo of my racing thoughts. At this rate, we could start a band with our fingers as the instruments.

"Words are easy, Aksel," I reply, my tone a guarded whisper. "How do I know this isn't just another one of your games?"

"Because I'm not the same person who played those games, Fallon." His hands clench into fists on the table, knuckles whitening as he struggles to convey the depth of his sincerity. "I can prove it to you if you give me the chance."

His gaze never wavers, but I can see the desperation lurking beneath the surface, a plea for redemption that echoes through the quiet space between us.

"Actions speak louder than words," I say cautiously, testing the waters. The memory of Mia's warnings flits through my mind, a reminder that trust is not easily won or given, her words based on the countless times I cried on her shoulder because of Aksel's cruelty and ultimate betrayal.

"Then let me show you," he replies, determination burning in his eyes. "Let me prove that I'm worthy of your trust, your forgiveness..." He pauses and suddenly looks nervous. "And maybe even your love."

My heart stutters in my chest, the fire of hope fanned by his words. Yet, doubt still gnaws at the edges of my resolve, a persistent shadow that refuses to be banished. I'm supposed to be plotting revenge against this man, not debating whether we can reignite our affection of years ago.

"Fine," I concede, swallowing hard against the lump in my throat. He needs to be warned, and this also might be the perfect way to lure him into my trap, to find out something that can ultimately bring him down. "I'll give you a chance to prove you've changed. It won't undo the hurt you've caused me." I pause, my eyes narrowing at him. "But if you betray me again, Aksel... there'll be no coming back from that."

"Understood," he murmurs, his relief palpable as he reaches across the table, his fingertips brushing mine with a feather-light touch that sends shivers down my spine.

"Thank you, Fallon," he whispers, and it's as if the entire coffee shop holds its breath, waiting for the outcome of this fragile dance between us.

As we sit there, surrounded by the soothing aroma of coffee and the muted hum of conversations, I can't help but wonder what the future holds for us. Will this confrontation be the key to unraveling the knotted threads of our past, or will it simply draw them tighter, binding us together in a tangle of pain and betrayal?

Only time will tell, and as Aksel's fingers intertwine with mine, I find myself both terrified and hopeful, caught in the whirlwind of emotions that has become an all-too-familiar part of our story.

The waiter returns and I order a cold brew. Two double espressos would have me tap dancing on the table so I need to mix things up.

As we sit there, I find my anxiety growing. Perhaps I've already had one too many espressos, but I suddenly feel agitated. The conversation grows more heated and I pull my hand away from his, the air between us thick with unspoken words and tension.

Aksel's eyes darken as he tries to clarify just one of the past misunderstandings that have haunted our relationship for years.

"Fallon, I told you the truth. I never meant to hurt you back then," he says, his hands gesturing wildly in an attempt to convey the depth of his regret. "I was young and foolish, but I loved you more than anything."

His hands move erratically, emphasizing his words, but in my heightened state of distress, I misinterpret his actions as dismissive, as if he's trying to brush away the pain he caused me so carelessly. He's not giving me specifics, just vague apologies about his immaturity and allusions to some of the ways he hurt me. I know he doesn't know the full story, but he knows enough to give me more than this. And I deserve more.

The waiter returns with my cold brew and I take a sip while I figure out how to respond.

"Is that all you have to say?" I snap, anger and hurt boiling within me like a tempestuous storm. "You think a simple generalized apology will erase everything? That we can go on like nothing ever happened and there hasn't been a chasm of time and layers of hurt to drive us apart? That stuff doesn't just go away, you know."

Aksel opens his mouth to respond, but my fury gets the better of me. In a fit of frustration, I impulsively grab the cup of cold brew from the table, tossing it at him without a second thought. The icy liquid drenches him, shock registering on his face as it seeps through his fancy suit, darkening the fabric like ink spreading across parchment.

The coffee shop falls into a stunned silence, the only sound the steady drip of cold brew onto the floor. My heart pounds in my chest, a wild drumbeat echoing my shattered emotions.

"Fallon..." Aksel murmurs, reaching out for me, desperation etched into every line of his face.

But I've had enough. Betrayal and anguish claw at my insides, leaving me feeling hollowed out and raw. I can't bear to look at him any longer—the man who once held my heart in his hands, only to crush it mercilessly beneath his heel and then have the audacity to try to weasel his way into my heart once again. He deserves much more than cold brew to be tossed at him.

"Stay away from me." My voice trembles, a fierce growl edged with tears. "Don't you dare come near me again."

With that, I storm out of the coffee shop, leaving Aksel bewildered and dripping with cold brew amidst the hushed whispers of onlookers. The door slams shut behind me, a final punctuation to our disastrous meeting. I never should have agreed to come in the first place. Nothing good was ever going to come from this.

As I walk away, my thoughts race, a jumble of pain, anger, and confusion. The shattered remnants of our fragile connection lie scattered in my wake, the cold brew staining the table and his suit as a bitter testament to the misunderstandings that continue to haunt us.

"Fallon!" Aksel's voice calls out from behind me as he runs after me, but I don't stop. I can't. The ties that bound us together have been severed, leaving only the raw, jagged edges of betrayal and regret.

And so I keep walking, away from the man who once held my heart, away from the ghosts of our past that refuse to let us go.

"Fallon," he cries out again, the sound echoing through the streets like a mournful lament, but I don't look back.

I won't allow myself to be ensnared by his lies and false promises any longer. It's time to forge my own path, free from the shadows that have haunted me for far too long. I never should have allowed myself to be drawn back in, and I'll cut it off now before he has the opportunity to disappoint me yet again.

As the physical distance between us grows, I find a small measure of solace in the knowledge that, despite everything, I am still standing—broken, but not defeated, ready to face whatever comes next. Now any conflicting feelings about future potential between us is well and truly gone, and I'm even more focused on revenge.

Chapter 11

FALLON

As I step into my office, an unexpected sight greets me. A tall, imposing figure clad in black and gray is comfortably seated in my chair, seemingly unfazed by my entrance. The man—Grave—is a walking enigma, and his presence immediately captures my attention.

"Nice of you to finally join me," he drawls, his voice a low rumble that sends shivers down my spine.

Grave's unsettling calmness permeates the air as he peels an apple with a flick knife, an oddly casual gesture that contrasts with the tense atmosphere it creates. Apple peelings are discarded haphazardly on the floor, symbolizing his nonchalant disregard for the sanctity of my office.

"I hate it when you do that, you know," I remark, my eyes narrowing at him. He smirks, revealing a hint of amusement beneath his stoic exterior. "It's a small price to pay for getting to work with me though, isn't it, when you really think about it?"

I sigh, shaking my head. Grave fascinates me. On one hand, he appears to be a straightforward guy driven by primal desires—yet on the other, there's a complexity about him that eludes complete understanding.

"Hey, get up. I want to sit in my own chair. I feel like a client over here. I can't think like this." I plop down on the overstuffed couch, watching as Grave, with a nonchalant shrug, complies, removing his massive legs from my sleek white desk.

"Now you know how the clients must feel," he replies, his tone sardonic. "You towering over them with your opinions and your advice."

I roll my eyes. "Haha, you're hilarious. Anyway, to answer your question, yes, we have a client. I think this is going to be a fairly simple transaction. A just desserts type of scenario."

"Aren't they all?" Grave's retort is laced with a dark humor befitting of his enigmatic persona.

As we discuss the details of our new case, I can't help but study him. The way he moves, the way he speaks—he pulls it off as casual, but in reality it's more like a choreographed dance, each step carefully calculated and executed. He's a mystery that I've been trying to unravel for years, and every time I think I'm getting closer, he slips through my grasp.

It's infuriating and intoxicating all at once, and I couldn't imagine anyone else working with me in the capacity he does. My sidekick. My fixer. My literal partner in crime.

As I sit here, observing the man who has become such an integral part of my life, I wonder what secrets still lurk beneath the surface, and what hidden depths he has yet to reveal. And as much as I crave the answers to these questions, I can't deny the thrill of the chase—the exhilaration that comes from trying to solve the enigma that is Grave.

"Fallon?" he asks, snapping me out of my thoughts. "You okay?"

"Fine," I reply, forcing a smile. "Just lost in thought about why I let you continue to flick apple peels all over the floor of my office. By the way, that's the part that contains the most fiber. Now, let's get back to business."

He crunches into his apple as he takes a seat in my overstuffed couch, leaning into the cushion with one of his burly arms splayed across the back.

"Alright, let's talk about this new case," I say, focusing my attention on the file in front of me. "Matilda Smith. Twenty-six years old. Real estate agent who works upstate. She's been a victim of revenge porn. Her ex-boyfriend decided to release some private photos and videos after their breakup. Some of them have gone viral, and she's getting harassed both online and offline. It's been damaging to her career and obviously embarrassing on a personal level having that kind of material released without her consent."

Grave's expression darkens as he listens intently, his eyes reflecting an understanding of the darker aspects of human behavior that I've come to rely on in our work together. Our partnership thrives on our complementary skills—my strategic mind and his tactical expertise—and together, we're pretty much unstoppable. "What do we know about the ex?" he asks, his voice low and dangerous.

"His name is Jacob Daniels. He's your typical entitled prick—rich family, never had to face any real consequences for his actions." My hands clench into fists at the thought of yet another woman being humiliated like this. There are people who do insane things out of desperation, but this man has financial means, and his actions have clearly been driven by malice. It fuels my desire for vengeance, pushing me to keep going despite the darkness that surrounds us. "Sounds like he needs a taste of his own medicine," Grave says, his tone laced with menace.

"Exactly," I reply, a grim smile forming on my lips. "We're going to make him regret ever crossing Matilda Smith."

The office door opens, and Mia walks in, her petite figure and curly dark hair a warm contrast to the somber atmosphere. She's accompanied by an attractive young woman who looks visibly shaken and vulnerable. The sight of her like this only strengthens my resolve.

"Matilda, thank you for coming in," I say, rising from my chair. "This is my associate, Grave. We'll be handling your case together."

Grave steps off to the side, allowing Matilda to take center stage while Mia discreetly steps out of the office. Despite the occasional irritation he causes, I can't help but appreciate the reliability and loyalty he brings to our unconventional partnership. He reads clients well, too, accurately judging their body language even while they're in high states of distress.

"Nice to meet you," Grave says, his voice surprisingly gentle given his imposing stature. Matilda manages a small smile, her eyes darting between the two of us.

"Thank you both for helping me. You can call me Maddie by the way," she mumbles, her voice quivering. "I'm here because I just can't take it anymore."

"Maddie, we're going to do everything in our power to make this right," I assure her, my voice firm and steady. "Jacob Daniels will pay for what he's done to you."

"Thank you," Maddie whispers, tears welling up in her eyes.

"Let's get started," I say, determination coursing through me. Grave nods in agreement, his presence a constant reminder of the unique bond we share—a bond forged in darkness, vengeance, an unspoken understanding of each other's pain, and a commitment to delivering justice and retribution for those who have been wronged. And perhaps, in doing so, we'll find our own salvation in the shadows.

"We have the basics from our intake information, but tell us again in your own words," I say, turning my attention back to Maddie, "what exactly did Jacob do?"

She swallows hard, tears welling up in her eyes. "He...he posted intimate pictures of me online. Pictures that were only ever meant for his eyes."

"Did you consent to those pictures being taken?" I ask quietly.

"Yes," she whispers. "But not to them being shared with anyone but Jacob. It's mortifying, having my naked body plastered all over the internet. My clients have seen them. My family has seen them. And they're not like... tasteful nudes where the most sensitive parts are obscured. You can see everything. And I mean *everything*." Her face somehow seems to redden and pale at the same time. "And that's just the photos. There are actual videos as well."

"Understood," I say, feeling a surge of anger on her behalf. "I promise you, Maddie, we'll make this right."

I can't help but steal glances at Grave as Maddie recounts her story. The dimly lit office seems to suit him, casting shadows across his chiseled features and making him appear even more enigmatic than usual. He stands off to the side, arms folded over his broad chest, his dark eyes never leaving Maddie's face. His stoic expression gives away nothing, and I find myself wondering—yet again—what he's thinking.

My mind drifts back to when I first met him—his sudden appearance in my life like a phantom in the night. My life had been teetering on the brink of chaos, and then he was there, standing beside me like an avenging angel with a dark twist. The connection between us felt electric, immediate and dangerous. Despite our close partnership, there are still so many questions about his past that remain unanswered, like an incomplete puzzle that refuses to be solved despite the fragments I've gathered over the years. The occasional mentions of fallen squadron comrades, black ops missions, and boot camp tyrants send shivers down my spine. It's clear that beneath his rugged exterior lies a vulnerability, a hidden side of him that he keeps carefully guarded. But he's far more comfortable discussing clients than himself, so there are many pieces to Grave still to be untangled.

"Are there any other details you think we should know?" Grave interjects, speaking for the first time since Maddie entered the room, other than in greeting, and bringing my focus back to her. His deep voice gives me goosebumps, a reminder of the power he holds—and wields—so effortlessly.

"Um, no. I think that's everything," Maddie stammers, her eyes darting between us nervously. The atmosphere in my office is heavy with anticipation, the weight of Maddie's grief hanging thick like fog. My eyes flicker between her tear-streaked face and Grave.

"Maddie, you did the right thing by coming here and you're in good hands." My tone is gentle but firm as I clasp her hands in mine, feeling her slight tremble in my grasp. "We'll handle everything from here."

"Thank you," she chokes out, gratitude shining through her pain.

With a nod, Maddie leaves the office, and I find myself alone with Grave once more. The tension in the room is palpable, but there's also a sense of comfort in his presence—a knowledge that we're in this together, no matter how high the stakes.

"Let's get to work," Grave says, his voice low and dangerous—a promise wrapped in steel.

"Agreed," I reply, feeling the fire of vengeance ignite within me. "There's no time to waste. Where do we start?" I ask, searching for some semblance of direction amid the chaos. "What's our plan?"

"Simple," he replies, his gaze narrowing as he leans against the wall, his hands clasped behind his back. "We expose the truth, and we make this Jacob scum pay."

I nod. "He embarrassed her online, so as much as I would like to beat the shit out of him, that doesn't seem right." I furrow my brow. "So it's a matter of finding something more fitting."

"Well, Jacob's crime against Maddie was virtual, right? And I think we can destroy him virtually in a way that makes him wish he'd only been on the receiving end of physical violence," Grave counters, his lips curling into a half-smile that sends shivers down my spine. "Once things are out on the internet, they're out forever. Whereas bruises and broken bones heal."

"Let's go for it, then," I reply, feeling the fire of determination ignite within me. "No time to waste."

As we dive into our plan, I can't help but feel the echoes of Grave's speculated past lingering in the air—whispers of a life shaped by darkness and decisions made in the shadows. I ache to understand him, to know the truth behind his enigmatic façade, but for now, I need to set those thoughts aside and focus on exacting revenge for Maddie.

Some time later

"Grave," I say, unable to contain my curiosity any longer. "Why do you always keep so much to yourself? I mean, we've been working together for years, and yet I feel like I barely know you."

He hesitates, his brow furrowing as he contemplates my question. Finally, he speaks, his voice low and measured. "There are things in my past, Fallon, that I don't want to think about—let alone share with others."

"Even me?" I ask, hurt flickering through me at the thought that he might not trust me enough to confide in me.

"Especially you," he replies softly, his eyes locking onto mine. "You deserve better than the baggage I carry."

"Grave, we all have demons," I say, my voice shaking slightly. "But we can't fight them alone. Let me help you, just like you've helped me so many times before."

For a moment, he doesn't respond, and I wonder if I've pushed him too far. But then he takes a deep breath and nods, a look of resignation in his dark eyes.

"I'll tell you more one day," he says, an expression passing over his face that I can't quite put my finger on. "But I'm a very private person and now's not the time. So if you don't mind, let's focus on destroying Jacob Daniels' life the way he did to Maddie."

He's right. Now is the time for our client, not satisfying my latent curiosity.

"Let's do this," I say, feeling the adrenaline surge through my veins.

In this moment, I know that no matter what lies hidden within our respective histories, one thing remains clear: we are bound by a common purpose, and together, we are unstoppable. Grave's gaze meets mine again, and for a moment, I see something in his eyes that makes my heart race—a fierce determination that mirrors my own. There's an unspoken understanding between us, a shared drive for justice that binds us together like the strands of a twisted rope.

As we sit, poring over our laptops in companionable silence, I realize I've been so wrapped up in planning revenge for Maddie, and contemplating Grave's dark past, that Aksel has barely crossed my mind.

Chapter 12

FALLON

The door to the dive bar creaks as I push it open, a cloud of cigarette smoke and the smell of stale beer engulfing me. It's perfect, just what I need right now. After hours in the office plotting with Grave, I need a change of scenery where my mind can process while I focus on other things. Revenge work is rewarding but draining.

"Whiskey, neat," I tell the bartender, sliding onto one of the worn stools. He nods, pouring me a shot of amber liquid. I knock it back, my throat burning from the heat of the alcohol, but it's a welcome distraction. The image of Maddie Smith, broken and distraught, lingers in my mind, her tearful words echoing through my head. I can't even imagine what it would feel like to have my most private photos and videos plastered all over the internet for whoever to see. Such an invasion of privacy, and most definitely intentional. Jacob Daniels will pay for what he did to her—I'll make sure of it.

"Another," I say, pushing the empty glass towards the bartender. He refills it without question, and I toss it back just as quickly as the first, the warmth spreading through my chest. The world shifts around me, blurring at the edges, and I let the haze take over as I continue to conjure up elaborate revenge plots against Jacob.

"Rough day?" the bartender asks, wiping down the counter with a damp rag.

"Something like that," I reply, my voice tight. "You ever had someone you just wanted to bring down?"

"Who hasn't?" he chuckles, his eyes crinkling at the corners. "But you know what they say—revenge is a dish best served cold."

"Or with a side of whiskey. I mean, both are said to be poisons that consume you from the inside out." I smirk, raising my glass in a mock salute before downing another shot. He laughs, shaking his head, but pours me another anyway.

"Can't argue with that," he says, leaning against the bar. "Just don't let it consume you, alright?"

"Too late for that," I mutter under my breath, my thoughts swirling around Jacob Daniels and the ways I could make him suffer. He deserves nothing less, and I won't rest until he's on his knees, begging for mercy.

"Hey," the bartender says softly, concern etched onto his face. "Whatever it is, just remember that you're better than them, alright? Don't let their darkness poison you too."

I nod, appreciating his words despite the anger boiling inside me. He has no idea of the darkness that swirls within. But I can't let go of the rage, not yet. Maddie deserves justice, and I'm the only one who can give it to her.

"Thanks," I tell the bartender, my voice rough. "But this is something I have to do."

Feeling looser and in need of a distraction while my brain plots against Jacob in the background, my eyes drift away from the bartender and scan the dimly lit room, landing on a mysterious stranger perched on a barstool in the corner. He's tall, with dark hair and an enigmatic smile and intense dark eyes, exuding an air of danger that immediately piques my interest. He wears a plaid shirt with the sleeves rolled up to his elbows, revealing tattooed forearms that make my heart race a little, and ripped jeans with scuffed, steel-toed boots. I need something to numb me, to make me forget the weight of what I'm about to do. Maybe this man can provide that temporary escape.

"Here goes nothing," I mutter under my breath as I stride towards him, confidence masking any lingering doubt. When I reach his side, I lean against the bar, close enough for him to notice the fire burning within me. I don't want there to be any room for misunderstanding about what I'm after. He's even better-looking up close and I feel a twinge of excitement at the thought of what I'm about to make happen.

"Hey there," I say without preamble. "You're looking for some no-strings-attached fun tonight?"

His eyes trail over me for a moment and I can tell he's pleased with what he sees. The man raises an eyebrow, clearly surprised by my blunt approach, but his lips curl into a knowing grin. "I might be. What did you have in mind?"

"Nothing too complicated," I reply, my voice dripping with seduction. "Just two people drowning their demons for a night."

He studies my face for a moment, as if gauging whether I'm serious. Whatever he sees must convince him, because he nods and drains the last of his drink. "Lead the way."

We exit the bar and make our way down the street, the cool night air doing little to quell the heat simmering between us. My thoughts are a jumbled mess, Jacob Daniels' name still echoing through my mind, but I force it all aside. The rest of tonight is about distraction, not revenge.

"Over here," I gesture to a nearby hotel, succumbing to its flickering neon sign like a moth drawn to a flame. It's cheap and divey and well-suited for the rough primal night I have planned. We walk in, and I saunter up to the front desk, giving the receptionist a tight-lipped smile. "Room for the night, please."

"Name?" she asks in a bored voice, her fingers poised over the keyboard.

"Jane Smith," I reply, a fake name to throw off any potential eavesdroppers. The receptionist nods and hands us our keycards, her face displaying no judgment or curiosity. This is not the kind of place where they check for IDs or charge for incidentals, because they don't care who you are as long as you have cash, and there definitely aren't any incidentals.

"Room 314," she says, her voice monotone. "Enjoy your stay."

"Thanks," I murmur, grabbing the man's hand and leading him towards the elevator, my heart pounding with anticipation. This isn't love, it's not even desire, although the man is attractive and has a certain energy about him. It's a desperate attempt to forget the darkness brewing within me, if only for a few hours.

But as the elevator doors close, sealing us in, I can't help but think of Aksel and the way he makes me feel alive. And I wonder if this night will be enough to wash away the emptiness consuming me from within. I quickly shove all thoughts of him down and I turn to face the man from the bar. "Are you ready?" I ask, my voice husky.

"I can't wait," he growls as we make our way out of the elevator and down the hallway.

The moment the hotel room door clicks shut behind us, an electric hunger surges through me. I grab the hot stranger by his shirt collar and pull him in for a rough, greedy kiss. Our lips crash together as our hands move with urgency, tugging at clothes that suddenly feel like barriers we must break down.

"Fuck," he breathes against my mouth, his fingers deftly lifting my racerback top up over my head and letting it fall to the floor. My own hands are busy tearing at his belt, yanking it free and discarding it with impatience.

Shirts, pants, underwear—all of it becomes a forgotten trail on the floor as we stumble towards the bed, still locked in a frenzied embrace. It's all action, no words; our mouths too preoccupied with kissing to bother speaking. The only language here is raw need, a primal craving that demands satisfaction.

His torso, like his arms, are covered in tattoos and he's sculpted as fuck. By his boots and his figure, and his rough, calloused hands, I can tell he works in something physically demanding like construction or landscaping or maybe heavy equipment. While in some ways I couldn't care less who he is, his ruggedness further sets off the primal urgency within me, although in ways he might not expect.

He lifts me up, and I wrap my legs around his waist, feeling his hardness pressing against me. My back hits the mattress, and he follows, not once breaking contact. His body covers mine, hot and heavy, and I arch beneath him, seeking friction. He reaches down to line himself up with my entrance and slams himself into me. I'm soaking, hungry with desire for an anonymous physical connection. Still, I gasp as his girthy cock stretches my walls, stinging in a good way as he slides into me to his hilt.

He groans. "Fucking hell, your pussy feels amazing," as he plows himself into me, my pussy clenching tightly around his sizable shaft.

"More," I gasp, digging my nails into his shoulders, urging him on without another word. He understands, responding with a thrust that sends waves of pleasure rippling through my core. Everything else fades away—the anger, the vengeance, the unrelenting ache in my heart—leaving only this base connection between two strangers desperate to feel alive.

Our bodies move together in a wild, urgent rhythm, each thrust erasing the memories of the day from my mind. His grunts are carnal, him needing me as much as I need him. This man is a balm to my bruised soul, a temporary reprieve from the darkness that threatens to engulf me. And yet, even as I lose myself in the pleasure he provides, there's an emptiness that lingers, a hollow feeling deep within that can't be filled by sex alone.

But for now, I push that thought away, focusing on the rough slide of skin against skin, the taste of sweat and desire on my lips. I cling to this stranger, drowning out the world with each gasp and moan, praying that for a moment, just a moment, I can forget everything else.

My mind starts to drift despite the pleasure he's giving me, and I know I need to change things up in order for this encounter to give me what I truly need: distraction and a sense of control. "Are you ready for what I have planned next?" I growl in the man's ear. "Can I dominate you for the rest of our time together?"

He raises an eyebrow, momentarily pausing his thrusting. "*You* want to dominate *me*?" He smirks, but also looks intrigued. I bet nobody has ever suggested that to him before.

"That's what I said, didn't I?" I growl, digging my nails into his back a little harder.

"Go right ahead," he growls.

The sexy stranger hops off me and I retrieve a few items from my bag and return to the bed.

"Get on your knees," I growl, and the man complies, turning his ass to face me. The sound of the leather straps slapping against each other echoes in the room as I secure the man's wrists to the bedposts. My hands shake slightly, but my resolve remains firm, unyielding. I need this, and so does he—this release from control, this surrender to something darker, more primal.

"Is this okay?" I ask, my voice rough with desire. He nods, his gaze locked on mine, a mix of anticipation and uncertainty in his eyes. I can't help but grin, feeling powerful, untouchable, as I reach for the harness and silicone toy I brought along. I don't normally carry a strap-on around with me, but I had a feeling I'd need a distraction tonight, and I wanted nothing more than to be in control of someone much bigger and stronger than me. Luckily, he's a willing participant. I can usually pick them out in a crowd, a hidden skill.

Adjusting the straps around my hips, I give him one last look, searching for any sign of hesitation. But there's none—only a wordless plea for me to take control, to give him what neither of us knew we needed until now. He doesn't flinch as he watches me apply a generous amount of lube to the dildo. And so, with a deep breath, I kneel behind him and line myself up between his legs, gripping his thighs as I push forward into him.

"Fuck," he groans, his body tensing beneath me. The sound of his submission sends a shiver down my spine, a surge of satisfaction that only fuels my hunger for more. I start slow, working my way in slowly and he moans a little each time I make my way further inside him. Before long, the dildo is fairly well into his ass, building a steady rhythm that has us both gasping for breath, our eyes locked in a dance of dominance and submission.

"Harder," he whispers, his voice strained. I oblige, increasing the pace, the force behind each thrust. It's exhilarating, intoxicating, this power I wield over him, and yet... it's not enough.

Aksel's face floats into my mind, his piercing gray eyes, his smug smile—a reminder of everything I've lost, everything I'm fighting for. I try to push the thought away, to focus on the man writhing beneath me, but the image lingers, taunting me, stoking the flames of my rage.

"Damn it," I hiss, frustration clawing at my chest. The man twists around, concern etched across his face, but I shake my head, refusing to let him in on the turmoil that threatens to consume me.

"Keep going," he urges, desperation in his voice. And so I do, pounding into him with renewed vigor, each thrust an outlet for the anger, the pain that courses through my veins. But it's no use—Aksel is there, behind every thrust, every gasp, mocking me even as I try to forget him.

I pause, and the man twists around again. "Please, I never knew this would feel so good—please keep going," he begs, but I can't, and instead, I shake my head.

"Fuck this," I growl, pulling out and unfastening the harness, throwing it aside and then unsecuring both of his wrists from the leather straps that held him captive and helped bend him to my will. The man flips around and watches me, confusion in his eyes, but I can't bring myself to care. All that matters is the fire that burns within me, the need for vengeance that refuses to be quenched by anything else.

I decide to give it one more try. Maybe if I come, the release will help to free some of my mental anguish. He's lying on his back at this point, so I climb onto him, straddling his hips between my thighs and feeling his hardness pressing against me. "We can keep going, but do you mind if I call you another name?"

"Call me anything you want," he says, his eyes dark with a combination of lust and residual confusion.

"Good," I say as I slam myself down on his cock, enjoying the sensation of his girth dragging against my walls. He groans as my pussy strains against his hardness.

"Fuck, Aksel," I gasp, my fingernails digging into the man's shoulders as I ride him, but it's not the nameless man beneath me that I see. Instead, it's Aksel's eyes that bore into mine, his lips that curl into a smirk as if he knows all my secrets, all my weaknesses.

The stranger reciprocates by grabbing me by my hips and plowing into me from below. "Harder," I demand, my voice raw and desperate, and the man obeys, thrusting up into me with a fierce power that has me teetering on the edge of release. Yet still, it's Aksel who dominates my thoughts—Aksel who I crave even as I punish myself for wanting him at all. Instead of anonymous sex with a stranger, I'm now using this man as a vessel for the only person's body I truly crave. And it seems to be working.

"Say my name," I order the man, needing to hear it out loud to banish Aksel from my mind.

The man hesitates, clearly unsure of how to respond to such a strange request, but eventually he complies, his voice strained and breathless as he gasps, "What is it again?"

I smirk. "Fallon," I pant.

"Fallon," he rasps.

"Again," I command, feeling the coil inside me tighten further with each utterance of my name. It should be enough—it should send me spiraling into oblivion, shattering me into a million pieces so that I can forget, if only for a moment, the twisted game that Aksel and I are playing.

"Fallon," the man repeats, his voice cracking under the strain, but it's not enough. I need more—I need the one thing I know I can never have.

"Jesus Christ, Aksel," I scream, finally giving in to the depth of feelings that have haunted me since the moment I laid eyes on him. And as I do, something snaps within me, releasing a torrent of pleasure so intense that I barely have time to register it before I'm collapsing onto the man's chest, my body wracked with sobs and tremors that refuse to be silenced. Just as quickly, I stop myself and push myself up to sitting, lifting myself off the stranger's softening cock.

"Hey," the man says softly, his arms coming up to hold me even as I try to push him away. I'm done with him, and have no further use for his body or idle chit chat. "That was...intense. I haven't done some of that stuff before. Can I, uh, have your number? Maybe we could do this again sometime?"

"Get out," I snap, wrenching myself free of his embrace and scrambling off the bed. "Just get the fuck out."

"Alright, alright," he mutters, gathering his clothes and pulling them on with clumsy, trembling hands. "No need to get so pissy about it."

"Out!" I repeat, my voice rising to a shriek as I throw open the door and gesture for him to leave. He does, casting one last, bewildered glance over his shoulder before disappearing into the night.

As soon as he's gone, I slam the door shut and lean against it, my breath coming in ragged gasps as tears stream down my cheeks. It shouldn't have been Aksel—it should never have been him—who's able to get to me like this. But somehow, despite everything, he's wormed his way into my heart, and now there's no room left for anyone else. Even a sexy rendezvous with a hot stranger isn't enough to get him off my mind.

"Fuck you, Aksel King," I whisper, my voice choked with grief and rage. "You've ruined me, and I swear to God, I'll make you pay."

After gathering my things together, I stride away from the motel, my body still thrumming with a raw, base satisfaction. But it's my heart that feels like shattered glass, an empty void echoing through my chest.

"Damn you, Aksel," I mutter under my breath, hugging myself against the chill of the night air. The city streets are eerily quiet, and it only serves to amplify the turmoil raging inside me.

"Hey! Watch it!" A passerby in a bulky coat and wool hat snaps as I bump into him, my thoughts too wrapped up in my own misery to notice where I'm going. I mumble an insincere apology and keep moving, the frigid wind biting at my exposed skin.

"Maybe I should've given him my number," I think aloud, the words tasting sour in my mouth. It's a fleeting thought, one that dissipates as quickly as it came. I know that man wasn't what I truly wanted or needed—not even close.

"Fuck, what am I doing?" I ask myself, feeling utterly lost. Revenge burns within me, but now, so does this twisted obsession with Aksel. Can I carry out my plans when my heart is betraying me?

"Get your shit together, Fallon," I chide myself, gritting my teeth as I make my way along the dark streets. "You're on a mission here."

Chapter 13

AKSEL

The ice clinks against the glass as I swirl my whiskey, a symphony of solace in my dimly lit apartment. As hard as I tried, work and the gym didn't drown out my feelings, so alcohol will have to do. The cityscape outside is a blur of lights and darkness, mirroring the turmoil within me. My memories pull at the edges of my mind, dragging me back to a time I both yearn for and despise. Yearn, because I had her. Despise, because I lost her.

"Fuck," I mutter under my breath, downing the last of the amber liquid before setting the glass on the sleek black coffee table. My eyelids are heavy, and I sink back into my comfortable couch.

--Freshman year--

Palm Falls High School looms before me, its colors and movement more vivid than any painting. I'm there again, smack dab in the center of it all—Aksel King, the guy everyone wants to be around. It's intoxicating, and I can't help but feel that addictive surge of power when people gravitate toward me. They don't see the cracks in my façade or understand the burden I carry beneath my leather jacket.

"Hey, Aksel!" someone calls out, snapping me from my thoughts. I plaster a smile on my face, nodding in response as I continue down the hallway. The laughter and chatter of my peers rings in my ears—a cacophony that somehow only intensifies the loneliness within me.

As I walk down the crowded corridor, I overhear snippets of conversations—whispers about my family's wealth, power, and the rumored mafia ties that cling to us like a dark cloud. The constant hum of gossip is both a source of pride and a reminder of the loneliness that grips me behind closed doors.

"Hey, King!" someone shouts in greeting, and I raise my hand in acknowledgment, plastering on another fake smile. My popularity and numerous friendships are a paradox. They provide a sense of belonging while simultaneously highlighting the emptiness I feel deep down.

"Hey, Aksel! Did you see that game last night?" one of my buddies asks, clapping me on the back.

I force a smirk. "Yeah, man. It was sick."

I have to build in extra time to get from class to class, and between my locker and practice. Everyone wants a piece of Aksel. Sometimes it's flattering, but other times it's an annoyance.

"Hey. Do you have a lighter?" I ask as I lean against the lockers, just another cool kid trying to fit in with another of my teammates. "I'm going to have a smoke out the back at recess." He nods and produces a lighter from his jeans pocket, handing it to me. But the truth eats away at me, gnawing at my insides like a parasite. I crave a connection, something real and honest, yet I keep everyone at arm's length. I'm trapped in this cage of popularity, and even though I long for escape, it's all I've ever known.

As I retrieve my practice gear from my locker, my eyes are drawn to a figure down the hall—Fallon Dempsey. Her red hair is a fiery beacon, and her spirit captivates me like a moth to a flame. My chest tightens as I watch her move through the crowd, turning heads with every step.

"Damn," I exhale, fighting the urge to follow her. "She's something else."

"Who, Fallon?" my friend snorts, stealing my gaze for a brief moment, and I realize I just spoke my thoughts out loud. "You've got a thing for her, don't you? She's a bit of a nerd, isn't she?"

"Shut up," I snap, my grip on the lighter tightening. The secret longing within me churns as I shove those feelings down, locking them away in the deepest, darkest part of my soul. There's no room for vulnerability here, not when I'm supposed to be untouchable.

"Alright, alright," he acquiesces, raising his hands in surrender. He smirks. *"Just saying, man. You two would make quite the power couple. Most popular guy in school and a complete freak show. Isn't she meant to be a witch or something?"*

I don't know exactly how she's developed a reputation for being different, but there's definitely something unique about her. I'm drawn to her magnetism, but it's like other people see her as an outsider no matter what she does. She has friends, but she always seems to be on the outskirts of the cliques that naturally form at a high school like this. Except for that one girl who follows her around like a lost puppy dog. Marsha or Mieke or Myra or something like that.

"Fuck that," I growl, pushing off from the lockers and stalking away. I won't allow myself to entertain the idea of being in a relationship with Fallon, not when it could open the floodgates to all the other emotions I've suppressed for so long.

--Sophomore Year--

I see a flash of red hair and she zooms down the hallway, power walking on her way to her next class. She doesn't seem to notice me as she charges determinedly through the crowd. I smirk at her insistence on being early to each lesson, eager to grab a seat near the front. While she dresses a little edgier than most, her behavior belies her studious, nerdy behavior. She's always putting her hand up to answer questions, referring to her meticulously curated notes with a color-coded tab system that would drive any librarian wild.

"Hey, Aksel!" another voice calls out, breaking me from my thoughts. I turn my head and see one of our teammates approaching, wearing his usual grin.

"Yo," I reply, forcing a smile and reminding myself that I have an image to maintain—the King of Palm Falls High School can't afford to be caught daydreaming about some girl. Especially one like Fallon fucking Dempsey.

"Party at my place tonight," he announces, slapping me on the back. *"You coming?"*

"Wouldn't miss it," I say, my tone dripping with arrogance. It's all part of the act—the cocky demeanor, the confidence, the swagger. They're the building blocks of my carefully constructed persona, a shield against the vulnerability lurking beneath the surface.

"Great! See you there, man." He jogs off, leaving me alone with my thoughts once again. I can still see her out of the corner of my eye, a flash of orange-red through the window of her

classroom.

"King," a hand slaps me on the back, nearly knocking me off balance. I turn to see one of my so-called friends chuckling at his own antics. "What are you staring at?"

"Nothing," I snap, my eyes flicking away from Fallon for a moment. It's infuriating how she manages to steal my focus, even when our paths never truly cross. The unspoken tension between us is like an invisible thread that tugs at me constantly, defying logic or reason.

"Damn, man. Chill. Just making sure you're still alive in there." He grins and continues down the hall, leaving me alone with my thoughts once more.

"I'm fine," I mutter under my breath, returning my gaze to the girl who has become an enigma in my life. A contrasting force to my brooding nature, a challenge to everything I thought I knew about myself.

As I walk away, down the hallway and past her classroom, I can't help but glance at Fallon one last time. She catches my eye through the open door, and our gazes lock, a silent recognition passing between us. For a fleeting moment, I wonder if she feels the same pull, the same inexplicable connection that tugs at my heartstrings. But then I turn away, burying my feelings beneath the façade I've spent years perfecting.

"Focus, Aksel," I mutter to myself, clenching my fists. "You're better than this."

Later that day

I round a corner and find myself face-to-face with Fallon once more. Our eyes meet, and for a moment, the world around us fades away. The pull between us is undeniable, but I know I can't let myself get lost in it. I need to stay focused, to remain untouchable.

"King," she says, her voice low and sultry, sending shivers down my spine.

"Dempsey," I respond, my tone equally measured. There's a challenge in her eyes, and I find myself rising to meet it. We're both playing our roles, maintaining the façades we've built up over the years. But beneath the surface, there's something else—a connection that threatens to break through and expose us both.

"See you at the party tonight?" she asks, as if reading my thoughts.

"Wouldn't miss it," I repeat, a little surprised she even knows about the party, and with that, we part ways—two lost souls drifting further apart, clinging desperately to the masks that keep us safe.

As I walk away, I can't help but think about Fallon and the way she makes me feel. It's unsettling. I get a lot of attention from other girls, but she's the only one who makes me feel anything like this.

"Rough day, King?" The voice is unmistakable—Fallon. She leans against the doorway, her fiery hair catching the dim light, her expression unreadable.

"Something like that," I admit, my defenses crumbling for a moment.

"Join the fucking club," she replies, crossing her arms over her chest. Her eyes meet mine, revealing a vulnerability that mirrors my own. For a split second, we're connected—two souls bound by a darkness that runs deeper than either of us can comprehend.

"Stay away from me, Fallon," I warn, fear and desire warring within me. The air crackles with tension, charged with unspoken emotions that threaten to ignite.

"Scared, King?" she taunts, that familiar fire dancing in her eyes as she pushes off the doorframe and walks away. And just like that, she's gone, leaving me grappling with the storm raging inside me.

I don't know when things got like this, some rivalry that appeared out of the blue.

"Fuck," I whisper again, slamming my fist against the locker. This game we're playing is dangerous, the lines between love and hate blurred beyond recognition. But it's a game I can't walk away from, no matter how much I wish I could.

I straighten up, pushing the swirling thoughts aside as I step back into the chaos of the hallway. A wolf in sheep's clothing, hiding my true nature behind a mask of arrogance and bravado. No one knows the truth—not even Fallon—and that's the way it has to be.

For now.

--Junior Year--

The bell rings in my ears, drowning out the conversations that fill the halls of Palm Falls High School. My gaze drifts down the hallway, drawn to the vivid red hair that still stands out like a beacon among the sea of students. Fallon Dempsey.

"Hey, Aksel!" I hear someone call out, but my attention remains locked on her as she confidently navigates the crowded space. She's always moving with purpose, head held high, seemingly oblivious to the whispers and stares that follow her every step.

"Fallon," I breathe the name, tasting it on my tongue like a forbidden fruit. I watch her laugh at something her friend has said, and I can't help but feel the magnetic pull between us. It's a dance of distance and proximity that neither of us seems willing to break.

"Fuck," I curse softly, tearing my eyes away from her as I make my way to my next class. I can't let her get under my skin, not when there's so much at stake. But it's not just her presence that haunts me, it's the unspoken emotions that linger in the air whenever our eyes meet.

"Get it together, Aksel," I warn myself as I take my seat in the classroom, focusing on anything but the burning desire to seek out Fallon's fiery gaze once more. "You can't let her win."

"Hey, King!" a voice calls from behind me, and I turn to see Fallon standing in the doorway, her green eyes locked on mine like a predator sizing up its prey. My heart hammers in my chest, but I refuse to give her the satisfaction of seeing me flustered.

"Fallon," I say coolly, offering her the same sly grin I've perfected over the years. It's a disguise, one that hides the storm raging beneath the surface.

"Looks like we're lab partners today," she says, stalking towards me with a confidence that sends shivers down my spine. Her proximity is intoxicating, but I mustn't let her get too close. "Try to keep up, King."

"Never had an issue before," I retort, allowing her challenge to fuel my own determination. This game between us is dangerous, a dance along the edge of a knife that could easily cut both ways. But I won't back down, not when revenge, justice, loyalty, and love are all tangled together in this twisted web we've woven.

"Let's see if you can handle the heat," she taunts, her eyes glistening with excitement. And as we begin our work, I can't help but wonder if either of us will ever truly escape the gravitational pull that binds us together, or if we'll simply burn in the flames we've ignited.

"Bring it, Dempsey," I reply, knowing full well that this battle of wills is far from over, and the stakes have never been higher.

I lean against the cool metal of my locker, trying to appear nonchalant as I watch Fallon breeze down the hallway. She's laughing with a group of her friends, her red hair catching the light and drawing eyes like moths to a flame. She's becoming more stunning with every passing semester. It takes everything in me not to stare openly, but I've become an expert at playing this game.

"Hey, King," a familiar voice interrupts my thoughts, and I turn to see my best friend, Jace, approaching with a smirk. "You daydreaming about your next conquest?" He nods towards Fallon, and my jaw tightens involuntarily. "That fiery freak show?"

"Hardly," I snap, forcing a laugh that sounds hollow even to my own ears. "She's not my type."

"Right," Jace says, his eyebrows raised in disbelief. But he knows better than to press me further, and we fall into conversation about the upcoming football game instead.

As the morning passes, my mind keeps returning to Fallon. Her presence is like a magnetic force, impossible to ignore. And while I try to convince myself it's just competitive rivalry, the truth is far more dangerous.

The lunch bell rings, flooding the hallways with students eager to escape their classrooms. I find myself standing outside the cafeteria, scanning the crowd for that flash of red that has become both my torment and my obsession.

"Hey, Aksel," Fallon's voice sends a jolt of electricity through me, and I curse myself for being so easily affected. She saunters up to me, her green eyes gleaming with mischief. "Ready to admit defeat in that bet of ours?"

"Never," I retort, desperately clinging to the façade I've built. "Just you wait, Dempsey."

"Keep dreaming, King," she smirks and walks away, leaving me feeling like I'm drowning in an ocean of my own desire and frustration.

Every time I see her talking to another guy a jealous rage swirls within me and I plot and plan against her, sure she's making conversation with them just to taunt me. I vow to hurt her in the same way but worse, in a way that will humiliate her. By doing so, I hope that my feelings for her will go away and she will stop occupying every corner of my mind.

Over the next few weeks, our rivalry escalates. I find myself going out of my way to one-up Fallon on every front—academically, athletically, socially. Each victory feels hollow, tainted by the knowledge that I'm fighting against the very thing I crave more than anything.

It's when I see her out at the town's diner with a male classmate that I snap. They're huddled together, laughing, and he feeds her a bite of his ice cream. She giggles and touches his arm. Gross.

Every time she wears a new outfit or hairstyle I find a way to make a subtle critique. "Oh, those are interesting bangs," and "What a unique color choice you've made today." I see the way my little barbs erode her self-confidence. On several occasions, she's changed her hair and clothing soon after I've made these remarks, and each time she does, a little victory band plays in my mind.

I see the way she reacts when I beat her at anything, her fiery hair a symbol of the simmering rage about to boil over at any moment. When the student election comes, I devise my magnum opus of pranks, drawing her in close and encouraging her to run for class president. She's reluctant at first, but I convince her she's the only real contender.

"Fallon, trust me, you'd make a great class president," I say, my voice smooth and encouraging.

"Are you sure?" she asks, uncertainty lacing her words. "I don't know if I can handle all the pressure."

"Of course you can," I assure her, placing a hand on her shoulder. "You're strong, smart, and dedicated. You'll do an amazing job."

But, while my belief in Fallon's abilities is genuine, it won't protect her from the destruction that follows, orchestrated by my own hands.

Secretly, I enroll myself in the election race. I then get to work, developing a vicious smear campaign against her. "Felony Dempsey," the posters slapped across hundreds of lockers proudly declare, alluding to her family's ties to criminal activity and alleging some type of promiscuous behavior that gets tongues wagging in the school's corridors but doesn't meet the threshold for libel.

It begins with whispers in the hallways—hints of incompetence, rumors of scandalous behavior—all designed to weaken her standing among our peers. Before I know it, the campaign has taken on a life of its own, with other jealous classmates embellishing and adding to the already cruel picture I've painted. The guilt gnaws at me, a constant reminder of the damage I've done.

"Did you hear what they're saying about Fallon?" one student mutters to another as we pass by, their eyes filled with judgment.

"Unbelievable," the other replies, shaking their head. And just like that, Fallon's reputa-

tion crumbles before my eyes.

Sure enough, I sail through to a clear win. I never even wanted to be class president. I just wanted to show off to her, to be better than her. To show her I could beat her at this along with everything else. It's a drive within me that I can't quite explain, a reaction to the amount of time I spend thinking about her, dreaming about her.

My cruel nickname for her sticks and I know she hates it. Our senior yearbook reads Felony Dempsey and deems her most likely to be a criminal once she graduates from high school. She's mortified when she reads it, and I feel a little surge of schadenfreude as I see her rip the page from her own yearbook, running out of the lunchroom in tears. Her puppy dog friend, Michelle or whoever, runs after her to provide comfort, and I scoff at her weakness.

As I watch Fallon's world unravel, I can't help but feel responsible for her pain. I was blinded by my own need for validation and power, unable to see the impact of my actions until it was too late. As she spirals further into darkness, my regret grows heavier, suffocating me beneath the weight of my past mistakes.

By the time junior year is nearly over, my thoughts are in turmoil, battling between the urge to draw her close and the need to keep her at arm's length. It's a war I'm losing with every stolen glance and heated exchange.

"Christ, Aksel," Jace mutters one afternoon as we stand on the football field, watching Fallon's lithe form sprint past us during track practice. "You've got it bad for her, don't you?"

"Shut up," I hiss, anger flaring at the all-too-accurate accusation. "It's just a game."

"Whatever you say, man," he says, shaking his head. But I can see the concern etched into his features, and I know he's right. This is no longer just a game—it's an obsession, a wildfire consuming everything in its path.

One night, after another bitter standoff with Fallon at a party, I return home to my empty house, the weight of my emotions bearing down on me like a crushing tidal wave. In the darkness of my room, I allow myself a moment of weakness, the tears spilling hot and unchecked down my face.

"Fuck," I whisper, the word choked and broken. "What the hell am I doing?"

But even as the question haunts me, I know there's no turning back. The lines have been drawn, the ante raised with every passing day. I'm pretty sure she hates me now. The girl I obsessed over has become my nemesis. The obsession has continued but in a different form. And though part of me longs for surrender, for the sweet relief of honesty and vulnerability, I know that I can never allow myself that luxury. Not when there's so much more at stake.

"Fallon," I whisper into the night, her name both an invocation and a curse. "One day,

you'll understand."

you'll understand."

Chapter 14

AKSEL

The fluorescent bulbs above cast an unforgiving light on the sweat-slicked equipment, illuminating the room with a cold, clinical glare. The hum of machinery and my labored breathing fill the air, drowning out the memories that threaten to swallow me whole. My playlist blares through the speakers, each bass note reverberating in my chest as I push through another rep, muscles straining against the relentless force of gravity. I don't know what I would do without my home gym, the place I retreat to for respite from the outside world, the pressures of my work and the dark thoughts that consume my mind.

The air around me crackles with tension, each breath infused with the bitter sting of regret. My fists clench at my sides as I stare at the row of weights that have become my confessional, their cold metal surfaces reflecting the storm of emotions brewing within me.

"Fuck," I hiss under my breath, the metallic clink of weights crashing onto the floor and echoing in the cavernous space. A fleeting shadow dances across the wall as a car goes by on the street below, taunting me like the ghosts of my past. I can't outrun them, not even in this sanctuary, where iron and sweat are my confidants.

"Damn it, Aksel," I mutter to myself, hands gripping a barbell as if it's the one thing keeping me grounded. "Get your shit together."

But it's easier said than done. In this dimly lit corner of my home gym, away from the prying eyes of the world, I'm confronted by the stark reality of my feelings for Fallon—feelings I never truly acknowledged, let alone understood, until now.

"God, I was so fucking blind," I say, the words barely audible over the thud of my heart and the grind of gears. I reflect on the flashbacks from the previous night that, for the first time, helped me to see my own behavior and emotional rollercoaster in more detail. The self-loathing is palpable, a bitter taste at the back of my throat. How could I have been so oblivious to my own emotions? It was such a build-up over time that I didn't even realize. And those years don't even accumulate to anything close to how I treated her in our senior year.

"Obsession," I spit out, the word tasting like venom. "That's what it was, right? That's what you'd call it?"

"Who are you talking to?" a voice interrupts, pulling me from my thoughts.

"Shit," I curse, spinning around to find my reflection staring back at me from the mirrored wall. "Just myself, apparently." I shake my head, pushing away the memories that threaten to consume me.

"Focus," I command myself, hands returning to the barbell. "Just a few more reps." But as much as I try to drown out the past with physical exertion, it seeps back in like a stain, creeping into the corners of my mind and refusing to be ignored.

"Fallon," I whisper, feeling the heat of my unspoken love for her burn through me like wildfire. I didn't know how to say it then, and I don't know if I can say it now. "What did I do to us?"

"Ask yourself that question, Aksel," my reflection sneers, eyes boring into mine with a cold, unrelenting stare. "What did you do?"

"Everything," I admit, feeling the weight of my actions press down on me with crushing force. "I pushed her away. I hurt her. And I never even realized how deep it went."

"Then maybe it's time to make amends," the voice suggests, its tone suddenly softer, more hopeful.

"Can I?" I wonder, my grip tightening on the barbell. "After everything I've done, can I really make things right?"

"Only one way to find out," the voice challenges, and I nod, drawing in a shaky breath. Great, I've gone insane. I hear voices now. But at least the voice inside my head seems to be talking some sense.

"Fuck," I mutter under my breath, a single word encompassing the depth of my self-loathing. "I never told her. I never fucking told her."

"Maybe you don't need words," the voice suggests, echoing my own thoughts. "Maybe actions speak louder."

"Actions?" I scoff, disdain dripping from each syllable. "Look where my actions got us."

"Then change them," the voice insists, relentless and unyielding. "Show her what she means to you."

"Fine," I growl, my resolve hardening into something fierce and unbreakable. "I'll show her. Let's see if I can fix this."

I approach the weight bench once more.

"Come on, Aksel," I coach myself, summoning every ounce of strength I possess. "You can do this. For her."

Gritting my teeth, I hoist the barbell from its stand, the weight bearing down on me like a physical manifestation of all the things I never said to Fallon. Each lift is a promise, each rep is an unspoken word, a plea for understanding, a declaration of the intense feelings that have been smoldering inside me for so long.

"Fuck," I grunt, testing my own limitations. My muscles strain and protest under the relentless onslaught. The metallic clang of weights hitting the floor resounds through the gym, a symphony of determination and struggle.

"You've got this, Aksel," I hiss to myself, once again pushing through the pain. "This is for her."

My hands grip the barbell, knuckles white with determination, as I lower it to my chest. The iron presses into my flesh, the harsh motion mimicking the tumultuous beats of my heart. As I push through the pain, continuing my relentless workout, I can't help but feel that I'm not just fighting against the weight of the barbell, but also against the crushing weight of my past. It's a battle I'm determined to win—for Fallon, and for myself.

"Damn it," I curse as the weight of my feelings threatens to overwhelm me. My heart races, and sweat drips down my brow, but I refuse to back down. "I will fix this," I pant, my breath ragged from exertion. "I'll fight for you. I'll make things right between us, no matter what it takes."

"Good," the dark voice murmurs, its tone laced with malice. "And when you finally have her, don't let anything stand in your way."

"Trust me," I growl, my muscles aching with the effort, "nothing will."

~~Senior Year~~

As I step through the doors of Palm Falls High School, the chaotic symphony of adolescent life washes over me. The scent of cheap cologne and sweat clings to the air like a heavy fog, while the voices of my classmates blend into an indistinguishable cacophony.

"Hey, Aksel!" one of them shouts, a blur of color and motion in the crowded hall. My lips twist into the same old practiced grin, but my insides churn with an unease that's become increasingly familiar.

"Sup," I call back, offering a casual wave as I continue down the polished linoleum floor. I'm acutely aware of the eyes that follow me, their assumptions and judgments hidden behind carefully constructed masks.

But there's one pair of eyes I seek out above all others: Fallon Dempsey, a beacon of fierce resilience in this sea of superficiality. It's like she doesn't even know how much power she wields, and it makes her all the more alluring.

"Fallon," I whisper under my breath, feeling the weight of our shared history and petty rivalries pressing down on my chest. I want to reach out, to bridge the gap between us, but the shadows of our past cling to me like chains.

"Yo, King!" someone shouts, jarring me from my thoughts. I force my gaze away from Fallon and plaster on another fake smile, giving a nod to whoever called my name.

"Hey," I say, not bothering to figure out who it was. They're just another face in the crowd—a crowd that's swallowed me whole and left me feeling emptier than ever.

"Class prez meeting after school!" one of the guys on the student council calls out as I pass by. I give him a thumbs up, pretending to care.

"Can't wait," I lie, my voice dripping with sarcasm that goes unnoticed.

My thoughts spiral, the churning confusion of my emotions threatening to overwhelm me. I want to scream, to tear down these walls that have been built around me—walls for which I'm the chief architect and principal engineer—but instead, I swallow it all down and lock my feelings away.

"Hey, Aksel," Fallon says as she approaches, her voice a soft melody cutting through the noise. My heart stutters in my chest, but I force a casual grin onto my face.

"Hey, Fallon. What's up?" I ask, trying to sound nonchalant. My mind races, searching for an escape route from the conversation. But deep down, some part of me wants to stay—wants to linger in her presence and soak up every moment I can.

"Nothing much," she replies, her eyes darting away for a moment before meeting mine

again. "Just wanted to remind you about our project for Mr. Thompson's class. We should probably start working on it soon."

I'm not sure what happened over the summer, but something's shifted between us this year. The animosity that oozed from her after my class president prank seems to have dissipated at least partially, like she's open to giving me another chance, or at least a truce. We're in a lot of the same classes, so maybe she just wants being in the same room as me to be more palatable.

"Right, the project," I say, pretending the thought of getting to work with her on something hadn't already consumed me for days. "We'll find some time, don't worry."

"Okay," she says, her lips quirking into a small smile that does nothing to ease the tension between us. If anything, it makes it worse.

"See you around, Aksel," she murmurs, and I can't help but think I hear something else in her voice—a hint of longing, maybe even regret. Or perhaps that's just my own wishful thinking.

"Later, Fallon," I reply, watching as she walks away, her curvy form disappearing into the throng of students. The ache in my chest grows stronger, fueled by the unspoken words that lie between us like a chasm.

I lean against the row of lockers, watching as Fallon maneuvers her way through the crowded hallway. The sea of students parts for her, their whispers carrying a mix of admiration and envy. She's an enigma, equal parts beauty and grace, a force that seems untouchable in this world of cliques and calamity.

"Hey, King." The voice cuts through my thoughts like a serrated blade, and I don't have to turn around to know who it is. Carissa. Her jealousy hangs thick in the air, a toxic cloud that threatens to choke me every time she's near. She's pretty, and I considered dating her at one point, but something about her has always seemed off. And she seems to have a bigger boner for Fallon than I do for some reason, which is obviously saying a lot, because at this point I find it hard to think about anything or anyone else.

"Carissa," I reply, my tone flat. I refuse to let her see how much she gets under my skin. That's what she wants—acknowledgment, power, control. I may be trapped in this web of high school social politics, but I won't give her the satisfaction of feeding into whatever game

she's playing today.

"Fallon looks good today, doesn't she?" She smirks, trailing her fingers along my arm in a sickeningly possessive gesture. I tense, fighting the urge to shove her away. I wonder what she's playing at bestowing compliments on her nemesis.

"Sure," I say nonchalantly, shrugging off her touch. "She always does."

Carissa frowns at the compliment directed toward Fallon. "Who do you think she's going to the dance with?" Carissa asks, her voice dripping with false innocence. I know she's fishing for information, trying to get a rise out of me.

"Does it matter?" I snap, my patience wearing thin. I would like nothing more than to take Fallon to the dance, but the thought of her rejecting me, which I probably deserve after the election, the insults and all the other pranks, is too much to bear.

"Of course it matters," she purrs, leaning in close. "After all, you're still pining after her, aren't you?"

"Fuck off, Carissa." My words are harsh, but she only laughs, seeing through my façade of indifference. She knows damn well how much Fallon means to me, how deep these unspoken feelings run. Call it womanly intuition, or call it a teenage girl being a jealous bitch, but she knows.

"Who are you going to the dance with, anyway?" she asks, still hanging onto my arm while Fallon walks back down the hall to retrieve a forgotten item from her locker. A nasty smile plays across her face as Fallon glances at us, her eyes growing wide as she notices Carissa's hold on me. "We could go together, you know. I think we'd make a cute couple." She winks.

"I—um, was thinking of asking someone else," I say, deflecting Carissa's advances. Her mouth curls into a cruel snarl and her eyes narrow as they flit in Fallon's direction.

"Oh well, have fun watching from the sidelines. I heard Fallon's been giving Jimmy all of the blowjobs, and he's planning on giving it to her on prom night," she taunts, sauntering away with a wicked smile. I watch her go, my fists clenched and jaw tight, every muscle in my body screaming for release.

The thought of Fallon bobbing up and down on another guy's cock twists my stomach and crushes my chest until I can barely breathe. Blood racing to my temples, I have the urge to hunt Jimmy down and knock his head off. But there's no evidence, not that I would expect there to be, and I question whether I can take Carissa's word for it. She seems far too interested in Fallon's every move—and in me—to be a neutral party even though she tries to play it off that way.

I can't shake the feeling that Carissa's venom is poisoning the already fragile connection *between Fallon and me, driving us further apart with each passing day. If she's making these types of comments to me, I can only imagine what she's saying to Fallon.*

The bitter taste of rage and regret lingers on my tongue as I sift through the memories, searching for answers. My once steady breaths grow ragged with each image that flickers across my mind's eye—a cruel montage of loss and betrayal.

"Carissa," I hiss under my breath, her name a venomous dart in my mouth. She was the architect of our downfall, the serpent in the garden that tempted me to stray from Fallon's side. She'd been relentless in her pursuit, fueled by jealousy and a twisted desire to possess something she could never truly have—my heart.

In hindsight, I see how she'd always find a way to insert herself into my life, slithering into conversations and lingering at the edge of my vision like a predatory shadow. She'd always do just enough to cause damage, but little enough that she could explain it away innocently. My teenage boy brain would always accept her carefully constructed lies at face value.

After everything that happened, her presence was constant and suffocating, always there to remind me of the destruction she had wrought upon my relationship with Fallon. But I still never dated her or took her home, as much as she might have tried.

"Hey Aksel, can I talk to you for a second?" Carissa would ask, batting her eyelashes and feigning innocence. But her intentions were far from pure, and I was too naïve to see through her performance.

"Sure, what's up?" I'd reply, playing right into her hands.

"Have you seen this?" she would say, producing a crumpled piece of paper or an incriminating photograph, fabricated evidence designed to drive a wedge between Fallon and me. "It looks bad, doesn't it?"

My stomach churns at the memory of those lies, how they spread like wildfire through the halls of our high school, sullying Fallon's trust in me. And I didn't help matters—I was weak, unable to resist the pull of Carissa's manipulative tactics. When I should've been strong for Fallon, I let doubt and confusion cloud my judgment, allowing Carissa's poison to seep into the cracks of our fragile foundation.

Why didn't I see through her games? Why didn't I fight harder to protect Fallon from the heartache she was destined to face?

"Damn it," I growl, slamming my fists against the wall of the gym, the pain a fleeting distraction from the storm raging inside me.

The truth is, I was too caught up in the whirlwind of teenage emotions to fully comprehend the consequences of my actions. I was blind to the web of deceit that Carissa spun around us, entrapping us both in a cycle of hurt and betrayal. And though I never meant to cause Fallon any pain, my inability to stand up to Carissa's schemes made me complicit in her suffering.

"Hey, Aksel, did you hear about that hot new transfer student?" Carissa's voice echoes in my memory.

"Yeah, I heard she's really into bad boys," I'd replied, allowing the rumor to spread, hoping it would stoke some kind of jealousy within Fallon. But instead, I only added fuel to the fire that consumed the innocence of our relationship.

My knuckles turn white as I squeeze the weight harder, trying to force the memories out of my head. I hate who I was back then—a pawn in a twisted game that I didn't even understand. I traded whispers with pretty girls like Carissa, all for the sake of cultivating an image that would make Fallon jealous. In reality, I never cared about any of them. It was always her—it has always been Fallon.

"Damn it," I curse aloud, slamming the dumbbell onto the ground. The clang echoes through the gym, but it does nothing to silence the guilt that gnaws at me.

Why didn't I just tell her how I felt? Why did I let my own insecurities and confusion lead to so much pain?

As the echoes of my past mistakes reverberate through the room, I steel myself for the battle ahead. I will not let Carissa's treachery define our fate. I will fight for Fallon, for the love that slipped through our fingers like sand, leaving only shadows and regret in its wake.

"Carissa," I vow, my voice barely more than a whisper, "you will pay for the damage you've done."

I know now that I can no longer hide from the truth, or from the part I played in Fallon's heartbreak. It's time to face the demons that have haunted me for so long, to confront the tangled threads of our shared history and unravel them once and for all. For Fallon, for the love we were never fully allowed to explore, I will make things right—no matter what it takes.

As I stand amidst the machines and iron weights, I can't help but feel like I'm teetering on the edge of a precipice. One where my past mistakes threaten to drag me down into an abyss of regret, and the only way forward is to confront the demons that have haunted me for years.

Carissa's words fail in their quest to augment my rivalry with Fallon. In fact, they do the opposite. I find myself defensive, and realize I want to protect Fallon. I feel some sort of ownership over her, a desire to keep her close to me at all times. With embarrassment, I realize I've been the living, breathing cliché of the boy toddler who hits a girl because he likes her. I've tormented her for so long, and for what? It's suddenly obvious to me. That's why I was so worried about Carissa destroying my connection with Fallon. It may be toxic, but it's the way I've been able to stay close to her all these years.

The truth is, I'm fixated on Fallon Dempsey because I really, really like her... if I'm honest, it's far more than that. And I'd like nothing more than to make her mine. Maybe, just maybe, I should lay off the jerk act and show her how I really feel.

The unrelenting beat of my heart drowns out the cacophony of the school grounds. Fallon's pulse races in tandem with mine, our breaths ragged and synchronized as we stand under the moonlit sky, shielded from prying eyes by the shadowy foliage. Our first kiss, a tentative dance between vulnerability and desire, is electric—a searing sensation that courses through me like wildfire.

For the next week, more meetings like this. More kisses that set my heart ablaze.

And then, one magical night under the stars, our naked bodies intertwined for the first time.

"Fallon," I breathe against her lips, drowning in the depths of her green eyes. There's so much I want to say, but words are elusive, slipping away like sand through my fingers. In this moment, I hope my actions can speak louder than words ever could.

"Wait," she whispers, a panicked edge to her voice. "Do you hear that?"

My senses sharpen, and I detect it too: the crunching of leaves, the sound of someone approaching. Moments later, Carissa emerges from the shadows, her face twisted into a malevolent grin.

"Look what we have here," she purrs, venom dripping from her every syllable. "Aksel and Fallon, sharing a secret rendezvous."

"Carissa, get the fuck out of here!" My anger flares, a burning heat that threatens to consume me.

"Fine," she snaps, her eyes narrowing to slits as she stalks away. "But don't think you can keep this a secret for long, Aksel. Everyone will know by tomorrow. And she's definitely not the only girl you've been doing this with. I could say the same for her."

As Carissa's footsteps fade into the night, Fallon's gaze hardens, her expression a mixture of hurt and confusion. "What did she mean, Aksel?"

"Nothing," I lie, unable to meet her eyes. "She's just being her usual spiteful self. Don't worry about it."

But the damage has been done. I can see it all over Fallon's face.

The fragile connection we'd forged shatters under the weight of Carissa's interference, and Fallon slips away as quickly as she'd appeared.

The unspoken rivalry between us festers, fueled by the complex dynamics of high school hierarchies and the labyrinth of emotions we're both too afraid to navigate. As I stand in the hallway, surrounded by the loud chaos of adolescent life, I can't help but wonder if there's any hope for me and Fallon. We're worlds apart, separated by a chasm of misunderstanding and resentment, and it feels like an insurmountable distance.

"Later, Aksel," Fallon calls as she passes me, her voice strained with forced neutrality. The sound of her name on my lips feels like a betrayal, a reminder of everything I've lost and can never get back. I watch her walk away, a ghost in a world that no longer belongs to either of us.

"Later," I echo, the word heavy with the weight of things left unsaid.

"Fallon, please talk to me," I pled back then, trying to bridge the chasm that had grown between us. But she refused, her pain palpable as she turned away, seeking solace in the company of others who would only bring her more harm.

I can't shake the feeling that I somehow drove her into the arms of danger. The rumors of promiscuity with unfavorable people and drug use circulated like wildfire, and though she never confirmed the details, I sensed the truth in her haunted eyes. The guilt is still a heavy burden, an unspoken reminder that my actions set her on this path.

"Fallon," I whisper to myself, her name tasting bittersweet on my lips. "I'm so sorry. I never meant to hurt you."

My heart clenches as I think about the fiery girl who captured my soul, and how my misguided attempts at gaining her attention only served to dim and risk permanently extinguishing her light. But I refuse to let this be the end of our story. My thoughts are a whirlwind of emotions—anger, regret, and most of all, love. I know I can't undo the past, but I can fight for a future where we find justice for the pain we've endured. If there's one thing I know for certain, it's that Fallon deserves justice—I don't know exactly what that looks like yet, but I won't rest until she gets it.

Years later, I can't shake the ghost of what we had and how it was destroyed. The memory haunts me, a persistent specter that refuses to fade in the recesses of my mind. From afar, I follow Fallon's life—her successes, her triumphs, her heartaches—unable to let go of the lingering question: what if Carissa hadn't interfered?

"Fuck," I mutter, scrolling through yet another article about Fallon's latest achievements. My hands tremble with barely suppressed rage, frustration gnawing at my insides like a relentless parasite. A part of me is proud of her accomplishments, but another part burns with the knowledge that I should have been there to witness it all.

$\mathcal{C}hapter\ 15$

FALLON

The golden chandelier casts shadows on the intricately patterned wallpaper, and as usual I feel dwarfed by the sheer opulence of my father's formal dining room. I can never quite bring myself to refer to it as also being my stepmother's home, just my father's. This home is anything but a sanctuary for me, a stark reminder that no matter how far I've come and how much I've tried to distance myself, there are still undeniable ties to my past. My stomach clenches as I take a tentative sip from the crystal wine glass handed to me by a waiter on my arrival.

"Congratulations, Fallon," my father says, his voice somber yet laced with a hint of pride. The entire room goes quiet, as if everyone collectively held their breath. "You did an exceptional job at the charity gala. You should be proud."

"Thank you, Father," I respond, trying to keep my voice even as I sense watchful eyes on me. My stepmother gives me a tight-lipped smile, her makeup immaculate as always. Link, my brother, narrows his eyes, obviously unprepared for the rare praise our father has bestowed upon me. It doesn't happen very often, and even though I did what my father asked of me at the event, I wasn't expecting this.

"Another toast," my father announces, raising his glass. "To Fallon and her success helping us to advance the Eternity Development Project. Farelli has awarded us the contract in the amount we anticipated. In fact, we received even more favorable terms than we would have accepted." The clink of glasses fills the space in the silence, and I can't shake off the feeling that there's something more beneath these words of praise.

"Cheers," I say, forcing a smile, though my gratitude is genuine. But the weight of his expectations feels like a noose around my neck.

As the dinner progresses, I can see the envy simmering in Link's eyes. He can't resist the urge to poke at old wounds, to find cracks in my armor. "What a little social butterfly you've become, Fallon. Running around diamond-encrusted charity galas securing lucrative contracts for the family firm by batting your eyelashes at wealthy men. Hard to believe this is the same little sister who spent more time with her nose in a book than enjoying high school, isn't it?" he teases, a smirk playing on his lips.

"Times change, Link," I reply, keeping my voice steady. "And maybe all that studying paid off. Besides, what's wrong with studying, anyway?" I refuse to let him drag me back into the past, where vulnerability and insecurities reigned supreme. I also refuse to engage in the misogyny of his other comments.

"Speaking of the past," Link continues, ignoring my attempt to shut him down. "Remember your little crush on Aksel?" My heart skips a beat, and I can feel my cheeks flush with embarrassment as memories of whispered rumors and stolen glances flood my mind. "I heard he's quite the successful businessman now. Must have been fun seeing your old high school sweetheart at the event. And wasn't Carissa meant to be there, too? That must have been exciting to have everyone in the same room after all these years." He grins, mischief in his eyes. "Nothing like a little drama to spice up a stuffy charity gala, right?"

"Link, that's enough," my oldest brother Cheston interjects, his voice sharp and disapproving. But the damage is done, and a storm brews beneath the surface of our seemingly perfect family dinner.

I clench my fists under the tablecloth, the anger threatening to spill over and ruin my carefully curated impenetrable persona that belies the more sensitive, real me that trembles just below the surface. There's no room for the pain of the past when so much is at stake, and Link always knows how to cut me right to the core. So I take another sip from my wine glass, swallowing the bitterness along with it, and vow not to let my brother's cruel words derail me.

The moment I step out of my father's opulent home, which I do as soon as I can excuse myself after dessert, the chill of the night air is a welcome reprieve from the stifling atmosphere that had filled the dining room. My hands tremble as I fumble for my keys, the weight of the evening's events pressing down on me like a tangible force. I slide into the driver's seat of my car, taking a deep breath to steady myself before starting the engine.

My fingers grip the steering wheel tight, knuckles turning white as I navigate the city streets. The kaleidoscope of lights reflecting off the buildings only serves to heighten the turmoil brewing within me. The silence in the car is deafening, giving way to the whispers of memories I thought I'd long locked away. Images of Aksel and our tumultuous youth together flicker through my mind, pulling me back to a time when rumors and misunderstandings shaped the narrative of our lives.

"Dammit, Aksel, and fuck you, Link," I mutter under my breath. I try to get my mind off all of them by turning on the radio, but the first song that comes on takes me straight back to those years, ironically one Aksel and I used to listen to together, and I shut it off immediately. The solitude of the car becomes a canvas for me to revisit the heartbreak that lingers from high school, the pain of betrayal fueled by the echoes of past rumors.

I remember the whispered conversations in the hallways, the sideways glances exchanged between classmates as they gossiped about Aksel's involvement with other girls and the smear campaign he waged against me, and all the ways I was made to feel less than. Each story left a searing ache in my chest that still weighs heavy on my heart, and worst of all was Aksel's role in it all.

"Forget it, Fallon, focus on work," I tell myself, shaking my head in an effort to dispel the intrusive thoughts. "You're not that naïve girl anymore."

But as much as I try to push them away, the memories refuse to be silenced. The ghost of Aksel's touch on my skin, the sound of his laughter, the warmth in his eyes when he looked at me—all these things come rushing back, making it impossible to ignore the bitter sting of betrayal and the longing that has remained dormant all these years.

"Shit," I hiss, feeling the tears threaten to spill over. "He doesn't get to do this to me again just because he's back in town."

I take a deep breath, forcing myself to focus on the road ahead. The city lights blur together as I speed through the streets, the pressure in my chest building with each passing mile. In this cocoon of conflicting emotions, I fight to hold onto the woman I've become—strong, determined, and fiercely loyal to the few who have earned my trust.

"Never again," I whisper, my voice barely audible above the hum of the engine. "I won't let him break me."

I contemplate pulling over and just letting all these emotions pour out of me like a torrential rainstorm. Would it be better to simply leave this life behind and start anew, far away from family expectations and the shadows of my past with Aksel?

But then I think about how many people I've helped through the course of my work, the countless hours spent building the company up from nothing. And most importantly, the unwavering loyalty of Grave and Mia, who have both been by my side through thick and thin. No, I can't abandon them—they're the reasons I keep going when everything else seems dire.

"Fuck," I exhale shakily, feeling the weight of my decision pressing down on my chest. "Fallon, you need to make a choice." My own voice startles me, echoing through the car as if it were an outsider's opinion.

At that moment, I reach a literal and figurative crossroads. The traffic light ahead turns red, and I bring the car to a stop. In the stillness, I feel the pull between continuing my vendetta against Aksel and letting go of the past entirely. This journey home has become a metaphor for the path I need to navigate—between the shadows of the past and the promise of a future where forgiveness and understanding might reshape the echoes of youth.

"Forgive or forget," I whisper to myself, watching the light turn green. "Which path do I choose?"

As I press down on the gas pedal, my mind steps back in time, revisiting moments with Aksel that brought both joy and pain. The laughter we shared, the stolen glances, and then the bitter taste of betrayal when rumors of his involvement with other girls circulated.

"Enough," I say firmly, shaking my head to clear the memories away. "I need to focus on the present. He's just a distraction and he's not worth it."

The city streets stretch out before me, a labyrinth of choices and consequences. And as I drive towards my condo, I know one thing for certain—I cannot avoid making this decision any longer.

"Get even or let go," I repeat, feeling a newfound determination rising within me. "But no matter what, I won't let Aksel break me again."

The lights of my condo building cast a warm, golden glow on the pavement as I pull into my reserved parking spot. The engine's hum dies down as I switch off the ignition, and for a moment, I sit in the silence, my heartbeat pounding in my ears. Tonight's emotional whirlwind has left me feeling like a tornado ripped through my chest, scattering debris in its wake. I hate that it's so easy for my brother to rile me like this, and that he takes the opportunity to do so regularly.

"Home," I sigh, gripping the steering wheel tighter and glancing up at my condo, temporarily paralyzed in the driver's seat. "But what the hell does that even mean anymore?"

I force myself out of the car, every fiber of my being longing to collapse onto the ground and let the pain swallow me whole. But no, I've come too far for that. I won't allow myself to break now.

I trudge toward the entrance, my heels clicking against the concrete.

"Hey, Fallon!"

My head snaps up, and I wince at the ache that shoots through my temples. It's my neighbor, Sadie. She's leaning over the railing of her balcony, concern etched across her face as she peers down at me.

"Are you okay? You look... well, you don't look great."

"Thanks," I reply, attempting a smile. "Just one of those nights, you know?"

"Ugh, I feel you. Family stuff?"

"Something like that." I hesitate before continuing. "Family, and old ghosts. The kind that never seem to stay buried."

"Damn, girl," she shakes her head. "Sounds rough. Maybe you need some kind of exorcism."

"Tell me about it." I sigh and look up at her. "But you know what? It's time to face them. I've decided I won't let my past define me anymore."

"Good for you," she says, her eyes filled with admiration. "You're stronger than you think, Fallon. Remember that." I don't know her well, having only spent time with her at a few condo association events, but her words echo Mia's earlier notes of encouragement, and I find them validating, soothing. Just what I need right now.

"Thanks, Sadie. I needed to hear that."

"Anytime, girl. Now go kick some ass."

With a renewed sense of determination, I stride toward my condo, the ghosts of my past nipping at my heels. But this time, I won't run from them. No, not anymore. I will face them head-on, and I will emerge victorious.

"Confront or let go," I whisper as my key slides into the lock. "I've come too far to turn back now."

The door creaks open, revealing the familiar sanctuary of my condo. But tonight, it feels different—no longer a refuge from the storm but instead a battleground for my own thoughts that I can't seem to escape.

Chapter 16

AKSEL

The sun dips below the horizon, casting long shadows across the sprawling grandeur of my family's estate. A mansion steeped in history and luxury, it conceals hidden rooms and secret passageways known only to a select few. As I walk the meticulously manicured grounds, the whispers of generations echo around me—hushed rumors of power, underground sex clubs, and polygamy. The air is thick with the scent of hidden mafia affiliations as I step inside the fortress that guards our family's secrets.

"Ah, Aksel, there you are," my grandmother announces as I enter the room. Her presence is formidable, her posture regal and foreboding. Her tailored suit drapes over her strong, elegant form like armor. The thought crosses my mind that I've never seen her in casual clothes. My siblings and I joke that she probably sleeps in a suit, and I'd probably fall over if I ever saw her in pajamas. Her sharp eyes observe me, missing nothing. "You're late for dinner, dear."

"Apologies, Grandmother," I reply, taking my regular seat at the grand dining table. The weight of her gaze is heavy, but beneath the steel lies a hint of warmth that belies the cool, unyielding façade she presents to the world. She has been both guardian and matriarch since my parents' deaths, and the bond between us runs deep. As we gather around the dining table with my siblings, I can't help but feel a surge of gratitude for the family that surrounds me. Despite our dark past and the weight of our secrets, there is love here—a fierce, unbreakable bond that holds us together in the face of adversity.

"Better late than never," Raine chimes in, offering a smile. My elder sister, her wisdom and care have guided me throughout my life. Her warm, resonant voice instantly puts me at ease. "What held you up?"

"Lost track of time while walking the grounds," I admit, returning her smile. Laughter bubbles at the table, lightening the tense atmosphere momentarily. Around the table, my siblings—Raine, Roxy, and Carson—each bear their own struggles within the shadows of our family legacy.

"Roxy, any new drama to report?" I tease, turning my attention to my beautiful, rebellious younger sister. Her blonde hair cascades around her shoulders, framing large blue eyes that sparkle with mischief.

"Please, Aksel, you know my life is always full of drama," she replies, rolling her eyes. "But at least it's never boring."

"True," I agree, though worry tugs at the corners of my thoughts. "Just promise me you'll think twice before making any life-altering decisions, okay?" I notice a new tattoo has appeared on her forearm. The way she's going, I think she'll likely run out of space by the time she's thirty.

"Fine, fine," she sighs, though I can tell she's humoring me. "No impulsive decisions without consulting my wise older brother first."

"Speaking of which," I turn to Carson, our youngest sibling on the cusp of adulthood. "How are things going for you? Any big decisions coming up?"

"Nothing major," he replies, avoiding eye contact. I sense his unease, knowing he's at a crossroads in his life. The desire to protect him from the darkness that looms over our family wars with the knowledge that he must eventually find his own path.

"Listen, Carson," I say gently. "I know there are people in our circles who might not have your best interests at heart. Just remember, you don't have to follow their lead. Trust your instincts and make choices that feel right to you."

"Thanks, Aksel," he murmurs, finally meeting my gaze. I nod, hoping my words offer some measure of comfort. But I also feel hypocritical, gently trying to lead him away from the family business and into something safer. It sounds like the easiest path, staying with King Enterprises, but from personal experience, although alluring, it slowly tears you apart from the inside.

The rest of the conversation at dinner is lighter, and I enjoy chatting about day-to-day things that Carson and Roxy are up to with their friends.

"Roxy, I saw your latest photo shoot online," Raine says with a teasing smile. "It was cute and all, but when are you going to give up modeling and join the family business?"

"Never," Roxy retorts playfully, flipping her blonde hair over her shoulder. "I'd rather pose in front of the camera than deal with all those boring meetings."

Carson chuckles, his eyes lighting up with amusement. "At least you're honest about it, sis."

"That's enough about me," Roxy grins. "Hey, Aksel," she turns to me, a mischievous glint in her eyes. "How's your love life? Found anyone to tame the great Aksel King yet?"

I roll my eyes at her persistence, trying to hide the small smile that threatens to spread across my face at her teasing. "My love life is none of your business, Roxy."

"Come on, big brother," Carson chimes in, grinning. "We're just curious."

"Fine," I relent, my lips twitching into a half-smile. "Let's just say I'm exploring my options."

"Ah, spoken like a true diplomat," Raine observes, raising her glass in mock salute. "To Aksel, the eternal bachelor."

We all raise our glasses to exploring our options, clinking them together in a moment of playful camaraderie. The laughter that fills the room warms my heart, a reminder of the light that exists even in the darkest corners of our family's legacy. I'm so used to presenting the cool bachelor act that I almost believe my own words. But deep inside I know they're hollow, just an act. Because the only woman I've ever cared about is Fallon Dempsey.

"Alright, enough teasing Aksel for one night," my grandmother interjects, her voice laced with gentle authority. "Let's enjoy our dinner and each other's company."

"Agreed," I say, raising my glass once more. "To family."

"To family," they echo, and the sound of clinking glasses melds with the murmur of voices as we settle into the familiar dance of conversation.

As the laughter dies down and the night edges on, I slip away from the dinner table, seeking refuge in the quiet solitude of the library. The dimly lit room is a welcome escape, a sanctuary where I can gather my thoughts and find solace in the stillness.

"Mind if I join you?" Raine's voice breaks the silence, her presence unexpected yet comforting.

"Of course not," I reply, gesturing for her to take a seat across from me. "I was just gathering my thoughts."

Raine settles into an armchair, her gaze penetrating as she studies me with concern. "You've been carrying a heavy burden, Aksel. I can see it weighing on you."

I sigh, running a hand through my hair. "It's just...everything. Roxy, Carson, our family's legacy...sometimes it feels like it's all too much to bear. Between Carson's future, Roxy's decisions, and the shadows of multiple mafia families lurking around every corner, it feels like I'm walking a tightrope."

"Believe me, I understand." Raine pauses, her eyes searching mine. "But you don't have to carry this weight alone. We're all in this together. And sometimes, you need to let others step up and share the load."

"Thank you, Raine." I nod, acknowledging the truth in her words. "But it's hard, you know? I can't help but feel responsible for everyone, especially after what happened to Mom and Dad. Not that you and Grandmother haven't done an incredible job of raising the rest of us. But I just feel an additional layer of responsibility being the oldest son, you know?"

"I understand that, and I've definitely felt the same way over the years as the oldest sibling. But responsibility doesn't mean control, Aksel. Learn from my mistakes," Raine replies softly, her words laced with wisdom. "You can't control everyone's choices or actions. You can only guide and support them. We all have our own paths to walk, and our own mistakes to make."

"Speaking of which," I say, shifting gears, "Roxy seems to be on a collision course with disaster. Her recklessness could endanger everything we've worked so hard to protect."

"Ah, our little firecracker," Raine smirks, though her expression remains serious. "She's always been impulsive, but she also has a heart of gold. I think she's just searching for something, even if she doesn't know what it is yet."

"Her latest antics are pushing the limits, though," I admit, my concern evident in my tone. "While I appreciate her free spirit, she needs to understand the consequences of her actions—not just for herself but for our family as well. The people she's hanging out with seem to be getting more dangerous, and each time I see one of her photo shoots it becomes increasingly pornographic."

"Then talk to her, Aksel," Raine urges, leaning forward. "Not as the overbearing older brother, but as someone who genuinely cares about her well-being. Help her see that there's more to life than chasing after the next thrill."

"Thank you, Raine. I'll do my best," I promise, my resolve strengthened by her words.

I'm also acutely aware that if I don't tread very carefully with Roxy I risk pushing her away from me and right into the arms of the people I most wish she'd stay away from.

"Remember, Aksel," she adds, her hand on my shoulder, "we're all in this together. Don't forget that."

I nod, our shared understanding a beacon of hope amidst the shadows that shroud our existence.

I take a deep breath as I approach Carson, who's perched on a window seat in the sitting room overlooking the estate. His youthful features are contemplative as he gazes out at the sprawling grounds. Even though he's reached adulthood, amidst the grandiosity of the estate he looks small and I'm acutely aware of his vulnerability at this intersection of his life. I can't help but feel a pang of protectiveness for my only brother, knowing the darkness that casts its shadow over our family and threatens to consume him. And I definitely don't want him to follow in my footsteps.

"Hey, Carson," I say gently, pulling his attention away from the view. "Mind if I join you?"

"Sure, Aksel," he replies with a small smile, shifting over to make room for me.

"Listen," I begin, choosing my words carefully. "I know you're at a crucial point in your life right now."

He nods. "What do you think about my plans for college? I've been thinking about majoring in business, following in your footsteps." He smiles expectantly, as if seeking my approval.

"Carson," I sigh, placing a hand on his shoulder, feeling the weight of responsibility as his older brother. "I want you to choose your own path, not just follow mine. And be careful with those new friends of yours. Like I said before, some people might not have your best interests at heart. There are going to be people who want to sway you one way or another. And they could be using our family's name and connections for their own gain."

He frowns slightly, sensing the gravity of my words. "Yeah, I guess I've noticed that lately."

My voice is firm yet gentle as I warn him. "We have connections to some dangerous people."

"Like those guys connected to the...?" he asks hesitantly, his voice trailing off and his eyes widening as the reality of our situation sinks in.

"Exactly," I confirm. "Some of them may seem like friends, or even business associates, but they have their own agendas. Don't let them lure you down a path that could lead to disaster."

"Are you saying I shouldn't trust anyone?" Carson questions, uncertainty clouding his expression.

"No, not at all," I clarify. "Just be cautious. Trust your instincts, and remember that we—your family—are always here for you."

He nods solemnly, understanding the gravity of what I'm saying, but I can sense his desire to prove himself. "I know, Aksel. I'll be cautious. Thanks for looking out for me."

"Always, little brother," I reply, ruffling his hair affectionately before we part ways.

As I stand in the dimly lit sitting room, surrounded by the echoes of my siblings and the whispers of our tangled past, I realize that it's these relationships that hold the key to unraveling what's lost within me. Beneath the veneer of power and wealth, I'm bound to my grandmother, Raine, Roxy, and Carson by threads of strength and vulnerability, love and loyalty. And as the shadows of the mafia loom large, it's these ties that will ultimately guide me through the darkness.

Chapter 17

FALLON

"Grave, we need to hit Jacob Daniels where it hurts." I lean against my desk, tapping my fingers on the surface. The urge for revenge courses through my veins like a wildfire, threatening to consume me if I don't act soon. The glow of the computer screen illuminates my face as I scour through Jacob's private information. My heart races, a dark satisfaction coursing through me.

"Agreed," Grave says, his voice low and dangerous. "Legal action won't cut it. I've been researching revenge porn laws and it's very clear that it's almost impossible to see any form of official justice for victims of this type of crime." Despite our willingness to engage in vigilantism, it's usually our first instinct to try and follow a legal process if there's one available. Unfortunately, sometimes that doesn't bode well for the victim and instead threatens to revictimize them, and this is one of those cases. "We're going to have to get creative."

Creative is an understatement. What Jacob did to Maddie is unforgivable, and we're not going to let him walk away without consequences. No, this bastard is going to have to pay.

"Remember, we need to attack him where it's actually going to leave more than a superficial dent," Grave responds, his voice dark and determined. "His business needs to crumble, his reputation needs to be shattered, and most of all he needs to be personally embarrassed."

"Agreed," I answer, beginning to hack into Jacob's company servers. It doesn't take me long to uncover a treasure trove of questionable business practices extending into nearly every aspect of his operations. "Looks like our dear Jacob has been cutting corners, cheating his partners, and exploiting his employees. There's hardly a shortage of material to work with."

"Perfect," Grave mutters, leaning closer to examine the screen. "We'll use that to paint him as the immoral bastard he is."

I nod, pleased with what I've found so far. Where there's smoke there's fire, and one quick look into Jacob is already revealing a blazing inferno.

"Fallon, look at this," Grave calls from across the room, his voice low and purposeful. I glance over, watching as he scrolls through some incriminating photos on his own screen. "Seems like our dear friend Jacob here has been sending these dick pics around like they're candy."

A grin spreads across my face. "Oh, this is perfect, and I'm not at all surprised to hear it." I saunter over to him, leaning in to take a closer look. "He's got no problem sending these to random women, but let's see how he likes them being spread all over the internet. Not that there's anything to be proud of there."

"Right?" Grave snickers, clearly sharing my amusement. "Not that I've seen a ton, but from what I've observed the guys who tend to send the most dick pics are the ones who probably shouldn't."

I laugh and nod.

"We have more to do, though," he continues. "It's one thing if we want to just embarrass him a bit, but we've got a lot of ground to cover if we want to ruin his career the same way he ruined Maddie's."

"Time to create a scandal," I whisper, feeling the rush of adrenaline as I start crafting anonymous emails and social media posts detailing Jacob's dirty dealings. I can see it now, the headlines screaming: 'Jacob Daniels—The Corrupt Businessman' or 'The Dark Side of Jacob Daniels' Empire.'

Together, we spend hours creating fake anonymous social media accounts, posting Jacob's dick pics alongside scathing denouncements of his actions. Every time I hit 'post,' I feel a thrill course through my body, a fire burning hotter within me. My fingers fly over the keyboard, driven by a need to see justice served.

"Fallon, what do you think of this caption?" Grave asks, drawing my attention to his screen. "'Jacob Daniels: The cheating scum who couldn't satisfy a woman even if he tried.'" We make sure that his dick pic contains links to Jacob's social media platforms—his LinkedIn, his Facebook, even his company website. By the time we're done, there'll be no way he can avoid his friends, family and professional acquaintances from seeing what he's been up to.

"Perfect," I reply, smirking. "I think it gets the message across."

"Exactly." He gives me a conspiratorial wink, hits 'post,' and leans back in his chair, satisfaction written all over his face. "Now watch the fireworks begin."

I tap away at my keyboard, creating my own anti-Jacob masterpiece.

"Make sure to mention his perverse interests, too," Grave reminds me, his eyes flaring with anger. "No one will want anything to do with him once they know the true extent of his depravity."

"Of course," I say, adding in allusions to bestiality and his inappropriate relationships with several business colleagues. I can feel bile rising in my throat just thinking about it, but this is necessary. This is justice.

"Being from a devoutly religious family, he won't escape the wrath of his church either," Grave says, an almost cruel smile on his face. "They'll turn their backs on him once they realize how far he's strayed from their teachings. Infidelity, impropriety, immorality—they won't be able to excommunicate him fast enough."

"Consider it done," I reply, weaving in subtle hints about Jacob's lack of faith and his hypocrisy. He may have fooled others, but he'll never fool us.

"Excellent," Grave praises me. "Now let's make sure everyone in the city knows exactly what kind of man Jacob Daniels is."

"Let's burn his reputation to the ground," I agree with finality, hitting send on the remaining emails and posts.

As we monitor the fallout, some of which is pretty instantaneous, I can't shake the feeling that there's still more to be done. The fire of vengeance still rages within me, and I know that it won't be extinguished until Jacob Daniels has paid for his crimes in full.

"Grave," I say, determination hardening my voice. "I don't think we're done here yet. There's still so much more we can do to make sure he never hurts anyone ever again. It's getting late, but Maddie's humiliation doesn't get a chance to rest, so neither should we."

"Agreed," he replies, his eyes dark with resolve. "We won't stop until justice is served."

And with that, we dive back into our mission, ready to bring the full force of our wrath down upon Jacob Daniels. For Maddie, for ourselves, and for everyone else who's ever been wronged by men like him.

"We need to get Maddie's video down as soon as possible. We can't let that keep haunting her," I say, my hands clenched into fists.

"Agreed. I'll make contact with the guy who runs the site. You know it won't be easy—or cheap, though," Grave replies, his eyes narrowing in determination.

"Whatever it takes," I growl. "Maddie deserves her life back."

Grave nods and starts working on making a connection with the shady character behind the popular revenge porn site. While he does that, I work on drafting a proposal for new legislation. While it's all fun and games causing humiliation for Jacob, if we want to make lasting change, we need to strike at the heart of this issue: the law itself. That won't solve Maddie's immediate problem, but it will hopefully give her some of her power back, knowing she's been instrumental in helping to protect others in future from this happening to them.

Less than an hour later, Grave bangs his fist on the table in triumph, rattling the work surface and causing my laptop to jiggle. "Fallon, I've got him," Grave says, an edge of victory in his voice, having successfully reached the revenge porn entrepreneur, Clark Diggins. He's a notoriously shady figure who brags about his achievements online, having accumulated substantial wealth from broadcasting other people's most private moments without their consent.

He's a slippery individual who, while willing to boast about himself, is, for obvious reasons, very hard to locate. If I weren't so focused on exacting revenge against people like Jacob and Aksel I might turn my focus to Clark. But I can only turn my attention to so much revenge at once. "He wants to meet in person. Says he doesn't trust anyone online."

"Can't blame him for that," I mutter, shaking my head at the irony. "Alright, set up the meeting. Let's get this done."

"Fallon," Grave murmurs, catching my eye. "We did good today."

"Yeah," I agree, feeling the weight of our actions settle on my shoulders. "We did."

The next day, we find ourselves in a grimy bar, waiting for the man who holds Maddie's future in his hands.

Twenty-five minutes after our set meeting time, he slides into the booth across from us, his eyes darting around as three burly bodyguards in suits and sunglasses flank his side of the booth. Guns poke out visibly from waist holsters.

Despite his extensive personal security detail, he peeks out at us from underneath a cap and hoodie. I can't help but notice he's wearing the most atrocious combination of designer clothing I've ever seen—like a luxury department store threw up on him after eating its clearance rack.

He wears a giant Rolex that dwarfs his bony wrist and small hand. What a little weasel. I narrow my eyes at him but keep from saying what I want to because we need his help.

He tents his fingers, his elbows resting on the table across from us, and quirks an eyebrow in my direction.

"You're that bitch who saves bitches. I had my guys look you up."

I do everything in my power to hold back from rolling my eyes. "Let's cut to the chase," I say, my voice cold as ice. "We want the video of Matilda Smith removed from your site. Permanently."

"Why would I do that?" he smirks. "It's proving quite popular."

"You didn't have her consent to post the images." Grave's tone is serious, to the point.

Diggins smirks, glances at one of his bodyguards and then cackles. His laugh is unfortunate, like a hyena crossed with a chicken. I bet he got picked on in school for it, which probably explains a lot of this. "That's my entire business model. Do you think I care about some dumb rules?"

"Listen," I press, my voice stern. "We insist you take them down."

He shrugs. "You can insist all you like, but you can't make me do anything. If I took down everything someone asked me to, well, I wouldn't have a website, let alone a multi-million dollar business."

I glance over at Grave, who calmly cracks his knuckles in front of him.

"I don't think you understand," Grave says, his tone stern. We aren't here about anyone else, although we think your little business is a disgusting cesspool of inhumanity. But we insist that you take all material featuring Matilda Smith down immediately."

Diggins glances back at his three bodyguards and smirks. "Or what?"

Before his bodyguards can make a move, Grave leaps up and swiftly deploys a picture-perfect roundhouse kick to the first man. Surprised, he grunts and staggers back into the table behind him. Grave reaches under the dining table and pulls out a baseball bat. He raises the bat high above his head and smashes it down on the disoriented man who groans as the wooden shaft connects with his skull with a satisfying crack. His skull is so thick that the bat shatters in half, splinters flying. He staggers and falls to the ground, blood running from his temple.

The other bodyguards leap into action, attempting to flank Grave. Before they can draw their weapons, though, Grave has grabbed the first guard's gun and has it cocked at the first man. "Don't move," he says, his voice like gravel, "or you're both dead, along with this try-hard."

The guards freeze for a moment. Before they can figure out their next move, Grave leaps onto one set of booth seating and off the other side, leaping at the second man. He smashes the barrel of the gun into his head. The man cries out in pain and crashes to the floor.

The third man backs away, fear in his eyes. Grave smirks at him and shoots the man in both of his feet. The man crumples to the floor, howling. Grave calmly approaches him and gathers his gun from his holster. "Your turn?" He turns and quirks his brow at Diggins, who has grown so pale he's almost translucent.

"No, please," he begs, his breath ragged. "Of course I'll take the posts down, straight away," the man throws his hand up in resignation. He narrows his eyes, stubborn despite his fear. "But you know that comes with a price."

"Name it," Grave snarls. His protective instincts are kicking in, and I love him all the more for it.

"Thirty grand. Cash," the man says, bolstered by the confidence of knowing how many people have paid this price before, sometimes more.

"Twenty," I say without hesitation, pulling out a fat envelope and sliding it across the table. Grave did his research before we came, and knew exactly what Diggins would accept. "Now delete the video, or we'll take you down, too."

"Alright, alright!" He scrambles for his phone and feverishly types away, sighing every now and then as if we're super annoying for our request. Within minutes, he shows us the confirmation that the video has been removed.

"Good," Grave says gruffly. "Now get lost. And if it comes up again on your site I will kill you." He cracks his knuckles and Diggins visibly pales.

As the man scuttles away, his guards still incapacitated on the floor in various states of consciousness, I can't help but smile. One more victory for Maddie.

"Good job, thanks Grave," I say. "They didn't stand a chance. But we're not done yet. Next up: getting the law changed." Determination fuels my every word.

"Let's do this, Fallon," Grave agrees, matching my intensity the way that only he can.

As our handiwork spreads like wildfire across the internet, I can't help but feel a sense of pride. Jacob's humiliation is only just beginning, and it's all because of us. We've taken matters into our own hands, refusing to let him continue hurting people like Maddie without consequences.

Within hours, the internet is ablaze with rumors and damning information about Jacob.

Within days, his business partners start distancing themselves.

Within weeks, his family turns their backs on him, and even his closest friends abandon him.

We lobby tirelessly for a new law targeting revenge porn. We call in favors, make impassioned speeches, and even get some media attention. Slowly but surely, momentum builds around our cause.

"Grave, they're calling it 'Maddie's Law'," I say in awe as I read the news headline a few weeks later. "It's going all the way to Congress and has a ton of high-profile support. Maddie has been able to channel this into a new career opportunity. We—and she—are really making a difference."

"Damn right we are," he replies, pride shining in his eyes. "For Maddie, and for everyone else who's suffered like her. Don't tell anyone, but doing this kind of work makes me feel warm inside."

"My lips are sealed," I laugh, and then I feel overwhelmed by more serious emotions. "Justice is finally being served," I whisper, knowing that all our hard work is starting to pay off. "And don't worry, I won't tell anyone you're secretly a big teddy bear inside. Thank you for your unwavering support. I appreciate you being here for me."

"Always, Fallon," Grave says, awkwardly tapping me on my shoulder in a side hug which is about as affectionate as he gets. "Always."

"Fallon, look at this," Grave says, showing me a news article that has just been published. "Jacob Daniels: A Life and Career in Ruins."

"Good," I say, my heart pounding with satisfaction. "He deserves every bit of this. Maddie can finally rest easy knowing her tormentor has at last been brought down."

Chapter 18

FALLON

The next day, adrenaline still surges through my veins, and I can't help but grin when I think of Jacob Daniels getting his just desserts. We've done it. Our most recent revenge is a success. I glance over at Grave, who shares a satisfied smirk with me before turning his attention to the door.

"Fallon," he murmurs, "the next client is here." We don't usually have them back-to-back like this, but it feels like the level of douchebag behavior in this city is at an all-time high.

"Send her in," I reply, anticipation curling around my heart like smoke from a burning flame.

The door swings open, revealing Janice Hopkins, our second client. She's a petite woman with layered brown hair and thin lips, and she's wearing a demure floral dress. Her eyes are red-rimmed from crying, and she clutches her purse tightly against her chest as if it were a shield. She has a slight limp as she makes her way into the office. She glances at my overstuffed couch but remains standing.

My anger ignites at the sight of her fragile state, and I know that we're about to embark on another dark path for justice.

"Janice, please, have a seat," I gesture to the chair across from my desk. She nods gratefully and sits, wringing her hands together in her lap.

"Thank you for seeing me," she whispers, taking a deep breath. "I've heard that you two... well, that you can help people like me."

Grave leans against the wall near the corner, arms crossed, and Janice glances at him nervously. He attempts a smile to ease her nerves and, despite the seriousness of the moment, I almost laugh out loud when I get a rare glimpse of his teeth. I forget he even has them sometimes.

"We can, Janice," I smile at her with a warmth that I hope contrasts with the darkness we deal in. "But to best help you, we need to know everything about what's happened. Who's hurt you?"

Tears well in her eyes, and she swallows hard before speaking. "My husband, Dickson Fineman. He's... he's a violent and rageful alcoholic. He goes on these drinking benders, disappears for days at a time. And when he comes back, he's not... himself. He's violent ...and I'm not sure whether it's just alcohol he's using at this point."

As she continues to describe the escalating abuse she's suffered at the hands of her husband, my blood boils with rage.

It emerges that Dickson's behavior started out with minor emotional abuse that left her feeling confused about whether he'd actually crossed a line. His verbal barbs soon became more severe, with increasingly frequent and derogatory comments being made at her expense. And then things turned physical.

Now he's beating her on a regular basis while also abusing her financially, draining her assets to fund his drug and alcohol addiction. He has access to all of her bank accounts, and has somehow had himself nominated as power of attorney through some type of conservatorship arrangement so she can't do anything about it.

Unlike Jacob Daniels, Dickson is a textbook narcissist with a gift of the gab. Janice has tried utilizing the court system and domestic violence resources, but every time Dickson gets in front of the police or a judge he sweet-talks his way out of the situation, making it look like Janice is the violent abuser in the relationship. Unfortunately, we see this all too often.

So here she is, abused and frightened with seemingly no way out. How dare he treat her like this? How can someone be so cruel to another human being? My blood boils as she recounts further details of her predicament.

"During the last attack," she continues, wiping at her tears. "He pushed me backwards, and I fell down the stairs and broke my leg. It fractured in several places and I'll... I'll never walk the same again. And then he tried to strangle me at the foot of the stairs when I was already barely conscious. An Amazon package happened to be being delivered right at that time, and the delivery person rang the doorbell, or I believe I would have died that night."

A shiver runs down my spine at how close she came to death. "Janice, I promise you," I say fiercely, leaning forward in my chair. "We're going to make Dickson pay for what he's done to you. We won't let him hurt you anymore."

"Thank you," she whispers, her voice cracking with emotion. "I don't know what I would do without you two."

Grave nods solemnly, and we all share a moment of understanding. This is why we do what we do—to help those who can't help themselves, to bring justice to the ones who've suffered.

"Leave it to us, Janice," Grave reassures her. "We'll take care of everything."

"Th-thank you both," she looks from him to me, her apprehension toward Grave now vanished.

As she stands up to leave, I feel a surge of determination flowing through me. Another chance to right a wrong, to make someone pay for their actions. Fuckboy only begins to describe the level of asshole we really deal with on the dark side of our operations. I'm glad we have my more lighthearted education programs as a cover for this most important work.

"Be safe, Janice," I tell her, watching as she limps out of my office, her head now held high despite the pain she carries.

"Another monster to put down," Grave says as the door clicks shut. And I couldn't agree more. Dickson Fineman will get what's coming to him.

I clench my fists, the fire of revenge burning hotter than ever.

I can't shake the image of Janice's tear-streaked face from my mind as I lean back in my chair, my fingers tapping restlessly on the desk. Grave's dark eyes meet mine, reflecting similar thoughts.

"Strangling her wasn't enough for that bastard," he growls, his voice low and filled with anger. "He had to tell her he wished she was dead. Can you believe the nerve?"

"Unfortunately, I can," I reply, my own voice dripping with disdain. "And we both know that it's not just about the physical violence. It's the psychological impact, too. The fear that comes from knowing the person who's supposed to love you could end your life in an instant." My heart aches for Janice, and I know that Grave feels the same way. "We've seen it too many times."

"Exactly," Grave agrees, rubbing his chin thoughtfully. "And the stats... someone who's strangled their partner before is hundreds of times more likely to eventually murder them. We need to act fast, Fallon. We can't risk him hurting her again."

"Agreed," I nod. "So, what's the plan?" I ask, my determination solidifying as we brainstorm how best to exact our revenge on Dickson Fineman.

Grave smirks, and I can tell he already has an idea forming in his mind. "Well, considering our friend Dickson likes his liquor so much, why don't we give the man what he wants?"

"Go on," I encourage, intrigued by his train of thought.

"Waterboarding, but with vodka," Grave suggests, a wicked gleam in his eyes. "Let him feel the same suffocating helplessness he inflicted on Janice. Let him drown in his own vice. He's been physical toward Janice—he's disabled her and almost killed her—so I feel like it's appropriate."

I can't help but grin at the poetic justice in Grave's plan. "That sounds perfect. It's time to make Mr. Fineman realize the gravity of his sins."

"Let's do it," Grave agrees, his voice filled with dark resolve. Together, we'll make sure Dickson Fineman pays dearly for the pain he's caused Janice. "And then, of course, we've got to dismantle this ridiculous conservatorship situation. But I'm sure Dickhead will be more amenable to signing away his 'rights' once we're done with him."

We work into the night mapping out our next steps.

With each plan we devise and execute, our bond grows stronger, fueled by our shared quest for justice. And as we prepare to face yet another monster, I know that together, we are unstoppable.

Chapter 19

FALLON

Although things are going well at work, the need for control in my personal life gnaws at me, a hunger I can't ignore any longer. I sit on my couch, scrolling through an online dating app on my phone. This is my answer—another night of no-strings-attached sex with a man I'll never see again. The perfect way to assert my dominance and forget about the smoldering gaze of Aksel King. As long as it goes better than last time when, no matter what I tried, I couldn't get that asshole out of my mind.

"Fuck you, Aksel," I mutter under my breath as I swipe left on yet another profile that reminds me of him. It's not even that the other guys really look like him at all. It could be merely one facial feature, the fit of their T-shirt, the fact they breathe air—anything at all—that brings him to mind. He's got me all twisted up inside and I hate it. I crave control, but he's thrown me off balance. I need to regain my footing, and prove to myself that I'm still in command.

My thumb hovers over the screen, hesitating for just a moment before swiping right on a man who looks absolutely nothing like Aksel. He's on the shorter side, and has a wild mess of bleached curly hair—the complete opposite of Aksel's tall, muscular frame and meticulously styled, closely-cropped dark hair.

The man messages me almost immediately.

Netflixandchillwyou: Hi there pretty lady. Wyd?

It's a douchey screen name but I guess it's to the point. I reply, keeping it short and detached.

Me: Fallon.

No personal details, no connection. Just two consenting adults meeting for one explicit purpose.

Netflixandchillwyou: Your place or mine?

He cuts straight to the chase. I appreciate his bluntness.

Me: Neither. Devereux Hotel. One hour.

The Devereux is an elegant boutique hotel on the other side of the city. I feel like doing something a bit more upscale this time.

Netflixandchillwyou: Works for me.

I shoot him a final message.

Me: You better be ready for me. I'm in charge tonight and anything goes. Do you understand?

Netflixandchillwyou: Sounds exciting. I'm in.

My pulse quickens as I prepare myself for the encounter. My heart races, my mind already running through all the ways I'll exert my power over the man. He doesn't know exactly what he's getting into, but I do—and I am more than ready.

"Control. Dominance. Power." I repeat these words like a mantra as I slip into my tight black dress and matching red-bottomed heels. I add a slick of bright red lipstick and black winged eyeliner that make me feel sexy and strong. I need this. I will have it.

I glance in the mirror one more time and smile at my reflection. If looks could kill, tonight I'd be an assassin. "Let's do this," I whisper to myself, stepping out of my condo with confidence and determination. Aksel King may haunt my thoughts, but tonight, he'll be nothing more than a memory as I take back control and remind myself who the hell I am—Fallon fucking Dempsey.

I stride into the dimly lit lobby of the Devereux Hotel, my stiletto heels clicking against the marble floor. I never enjoy wearing heels, but sometimes they come in handy, especially for nights like tonight. The chandelier above casts a sinister glow on the opulent surroundings, but I barely notice. My thoughts race, focusing solely on the night ahead.

"Room 237," I murmur to myself, heading towards the elevator. As the doors close behind me, I take a deep breath and steel my resolve. This is what I need—control, dominance, power. Tonight, it's all mine for the taking.

The door to room 237 swings open, revealing the man from the dating app standing there in a plain white T-shirt and baggy jeans, his curly hair tied back in a slightly disheveled man bun. He grins nervously at me as I enter, and his smile crinkles the corner of his eyes and reveals dimples on both cheeks. I can't help but smirk back. He's adorable, and he has no idea what he's in for.

"Hi, Fallon," the man says, his gaze appreciatively traveling over my body. "You look as hot as you did in your pictures, even moreso actually. My name is Bun, by the way."

Of course his name is Bun. I wonder which came first, his name or his hairstyle.

"Of course I do." I snap back, not interested in pleasantries. "I have no concern for your name or any other personal information. Now strip." His jaw drops as I push him backward into the room and let the door click closed behind us.

I turn and latch the security lock, and then toss him a black mask from my purse, and he fumbles before catching it. "Put this on and then take off your fucking clothes."

"Okay," he replies hesitantly, turning the mask over in his hands in surprise before slipping it over his head. It covers his eyes and leaves only his mouth exposed. I'll have time to see his cute face later, but for now I need to show him who's in charge.

As he undresses, I let my gaze roam over his body, taking in every inch of his lean but muscular form. So different from Aksel's towering frame, and yet, my desire burns just as fiercely in my hunger for a casual connection. When he removes his underwear, a smile passes over my lips. The man may be on the shorter side, but he's packing, girthy. I'm going to have some fun with him.

"Get on the bed. Lie on your back. Hands above your head," I command, watching as he obeys without question. I feel a thrill run through me at the sight of him lying there, vulnerable and completely at my mercy. I've chosen well.

Retrieving silk ties from my purse, I secure each of his wrists and then his ankles to the bedposts.

The dim light casts shadows across the hotel room, highlighting his muscular form as he lies bound on the bed. I stand at the foot of the bed, taking a moment to admire my handiwork.

"Please," he whispers, his voice barely audible as I move toward him. "I want you."

"I'll decide if and when that happens."

"Oh—okay?" he says nervously.

"So, you're lying on a bed, tied up, wearing a mask, at the mercy of a complete stranger. Is this what you wanted?" I ask, my voice cold and authoritative.

"Y-yes, I didn't know it until now but yes," he stammers, anticipation and arousal dripping from every syllable.

"Good," I reply, stalking toward him with predatory grace. My hands run over the lengths of the silk ties binding him, ensuring they're secure. I won't tolerate any interruptions tonight—not when I need this encounter to satisfy my craving for control.

"You'll get what I give you," I reply sharply, my fingers trailing down his chest. "And you'll thank me for it," I add, making sure my fingers dig in just enough to leave thick pink lines down his torso. I don't wait for a response as I slip off my dress and then climb onto the bed and straddle his hips, still wearing my black lace panties, feeling his hardness beneath me and reveling in the power I hold over him.

"Thank you," he breathes out, and I smirk at his eagerness.

"Good boy," I murmur, leaning down to kiss him roughly. He moans into my mouth, but I pull away before he can get too comfortable. This isn't about pleasure—not for him, anyway. Tonight, it's all about control.

As we continue, I let go of my thoughts of Aksel and immerse myself in the moment, taking what I want and leaving no room for doubt or regret. In this room, with this man, I am powerful, dominant, and free.

"Open your mouth," I command, and he obeys without hesitation. I stand over him and slide off my underwear, then I straddle his face, lowering myself onto him with my thighs on either side of his masked head. His tongue meets me eagerly, exploring my pussy.

He moans at the way I taste, sliding his tongue along my folds and slipping it in between. I grip the headboard, letting out a throaty moan as his mouth works its magic on me. He flattens his tongue and licks me from my entrance all the way up to my clit. I gasp as he gently sucks my clit into his mouth and licks and sucks at it.

Thighs shaking, I grind my hips so my pussy mashes against his tongue. He'd better watch it, or I'll suffocate him. He moves his head in rhythm with the gyration of my hips.

"Tongue fuck me," I growl, continuing to ride his face. Obediently, he shapes his tongue into more of a cylinder and plunges it into my pussy. I ride it, allowing it to slide into me as far as it can before gliding back out, over and over again. I moan at the feeling of his tongue against my entrance. "Now focus back on my clit," I command, "and make me come."

All the while, Aksel continues to haunt my thoughts. His disapproving gaze, his simmering anger—they fuel my desire for dominance and control. And as much as I want to push him away, I can't help but find some twisted satisfaction in knowing it's his lingering presence that drives me to this level of ecstasy.

Bun complies, once again flattening his tongue and my hips buck as he laps at my clit. My thighs shudder as the coil builds in my core. "Fuck, that's it," I growl, my thighs tightening around the man's face as my climax continues to build. His muffled moans are like music to my ears, a tangible reminder of the power I wield over him.

Each thought of Aksel intensifies the sensation until I'm teetering on the edge.

"Say my name," I order breathlessly, needing to hear him acknowledge the woman who has brought him to his knees—metaphorically, at least.

"Fallon," he gasps, his voice muffled by my body. And that's all it takes. Thoughts of Aksel and the fire he ignites within me push me over the edge, and I come undone. I mash his head between my shuddering thighs and smother him as waves of pleasure crash down around me.

It's a moment of pure, unadulterated release—one fueled by anger, resentment, and an insatiable hunger for control. The heat of the moment has a way of making you forget about everything else, of blurring the lines between right and wrong.

As I stare down at the man beneath me, his once confident expression now replaced with a mixture of lust and fear, I can't help but revel in the sensations coursing through me. The hunger for control. The need to assert my dominance.

"What happens now?" he rasps.

"Did you think you could just make me come and walk away?" I sneer, the words dripping with venom. I yank the mask off and, as he looks up at me, my hand cracks across his face, leaving behind a stinging red mark that only serves to fuel my desire.

"Fuck," he gasps, his eyes widening in surprise. But there's no denying the excitement that flickers in his gaze. "I know you said you'd be in control tonight, but I didn't know you were into this."

"Neither did I," I admit, an almost feral grin spreading across my features. It's true—until tonight, I had no idea just how thrilling it could be to hold someone else's fate in my hands to quite this degree. And as I tighten the silk ties around his wrists, binding them even more securely to the headboard, I can't help but feel a spark of anticipation ignite within me.

"Tell me you want this," I demand, my voice low and dangerous. The power I wield over him is intoxicating, consuming every fiber of my being.

"I—I want this," he stutters, his chest heaving with each ragged breath. "Please, Fallon...give it to me—"

"Good." I lean in close, my lips hovering just above his. "Because you have no idea what I'm capable of."

And then, without warning, I spit in his face. The action is crude, vulgar even, but it sends a shiver down my spine nonetheless. I watch as a mixture of shock and desire contorts his features, his pupils dilating with each passing second.

"Is that all you've got?" he taunts, a wicked grin tugging at the corners of his mouth as my saliva trickles down his cheek. It's as if he's daring me to push him further, to test the limits of our twisted little game.

"Careful what you ask for," I warn, my voice barely more than a whisper. And with that, I slap him once more, relishing in the way his body jerks in response. The sound of flesh against flesh echoes throughout the room, a stark reminder of the control I now wield over this man.

Reaching back, I'm not surprised to find he's harder than ever. I stroke his girthy cock and he groans with pleasure. "I'm going to ride your cock now and you're going to make me come again. Do you understand?"

"Fuck, yes," he groans, his muscles tensing beneath me as I move backward and slide my pussy down onto his cock. I moan at the sensation of him dragging against my walls, stretching me.

It's clear he enjoys this power play just as much as I do—perhaps even more so. But as I stare down at him, bound and vulnerable, I can't help but think of Aksel, and the way he'd made me feel so powerless. So weak.

I begin to glide up and down, impaling myself on his hardness, and he bucks his hips in rhythm with my movements. Raking my nails over his chest, I grab onto him by the shoulders and slam myself down on him forcefully.

He moans, "Fucking hell," as I ride him, over and over again, my pussy tight around his shaft. I angle my hips so my clit rubs against him and I feel the coil deep within me tightening again as our bodies build friction. I dig my nails into him until I feel his blood underneath them, squeezing my thighs tight against his hips as I come hard again, my body quaking against his.

His body tenses and he grunts as he releases, his thighs shuddering as his cock pulsates.

The moment his orgasm subsides, I climb off him and untie his ropes. "It's time for you to go now, but remember my name," I lean down and whisper into Bun's ear as our encounter draws to a close. My voice is cold and distant. "Fallon fucking Dempsey."

"Fallon," he repeats, his voice shaky and filled with awe. "Fallon fucking Dempsey. I'll remember you forever." I smile, satisfied with the night's events. The control I've sought is mine, and with that, I throw myself into the darkness.

Chapter 20

AKSEL

The sharp sting of cold air slaps my face as I step outside, clutching my phone. I can't shake the urge to talk to Fallon, but I know there's only a small chance she'll answer when she sees it's me calling. With a deep breath, I select her name in my contacts and wait for her voice to fill my ear.

"Hello?" she answers, sounding distracted. But that's better than nothing. At least I get to hear her voice.

"Hey, Fallon, it's Aksel." I try to hide the desperation in my tone but fail miserably.

"Yeah, I can see that. Your name came up on my phone even though I really should have you blocked. What do you want? Make it quick, Aksel. I'm busy," she snaps, her tone void of any warmth.

"Is everything okay? Things left off kind of..."

"Of course," she snaps. "Everything's fine. I've just got a lot on my plate right now with my clients. Can't chat." The line goes dead before I can even respond.

"Fuck!" I scream, letting the phone slip from my fingers onto the frozen pavement. My chest tightens with every heartbeat, and an overwhelming sense of hurt consumes me. She seemed so cold, so distant. Like I was nothing to her, when she is everything to me.

"Get your shit together, Aksel," I mutter under my breath, forcing back the tears that threaten to spill over. "You're living on memories." I scoop up my phone, wiping away the dirt and snow, then shove it into my pocket. What was lost back then is long gone. It's time to drag myself into the present.

I march back inside, slamming the door shut behind me. My office, typically meticulously organized, is a mess, papers strewn across the desk, a testament to my scattered mind. I didn't think I'd be this affected by Fallon's dismissiveness. But here I am, consumed by the thought of her, and she doesn't even give a damn.

"Enough," I growl to myself, plonking myself heavily into my chair. I need to focus on work, not her. "Don't let her get to you, Aksel."

My fingers fly across the keyboard, typing furiously as I lose myself in my work. I crush my way through my extensive to-do list, even crossing off items that I've been putting off for a while. Hours pass like minutes, the glow of the computer screen casting eerie shadows on the walls. I can't keep letting Fallon control my emotions. She's volatile, she's clearly pissed at me even though I'm not sure why, and I need to protect myself.

"Fuck her," I whisper, trying to convince myself that I don't care. But deep down, I know I'm lying. The ache in my heart persists, no matter how hard I try to ignore it.

"Focus, Aksel. Focus on what matters." I take a deep breath and throw myself back into my work, letting the darkness of my thoughts fuel my determination.

The Next Day

The large conference room outside my office is swarming with people here for a key meeting, but all I hear is the pounding of my heart in my ears. My eyes remain fixated on the stack of accounting books and financial statements on the large desk in front of me, as if they're a code waiting to be deciphered.

"King Enterprises has its fingers in a lot of pies," I mumble to myself, flipping through the pages. "Where is the truth hidden?"

"Is everything alright, Mr. King?" Darren, my assistant, asks as he pops his head into my office and notices the concerned look on my face. As always, he's dressed in an immaculately pressed collared shirt and khaki trousers. He raises an eyebrow at me, his icy blue eyes piercing into mine. "The meeting's about to start and just about everyone else is there."

"Everything's fine, Darren. Just reviewing some numbers. I'll be there in ten minutes. They can start without me." I force a smile, though it feels like sandpaper against my skin.

"Very well, sir. If you need any assistance, I'm here for you."

I trust Darren implicitly. And wish I could say the same about everyone in the adjacent conference room. But I can't let any of them know exactly what I'm looking into, at least not until I find out more.

Kent Farrington knocks on my door frame and pokes his head in. "Hey Aksel. See you in the meeting. You need anything before we go in?" He scans his eyes over my desk and I discreetly shuffle a pile of papers that are none of his business. He can't know what I'm looking into just yet.

"No thanks, Kent. See you in there." I force a smile, although it pains me to extend even a minor courtesy to someone who is likely plotting to take my family's entire company down from the inside.

"Okay, well, see you in there." Kent jerks his head toward the boardroom and returns my smile with a sinister smirk before walking away, leaving a trail of unease behind him.

I continue to pore over the documents, searching for any discrepancies that would point to foul play. As much as I want to believe that my family is innocent, I can't shake the feeling that there's more going on than meets the eye.

Twenty minutes or so later, I glance over to where Kent is chatting with our Chief Marketing Officer. His eyes flick over to me, but he quickly looks away when he sees me returning his gaze.

"Perhaps it's Isabella?" I think out loud, my gaze moving towards our Chief Operating Officer, who is busy conversing with another group of executives. Her dark hair is pulled back into a tight bun, her eyes calculating and cunning. Could she really be part of this too?

My phone beeps.

Raine: How are things going over there? Has the meeting started? I bet you're procrastinating on going into the conference room.

Me: Ha. You know me too well. Or did you have surveillance cameras installed in my office? ;)

She's the only one in the family other than my grandmother who seems to understand the weight of the situation, and I'm grateful for her support.

Raine: Have you found anything yet?

Me: Nothing concrete. But I'm getting closer. I can feel it.

Raine: Keep digging, Aksel. I'm getting started on my end today. We'll get to the bottom of this together.

Her words are a promise, like a virtual reassuring squeeze of my hand. Her loyalty, a beacon in the storm, guiding me through these treacherous waters.

Aksel: Thanks, Raine. I don't know what I'd do without you.

I push myself up from the chair, and I muster up a genuine smile for my sister that she can't see through the phone. I think of Carson and Roxy and my grandmother, and all that's at risk if my instincts are right. In this moment, I make a silent vow: no matter what it takes, I will uncover the truth and protect my family at all costs.

The air is thick with tension as I make my way to the private conference room, my heart pounding in my chest like a caged animal. I need answers, and I'm not going to get them sitting around waiting for something to happen.

"Kent, Isabella," I greet them as I enter, trying to keep my voice steady. They both look up from their respective piles of paperwork, the shadows under their eyes betraying their exhaustion—or perhaps it's something more sinister.

"Ah, Aksel, just the man we wanted to see," Kent says, his voice dripping with false cheerfulness. Isabella shoots him a quick glance, her expression unreadable. "We were just discussing some... discrepancies in the financials. We thought we'd get started in five or so minutes. Prentice got stuck in traffic."

"Discrepancies?" I question, my mind racing through every possible scenario. What are they hiding? Are they trying to get ahead of their fraudulent activities by throwing red herrings my way?

"Nothing major," Isabella interjects quickly, her voice smooth as silk. "Just a few minor errors we're working to correct."

"Errors that shouldn't be there in the first place," I snap, my suspicions flaring. "I trust this group to ensure our contracts and compliance documents are ironclad and entirely accurate. What's going on?"

"Relax, Aksel," Kent says, leaning back in his chair. "Sometimes things slip through the cracks, especially when you're dealing with a company as large as ours. It happens."

I shake my head. "Unacceptable. And I know mistakes happen, but," I say, glaring at them both, "it doesn't sit right with me."

"That's understandable, Aksel," Isabella replies, her eyes locked onto mine. "But you can be assured that we have it under control."

"Fine," I concede, though the unease in my gut tells me otherwise. "I'll leave you two to it then."

"Thanks, Aksel," Kent says, nodding at me. I turn to leave, but as I reach the door, I hear their hushed whispers begin.

"Keep an eye on him," Isabella murmurs, her voice barely audible. "He's getting too close."

"Relax," Kent responds, his tone just as quiet. "We've got this under control. The plan is already in motion."

"Good," Isabella says, her voice laced with venom. "The sooner we bring the Kings down, the better."

My blood runs cold at their words, and it takes every ounce of my willpower not to barge back into the room and confront them. Instead, I slip away silently, my mind racing with a thousand thoughts.

What the hell have I stumbled onto? Are they really trying to destroy my family from the inside? And it can't be just the two of them, so which rival mafia family are they working for?

I need answers—and I'm going to get them, no matter what it takes. But first, I need to keep my enemies closer than ever before.

Chapter 21

FALLON

The air in the dimly lit abandoned warehouse on the outskirts of the city chills my bones as I watch Grave secure Dickson Fineman to a rickety wooden chair. The smell of damp mold and fear fills the room, making my stomach turn. My heart races with anticipation, knowing that tonight we'll exact our revenge on this vile man.

"Are you sure about this, Fallon?" Grave's voice was low and steady as we drove to the man's residence earlier in the evening, but I could sense his concern for me deep within his words.

"Positive," I had replied with a conviction that still shakes me to my core. "He deserves everything he's about to get."

Grave had merely nodded, understanding the depth of my hatred for Dickson, and we'd driven the rest of the way in silence. Dickson, understandably surprised by our arrival at his home, was easily subdued. It's ironic how the men quickest to use their fists against people weaker than them, are usually also the most useless when it comes to defending themselves.

Grave takes a bottle of vodka and pours it into an industrial basin nearby, the liquid splashing against the metal surface. The sharp chemical smell of alcohol invades my nostrils, making me shudder.

"Last chance to change your mind," Grave offers me one final out, but I know there's no turning back now.

"Let's do this," I say, determination surging through my veins.

Grave hands me a rag soaked in the vodka, its frigid wetness seeping through the fabric and numbing my fingers. As I approach Dickson, his eyes flicker open, confusion and terror clouding his gaze. It's a look that sends a twisted thrill down my spine.

"Remember Janice, you sick bastard?" I spit the words at him like venom. "This is for her."

"My wife, Janice? Oh my god. This is because of her? Please," he sobs, his voice hoarse and broken. "I'm sorry. I didn't mean to hurt her."

Dickson's pathetic pleas for mercy slice through me, igniting a wildfire of fury that I struggle to contain.

"Didn't mean to?" I spit back, the venom in my words thick and lethal. "You nearly killed Janice, you piece of shit!" I can't help but imagine the pain she went through—the bruises, the broken bones, worst of all the psychological anguish—and it fuels my rage further.

"Fallon, let him speak," Grave says, an eerily calm presence beside me. But I can hear the edge in his voice too. He's as invested in this as I am. We're both seeking justice for our client.

"Alright, Dickson. Tell us what happened," I demand, my tone cold and unforgiving.

"Janice... she provoked me. She said things... made me mad." His excuses are weak, pathetic attempts at justifying his monstrous actions.

"Made you mad? So you decided to beat her within an inch of her life, is that it?" I seethe, digging my nails into my palms so hard that they draw blood. "Took away all of her financial independence so you could control her completely, even after you permanently disabled her?"

"Okay," he finally admits, choking on his tears. "I did it. I hurt her. But I swear, I'll change. I'll get sober, and I'll stop putting hands on her. Just please... don't hurt me."

"Change?" My laughter is bitter, hollow. "You think getting sober is going to erase the years of pain you've inflicted on people? You think it'll make up for what you did to Janice? That it will somehow cure her permanent disability and take away the mental scars you've inflicted on her?"

"Fallon..." Grave warns again, his hand gripping my arm. But I can't let this go, not when Janice still bears the scars of Dickson's cruelty.

"You're lying," I snarl, stepping closer to him. "You don't want to change. You just don't want to suffer the consequences of your actions."

"Please!" Dickson wails, desperation lacing his voice. "I'll do anything. I'll stay away from her. I won't touch another drop of alcohol ever again. Just please... don't kill me."

I place the alcohol-drenched rag over Dickson's face, covering his nose and mouth. His muffled pleas for mercy are barely audible beneath the thick fabric. I signal for Grave to begin pouring the vodka from the basin. The clear liquid cascades over Dickson's face, his choked gasps becoming more desperate by the second.

"Stop! Please!" he manages to gurgle between tortured breaths, but his pleas fall on deaf ears.

"Did you stop when Janice begged you?" I growl, my voice laced with fury as I watch the liquid pool around Dickson's head. "No, you didn't."

I press the rag down harder, ensuring that every ounce of vodka seeps into Dickson's airways. His body convulses violently, the chair creaking beneath him. The sight of his suffering fuels my rage, pushing me to continue this torment. He coughs and splutters beneath the rag which only makes me hold on tighter and pour faster.

"Fallon," Grave warns, his hand on my shoulder. I know he's concerned that I'm going too far, that I might lose myself in this darkness. But the thought of stopping now feels like a betrayal. Dickson's head lolls to the side, his eyes bloodshot, tears streaming down his face as he continues to gag. Noxious vodka fumes threaten to overwhelm me as I stand just inches away from him, and I resist the urge to gag myself.

"Almost there," I snarl, refusing to relent. The vodka-soaked cloth smothers Dickson's face once more, and his body writhes in agony. I feel a sick satisfaction in watching him suffer, but it's not enough—not yet.

"Stop!" Dickson chokes out between desperate gasps for air. "I'll do anything you want—just please stop this!"

"Fallon, he's had enough," Grave insists, his hand tightening on my arm, pulling me away from the madness that threatens to consume me. My heart races, fueled by anger and adrenaline, but I reluctantly let go of the rag and step away from Dickson. His body slumps forward as he gasps for breath, blood trickling from his nose and mouth.

"Fine," I snap, throwing the cloth aside and unfastening his restraints. "Get up, Dickson."

Dickson struggles to push himself upright, coughing violently as he tries to regain his breath. His tear-filled eyes meet mine, and I can see the fear that has taken root in his soul. Good.

"Remember this pain, Dickson," I hiss at him. "And listen carefully," I growl, moving closer until our faces are mere inches apart. "You will stay out of Janice's life. And you have five business days to have the conservatorship reversed and everything put back in Janice's name, including the assets you've been hiding from her. You will send her financial assistance in perpetuity for your criminal actions. Do you understand?"

He nods weakly. "Y-yes," he stammers, trembling beneath my glare.

"If you try to go to the authorities, we will know. We have evidence of your crimes, and we will not stop at torture next time. Is that clear? Your life, your family's lives, will be ruined. Do you understand you have no choice but to go through with our demands?"

"Ye—yes. I understand." He nods, his eyes wide.

"Grave, do you believe him?" I ask, my eyes never leaving Dickson's tear-streaked face.

"Fallon," Grave sighs, his grip on my arm tightening. "We've made our point. It's time to leave."

"I—I swear, I'll never bother her again." The man's breathing is ragged. "And I'll pay... whatever she needs."

"Damn right, you will," I spit, my voice venomous. Before we leave, I lean down, my lips brushing his vodka-soaked ear as I whisper, "Because if you don't do right by Janice, or if I hear of you hurting someone else ever again, I will hunt you down and I won't be so merciful next time."

As we leave the basement, the sounds of Dickson's labored breathing and shuddering sobs echo behind us. I feel a warped sense of satisfaction.

"Are you okay?" Grave asks, noticing the twisted smile on my face, his voice gentle and concerned as we make our way back to his truck.

"Better than ever," I admit, my heart still pounding with adrenaline. "Justice has once again been served."

Chapter 22

FALLON

The sun filters through the tall windows of Eden Cafe, casting warm rays across the small metal table I've claimed as my own. It's a stark contrast from the dark, dingy warehouse where Grave and I tortured Dickson Fineman only hours ago. I sip my espresso and watch the door, anticipation prickling beneath my skin. Bronson had mentioned this place a few times, but I'd never bothered to check it out until now.

I'm beginning to see why he likes it so much. It's trendy but cozy, local street art splashed across the brightly colored walls, rustic brick adorned with twinkling fairy lights and potted plants, and vintage chandeliers perched above an eclectic mix of vintage tables and chairs.

Music by local artists plays softly in the background as baristas roast organic, fair-trade coffee beans onsite, expertly crafting beverages served in mugs handcrafted by local artisans. It's bougie, but it works.

Bronson and his fairly new girlfriend, Wren, are due to arrive any minute now. I'm excited to get to know her, but also cautious. After all, we've seen how quickly relationships can go sour in our family. I was worried I'd be tired for this meeting after last night, but the heady combination of revenge-fueled motivation and potent caffeine have me feeling lively.

The door swings open, and there they are—Bronson, tall and confident, with a protective arm around Wren, her delicate features framed by golden curls that cascade down her back. She offers a tentative smile in my direction, her green eyes curious yet cautious. There's something captivating about her, like a hidden fire waiting to be unleashed.

"Hey, Fallon!" Bronson greets me with a grin as he pulls out a chair for Wren. "Thanks for meeting us here."

"Bronson," I greet him warmly, standing to embrace my older brother. His arms wrap around me protectively, the bond between us palpable. "It's good to see you."

"Always a pleasure, Fallon." He grins as we break apart, his gaze flicking toward Wren. "You remember Wren, right?"

"Of course," I say, extending my hand to her. I met her once in passing at an event, but this is the first time we're spending time in a more intimate setting where we can have more than cursory small talk. "Nice to see you again, Wren."

"Likewise, Fallon," she replies, her grip surprisingly firm despite her delicate appearance. Although she's smiling, she seems to be sizing me up. Her posture is slightly tense, as though she's afraid she might say or do something wrong. I can appreciate how daunting it must be to meet your significant other's only sister for the first time, and I make a mental note to put her at ease because, after all, she's important to my brother.

"I'm glad we get to spend some time together today," I smile. "I've heard so much about you and we haven't really had a chance to chat!"

"Likewise," she murmurs, her eyes locked on mine for a moment before darting away. It's clear she's nervous, but there's also a spark of excitement behind her gaze. She fidgets with her silver bracelet, her eyes darting from Bronson to me and back again.

The server stops by to take their order, and when they hurry off there's a lull in the conversation.

"Hey, Wren," I say, aiming to dissipate the tension. "Bronson mentioned you're quite the artist. What kind of stuff do you like to create?"

Her face lights up at the mention of art, and she visibly relaxes. "Oh, I love working with all sorts of different mediums, but my favorite is probably watercolor. There's just something so calming about it."

"Watercolor, huh?" I grin, recalling a memory. "Bronson once tried his hand at painting with watercolors. Let's just say he ended up looking like a smurf. In fact, if I look around hard enough I might still have a photo of him, his face smeared in bright blue, wearing some ridiculous white beret our mom made him wear while doing his beloved art projects."

"Hey!" Bronson exclaims, feigning offense. "It was an accident! And you're not meant to tell people about that!"

Wren giggles at the mental image, and I can't help but join in. It feels good to include her in our laughter, and I notice her shoulders loosen as she becomes more at ease.

I turn my attention to her as she watches our exchange with an air of bemusement. She's dressed in a simple yet elegant sundress, her golden curls tamed by a thin headband. There's an understated beauty about her, one that both intrigues and intimidates me.

"Sorry about that, Wren," I apologize, feeling a twinge of guilt for excluding her from our conversation. "Bronson and I have years of embarrassing stories to share."

"Hey, it's okay," she assures me, her smile genuine. "It's nice to see you two getting along so well."

"Anyway," I continue, "I've always been fascinated by art, but I'm not exactly talented in that department. Maybe you could give me some pointers sometime?"

"Of course!" Wren beams, her blue eyes twinkling with enthusiasm. "I'd be happy to teach you a few techniques."

"Are you into photography too?" I ask, recalling Bronson mentioning her interest in capturing images.

"Absolutely," she nods with contagious enthusiasm. "I love experimenting with light and shadow, finding unique perspectives to showcase the beauty in everyday life."

"Wow, that sounds amazing," I comment genuinely. "I've always admired people who can see the world through a different lens. You'll have to show me some of your work sometime."

"Definitely," Wren agrees, her smile reaching her eyes. "I think you might enjoy some of the more abstract pieces I've been working on."

"Abstract photography?" I question, my interest piqued. "That sounds fascinating."

"Wait until you see it," she says, her excitement near bubbling over. "It's like nothing you've ever seen before. Actually, here are a couple of pieces I have on my phone...". She pulls her smartphone out of her purse and opens her photography app. "See, here are some of my favorites. They all have a meaning behind them. So for example, this one," she flashes up a photograph of a single drop of water suspended in mid-air, captured in crisp black and white. "It's meant to evoke a sense of isolation and reflection."

I nod. "It's really clever, and it does evoke those feelings."

"And this one..." she pulls up another black and white photo of a lone tree in a desolate, dry landscape, "is meant to reflect the emptiness and isolation of modern society. And," she turns a little pink, "before you think I'm all emo and that everything I do is in black and white, here are a couple of my colorful pieces—this blurred and distorted one is meant to represent a distant dream or memory, and this softer, more ethereal blur is meant to invoke a dreamlike haze."

I'm mesmerized by each of the pieces, all a combination of unabashed creativity and technical expertise. "Wow," I breathe, "Wren, you should be very proud of yourself. These are exceptional. I'd actually love to put some of these up in my office. I think clients and employees would love them."

Wren blushes. "Oh goodness, I'd be honored."

Bronson beams in the background. I can tell he's tickled the two of us are getting along so well.

As we settle into the conversation, I notice the way Bronson and Wren interact. He's attentive to her, his eyes never straying far from her face. She, in turn, leans towards him, her laughter bright and genuine. I can't help but feel a pang of envy. Their happiness is evident, and it's something I've always wanted for myself. I even thought I had it for a brief time, but it was ripped away, only an illusion.

But I push those thoughts aside as I focus on getting to know Wren. She's intelligent, witty, and kind—qualities that make it easy to see why Bronson was drawn to her. And as our time together progresses, her initial wariness rapidly fades, replaced by a more relaxed demeanor. She seems genuinely interested in my life and opinions, which is refreshing. And she has a great energy about her that I can't quite put into words, I can just feel it.

"Fallon," Wren says at one point, "I've heard you're quite the chef."

"Bronson told you that?" I ask, surprised.

"Of course," he chimes in, a proud grin spreading across his face. "My little sister's got mad skills."

"Stop," I laugh, swatting his arm playfully. "You're making me blush. And I can't even remember the last time I cooked for you, Brons!"

"Seriously, though," Wren interjects, her eyes shining with interest. "I'd love to cook with you sometime. I'm okay at the basics, but I'd love to be able to cook Brons something a little more exciting than my mom's spaghetti bolognese recipe..."

"Hey, I love that recipe!" Bronson smiles. "You're making me hungry just thinking about it! Especially when you do the garlic bread with it!"

"Absolutely, I'd love to cook with you," I agree, warmed by her enthusiasm. There's a connection forming between us, something that hints at the possibility of a deep friendship.

And as the afternoon sun begins to dip toward the horizon, I find myself hoping that Wren will become a permanent fixture in our lives. Not just for Bronson's sake, but for mine as well.

Wren stands up, slinging her purse over her shoulder. "This was really nice, guys. I need to get to work, but I hope we can do it again soon."

"Definitely," Bronson agrees, pulling her in for a quick hug and a kiss before turning to me. "You're always welcome to join us, Fallon."

"Thanks," I say, genuinely touched by the invitation.

Bronson turns to me, his expression serious as he leans in for a hug. "Thanks for giving Wren a chance, Fallon," he whispers into my ear. "It means a lot to me."

"Of course," I reply, giving him a reassuring squeeze on the arm. "I can see how much she cares about you, and I'm glad you found someone who makes you happy."

As we part ways and I watch them walk away hand in hand, I can't help but feel a twinge of excitement for the potential friendship blossoming between Wren and me. It's a new chapter for all of us, and I'm eager to see where it leads. With Wren by Bronson's side, I have a feeling that our family dynamics are about to change for the better—and I couldn't be happier.

Chapter 23

FALLON

The door to my office opens, and Teri Thickett steps inside, her eyes burning with a mixture of pain and determination. She's a woman who has been through hell and back, all because of one man—Jared Carlson. Her once vibrant life has been reduced to a series of devastating doctor's appointments and bitter tears, but she's here now, ready to take back control and make Jared pay for what he's done.

"Please, have a seat," I say, gesturing to the chair across from my desk. Grave stands stoically beside me, his presence a silent reassurance that we're here to help.

"Tha—thank you for seeing me," Teri says, her voice wavering slightly as she sits down. Her fingers nervously fidget with the purse that she clings to like a lifeline, betraying the turmoil beneath her composed exterior. Now and then, she tucks a rogue strand of hair behind her ear as if it's one action she still has control over.

"Ms. Thickett," I begin, my voice calm yet firm, "I understand that you've come to us seeking justice against your former partner of many years, Jared Carlson. Please, call me Fallon, and tell me how we can help you."

The woman's eyes fill with tears, but she blinks them away with determination. "You can call me Teri. And yes, I'm here about Jared. I want him to pay for what he's done," she says, her voice wavering but strong. "I don't want him to be able to just walk away and forget about me. He ruined my life, Fallon, and I'll be damned if I let him get away with it."

"Teri," I say, my voice filled with empathy and determination, "I promise you, we will make him pay for what he's done to you. No one deserves to go through what you've experienced, and we won't rest until Jared faces the consequences of his betrayal."

I glance over at Grave and see his usual stoic expression, but there's a flicker of understanding in his eyes as he listens to Teri's words. His relentless dedication to righting wrongs is one of the reasons I trust him implicitly. He truly cares about each of our clients.

"Of course," I say, trying to exude both professionalism and empathy, "we want to help you, Teri, but first, we need to understand your story. We know the basics—what Jared did, how it affected your health—but we need to hear it from you."

Teri takes a deep breath, swallowing hard before she begins. "Jared was...my everything," she starts, her voice barely above a whisper. "Well, the person who he showed me... who he pretended to be... was my everything, I should say. We were together for five years, and I truly thought he loved me as much as I loved him. I thought we were soulmates. We built a life together, a home, dreams for our future... but one day, I found out he'd been cheating on me." She pauses, her face contorting with anger and grief as the memories wash over her. "Not just with one woman, but several, including some for the entire course of our relationship."

Her hands grip the armrests of the chair, knuckles turning white from the pressure. The weight of her words hangs heavy in the air, and I can feel the anger and betrayal simmering beneath her calm exterior. She begins to tremble slightly.

"I confronted him, and he promised he'd change. He swore he loved me, that it wouldn't happen again. But he couldn't keep his promises. The lies and the cheating continued. And then..." She swallows hard, tears pooling at the corners of her eyes. "Then I found out I'd contracted two STDs from him—including one that's made it impossible for me to have children, which was always one of my dreams."

The room falls silent as the gravity of her words settles over us. My fists clench in response, and I can see Grave's stoic demeanor crack ever so slightly. I feel my own rage bubbling up inside me, threatening to spill over, but I keep it contained—for now.

The familiar fire of vengeance ignites within me, because although I've heard countless stories of betrayal, each one still feels like a fresh wound. Jared's cheating alone is reason to be devastated in her relationship, but the health implications, and the inability for Teri to have children far beyond her time with him, is even more unforgivable. Teri doesn't deserve the pain she's been forced to endure, and I'm more than ready to make sure Jared gets a taste of his own medicine.

"Teri," I say softly, leaning forward in my chair. "We're here for you. We understand what you've been through, and we want to help you get the justice you deserve."

Her gaze flickers between Grave and me, her skepticism evident as she crosses her arms protectively over her chest. "So, what exactly is it that you two do? I mean, how can I trust that you're not just... playing with my emotions? That this isn't some type of scam?"

"Teri, we understand your concerns," I say gently, feeling the weight of responsibility settling on my shoulders. "Our sole purpose is to deliver justice to those who have been wronged by people like Jared. We're not here to exploit your pain. We're here to help you heal."

"Can you really guarantee results, though?" she asks, biting her lip nervously. "I'm scared to get my hopes up after everything he's done."

"Nothing in life is guaranteed," I admit, "but we've been quite successful in our missions so far, haven't we, Grave?"

"Yes, we have," Grave chimes in, his voice steady and sure, his expression stony with determination. "We won't stop until we've achieved your target result."

As the meeting continues, I can see the skepticism in Teri's eyes begin to transform into a steely resolve. She asks question after question, probing our methods and motivations, but with each answer, her trust in us grows stronger.

"Thank you," Teri says as she stands to leave. "I never thought I'd find people who would understand what I'm going through, but you two... you're different. Thank you for giving me hope."

"Remember, Teri, you're not alone anymore," I tell her, my voice filled with conviction. "We're in this together, and we won't stop until justice is served."

As the door closes behind her, Grave and I share a look of quiet determination. We've taken on the responsibility of avenging Teri's pain, and we won't let her down. The time for her suffering is over. Now, it's time for planning and action—and there's no turning back.

Grave and I barely wait until Teri has left my office before we begin delving into the specifics of our plan. My strategic mind begins to whirl, considering every angle and possibility while Grave's tactical expertise ensures that no detail is overlooked.

"Fallon, how far are you willing to go to take Jared down?" Grave asks, his eyes searching mine for any hint of hesitation.

"Far enough to make him feel the same pain he inflicted on Teri, and definitely something with similar long-term repercussions," I reply, my voice dark and unwavering. I frown. "But we can't cross certain lines, as tempting as it might be. We're not murderers after all, are we?"

"Agreed," Grave nods, although I see an odd flash in his eyes that gives me goosebumps. "We'll need to be creative in our approach, then. What if we expose his infidelity to his high-profile clients? Ruin his reputation, both personally and professionally?"

"Good start," I say, mulling over his suggestion. "But we need something more... personal. Something that will hit him where it hurts the most."

"Perhaps targeting his finances?" Grave suggests, a calculating glint in his eye. "Find a way to drain his bank accounts, leaving him with nothing?"

"That could be poetic... he's made Teri bankrupt from a fertility perspective, and we could do the same with his wallet," I agree, a wicked smile curling my lips. "And once he's lost everything, we'll ensure that everyone knows exactly why. No one will want to associate with him after they learn the truth about what he did to Teri." I pause and furrow my brow. "But I still think we need to make this more eye for an eye. There need to be physical implications."

"Fallon," Grave begins, his voice low and serious, "we need to consider the legal implications of what we're doing. If we get caught, there could be severe repercussions for all of us—especially Teri."

I clench my fists, nails digging into my palms. The thought of Teri being dragged down with us is unbearable. She's already endured so much pain at the hands of Jared, and now she's entrusting us with her hope for justice. "We'll have to be meticulous about covering our tracks," I say firmly. "No room for mistakes."

"Agreed," Grave nods, studying me intently. "But there's something else we should discuss—the emotional toll this might take on Teri. Are you prepared for that possibility?"

My heart clenches at the thought, but I know he's right. "She deserves justice, Grave," I reply, my voice cracking slightly. "If there are side effects, we'll help her through them. Together."

Grave's eyes soften, understanding the weight of my words. As much as I want to protect Teri from any further harm, I also know that sometimes, seeking vengeance can leave scars on the soul.

"Fallon," Grave says, placing a hand on my shoulder, "you can't save everyone. Remember that this mission might affect you too. You're not immune to the emotional consequences."

I swallow hard, feeling the sting of tears threatening to spill over. He's right. With each case I take on, a part of me becomes entwined with the pain of those I seek justice for. And yet, I can't help but press forward, relentlessly fighting for what's right.

"Thank you, Grave," I whisper, my voice barely audible. "I'll keep that in mind."

I can't help but wrestle with the ethical lines we're about to cross. Will our actions truly bring Teri the closure she seeks, or are we simply feeding the cycle of vengeance? And what if something goes wrong, causing even more pain for our client?

For now, however, these questions must remain unanswered. Our focus is on the task at hand—to exact revenge on Jared Carlson and bring justice to a woman who has suffered far too much. He needs to be humiliated and physically harmed, just like he did to her.

As we finalize our plans, I feel a sense of resolution settling over me. Our revenge against Jared Carlson is taking shape, and though it may be dark and twisted, it's necessary. For Teri. For all the women he's hurt.

As we continue to plot our revenge against Jared, I'm reminded of why I chose this path—the fierce determination to right the wrongs inflicted upon the innocent, to stand up for those who have been silenced by their oppressors. With each calculated step, we're inching closer to retribution on Teri's behalf. And as I watch the fire burning brightly in Grave's eyes, I know that together, we remain unstoppable.

But whatever lies ahead, one thing remains certain: Jared Carlson won't know what hit him.

Chapter 24

FALLON

The moment I dial Aksel's number, my heart races with anticipation. The phone rings and rings, but there's no answer. With each unanswered ring, my anxiety grows and I feel increasingly stupid for wanting to hear his voice on the other end of the phone. I know Aksel is a busy guy, but he always answers my calls. Unless, of course, he's playing games with me again, just because I didn't have time to spare to chat with him the other day.

"Fuck," I mutter under my breath as the call goes to voicemail. My hands tremble with anger, and without even thinking, I swipe through my contacts and block his number. "You wanna play games, Aksel? Fine. Consider this my opening move."

I need a distraction, something to get him out of my head. I can't let him win whatever stupid little rivalry this is. As I storm out of my condo, I decide to hit up a bar, knowing full well what I'm looking for. Revenge. It's not just about getting back at Aksel, it's about taking control of the situation. And maybe, just maybe, finding someone who won't treat me like I'm disposable.

The bar is dark and smoky, filled with couples huddled in corners and groups of friends laughing over drinks. I slide onto a stool at the counter and order my usual whiskey, downing it in one quick gulp. My eyes scan the room, searching for a target. Someone to spend a few hours with and use as a pawn in this twisted game.

"Can I buy you another drink?" a deep voice asks from behind me. I turn around to find a tall, muscular man with a mischievous grin plastered on his face. He's attractive, but there's something dark lurking behind those eyes that makes me wary. He wears a scruffy black T-shirt with an old metal band's logo and black jeans with tattered black sneakers. Tattoos adorn both of his arms as well as his neck, and he also sports hand tattoos. Oh god, they're one of my major weaknesses. I wonder if he has a pierced cock, too, and I'm planning to find out later.

"Sure," I reply, feigning a smile. "Why not?"

He orders two more whiskeys and leans against the edge of the bar, studying me intently. "You seem...angry," he observes, his eyes trailing languidly over me as he takes a sip of his drink, a trace of amusement in his expression.

"Am I that easy to read?" I scoff, downing my second whiskey.

"Maybe I'm just good at reading people," he smirks. "Or maybe you're looking for the same thing I am."

"Which is?"

"Distraction. Maybe a little revenge," he suggests, his voice low and seductive.

"Maybe," I admit, my heart pounding in my chest. The thought of using someone else to get back at Aksel both excites and terrifies me. It's a dangerous path to go down, but I can't help myself. "You up for it?"

"Definitely," he says, finishing his drink and slamming the glass down on the counter. "Let's get out of here."

As we leave the bar together, I can't help but feel a strange sense of satisfaction. If Aksel wants to play games, then so can I. And tonight, I've found myself exactly what I need.

The dimly lit hotel room is a far cry from the opulence of Aksel's penthouse that I've seen featured in several annoyingly eye roll-worthy magazine articles about the 'eligible bachelor's net worth' and his 'tryst pad', but it suits my current mood perfectly. The nameless stranger wastes no time in pinning me against the wall, his rough hands tearing at my clothes as he smashes his lips to mine, his tongue slipping through to explore my own.

"Tell me what you want," he growls into my ear, and I can't help but think of how Aksel would say those same words. But this isn't Aksel, it's just a random guy who's going to give me exactly what I need tonight.

"I want you to fuck me hard," I demand, desperation and anger fueling me. "Make me forget everything."

"Your wish is my command," he smirks, pushing me onto the bed and climbing on top of me. He lines himself up and slams himself into my pussy, his fingers digging into my hips as he thrusts inside me, causing a mix of pain and pleasure to wash over my body. This is not tender, slow lovemaking by any means. It's primal, raw, and exactly what I've been craving.

As the hot stranger continues to pound into me, my thoughts keep drifting back to Aksel. The way he touched me, kissed me, made me feel like I was the only woman in the world. I hate that I can't get him out of my head, even now. It's a stark contrast with the way this man is dragging himself in and out of me. I don't need tenderness when I'm fucking, and often I don't want it, including now. But he's making me feel interchangeable, like a hole to stick himself into.

"Harder," I demand, my voice cracking, determined to get what I need out of this empty interaction. The stranger complies, his massive calloused hands spanking me on the side of my hips with such force that I can already feel the red welts forming. It's painful, but cathartic—every hit feels like a release from the anger and resentment I've been holding onto.

"You like that, huh?" he asks, his breath hot against my neck. "You're a dirty girl, aren't you? I could tell by the way you were looking at me in the bar."

"Shut up and keep going," I snap, not wanting to hear his voice. But as much as I try to focus on the physical sensations, my thoughts refuse to cooperate.

His roughness only increases, and I find myself struggling to keep up with him, which is rare for me. His grip on my wrists becomes almost painful, and as his groans turn into roars, I realize that I've lost control of the situation. Panic sets in as I struggle to free myself from his grasp, fear clouding my judgment. "Take my giant cock, you stupid slut. You're a dumb fucking cunt just like the rest of them!" He growls, his tone feral, and he sinks his teeth into my neck.

"Stop," I say, wriggling my neck and managing to dislodge his teeth from my flesh. "Don't bite me. And let go of my wrists. I've had enough."

"You'll have had enough when I say you've had enough, bitch!" His eyes flash with anger and he tightens his grip on my wrists. They're stinging under his clamp-like grasp.

I wriggle and squirm in an attempt to find a weak spot. I manage to bend my knees high up near my waist and place them against his hips for leverage.

"Let go!" I gasp, finally managing to shove him off me with my hands and feet. He looks momentarily stunned, but I don't give him a chance to recover. In a flash, I shove him down on the ground, grab one of the silk ties from my purse and bind his wrists to the bedposts.

"Hey, what the fuck are you doing?" he splutters, trying to break free of his restraints. But I've learned a thing or two from Grave about how to tie a proper knot in the course of our work, and, regardless of his massive stature, there's no way he's escaping without help.

"Consider this payback, you fucking creep," I say coldly, pulling on my clothes and leaving him lying there naked and helpless. On the door, I pin a note for housekeeping: 'You probably want to call 911 before you go in there. But there's an abuser of women inside.' I don't want him to hurt anyone else, and nobody deserves to walk in on that in the course of their job.

As I stride down the hallway, adrenaline pumping through my veins, I can't help but feel both a twisted sense of satisfaction and a pang of regret. Aksel may have hurt me, but tonight perhaps I acted too hastily to try and take back some of the power I perceived he'd stolen. Maybe there's a totally reasonable explanation why he didn't answer my call, and I just put myself in danger... but to prove what to whom, exactly?

As I step out into the cold night air, my body shuddering from a mix of excitement and the lingering sensation of the stranger's rough hands on me, I can't help but feel I might have put myself in a needlessly risky situation that thankfully I was able to get myself out of. It would be much nicer to have Aksel dominate me than a random nameless stranger who could turn violent. I knew nothing about the guy and he was basically twice my size, after all, and was talking about revenge.

God knows I could have just dodged a misogynistic serial killer. I know I wouldn't need to worry about that with Aksel. Maybe I do have a little kernel of trust in him buried somewhere deep inside.

Chapter 25

AKSEL

My heart skips a beat as I notice a missed call from Fallon. My pulse quickens, and for a moment, I'm hopeful that she wants to reconnect. But when I try to call her back, I find that she's blocked my number. The realization slams into me like a freight train.

"Fuck," I mutter under my breath, unable to shake off the feeling of despair that's slowly taking over. Her quick deletion of our main means of contacting each other intensifies my sense of isolation and longing.

Desperate to distract myself, I throw myself into work, trying to focus on the numbers and spreadsheets that usually occupy my mind. But it's no use—thoughts of Fallon keep creeping in, poisoning every moment of my day. I hate that she's so easily able to pull me away from what's meant to be most important, just by one simple action.

"Damn it," I hiss, slamming my fist onto my desk. I need something else, something more physical to keep my mind occupied.

I head home to my gym, hoping that an intense workout session will help ease the turmoil inside me. As I lift weights and pound the treadmill, sweat pouring down my face, my muscles scream in agony. Yet, despite the pain, my troubled mind refuses to let go of Fallon.

"Come on, Aksel! Focus!" I scold myself through gritted teeth, pushing my body even harder.

But it's not enough. None of it is enough. No amount of work or exercise can erase the image of her face, the hurt in her eyes the last time we spoke, the sound of her voice when she told me she never wanted to see me again. And the blocked number that renders me incapable of getting in touch with her. But then the most precious of moments pop into my head, including the dinner at her place, the way we moved together on the dance floor at the gala. I'd give almost anything to relive those moments again, just for a split second.

"Fallon," I whisper, my voice cracking with emotion.

No matter how hard I try to fight it, the truth remains: I've lost her, and all I have left is the emptiness that comes from knowing she's gone. In this dark space, my thoughts are my own worst enemy, taunting me with memories of a love that's now out of reach.

"Get it together, Aksel," I tell myself firmly. "You'll be fine. There's someone else out there for you." But even as I say the words, I know that they're lies, hollow attempts to mask the pain that refuses to be silenced.

As I continue to work and push my body to its limits, the days turn into nights, and the darkness in my heart grows ever deeper. And all the while, Fallon remains unreachable, her absence a constant reminder of the love we once shared, and the actions and inactions that tore us apart.

My heart races as I pace the floor of my office, phone in hand. The weight of Fallon's absence remains a relentless burden on my soul. It's been weeks since we last spoke. I can't shake the image of her teary eyes from my mind, and it fucking kills me.

"Damn it," I mutter under my breath, slamming my fist against the desk. I need to get out of here, away from these walls that only serve to remind me of what I've lost. But where would I go? What could possibly distract me from the deafening silence that has taken hold of my life? Neither work or the gym—the two things in my life that typically give me solace—are working.

My phone beeps.

Carissa: Jesus, Aksel. You look like shit.

I glance around as if expecting to see her hiding in a corner. Three dots flicker on my screen to indicate another message is incoming. She's one of those people who messages a few words at a time and takes up the whole screen.

Carissa: I saw you rushing by

Carissa: downtown

Carissa: with your face in your phone earlier.

Carissa: Tried to call out

Carissa: but you were absorbed in a call

Carissa: or something.

Carissa: Anyway...

Carissa: We need to talk.

The messages continue to flood in. Lucky for her, phone companies don't charge by the message these days. I frown, scrolling through her lengthy note. It's filled with warnings about corporate espionage within my company, details she's apparently uncovered during her own investigations.

Given she's a PR executive I'm not entirely sure why she's involved in my business, but she occasionally forays into investigative journalism and she does have a reputation for enjoying digging up a scandal, so it's not entirely implausible she funded an investigation on a whim. Still, I'm skeptical. It's only when I see mention of Kent Farrington and Isabella Warner's names in the messages that my interest is truly piqued. Carissa insists we meet:

Carissa: Meet me at Luna's.

Carissa: I'll fill you in.

Carissa: Too busy to text

Carissa: and

Carissa: This is too important

Carissa: to discuss over the phone.

My instincts scream at me not to trust her, but desperation takes hold and I agree. I'm deeply invested in the family company and bear a great sense of responsibility to address any speculations of wrongdoing, especially knowing about the secretive operations that go on behind the scenes. At the very least, this unexpected development might offer a temporary reprieve from the constant ache in my chest.

Aksel: Fine. But you'd better be telling the truth.

Carissa: Of course. Why wouldn't I?

Carissa: Meet you at 8pm.

Carissa: Luna's on 8th.

As I enter Luna's—an upscale restaurant with dim lighting and plush seating—I scan the room nervously, searching for any sign of Carissa. I got here at eight on the dot, and the place is packed tonight. A live jazz band plays in the corner while patrons chat animatedly over their meals. In this sea of warmth and laughter, I feel even more isolated, more alone.

"Over here, Aksel," Carissa calls out, waving me over to a secluded booth near the back. Her eyes flicker with something unreadable, a hidden agenda lurking beneath the surface. As I approach, I notice that she's chosen a seat with a clear view of the entrance—likely a calculated move designed to ensure that anyone walking in will see us together.

"Nice spot," I mutter, taking my seat across from her. "You always were one for theatrics."

Carissa smirks, all too aware of the power she wields in this moment. "I thought it might be best if we discuss things... privately."

I roll my eyes at the hypocrisy of her words juxtaposed with the seating she's chosen for us. "Fine, let's get this over with," I say. "What have you found out about King Enterprises?"

"Slow down, Aksel," she purrs, a wicked smile playing on her lips. "Let me explain."

"Fine, explain. I'm waiting. Your texts were pretty cryptic," I growl, my fists clenched beneath the table as she weaves her tale of deception and betrayal within my family's company. It's a twisted web that threatens to pull me under if I'm not careful. For whatever reason she's chosen to do it, Carissa's investigation has reinforced some of my fears about Kent and Isabella and things are even worse than I thought. The entire company really could be at stake.

"Are you going to do something about it?" Carissa asks, her expression suddenly serious. "You can't just let them get away with it."

"Of course I am," I snap, my thoughts racing as I try to formulate a plan. "But why look into this at all? What's in it for you?"

"Maybe I just care about the company and want to see my friends doing well," she replies coyly, her eyes never leaving mine. She places her hand on top of mine. "Or maybe I'm just tired of seeing you so miserable all the time."

"Whatever your reasons," I say, my voice cold and detached, "I'll handle it."

"Good," Carissa smirks, raising her glass in a mock toast. "Cheers to digging up deep dark secrets and bringing them into the light. And to the histories and memories we keep burning bright."

Histories, memories... two things I can barely stop thinking about. As I reluctantly clink glasses with her, one thing becomes painfully clear: no matter how deep I dive into work or the complexities of my professional life, there will always be an insatiable void where Fallon once was. And as much as I want to forget, to move on, I know that the only way to truly heal is to face the darkness head-on—and find a way to make things right.

"Here's to memories," I mutter, downing my drink and steeling myself for the battles ahead.

Taking another sip, Carissa looks around, smirks and then moves her hand to my thigh, which I shrug off immediately.

My eyes scan the room as I try to shake the feeling that we're being watched. It's then that I spot her—Fallon, sitting at a nearby table with a group of women each with a copy of the same book. They're flipping between pages and talking animatedly, gesturing at the covers as they sip their wine. The breath catches in my throat, and I can't help but think that this meeting was never about corporate espionage at all.

"Wait, is that Fallon Dempsey?" Carissa asks innocently, following my gaze. "What a coincidence."

"Coincidence?" I hiss, my anger rising. "You planned this, didn't you?"

"Whatever do you mean, Aksel?" She feigns ignorance, but the glint in her eyes betrays her intentions.

"Carissa, this isn't a game," I growl, my hands clenched into fists beneath the table. "Fallon and I—"

"Are history. And maybe, just maybe, it's time you both moved on," she interrupts, her voice dripping with bitterness. "Maybe she just needs a bit of extra encouragement to extract you from her life. To free you, so you can truly move on to... other things." Without warning, she grabs my hand from the table and places it between her thighs. I feel heat emanating from her center and I jerk my hand away.

"Enough!" I snap, my voice louder than intended. In that instant, Fallon's eyes meet mine, her expression a mix of hurt and confusion. She glances from me to Carissa and back, watching my hand emerge from Carissa's side of the table. It's as if the air has been sucked out of the room, and I can't breathe.

"Fallon," I call out, desperate to explain the situation. I leap up from the table and run over to her group. "Fallon, it's not what you think."

"Save it, Aksel," she whispers, tears welling in her eyes as she pushes back from the table, her chair scraping loudly against the floor. She bolts toward the exit, leaving a trail of devastation in her wake as her swift movements cause a glass and some silverware to clatter to the floor. Her fellow book club members stare at me, at Fallon's path, and a few of their jaws drop.

"Damn it," I mutter under my breath, my chest tightening with regret. I look back at the booth where Carissa sits, smirking, relishing the chaos she has caused.

"Looks like you've got some explaining to do," she calls out, her voice sickeningly sweet. "Good luck with that. You could have just had me instead of all this silly drama. We could be really great together, Aksel. I can tell you're so close to feeling the same way."

I glare at her for a moment before turning on my heel, my mind racing as I contemplate how to salvage the wreckage of my budding relationship with Fallon. As I step into the dark night, I know that our story is far from over—and I will do whatever it takes to make things right.

The heavy door slams behind me, the sound echoing through the empty parking lot. My heart races as I scan the area for a glimpse of Fallon, her light blue dress catching the dim glow of a streetlight in the distance. She's running toward her car, desperation etched on her face.

"Fallon!" I shout, my voice cracking with emotion. "Please, just let me explain!"

Her steps falter, but she doesn't stop. I sprint after her, my muscles burning from exertion and frustration. As I catch up to her, I reach out to grab her arm, desperate to make her understand.

"Fuck off, Aksel! Go back to your stupid bitch friend Carissa. I knew you were all over her all along. Get the fuck away from me!" She shrugs herself off me and runs the rest of the way to her car, beeps it unlocked, climbs in and quickly locks it again. Before I know what's happening, she's started the engine and her vehicle is bearing down on me, high beams blinding me. I leap out of the way just in time as her car roars by.

She's a fucking lunatic. A complete psycho. Her jealousy got me more than a little excited. And I've never been as attracted to someone in my entire life.

Chapter 26

FALLON

The dim lights of the spa cast eerie shadows on the walls, flickering like an ominous heartbeat. I can feel my pulse quickening as I glance at Grave. His face is a mix of determined focus and bittersweet satisfaction. This is it. The day we've been planning for weeks.

"Are you sure Jared will show up?" I ask, trying to keep my voice steady despite the wild storm brewing in my chest.

"Positive," Grave replies, his voice low and confident. "He's so eager to meet his online dream girl, he won't suspect a thing."

I nod, biting my lip, unable to shake the unease that has settled in my stomach. We've meticulously crafted every detail of this revenge plot, luring Jared Carlson to this private spa we booked just for tonight. He thinks he's meeting the woman of his dreams for some sexy spa time, but instead, he's about to experience a terror he'll never forget.

"Fallon, are you ready?" Grave asks, locking eyes with me. I can see the fire of vengeance burning within him, and I'm reminded of why we're doing this. For Teri, and for all the other women Jared has hurt and discarded without a second thought.

"Let's do it," I reply, my voice stronger now.

We wait in silence, hidden in the shadows of the spa's entrance. Moments later, the door opens, and Jared steps inside, scanning the room with a smirk plastered on his face. He's completely oblivious to the trap he's walking into.

"Hello?" he calls out. "Is anyone here? Bella?"

"Over here, Jared," I say, disguising my voice to sound sultry and seductive like the imaginary persona, Bella, that I've created for the evening. He follows the sound, his eyes lighting up with anticipation when he spots me, draped across a lounge chair, wearing a form-fitting sheer black swimsuit coverup that leaves little to the imagination.

"Wow," he breathes, his gaze raking over me like a predator. "You're even more stunning than your pictures."

"Thank you," I purr, playing the part of the eager vixen. Inside, my stomach churns with disgust, but I push through it. This is for Teri. For justice.

"Come join me in the pool," I suggest, gesturing towards the water that shimmers under the dim lighting. "We'll have so much fun together." I stand and let the coverup drop from my body and crumple to the floor, revealing my swimsuit underneath.

Jared's eyes practically bulge from their sockets as he admires my curves, and he wastes no time in stripping off his clothes. I can barely contain my contempt as I watch him strut towards the pool, completely unaware of what awaits him.

"Let's spice things up a bit," I suggest, my voice dripping with seduction. "Put this on." I hand Jared a silk blindfold, and he grins eagerly, his eyes gleaming with excitement.

"Kinky," he chuckles, securing the blindfold around his head. "I like it."

"Step into the pool," I instruct, my tone firm yet sultry. "I'll be right there with you."

As he steps into the water, Grave emerges from the shadows, his expression stony and resolute. We exchange one last glance before locking our gazes on Jared, who still believes he's about to live out his wildest fantasies.

Little does he know, we're about to turn those fantasies into his darkest nightmare.

As Jared wades into the water, his hands outstretched to guide him, I shoot a glance at Grave. He nods, understanding our unspoken signal, and retrieves the small container holding our secret weapon—one tiny, almost invisible, candiru fish.

"Ready?" I whisper to Grave as we both approach the edge of the pool. He gives me a curt nod, his jaw set with determination.

"Okay, Jared," I call out sweetly. "Stay right where you are, sexy. I'm coming in."

Jared grins, his anticipation palpable as he stands alone, blindfolded and vulnerable.

I can't help but feel a sick satisfaction knowing that he's completely unaware of his impending fate.

"Three... two... one..." I count down softly, and Grave releases the candiru fish into the pool with a barely perceptible plop. The tiny, parasitic creature swims swiftly towards Jared, drawn by the scent of his urine, which he's unknowingly released in his arousal.

Suddenly, Jared screams, a guttural, horrifying sound that echoes through the empty spa. His hands shoot down to his groin, frantically trying to alleviate the excruciating pain.

"Please!" he begs, his voice cracking. "Make it stop! Make it stop!"

"Oh, we've only just begun," I say calmly as he writhes, water splashing on the walls around him.

He rips his blindfold off and stares in alarm at me and then Grave.

"Who is that?" he shrieks and points at Grave, the other hand still futilely trying to stop his penis from hurting.

"Interesting thing about the candiru fish," I say coolly, watching Jared writhe in agony. "It's attracted to the scent of urine, so when it finds its way into a urethra, it lodges itself in there with its small spines. Even if it wants to, it can't swim backwards. It can only move forwards."

"What the fuck? You put a fish in my penis? Get it out!" Jared howls, his face contorted with pain. "Please, I'll do anything!"

"Technically, it's a parasitic fish. And 'unfortunately'," I use air quotes to show I mean the opposite, "there's no way to remove it without causing even more damage. Also now, just like Teri, you're going to be infertile."

Recognition flares in his eyes at the mention of Teri's name, and fury contorts his face as he struggles to catch his breath between sobs. "You crazy bitch!" he snarls, hurling vitriol at me. "You've lost your fucking mind! You think this is going to make anything better?!"

I watch him with a cold detachment, my heart hardened against his pain. He deserves every ounce of anguish he's experiencing. "You brought this on yourself, Jared. You destroyed Teri's life. I'm just evening the score."

"Evening the score?" he scoffs, tears streaming down his cheeks. "You're psychotic! You don't know what you're doing!"

My hands clench into fists at my sides, and I resist the urge to jump into the pool and strike him. Instead, I focus on maintaining my composure. "Oh, I know exactly what I'm doing," I assure him, my voice cold as ice. "And I won't stop until you truly understand the consequences of your actions."

As Jared's anger begins to subside, desperation creeps into his expression. "Please," he begs, his voice hoarse and trembling. "I'll do anything. Just... please help me."

"Anything?" I challenge, raising an eyebrow. "Would you admit that you were wrong to treat Teri the way you did? That you abused her and took advantage of her trust?"

"Of course," he stammers, his eyes pleading for mercy. "I'm sorry. I never should have done any of it. I was... I was a monster."

"Sorry doesn't begin to cover it," Grave interjects, stepping forward to loom over Jared menacingly. "You need to feel the weight of your actions, not just spout empty apologies."

"So let me tell you what's going to happen, Jared," I say. "We're going to leave you with your fate in your hands, literally. My associate is going to place a knife by the edge of the pool. If you leave your penis intact with the candiru fish inside it, it will cause you to hemorrhage until you die. Or, you can chop your penis off and live. It's all up to you." I smile sweetly as Grave places a knife with a rusty, serrated blade on the poolside cobblestones. "And we'll call an ambulance in about fifteen minutes, just in case. We're not monsters after all."

"Please," Jared repeats, his desperation growing. "I can change. I will change. I swear it."

Part of me wants to believe him, wants to think that this act of retribution might actually lead to some sort of redemption. But I know better. People like Jared don't change. They only learn to hide their true nature more effectively. Although having a detached penis will almost certainly throw him off his game.

"Your word means nothing to me," I inform him coldly, watching as the last vestiges of hope drain from his eyes. "You had your chance to be a decent human being, and you threw it away. Now, you're paying the price."

Jared's chest heaves as he sobs, his body wracked with anguish—both physical and emotional. And while a part of me feels sickened by the scene before me, another part of me revels in the knowledge that we've succeeded in exacting our revenge.

"Remember this pain, Jared," Grave growls, his voice low and menacing. "Remember what you did to Teri and know that this is nothing compared to the suffering you caused her."

As Grave and I turn our backs on Jared's pitiful cries for help, leaving him alone in the deserted spa with his fish friend and a life-altering choice to make, I can't shake the feeling that we've crossed a line, that there's no coming back from the darkness we've embraced in our most recent quest for vengeance. We just rendered a man infertile while simultaneously causing irreversible physical damage and a shitload of pain. But if this is the price we must pay to see justice done, then so be it.

Chapter 27

FALLON

"**B**lack roses?" I whisper under my breath, staring at the giant aromatic bouquet sitting on my desk. A note dangles from the black satin ribbon, and I already know who it's from without reading it. Aksel.

"Who sent you those?" Mia asks, peering at the bouquet with a curious gaze as she enters my office.

"None of your business," I snap before ripping the note off the bouquet and stuffing it into my pocket. I don't need her prying eyes to see what he's written.

"Fallon, are you sure you don't want to read it?" Mia presses, her voice laced with concern. "You didn't even take the note out of the envelope."

"Positive," I reply through gritted teeth, grabbing the bouquet and tossing it into the trash with a defiant flourish. It's an empty gesture, one that's just for show. I'm surprised he remembered my preference for black roses, but it doesn't change anything between us. Probably just one of those snippets of information a manipulative narcissistic prick like Aksel files away without a thought, ready to pull out the moment he needs to manipulate his current target.

"Jesus, Fallon." Mia's eyes widen as she watches me discard the flowers like they're nothing more than garbage. "That seems a bit extreme."

"Does it?" I challenge, folding my arms across my chest and narrowing my eyes at her. "Maybe you should focus on your own life instead of mine."

"Fine." Mia sighs, hurt and defeated by my cutting remark and my general animus. "I was just trying to help."

"By sticking your nose where it doesn't belong? Thanks, but no thanks."

"Okay, I get it," she says, frowning and raising her hands in surrender. "But can I ask why you threw them away?"

"Because I don't need Aksel in my life. He should know I don't like flowers. They're such a waste. They die after a few days, anyway."

"True, but black roses aren't exactly common. Maybe he thought—."

"It doesn't matter what he thought," I interrupt, my irritation mounting. "He's always been like this—assuming he knows what I want and need, when in reality, he doesn't understand me at all. He never has."

"Alright, Fallon," Mia murmurs, backing away from my desk. "I won't bother you about it anymore." I swear I hear her mutter 'it's not my battle to fight' as she turns away.

"Good." I nod curtly, turning back to the pile of paperwork on my desk. She doesn't understand the depths of the darkness between Aksel and me, the twisted dance we're locked in. And I don't intend to fully let her in on the secret anytime soon.

As she leaves my office, I can feel the weight of those black roses in the trash like a heavy cloud hanging over me. But it's better this way. There's no room for Aksel in my life, and there never will be again.

The sunlight filtering through the blinds in the late afternoon casts a striped pattern on my desk, highlighting the stark contrast between the pristine white sheets of paper and the black ink of my pen. After a few hours of productive work, my thoughts once again swirl around Aksel and the darkness that envelops us both, tugging at my concentration and causing my focus to wane. Mia's soft footsteps approach my office, pulling me out of my reverie.

"Fallon," she says hesitantly, lingering in the doorway. "Can we talk?"

"About what?" I ask without looking up from my papers, masking my growing unease with irritation.

"About Aksel. And the flowers."

I sigh, finally meeting her gaze. Her dark curls frame her face, amplifying the earnestness in her eyes. "We already discussed those, even though I'm not quite sure what they have to do with you and why you want to keep talking about them." I frown. "What about the stupid flowers?"

"Look, I know you're angry at him, but sending you black roses—that was a thoughtful gesture. You have to admit it."

"Thoughtful?" I scoff, feeling the anger surge inside me like a tidal wave. "He doesn't understand me, Mia. If he did, he wouldn't have sent flowers in the first place. He would have sent a plant. Or maybe launched himself to the moon in a spaceship."

"Maybe he's trying to make amends," she suggests gently, her freckles standing out against her flushed cheeks. "He remembered that you like black roses. That has to count for something, right?"

"Fine," I concede, clenching my pen tightly. "Maybe he remembered. But it doesn't change anything. I have memories of him as well. Memories of how he hurt me, how he used me, how he broke my heart. He's still the same selfish, manipulative man he's always been. Flowers could never scratch the surface of fixing that."

"Have you considered that maybe having him in your life could be a good thing?" Mia questions, a determined glint in her eyes. "You've been so focused on the darker aspects of your job lately, it might help to have someone who cares about you around."

"Someone who cares about me?" I snort, bitterness lacing my words. "Aksel only cares about himself. I don't need him, and I certainly don't want him in my life."

"Fallon," Mia sighs, her voice softening. "I know you're hurt, but don't let your anger blind you to the possibility of forgiveness. Maybe Aksel has changed. Maybe he's learned from his mistakes and wants to make things right."

"Or maybe he's just playing another one of his games," I shoot back, anger flaring once more. "I'm not interested in finding out, Mia. I have enough darkness in my life without adding Aksel to the mix."

"Alright," she says, raising her hands in surrender. "I won't push it anymore. But just remember that people can change, Fallon. And sometimes, letting them back into your life can be a healing experience for both of you."

"Thanks for the unsolicited advice," I mutter, turning back to my work as an uneasy silence fills the room. Mia's words echo in my mind, but the thought of trusting Aksel again is like willingly stepping into a snake pit.

"Take care, Fallon," Mia whispers before slipping out of my office, her voice low, leaving me to wrestle with the darkness alone.

The scent of the black roses still lingers in my office, a cruel reminder of Aksel's manipulations. I try to focus on the case files spread across my desk, but my thoughts keep drifting back to Mia's words. They gnaw at me like a relentless itch under my skin.

"Fallon?" Mia's tentative voice breaks through my concentration, and she pokes her head into my office. "Can we talk?"

"About what?" I snap, bristling at the thought of discussing Aksel or the flowers any further. "If it's not about work I'm not interested. You need to stop coming in here and trying to counsel me on my personal life."

"Look," she says, stepping inside and closing the door behind her. "I know you didn't want to hear what I had to say earlier, but I can't just stand by and watch you push everyone away. And you need to hear this."

"Everyone? Or just Aksel?" I challenge, narrowing my eyes at her. She hesitates for a moment, clearly choosing her words carefully.

"Both," she admits. "But especially Aksel. He's trying, Fallon. Can't you see that?"

"Trying to do what, exactly?" My voice drips with sarcasm as I cross my arms over my chest. "Win me back with some cheap theatrics? Next thing he'll be sending me a heart-shaped box of chocolates or lifting a boombox up outside my room playing '*In Your Eyes*'. Sorry, but I'm not interested."

"Fallon, please," Mia pleads, her eyes glistening with unshed tears. "Just give him a chance to explain himself. Maybe he really has changed. You'll never know unless you talk to him."

"Enough, Mia!" I slam my hand down on the desk, making her jump. "This is none of your business! Keep your nose out of my relationship with Aksel! You hardly even know the guy, and you're acting really weird about him. If you like him so much, maybe *you* should date him!"

Her face crumples, hurt flashing in her eyes. I immediately regret my harsh words, but my pride won't let me apologize. Instead, I force myself to hold her gaze, daring her to challenge me further.

"Fine," she whispers, her voice wavering. "I'll stay out of it. But just remember, Fallon—you're the one who's choosing to shut people out. And when you're left all alone, don't say I didn't warn you."

With that, she turns on her heel and marches out of my office, leaving me to stew in my own bitterness. My hands tremble with a mix of anger and guilt as I try to focus back on my work, but the words on the pages blur together as my thoughts consume me.

Maybe Mia's right. Maybe I am pushing people away. My family. Aksel. Mia herself. But can I truly afford to trust Aksel again? To let him back into my heart, only for him to tear it apart once more? I don't know that I could physically or mentally withstand it.

My grip tightens around the pen in my hand, the plastic creaking under the pressure. No. I won't give Aksel that power over me again. He had his chance, and he blew it. And now, it's time for me to focus on what really matters—my job and my quest for justice.

No matter how lonely it is. And no matter how much it hurts.

Chapter 28

"Fuck this," I mutter under my breath, tossing my phone onto the bed after another failed attempt to reach Fallon. The screen taunts me with its unyielding display: *"User is unavailable"*—a cold reminder that she still has me blocked.

My chest feels tight, like an invisible hand is crushing my heart with every beat. It's not just the frustration eating away at me, but also the crippling uncertainty of whether she'll ever speak to me again. The weight of her absence drapes over me, a constant shroud of shadows that follows me everywhere.

"Come on, Fallon... just give me a chance," I whisper to myself, raking my fingers through my hair. "This can't be it for us." The desperate plea echoes in the empty room, mocking me with the silence that follows.

I pace back and forth, my mind racing as I try to sort through the tangled mess of emotions. Anger, sadness, regret—they all mingle together like some twisted symphony playing on repeat. But what stands out the most is the fear. The fear of losing her forever.

"Maybe if I try calling from a different number..." My voice trails off as I consider the possibility. But even as I think it, I know it's a futile gesture. She'd recognize my voice immediately and likely hang up without a word. It would make me seem like some type of catfish, or a stalker. Besides, I don't want to resort to deceit. I could show up at her condo again, but that feels intrusive given she's made it clear she doesn't want to talk to me. And I don't want to get in the middle of her and her work. That feels like it would be crossing a line. I could wait for her in the parking lot, perhaps. But that seems kind of stalkerish too.

"Fuck," I mutter under my breath. The emotions she evokes in me are unparalleled—a potent mixture of lust, admiration, and something deeper, more profound. I clench my fists, feeling the rage boiling inside me at the thought of losing her forever.

"Is this really it?" I ask aloud, desperate for answers I know I won't find. "Have I lost her for good?"

The question hangs heavy in the air, unanswered, leaving me with an overwhelming sense of emptiness. The silence is deafening, mocking me as I struggle to come to terms with the possibility of never hearing her voice again.

The room seems to close in on me, suffocating me with memories of our time together. My heart races as I replay the moments we shared—her gentle touch, her intoxicating scent, and the fire behind those fierce green eyes that seem to see right through me, exposing every vulnerability I possess. I can't help but be drawn to the memory of our first heated kiss, a moment that sparked a wildfire of desire within me. All of that was a long time ago, but our more recent times together had given me a renewed sense of hope that reconciliation was a real possibility.

"Fallon," I sigh, her name escaping my lips like a desperate plea. The longing for her threatens to consume me.

"Get your shit together, Aksel," I whisper to myself, wiping my face roughly with my hands. "You're not giving up on her that easily."

My resolve hardens as I stand up, pacing the room once again. This isn't over—not by a long shot. Fallon Dempsey might be stubborn and unyielding, but she's met her match in me. If I have any say, I won't let our story end like this.

But for now, all I'm left with is the deafening silence of blocked calls and the torturous uncertainty of whether our story really has come to its bitter end.

My hand reaches for the drawer beside my bed, retrieving a picture we took together during one of our happier moments long ago. We were laughing, her head thrown back in pure joy and her arm wrapped around my waist. It's a memory that feels so distant now, like a cruel reminder of what I've lost.

My eyes trace the outline of her body pressed against mine in the picture. Her warmth, her scent, and the taste of her lips consumes me. I'm torn between wanting to rip up the photo and hold onto it with every fiber of my being.

"Is this all I have left of you?" I ask the version of Fallon that exists only in the frame. There's no answer, of course, just the unending silence that has filled the void she left behind.

"Damn you, Fallon," I whisper, my voice cracking slightly. My heart races, and I can feel sweat beading on my brow. The intensity of my desire for her is overwhelming, consuming me like a wildfire.

My fingers tighten around the edges of the photograph as my free hand drifts down my body, seeking some form of release from the torment. I remember how her hands used to feel on my skin—gentle, yet demanding, driving me wild with desire.

"Damn it, Fallon," I growl, frustration boiling over as I give in to the carnal impulse. My hand moves rapidly, each stroke feeding off the memories of our shared passion. The sound of her moans echoes through my mind, fueling my desperation for even a fleeting taste of what we once had.

"Fallon," I moan, closing my eyes as the pressure mounts. I envision her beneath me, her body pressed against mine as I thrust into her, her breath hot on my neck. And then she's riding me, gliding herself onto my cock from above while I grab onto her gorgeous, curvy waist. It's a fantasy that only serves to intensify my longing for the real thing, but for now, it's all I have.

"God, I need you," I groan, each word spoken as if it could somehow summon her presence.

My breathing turns ragged, my grip on the picture tightening. The world around me fades away, leaving only the memory of Fallon and the desperate desire for what we once had. In that moment, I'm not just chasing physical satisfaction, I'm chasing the ghost of the connection we shared. I want to feel close to her again, even if it's just an illusion. As my breathing grows ragged, I can almost imagine her there with me, whispering my name, urging me on.

"Fuck, Fallon... I miss you," I rasp. With a final gasp, I surrender to the release, my body trembling from the intensity of it all.

Panting, I stare at the photograph once more. The emptiness inside me feels even more pronounced now, like a gaping chasm that can never be filled. Even as the physical intensity fades, the emotional ache remains, leaving me raw and exposed.

With a heavy sigh, I peel myself off the bed, my skin still slick with sweat and the memory of touch. My heart races as I grapple with the bittersweet aftermath of my indulgence. The photograph of Fallon remains on the nightstand, its presence both comforting and taunting me.

"Christ, what have we become?" I mutter, running a hand through my disheveled hair, feeling the weight of our fractured relationship.

As I step into the shower, I allow the scalding water to cascade over me, washing away the residue of my actions. But no matter how hard I scrub, the emotional filth clings to me like an unwelcome shadow. In the steam-filled enclosure, my thoughts drift to Fallon and the uncertain future that lies ahead.

"Can we ever find our way back?" I ask myself, my voice barely audible above the rush of water. The question lingers in the air, unanswered and tormenting. But despite it seeming futile, I can't help but hang on to a tiny kernel of hope.

Chapter 29

FALLON

The chill of the evening seeps through the windows, settling on my skin like a heavy cloak. I can feel it in my bones, mirroring the tension that hangs in the air. The Dempsey family estate feels different tonight. Although I never feel completely at home here, the stilted laughter and warmth that typically fill its halls have been replaced with a palpable unease.

"Fallon," my father's voice cuts through the silence like a knife. We're in the study, surrounded by mahogany walls that seem to close in around us, bearing witness to the cracks forming in our family portrait. He levels his gaze at me, disappointment etched across his face, and he shakes his head. "These numbers, Fallon, they're not good."

I force myself to meet his eyes, knowing full well that the financial records he's scrutinizing are a ruse. A necessary deception, designed to conceal my clandestine activities. But I keep this knowledge locked away, hidden beneath a mask of composure. He can't know anything about my revenge operations or he'd almost certainly cease all funding immediately. He'd see it as too big of a risk to have those activities potentially linked to the family name. Just another thing for the rest of the family to judge me for. Just another reason I'm the black sheep.

"Look at your brothers, Fallon," he says, gesturing towards Lincoln, Cheston, Fenton, and Bronson, who stand like statues against the far wall, their expressions carefully schooled. "They've each built successful careers, earned the respect of their peers. And you? You're floundering, chasing after some misguided dream. It's time you followed their example. Maybe you should consider quitting and come and join the family business," he suggests, oblivious to the true extent of my success, even if it's more intrinsic than financial. It grates on me, the way he dismisses my efforts so easily, pitting me against the boring, conventional and nepotistic achievements of my brothers.

"Quitting?" I scoff, my voice edged with defiance. "This is about more than just the profits, Father. I'm focused on long-term outcomes—something you'd understand if you took the time to look past your own narrow expectations for me. I have a roster of repeat clients and a flourishing referral business. This is just the beginning."

What I'm saying is true. Personal development courses just aren't as lucrative as hedge funds and celebrity-endorsed burger brands, I suppose. Speaking of which, I find it ironic that he frowns on my business empowering women, but Link's decision to go rogue and hawk bougie gluten-free sesame buns stacked with lab-grown meats is somehow okay.

His jaw clenches, and for a moment, I think he might relent. But instead, he doubles down, unable to see beyond the boundaries he's drawn for himself and his children. "Your brothers have done well for themselves, Fallon. They've followed the path I set out for them," he glances in Link's direction, "or at least constructed something financially viable."

He furrows his brow. "Why do you have to be so difficult and contrary about everything? Why can't you just make things simple and do the same?"

The words slice through me like a knife, the jagged edges tearing at the fragile threads of my self-esteem. I'm humiliated that he's having this conversation with me in front of all of them, as if he's trying to shame me, and I can feel my frustration boiling beneath the surface, a molten tide threatening to erupt and scorch everything in its path.

My pulse quickens, anger boiling up inside me as the chasm between us widens. How can he not see how suffocating his expectations are? How they threaten to snuff out the fire that drives me? I would rather die than have my father dictate what job I do day in and day out. As it is, I feel the suffocation of his breath on the back of my neck on a daily basis.

"Because I'm not them," I spit out, my words laced with venom. "And I don't want to be. They've made their boring choices, and I've made mine. Just because our paths are different doesn't mean mine is any less valid."

"But things could be so much easier for all of us if you made better choices, Fallon," his voice is stern. "Come now, join the family company. Close down this... money-sucking pipe dream."

"Is that what you want?" I snap, my voice rising to a fever pitch. "For me to become just another faceless cog in the Dempsey machine? To sacrifice my own dreams and desires in pursuit of some twisted notion of family honor?" I smirk in my brothers' direction. "Clearly I don't look the part, let alone act it."

"Sometimes we have to make sacrifices, Fallon," he retorts, his tone cold and unyielding. "Your brothers understand that. Why can't you?"

"Like I said, because I'm not them!" I scream, the words ripping from my throat in a violent torrent. "I will never be them!"

My heart pounds wildly in my chest, each beat a thunderous echo of the rage that courses through my veins. This isn't about my business or my brothers—it's about my father's need for control. About bending me to his will and forcing me to become something I'm not.

But I won't let him.

"Maybe this is the root of the problem," I say icily, my gaze locked onto his. "Maybe you've spent so much time trying to mold me into a carbon copy of my brothers that you've forgotten who I really am. Well, let me remind you: I'm not Lincoln, Cheston, Fenton, or Bronson. I'm Fallon. Why did you give us all -on names anyway? They sound stupid and stuffy and uptight which seems fitting for the rest of you."

I glare at my brothers, who all avert their gaze. "And I will not be held captive by your expectations any longer."

The air in the study grows colder still, as if the temperature has dropped several degrees. My father's eyes bore into me, a storm of emotions brewing behind them. But instead of relenting, he only digs his heels in further, tightening his grip on the reins and reinforcing his reputation as an extremely stubborn bastard.

"Fallon, you need to understand that this isn't just about you," he says, his voice tense and unyielding. "This is about our family legacy. It's about carrying on the name and the reputation we've built. You can't risk it all for some misguided venture because it makes you 'feel good'. Altruism is for the weak."

My heart slams against my ribs, fury at his words threatening to burst forth like an unstoppable torrent. The weight of his expectations, and the relentless pressure to conform—it's all too much. And yet, I can't bring myself to reveal the truth, to expose the hidden depths of my success. Instead, I steel myself, determined to prove him wrong on my own terms.

Yet I'm worried about pushing things too far. It's a delicate tightrope, and if I don't play it just right I risk him pulling all funding from my business, and everything that I've worked so hard for crashing down around me. But I'm angry, and if there's one thing I know about myself it's that my anger leads to recklessness. Damn this all to hell.

"Legacy?" I hiss, my fists clenched at my sides. "You're so concerned about maintaining appearances that you'd rather see me fail than forge my own path? Well, I won't do it. I won't be another pawn in your game."

As the words leave my lips, I realize the enormity of what I've just done. A line has been crossed.

My father's mouth sets in a firm line, his eyes blazing. He's not used to anyone speaking to him this way. In this moment, the fragile bonds that once held us together begin to fray, threatening to snap under the strain of unspoken tensions and unresolved conflicts.

The room feels as though it's closing in on me, the weight of my father's disapproval bearing down like a suffocating blanket. His eyes bore into mine, searching for any sign of weakness, any indication that I might succumb to his demands.

My eyes flick to my brothers, who are all doing their best to maintain their composure. They know better than to try to intervene in a showdown like this, lest they become the next target of our father's wrath.

"Very well," he says finally, his voice strained. "Have it your way. But don't come crying to me when it all comes crashing down."

I watch as he turns on his heel and stalks from the room, the door slamming shut behind him with a resounding bang. The sound reverberates through the study, a bitter reminder of the chasm that now divides us, my status as the nonconformist ne'er-do-well of the family more firmly entrenched than ever.

The clink of silverware against fine china fills the dining room, punctuated by animated chatter between my brothers. I sit in relative silence, picking at my food, acutely aware of the empty chair at the head of the table. My father's absence speaks volumes. I should have left right after my father stormed out, but I thought maybe we could put a Band-Aid on things over dinner. Hard to do when he doesn't even show up.

"Hey, Fallon," Link smirks, a glint in his eye betraying the cruel intentions behind his words, "Daddy's little princess is awfully quiet tonight. Did that little tantrum earlier tire you out?"

I glance at him briefly, but refuse to take the bait. Instead, I focus on my plate, stabbing my fork into a piece of roasted chicken with more force than necessary. The strain in my hand mirrors the tension suffocating the room, and my heart clenches in response. This isn't who I am—it's who they've made me.

As dinner drags on, I retreat further into myself, shutting out the world around me. Let them have their victories, their laughter—let them believe they've won. In the end, it'll only make my revenge that much sweeter.

After we've finished eating, I slip away from the others, making an excuse about needing to leave early.

Escaping to the solitude of my condo, it's there that I finally allow the façade to crumble, revealing the raw, vulnerable woman beneath. My hands tremble as I reach for the bottle of whiskey from my vintage bar cart, desperate for the numbing embrace of alcohol.

"Fuck them," I whisper to myself, taking a swig straight from the bottle. The fiery liquid burns its way down my throat, igniting a spark within me. It's not enough to erase the pain, but it's something.

The days pass in a blur, each one melding into the next as I continue to plot my revenge—against fuckboys, my family, Aksel, anyone who has ever done me or anyone I know wrong. The routine becomes second nature: punishing workouts, numbing alcohol, and stolen nights with strangers, all in an attempt to keep the demons at bay. I venture out to clubs, seeking the company of strangers who offer fleeting moments of connection beneath the dim lights and pounding bass. Their hands on my body, their breath hot against my skin—it's a temporary reprieve from the ache in my chest, a way to forget, if only for a little while. But even as I indulge in these vices, I can't shake the feeling that I'm teetering on the edge of something dangerous, something I might not be able to come back from.

Despite my efforts to distract myself, it isn't enough. The fog of my emotions remains thick, suffocating me, and I find myself drawn to darker thoughts. Revenge becomes an obsession, a lifeline in the chaos threatening to consume me. Each step I take down this path carries me further away from the woman I once was, but I can no longer turn back. I will destroy Aksel for hurting me, and I'll address my family pain in the process. I'm not sure exactly how yet, but I will. In the meantime, my clients' abusers will serve as proxies and guinea pigs.

"Fallon," I whisper to myself more than once while at work, gripping the bathroom sink for support, my knuckles white with strain, "you have to keep it together."

But the cracks are starting to show to others, too. My brothers notice how quiet I've become at the family dinners that I still drag myself to, and the way I avoid their gaze when they try to engage me in conversation. Link, in particular, seems determined to break through my carefully constructed walls, but I refuse to let him in, letting his barbed words wash over me like water off a duck's back.

"Come on, Fallon," he taunts one evening, smirking as he tosses a casual insult my way, "where's that fire you used to have?"

I simply stare at him, my face a blank mask, before turning away without a word. Let them think I'm broken, that I've finally succumbed to the weight of their expectations. It will only make my eventual triumph all the sweeter.

"Link," I murmur one night, staring blankly at my reflection in the mirror, "you've underestimated me. You all have."

With each passing day, I grow colder, harder. I embrace the darkness within me, allowing it to shape me into something new—something fierce. And as the storm clouds gather overhead, I know that there's no going back.

This is who I am now. This is who they've made me. And when the time comes, I will make them pay for what they've done.

Chapter 30

FALLON

The city lights cast a seductive glow on the sleek glass windows of my office, painting the room in shades of midnight and desire. I lean back in my chair, restless in the growing silence. It's late, but sleep is a luxury I can't afford. Not when there's so much at stake.

"Fallon." The single word slices through the quiet like a razor-sharp blade. My head snaps up at the sound of Grave's voice, low and gravelly as it always is. He stands in the doorway, face shrouded in shadows, a harbinger of secrets hidden in the darkness.

"Grave," I acknowledge him, my tone clipped and impatient. "What is it?" His gaze never falters, even though I know he senses my irritation.

"It's Link," he begins, folding his arms across his broad chest. "He's been digging into your business."

My blood runs cold. Fury coils in the pit of my stomach, igniting a fire that quickly spreads throughout my entire body. How dare he? I clench my fists, nails biting into my palms, as I fight the urge to lash out. Instead, I focus on the poison swirling inside me, channeling it into a deadly venom that drips from every word I speak.

The fury boils within me, a firestorm threatening to consume everything in its path. I pace my office like a caged predator, the truth of Link's betrayal echoing through my mind. That he would stoop so low as to investigate me and my company... it's beyond comprehension.

"Are you sure?"

"Positive. He hired a private investigator to look into your dealings. *Our* dealings."

I grit my teeth, jaw clenched tight enough to shatter bone. This isn't just betrayal, it's a goddamn declaration of war. Link may be my brother, but he's crossed a line that can't be uncrossed. I won't let him destroy all I've worked for. Not now, not ever.

"Find out what he's discovered," I command, my voice a barely contained snarl. "Then we'll deal with him."

"Consider it done," Grave replies, his loyalty unwavering even in the face of this treachery.

"Good." I release a breath I didn't realize I was holding, the weight of my rage still heavy on my chest. "Now get out."

"Fallon, it's not my fault," he says quietly, carefully. "I only brought you this information because I thought you should know."

"Of course it's not your fault, Grave!" I snap, my anger flaring despite my knowledge that he's done nothing wrong. "But you're here, and he isn't, so you get to deal with the fallout!"

His eyes flash with something akin to hurt, though he quickly tries to mask it. I can tell he doesn't understand why I'm lashing out at him—hell, I don't even understand it myself. But the rage inside me demands an outlet, and he's the only one within reach.

"Believe me, Fallon, I'm just as upset about this as you are," he says, his voice steady, unyielding.

I scoff, my hands balling into fists as I continue to pace. "You think there's any coming back from this? From him spying on me and trying to tear apart everything I've worked so hard for? My family was already fucked up, but this is next level! If he finds out about our revenge ops, and he tells my father—which he almost certainly will—goodbye to this company. Goodbye to everything!"

"I didn't say it would be easy," he replies, a slight edge creeping into his voice. "But we have to try. You're stronger than this, Fallon. You always have been."

"Stronger than this?" I breathe, incredulous. "Grave, he could ruin us. Do you understand that?"

"Of course I do," he says softly. "And I'm here to help you in any way I can. But taking your anger out on me isn't going to solve anything. We're partners in this, and if he takes us down I'm fucked, too. Nobody wants to hire a grizzled old ex-military guy with a questionable criminal record and homicidal history. Except for you," he smirks.

His words hit me like a punch to the gut, the truth of them cutting through my rage and leaving me deflated. He's right—Grave has always been loyal, steadfast, and true. He doesn't deserve my wrath.

"Grave... I'm sorry," I murmur, my voice softening as I finally come to a halt, my legs trembling with pent-up energy. "This isn't your fault. I shouldn't have taken it out on you."

He nods, his eyes still holding a trace of hurt but also understanding. "We all have our breaking points, Fallon," he says gently. "Just remember who your real enemies are."

I take a deep breath, allowing his words to seep into my consciousness until they become a mantra. My enemy isn't Grave. It's Link, and the festering pit of betrayal he's dug between us. Sad, considering he's my brother and all. Regardless, I'll make him pay for his actions, one way or another.

I can't help but wonder what drove Link to this point, though. His insecurity? His need for control? Whatever it is, it's going to cost him dearly. A wicked smile curls my lips as I imagine the sweet satisfaction of revenge. He wants to play dirty? So be it.

"Thank you, Grave," I say, steeling myself for the battle ahead. "Now let's figure out how to strike back."

Link, you have no idea what you've just unleashed.

I pause, my mind racing, calculating the best way to retaliate for my brother's actions. An idea takes root, growing stronger with each passing second. A slow smile spreads across my face as I lock eyes with Grave. "I'm going to find out every dirty little secret my dear brother's been hiding. And when I have enough ammunition, I'll confront him. He won't know what hit him."

"Are you certain you want to go down this path?" Grave questions again, his brow furrowed with worry. "It could change everything between you and Link."

"Everything's already changed," I reply coldly, my voice heavy with bitterness. "He started this war, Grave. I'm just going to finish it."

"Very well," he sighs, resigned to my decision. "If this is the path you choose, I'll stand by you. We'll need to be careful, though. If Link finds out what we're doing before we're ready, it could backfire."

"Trust me, Grave," I say, a fire burning in my chest as determination surges through my veins. "He won't see it coming."

Together, we begin to plot, our voices hushed and our words carefully chosen. The air around us crackles with the tension of secrets and betrayal, and I can't help but feel a thrill at the thought of bringing Link to his knees. He may be my brother, but he's chosen to make an enemy of me—and I have no intention of going down without a fight.

Chapter 31

FALLON

The glass in my hand feels cold and heavy, the amber liquid swirling inside it like a tempest. It's been weeks since I stormed out of the restaurant where I saw them together, but the images of him and Carissa still plague me. Every time I blink, it's like a cruel reminder of what I witnessed. To make matters worse, my brain never stops at what I actually saw—them sitting intimately in a booth, Carissa with her hand possessively on Aksel's thigh.

That on it's own would be enough to make my gut revolt. But my mind embellishes different versions of the story. They're nearly always in the booth, but they're kissing passionately with very visible tongue action, she's sucking his dick, he's going down on her, he's shoving all the plates off the table and taking her right there in front of everyone. Oh, there's even one where I return to my condo and they're in my bed, sitting up boltright in shock when I enter the room and catch them. He's in his suit, he's naked, she's in sexy lingerie, they're role playing in costume.

Ugh. Let's just say the two of them have a very active sex life rent-free in my head.

"Damn you, Aksel King," I curse under my breath, downing the rest of the whiskey as if it'll help me forget.

It doesn't. If anything, it only stokes the fire that's been raging inside me since I saw them together. It's not just anger—it's something deeper, a primal hunger that courses through my veins, consuming me. And it terrifies me. Because I realize the rawness and depth of my emotion comes from the subconscious belief that Aksel King is mine. *Mine.*

"Fuck it," I mutter, grabbing my phone with unsteady fingers. A part of me knows this is a terrible idea, but logic has long since taken a backseat to the storm of emotions inside me.

Me: Be at your place in 20.

I don't have to wait long for his response.

Aksel: See you soon.

No questions, just acceptance. Maybe he's just happy to take what he can get. Possibly he thinks I just want to talk, give him an earful. In that case, he's in for a pleasant surprise, because words aren't on my agenda at all.

When I arrive at Aksel's apartment, the door is unlocked, waiting for me. As I step inside, I find him standing there, as if he's been waiting for me all night. He looks like a dark angel, his carefully styled dark hair reflecting the dim light, his warm smile a stark contrast to the ice in his eyes.

"Fallon," he says, his voice low and velvety.

"Aksel," my own voice is sultry.

"What are you doing here?" he asks, and I can't tell whether he's feigning innocence or he really doesn't know. Given how I've been acting lately, that's fair.

"Cut the bullshit, Aksel," I snap, my chest tightening with every step I take towards him. "You know why I'm here. We have some unfinished business to attend to," I add, my heart racing.

"Are you sure about this?" he asks, raising an eyebrow. In that moment, I see his resolve wavering, but I need this. I need to feel something other than this gut-wrenching pain. And seeing I can't stop imagining him while trying to fuck anonymous strangers, I may as well take it straight from the man himself.

Then, he grabs my hand and pulls me further into his condo. The door shuts behind us with a soft click.

Inside, it's cool and quiet, the only sound our heavy breathing. Aksel drops my hand, and we're face to face. I can smell his cologne, mixed with the scent of his skin. I want to taste him. I want to make him suffer.

"Fallon," he whispers, his eyes darkening. "What do you want?"

"You," I say, my words barely audible.

"Are you sure?" He steps forward, too slow, and captures my lips in an agonizingly gentle kiss. My blood boils.

"Positive," I growl as I push him back against the door, closing the remaining distance between us, my fingers tangled in his hair as I deepen the kiss, desperation seeping into every inch of my being. His body responds to mine, hardening against me. His lips are warm and soft against mine, but there's an edge to it—a dark promise that sends shivers down my spine.

"Remember," he whispers as we part, his breath hot against my ear, "you asked for this."

I nod, unable to form words, my heart pounding in my chest as our eyes lock. In that moment, all the anger, all the betrayal, everything else fades away, leaving only the raw, unspoken connection between us.

"Are we really doing this?" I ask, my voice wavering despite my best efforts to keep it steady. Now it's my time to falter. I want to do this but I'm also terrified.

"Tell me to stop, Fallon," he challenges, his hands skimming my waist as if daring me to push him away. But I can't. And he knows it.

"God damn you, Aksel King." My words are a choked whisper as he leans in, his lips hovering tantalizingly close to mine.

"Damn me, then," he murmurs before claiming my mouth in a searing kiss that banishes all thoughts of resistance. His tongue swipes through my lips, desperate, starving for me.

I trail kisses down his jawline, sucking marks into his skin, slowly working my way towards his neck. *Mine.* He moans softly, arching into my touch. This man, who once owned my heart, now belongs to me, and I don't give a fuck who sees. In fact, I want everyone to see.

I bite down hard on his neck, drawing blood. He gasps, but doesn't pull away. Instead, he grips my hair tighter, pulling me closer. I lick the wound, tasting his sweet saltiness.

"More," he demands.

I oblige, sucking harder and taking more of his precious life force. The taste fills me with an unholy power.

Aksel's eyes roll back, and he grabs my hair again, this time roughly yanking me closer.

"You're mine now," he growls, his voice raspy with desire and pain.

I smile, my fangs piercing his skin again.

"No, Aksel," I whisper. "You're mine."

With that, I take control, pinning him to the wall and tearing through his clothing. My need for vengeance morphs into a lust so fierce it burns through me. He is mine to do with as I please. I trail my teeth along his freshly bruised collarbone, biting softly as I tug down his pants.

His erection springs free, thick and long. I take him in my hand, stroking gently at first, reveling in the power coursing through me. His chest heaves with each ragged breath as I circle the head of his cock with my tongue, tasting the pre-cum that beads at the tip.

"Fucking hell, Fallon," he groans, his hips jerking forward.

I look up into his eyes, challenging him. "You like that?"

He nods, his eyes wild with want and need.

I lower my mouth over him, taking him deep into my throat, bobbing up and down as I suck and lick every inch of him. He grabs my hair, fingers tightening as he thrusts into my mouth, fucking my face.

"Fuck..." he breathes out, the word sounding like a curse. "Oh yeah...."

I increase the pressure on his shaft, emphasizing the tip, and loving the power I have over him. This is how it was always meant to be—me in control.

He grabs my face, holding me still as he comes hard down my throat, pushing against the back of my mouth and filling me with his seed. The taste is bittersweet, delicious, and I swallow it all down which seems to please him.

"Fallon," he moans softly, pulling away.

I grin up at him, a cold smile playing on my lips. "You don't own me, Aksel. I'm my own woman."

He growls in response, guiding me over to his dining room table and hoisting me up on the end. "Then prove it."

I blink up at him, unsure what he means.

His hand lands on my shoulder, forcing me down as he yanks my dress up and parts my legs roughly. His lips find my aching pussy, tongue pushing inside me as he buries his face between my thighs. He starts off slow, licking and teasing, but soon his fingers are thrusting inside me too, finding my g-spot and massaging. I cry out, shockwaves of pleasure and anger washing over me as he takes control once more.

"Fuck," I groan, arching into his touch. "Aksel!"

He growls, his free hand slapping my ass hard. "Mine."

I pull back, pushing him away. "No, not yours."

His eyes flash with fire. "Then show me how much you don't want me."

I glare at him, caught off guard by his challenge. But then desire washes over me, drowning out my fears. I'm done playing nice. It's time for payback.

I growl, "Get on the couch," and he complies, pulling me by the hand over to the leather sectional. I push him back and he sits, facing me. I straddle him, positioning my wet pussy over his rock-hard erection. He doesn't protest as I lower myself onto him, impaling myself on his cock. Slowly, I ride him, taking back control of the situation. The couch creaks beneath us as I move up and down.

"Fuck, Fallon," Aksel growls as I dig my nails into his shoulders, unable to contain my desperation for him. "You're going to ruin me."

"Good," I pant, the word a declaration of war.

This time, I can focus on the sensation, and god he feels good. Images of him are no longer floating through my mind, because he's here right in front of me. He's inside me. The man who haunts my dreams and preoccupies my every waking thought is inside me. But he's a means to an end. This is simply to keep my distraction at bay while I plot how to take him down for the pain he's caused me, after all. His very nice cock is just coming in handy in the process.

"Holy fuck, Fallon." He grits his teeth.

I lean forward, my breasts brushing against his chest as I kiss him hard, tasting myself on his lips. Our tongues wrestle together, a violent dance of dominance and submission. His hands grip my hips, pulling me closer as he fills me completely. I feel every inch of him inside me, stretching me in ways I didn't know were possible.

"You like that, Aksel?" I whisper against his neck, nipping at the skin. "Being owned by a woman?"

He growls, his voice low and full of lust. "Fuck yes."

With each thrust, I feel him hitting my cervix, claiming me as his own. I grip the back of the couch, my nails digging into the plush leather as I take him deeper. We're both panting now, our bodies moving together in a rhythm of catharsis and lust.

"That's it," he mutters, his voice rough. "Ride me, baby."

I do just that, riding him harder and faster, determined to make him see that I've never been his. I've always been my own person. And I've learned a thing or two since high school and college.

His hands slide down to my ass, squeezing me tight as he slams into me from below with rough strokes. I cry out, my body betraying me as the sensations build. He's not gentle, but neither am I. We're both animals now, seeking release from this tension between us.

"You're mine," he says, his voice harsh. "Always have been."

I bite my lip, feeling the sting of his words. But I won't let him take away my freedom.

I won't let him define me.

He grabs my hair, pulling my head back roughly, exposing my neck. I taste blood in my mouth. "Say it," he whispers, his hot breath on my skin.

"No," I whisper back, but I can't deny the pleasure coursing through me.

He growls again and slaps me hard across the ass, leaving a stinging that only fuels our passion. We continue like this, our bodies moving together in a primal dance of hate and love. Of desire and anger. It's confusing and exhilarating all at once.

He grunts my name as he releases inside me. I scream, "Aksel," feeling him pulsing inside me which sends me over the edge, the coil within me snapping and sending bursts of white-hot electricity coursing throughout my body. The stings from his slaps are momentarily sensitized even further. The pain and pleasure blend together until I can't tell where one ends and the other begins.

As we catch our breath, he pulls out slowly, his eyes full of lust and something else—possessiveness, maybe? He slaps my ass again, marking me like a brand.

"Remember this," he says, his voice hoarse. "You're mine."

I push myself up from the couch and begin to walk away from him. While he can't see my face, I mouth, "I'll never forget it." I'd never give him the satisfaction of saying it out loud. And I can't possibly mean it. It must be the afterglow of what I have to admit was some pretty amazing sex.

He collapses back onto the couch, sweaty and spent, and a large part of me wants to join him. But this isn't over. Not by a long shot. I still have a score to settle.

As I put on my dress, I feel his eyes on me. They follow every movement, drinking me in. I feel heat rising up my chest and onto my face under the scrutiny of his gaze.

"You're leaving?" he asks, his voice broken.

I turn to face him, and purse my lips into a smirk. "I'm just getting started."

He looks at me quizzically as I slip out of his condo, my heart pounding. This isn't the end of our twisted game. It's a continuation.

As I step out of Aksel's apartment, the night air hits me like a slap in the face. It's cold and unforgiving, a stark contrast to the heat we just created inside those walls. The door clicks shut behind me, sealing away our momentary fulfillment. As the reality of my situation sinks in, I wrap my arms around myself, trying to hold onto some semblance of warmth.

"Fuck," I mutter under my breath, the word carried away by the wind. With each step I take, the distance between Aksel and me grows, but the lingering sensation of his touch remains. This unspoken connection we share is as dangerous as it is thrilling, and I can't help but feel like I'm playing with fire.

In my car, my hands tremble as I grip the steering wheel. I'm shaking with excitement and fear. What if this goes too far? What if he doesn't understand? But he has to. He deserves to understand.

As I drive off into the night, I replay our encounter over and over again in my mind. The way he took me from below while I was riding him—so rough, so raw. The way he growled my name. The way it felt to be his completely. It was intoxicating... and horrifying all at once. The memory of his hands on me, his lips against mine, both excites and terrifies me. How can something that feels so right be so undeniably wrong?

But I need to get over it. It was a means to an end. I didn't fuck Aksel to catch feelings. I did it because every time another guy touches me I wish it was his hand. His mouth. His cock. So I took it, in hope doing the real thing would get him out of my mind. I just hope it doesn't have the opposite effect.

"Get a grip, Fallon," I tell myself, shaking my head in an attempt to dispel the dangerous thoughts. "You're here for revenge, not a fucking love story."

But even as I speak the words, I know they ring hollow. The truth is, no matter how much I deny it, there's a part of me that longs for more than just vengeance. A part of me craves forgiveness, redemption, and yes—maybe even love.

"Shit," I whisper, my voice barely audible over the sound of my own pounding heart. As I continue to drive through the dark streets, the weight of my complicated emotions settles heavily on my shoulders, leaving me with one undeniable fact: I may have found momentary satisfaction in Aksel's arms, but this twisted game we're playing is far from over.

Chapter 32

FALLON

The chandelier's cold light casts fractured shadows across the grand dining hall, as if foreshadowing the growing fractures in our own family. As usual, we're gathered around the long mahogany table, dressed up for just another one of our ostentatious weekly family dinners, and the tension hangs thick in the air like a noose waiting to be tightened.

"Pass the gravy, please," my father murmurs, his voice barely audible over the clinking of silverware.

"Of course," I reply, my tone curt, handing him the white ceramic vessel. My gaze darts to Link, who sits at the opposite end of the table, his eyes hooded with a darkness that sends a shiver down my spine. This is the first time I've seen him since I found out he's been watching me––following me, or at least hired people to do it. Always jealous since we were children, for whatever reason, his envy has grown into a sinister serpent, ready to strike at any moment. But he doesn't know I know the full extent he's gone to. He thinks I'm an oblivious idiot. And I intend to have him think that until I'm ready for the big reveal.

"Fallon, dear, how's your company doing?" Zara asks, my stepmother's voice dripping with feigned interest. She's a great actress when she can be bothered. In fact, I almost give her kudos for not referring to it as my 'little company' or 'charming small business' or one of the little disparaging remarks she usually makes. "I read an article about a serial killer who terrorized women on one of those dating apps, and now companies are being sued by the families of the victims. Isn't that wild? I hope you have some excellent liability insurance." There we go. I knew she couldn't resist.

"Business is booming," I respond with a tight smile, my focus never wavering from Link's brooding form. "It seems that people can't get enough of feeling empowered." I refuse to get into a defensive position where I'm once again explaining to the room that I don't run a dating app or even a dating service. I'll let them construct their own narrative.

"Ah, well, it's good to see you succeeding," Zara says, though the malice in her eyes betrays her true feelings. I don't know why she's always been so irritated by me. Maybe because I'm the only other woman in her little 'family' bubble.

"Thank you, Zara. Your support means so much to me," I say, my words laced with sarcasm.

"Speaking of support, Fallon," Link interjects, his voice smooth but icy. "I've been hearing some... interesting rumors about your business practices."

The table falls silent, all eyes turning to me. I feel the heat of their gazes, invasive and judgmental, searing into my soul.

I'm so glad Grave gave me a heads up, but still, my stomach flip-flops as my mind races to think of what he might be talking about. "Really, Link? Do tell," I challenge, refusing to let him undermine me.

"Word on the street is that your success hasn't come without its fair share of... underhanded deals... or let's say, special operations?" he says, a cruel smile playing on his lips.

"Sounds like you've been listening to the wrong people," I retort, my heart pounding in my chest. I can't tell if he's bluffing or if his private investigators have already been able to find out more about our revenge ops business arm.

"Perhaps," Link concedes, but his eyes gleam with malicious intent. "But wouldn't it be wise for your family to look out for you, especially if those rumors turn out to be true?"

I can see he has my father's attention, and I shift uncomfortably in my chair.

"Link, are you suggesting that you've been spying on me?" I hiss, my anger flaring like a wild inferno.

"Of course not, Fallon." He leans back in his chair, the picture of smug satisfaction. "Public information spreads like wildfire around here. Just looking out for my dear sister."

"Enough!" Cheston interjects, his voice commanding. "This isn't the time or place for accusations. We're here to have a nice family meal and catch up on a personal level."

"Agreed," Zara adds, her eyes darting between us warily, likely relieved at the opportunity to get the attention back on her. "Let's just enjoy the dinner and each other's company."

"Fine," I grit out, my gaze never leaving Link's. The serpent has slithered into the light, but I refuse to let it sink its venomous fangs into me.

"Cheers to that," Link replies, raising his wine glass mockingly. His eyes meet mine, dark and vengeful, promising a battle yet to come.

And in this moment, I know that nothing will ever be the same between us. The bonds that once held our family together are corroding, eaten away by the toxin of jealousy. Dad seems oblivious, but the toxicity between Link and I is festering, as well as between me and Zara. Cheston plays mediator, but the guys always ultimately end up banding together. I thought things would mellow out as we matured, but they're only getting worse.

As we finish up our meal together under the chandelier's cold light, I can't help but wonder if there's any hope left for the Dempseys. Or at least a version of the Dempseys where I truly feel like I belong.

After dinner, despite wanting nothing more than to run away, I find myself in the living room with Cheston and Link. I'm feeling confrontational, a little emboldened by the wine that flowed freely during dinner, and I feel the need to say something in this more intimate setting.

"Would either of you care for more wine?" Cheston's voice cuts through the silence like a lifeline, his eyes darting between Link and me, searching for a way to mend what's already fraying at the seams.

"Thank you, Cheston," I say, my words clipped, as I offer him my empty glass. He pours the deep red liquid with steady hands, but I can see the worry etched on his face. He's trying so hard to keep our world from unraveling, to keep Link and I from saying or doing something truly irreparable, but some things are simply beyond repair.

"Link, Fallon, don't you think it's time you two clear the air?" Cheston asks, glancing at me and then turning his attention to our brother. Link's jaw clenches, but he doesn't respond. The ticking of the grandfather clock behind him becomes deafening.

"Alright, then." I slam my hand down on the table, making the wine glasses shudder. "You want to talk about clearing the air? Fine. Link?" I glare at him, eyes flashing. "Let's start with you hiring a private investigator to snoop in my company's affairs."

Link's eyes narrow, dark and dangerous, while his lips twist into a cruel sneer. "And just what did you expect me to do, Fallon? Stand idly by while you destroy yourself and take this family down with you?"

"Destroy myself?" My voice trembles with rage. "My company is successful because I built it from the ground up!"

"By any means necessary, it seems." Link's gaze pierces right through me, and I feel the weight of the accusations he leaves unspoken. "And definitely not with the degree of transparency expected in a Dempsey-owned business."

I bristle at the accusation, my nails digging into the wooden frame. "You don't know anything about my business."

"Then enlighten me," he challenges, his gaze unyielding. "Tell me why you've been meeting with some very dangerous people. Tell me why I had to hire a private investigator to find out what kind of twisted game you're playing."

"Link, please..." Cheston pleads, his brown eyes imploring us for peace. But as much as I love my eldest brother, I can't back down now. Not when the truth is so close to the surface.

"Fine." I shrug. "You want the truth? My company is built on taking down those who abuse their power. Those who have hurt others and gotten away with it. People like our dear father."

"Except," Link bites out, pushing away from the table, "you're not just going after them legally, are you? You've crossed lines, Fallon. Dangerous lines."

"Let's play devil's advocate here... who cares how she gets justice as long as she gets it?" Cheston interjects, but his words are lost in the storm of emotions raging between Link and me.

"Because it could destroy her!" Link bellows, and for a moment, the room falls silent. "Do you think I wanted to pry into your affairs, Fallon? Do you think any of this brings me joy? I did it because I love you, and I can't stand to see you throw your life away like this!"

"Love?" I scoff, my voice trembling with a toxic mix of rage and betrayal. "You don't know the first thing about love or loyalty."

"Fallon, it sounds like he's just trying to protect you," Cheston pleads, his hands raised in a futile attempt to mediate.

"Protect me?!" I whirl on him, feeling my blood boil beneath my skin. "By spying on me? By undermining everything I've worked for? I don't need his protection! I don't need any of you!"

"Maybe if you'd been more open with us from the beginning, we wouldn't be here right now!" Link snaps, his anger mirroring my own.

"Enough!" Cheston's voice cuts through the tension, but it's too late. The damage is done; the Dempsey siblings are no longer united by blood, but divided by jealousy and deceit.

"Listen, Fallon. I don't like what you're doing or how you're going about it, but Cheston's right. I've had enough as well," Link snaps, his composure cracking. "We're family, whether you like it or not."

"Family?" My laugh is hollow, devoid of any warmth. "You have a twisted idea of what family means, brother." I place my wine glass down onto the coffee table and rise to my feet. "This conversation is over."

"Fallon, wait—" Cheston tries to reach out to me, but I'm already storming out of the room.

I turn to glare at both of my brothers, letting my fury fuel me. "If you want to side with him, Cheston, then do it. But remember this: I won't forget who stood beside me and who stabbed me in the back."

I slam my childhood bedroom door shut, the sound echoing through the hollow chambers of my heart. My breathing is ragged, my hands shaking, as I pace back and forth across the cold hardwood floor. The one room in the house where I've ever felt truly welcome. My own space.

"Fucking dickheads," I mutter under my breath, the words tasting like poison on my tongue. "My own brothers..."

Tears threaten to spill, but I refuse to give in. Instead, I ball my fists, nails digging into my palms, as I struggle to contain the maelstrom of emotions that churn within me.

"Fallon?" The soft, hesitant voice of Zara drifts through the door. "Can I come in?"

"Go away!" I snap, my throat raw from the effort of holding back tears. My stepmother is the last person I want to be talking to right now. But she doesn't listen. The doorknob turns slowly, and Zara steps into the room, her doe-like eyes filled with concern.

"Please, Fallon, talk to me." Her words are gentle, a balm for the wounds my brothers have inflicted.

"Didn't you hear me, Zara?" I hiss, my anger flaring once again. "I said go away!"

"Stop pushing everyone away, Fallon," she pleads, stepping closer. "We're all hurting in our own ways, not just you."

"Are you seriously defending them? After what they did?" I can't hide the disbelief in my voice.

"Listen, I couldn't help but overhear all the yelling." I redden as I realize the conversation wasn't just between Cheston, Link and me, and the whole house was likely privy to it. "Link was wrong to spy on your business, and I know you hate it when they all double down and defend each other even when they're wrong," Zara says, her voice wavering. "But can you honestly say you'd never act out of love and concern for us, even if it meant making mistakes?"

"Love? This wasn't love, Zara!" I seethe, my chest tightening with every word. "This was betrayal, plain and simple. They chose their side, and now they have to live with it."

"Fallon, please..." Zara's voice cracks, and I see fresh tears in her eyes. "Don't let this destroy our family." It's only now that I realize she sees herself as belonging to the group much more than I ever gave her credit for. It always seemed like her and dad, and then the rest of us. But she views herself as part of the larger unit. Interesting. Although we all are about the same age—Cheston's older than her in fact—so it kind of makes sense.

"Maybe it's too late for that," I whisper, the words heavy with regret and pain. As I turn away from her, my gaze falls on the mirror above my vanity. The reflection staring back at me is a stranger—eyes darkened by vengeance, lips twisted into a snarl of contempt.

"Get out, Zara," I say quietly, unable to bear the sight of her any longer. She hesitates for a moment, then turns and leaves me alone in the darkness.

As the door clicks shut behind her, my resolve hardens like ice around my heart. This isn't just about Link anymore, it's about all of them. I feel more on the outside than ever.

"Watch your backs, brothers," I murmur, my voice low and cold as the shadows that now envelop us all. "You've awakened something you'll come to regret."

Chapter 33

FALLON

The cold steel of the knife glints in my hand as darkness beckons me, urging me to embrace the shadows. My heart pounds in anticipation, a twisted excitement building within me. I've always been one to toe the line between right and wrong, but now that line is blurring, leaving me with an odd sense of satisfaction.

"Isn't this what you wanted?" I taunt, my voice barely above a whisper. The man before me, bound and helpless, trembles as terror consumes him. This pathetic creature once caused me so much pain, and now, it's my turn to return the favor.

"Please... Fallon, don't do this," he pleads, tears streaming down his face. I smile, reveling in the power I now hold over him.

"Your words mean nothing to me anymore," I spit, my anger fueled by the emotional wounds he inflicted on me and the weight of family expectations that linger like a heavy fog. "You're going to pay for everything you put me through."

My mind races with thoughts of vengeance, each new idea more sinister than the last. Every fiber of my being yearns to see him suffer, just as he made me suffer. I take a deep breath, steadying my trembling hands, and approach him with a newfound sense of purpose.

"Let's see how you like having your world turned upside down," I say, grinning wickedly as the blade dances dangerously close to his skin. He whimpers, trying to keep his composure in the face of impending doom.

"Fallon, please... you don't have to do this," he begs again, desperation etched on his

tear-stained face.

"Ah, but you see..." I reply, my voice dripping with malice, "I want to." My grip tightens around the handle of the knife as I prepare myself for the delicious thrill of taking control, of watching him squirm and writhe beneath me.

"Remember when you said I was weak?" I hiss, my lips curling into a sinister smile. "You were wrong." And with that, I drive the knife into his thigh, watching in rapturous delight as he screams in pain. The sound is music to my ears, a symphony of revenge that resonates within my soul.

The man whimpers in shock and agony as I yank the blade out and plunge it into his other thigh this time, leaving a matching wound. I yank the lengthy blade out and this time I plunge it into his chest. He shrieks as blood begins to shoot from his legs. I hook my arm and stab the knife through the side of his head this time, just to mix things up.

I'll always remember his screams. The shrieks of excruciating agony. The way his neck feels as I step around behind him, hold his head steady and slit his throat, enjoying the view of crimson liquid gushing from the wound. The way his eyes grow large, bulging, his breath ragged, before his head lolls to the side and he grows increasingly still.

The lines between right and wrong have vanished, leaving me adrift in a sea of murky gray where morality is but a fleeting memory. It's intoxicating, this newfound power I wield, and as I stare at the man who once held dominion over me, I can't help but feel an unsettling pleasure coursing through my veins.

"Welcome," I whisper, my voice barely audible amidst his cries of agony, "to the darkness."

I wake with a start, bolting upright, and, as my eyes adjust to the light, I realize I'm in the safety of my own office chair. As in, not stabbing a guy whose face seemed to alternate between that of the many men I've sought revenge on before: my dad, Link, and of course, Aksel. Even Cheston's face swirled into focus for a moment. The guys who hurt me back in school. Every guy who has ever wronged me... like a dream punching bag, but with murder.

But as disturbing as the nightmare was, it leaves me feeling a little excited. Maybe some people would say I need help. But I'm just fine with the way I am.

The night air is crisp, the shadows stretching across the ground of my office like long fingers grasping for something to hold onto. As I stand in the dimly lit room, I can feel the darkness seeping into my very being, filling the void left by a lifetime of disappointments and pain. I'm still a little thrown that I fell asleep at work, but the mental exhaustion of the past few weeks has been intense.

I feel a little groggy and also a bit giddy. Unusual. That dream or nightmare or whatever it was seems to have awakened something inside of me. A bloodlust, an invincibility. Maybe it's a sign from the universe, or from my subconscious, that my revenge plans are exactly what I should be doing.

"Fallon?" Mia's voice floats through the gloom, a lighthouse offering safe harbor amidst the encroaching shadows. Her petite frame appears in the doorway, her soft features etched with concern. "You're still here? It's late."

"Ah, Mia," I murmur, a cruel smirk playing on my lips. "Just the person I wanted to see."

"Fallon, what's going on? You seem... different," she says cautiously, her dark curls framing her delicate face.

"Have you ever felt the power of absolute control, Mia? The kind that sends shivers down your spine?" My laughter, tinged with an eerie delight, resonates in the room. I feel a little unhinged as I give into my compulsion to say whatever's on my mind.

"Fallon, you're acting like you've discovered some dark secret. What's happening?" She presses, her freckled face creased with worry. "Did something happen with Aksel?"

"Darling Mia," I lean in, whispering conspiratorially, "Not everything is about Aksel. I've embraced the shadows, and it's intoxicating. The power, the control—I can almost taste it." I feel theatrical as the words dance off my tongue.

"Fallon, I don't understand." Her eyes dart around the room, searching for answers that remain shrouded in mystery. "This isn't you. What happened?"

"Who I was before doesn't matter anymore." I step closer to her, feeling the thrill of fear emanating from her as she backs away. "There's no turning back now, not for me."

"Please, Fallon, tell me what's going on. We can work through this together." Her voice trembles, a testament to her unwavering loyalty and love.

"Isn't it clear? I've found my calling, Mia. I've found the power to take what's mine, to exact revenge on those who've wronged me." My voice drops to a low growl. "And I won't stop until I've had my fill."

"Fallon, please, think about what you're saying. This... these feelings aren't something to embrace. They'll consume you." Her eyes brim with tears, her expression pleading.

"Perhaps," I concede, my gaze never wavering from hers, "but I'm willing to take that risk."

"And you're acting weird. Are you okay? Can I get you a glass of water or something?" I watch as she shakes her head, disbelief etched on her face. She opens her mouth as if to say something more but hesitates, her words lost in the oppressive silence of the room.

"Fallon—"

"Enough!" I snap, my patience worn thin. "I don't need your help or your pity. I am in control here, and nothing will stand in my way."

"Fallon," she whispers, her voice barely audible above the oppressive silence that fills the room. "I'm scared for you."

"Then be scared." My words are cold, devoid of emotion. "But don't expect me to change because of it. This path is mine, and I'll walk it alone if I have to."

"Is that what you really want?" Her eyes, once bright with hope, now glisten with unshed tears.

"Maybe it is," I answer, my heart aching with a pain I refuse to acknowledge.

"Please," she murmurs, taking a step back, her expression a mixture of sorrow and resignation. "Don't let the darkness consume you."

"Perhaps," I concede, my gaze never wavering from hers, "but I'm willing to take that risk."

The shadows continue their relentless march across the floor, an endless dance of power and control. And though Mia remains rooted to the spot, a lone figure amidst the encroaching darkness, I know that this dance has only just begun.

Because there is no escaping the allure of the shadows, and I am far too gone to ever return to the light.

Finally, with a frown, Mia turns and leaves the room.

My eyelids grow heavy again until, once more, there is only darkness in front of me.

I snap to attention, loosely aware that I'm in the office. I seem to recall something about a knife, and some conversation with Mia.

"Mia?" I call, stepping out into the dimly illuminated hallway.

I hear footsteps off in the distance.

"Mia?" I repeat. Only she would work this late, other than myself of course.

I run in the direction of the noise and reach the back door just in time to see Mia in her pink and purple wool two-piece disappearing out of it. She's sniffling in a way that I would guess means she's been sobbing. Without stopping, she slips through the door and I hear the lock click behind her.

Chapter 34

Grave watches me with wary eyes, scanning for cracks in my veneer. The shift in my demeanor hasn't escaped his notice, and I sense he's suspicious. An electric current thrums between us, charged with an unsettling energy.

He searches my face, probing. "There's something different about you." His voice is a low rumble, gravelly with unease. "An edge I haven't seen before."

I'm impressed that he knows me so well he can see I was changed by a nightmare or whatever that was. And he's not beating around the bush. But his words make me feel defensive. "You wanted to be part of a cause where we sought revenge on people who deserve it, Grave. Now you have it."

A muscle ticks in his jaw, tension gathering in his shoulders. "This goes beyond revenge, Fallon. I don't like what I see. There's something about you that's increasingly off. It's like your boundaries keep shifting further and further out. I was okay with the candiru fish plan at the time, but the more I think about it, the uneasier I get. We disabled someone, Fallon. How much further are you willing to go? For years, I've felt like I was the one that needed to be reeled in. And that's the way it was meant to be. But now, it feels like it's becoming you that needs to be stopped before you go too far. Before you go somewhere impossible to come back from."

Irritation flares in my chest at his judgment. "People are dynamic, and they change over time. Including me. You don't get to decide who I become, Grave." I step into his space, tilting my chin up in defiance. "Only I can do that. And here it is. Here I am." I spread my arms wide, spinning slowly. "Take a good look, Grave. Do you still recognize me?"

He inhales sharply and closes his eyes, pain etched into the lines of his face. A wave of nausea washes over me as understanding dawns—he sees himself in the creature I'm becoming. The ghosts of his past are awakening from their slumber, stirred by the echoes of a familiar darkness.

When Grave opens his eyes again, shadows cling to their depths. His voice is rough with emotion, threaded with anguish and longing. "I don't want to lose you to these feelings, Fallon. Not like I lost myself."

"Don't be so dramatic, Grave," I say dismissively, "it doesn't suit you."

The next morning dawns pale and weak, a grim reminder of the shadows now lurking within. As I drive along the city streets, I glance at my reflection in my rear-view mirror, searching for traces of the woman I used to be. All I find is a stranger with dead, hollow eyes and a twisted smile.

When I get to work, Grave is waiting in my office. But today he's not flicking apple peels onto the floor or sitting with his feet on my desk. He's standing, almost nervous.

"You again? So early?" I smirk, trying to dissipate the tension that is way too much this early In the morning, especially pre-coffee.

He studies me for a long moment before speaking. "What we talked about yesterday... I want you to promise me something." His voice is strained, as if forcing the words out causes him physical pain.

I arch a brow. "And if I don't feel like promising you anything?"

Hurt flickers in his gaze, but he swallows it down. Resignation settles over his features as he realizes he can no longer reach the woman trapped inside this shell. "Don't lose yourself completely, Fallon. No matter how deep you descend into the darkness... there's always a way back."

"Maybe I don't want to come back, Grave," I say. "I've left that person behind. The less cynical person who truly believed in being able to change the world through good intentions. Now I've learned that in order to make a real difference you have to be ruthless, willing to do whatever it takes. That's how we really help these women, Grave. And that's how I'll fix things in my personal life."

"There was nothing wrong with how you were before, Fallon," Grave furrows his brow. "You're beginning to scare me."

"The only way out is through, Grave. There's nothing I need less than a scared partner or a cowardly confidant. I need bravery and ruthlessness." I meet his eyes, allowing him to glimpse the shadows writhing beneath the surface. "And there's no turning back now. You're either with me or you're not."

He frowns, and I see a battle play out on his normally blank face, a duel between loyalty and fear.

"Well, I'm here for you if and when you need me," he says, his voice uncharacteristically soft.

I guess loyalty wins today.

Chapter 35

FALLON

The phone rings, startling me from my restless sleep. It's Mia. She rarely calls, preferring to text, and when she does it's definitely not late at night. Something must be up.

I answer immediately.

Her choked sobs crackle through the line. "Fallon, I'm so sorry to call you this late. But I really need to talk to you..."

My senses sharpen. "Don't be sorry. Are you okay? What happened?"

"I went on a date tonight and it was a disaster. He wouldn't stop touching me, and he said the most disgusting things. I feel so violated." Her words tumble out in an anguished torrent.

Rage boils in my veins, searing away the last vestiges of drowsiness. My fists clench, nails biting into my palms.

"Did that bastard hurt you? Who was he? Where did you meet him? Where does he live? Tell me everything, Mia. Now."

She inhales sharply. "No, I got away before he could do anything worse. But Fallon, the way he looked at me..." A shuddering breath. "Like I was nothing but a piece of meat for him to devour. He seemed so nice online and then he was just so different in person and I—"

"I'll kill him." The words slip out unbidden, borne of a possessiveness bordering on obsession. Mia is my best friend and therefore mine to protect, and anyone who dares violate her will face my rage. My clients' fuckboys should fear my wrath, but someone who hurts my best friend can expect a whole new level of hell to rain down on them.

"No, please don't do anything rash!" Mia pleads. "I just needed to hear your voice. You always make me feel safe and I knew you'd understand. I'm home now and I'm going to be okay. I blocked his number and he doesn't know where I live or anything."

Her words pierce the raging storm inside me, a bolt of lightning amidst the darkness. My breathing slows as I focus on her, pushing aside my murderous thoughts. She comes before all else.

"I'm here for you, always." My voice is gentle. "Do you want me to come over?"

A soft sigh. "Would you? I don't want to be alone right now."

"Give me ten minutes." I hang up, throwing on the first clothes I grab and rushing out into the night.

The city streets blur as I race toward Mia, only one thought in my mind. To hold her close, keep her safe in my arms, and never let go. She is mine to look after, mine to protect.

And whoever this 'date' was is going to pay.

I burst through Mia's front door without knocking, frantic eyes scanning the room until they land on her curled up on the couch. She looks up at the sound, face pale and drawn, but a flicker of relief lights her eyes when she sees me.

I'm at her side in an instant, pulling her into a hug. "I'm here now. You're safe."

Her body relaxes against mine, tremors wracking her delicate frame. "Oh Fallon, it was awful. The way he spoke to me, the things he did..." A choked sob escapes her. "I felt so helpless, so afraid."

She recounts the story of how she met the guy at a bar, purposely choosing a public place seeing it was their first time meeting. But he'd insisted on this particular venue, and it soon became evident he'd picked it for a few different reasons. Dark, secluded, he knew the people who worked there. And overall it gave Mia a creepy vibe she couldn't put her finger on. She was terrified of leaving the guy alone with her drink, and when he cornered her in their booth in the dark corner of the bar and started making moves she was terrified.

Rage ignites anew, flames licking at my insides. I tighten my hold on Mia, struggling to contain the inferno threatening to consume me. She needs me, not the avenging fury I feel inside. I take a deep breath, then another, the tumult within settling into a slow, simmering burn.

Vengeance can wait, I'll just add him to the ever-growing list. Mia comes first. She always comes first. Or at least she used to.

I stroke her hair, murmuring soft reassurances as she cries.

When at last her tears subside, I gently lift her chin so our eyes meet. "You are the strongest, bravest, most incredible woman I know. No one, not a single soul, has the right to make you feel otherwise. Especially not that pathetic waste of flesh." My lips curl into a snarl at the thought of him, and I'm overcome with rage fueled by the protectiveness of a long-term friendship.

I want to tell her all the things I want to do to this man to avenge how he treated her. There are far too many men out there like this, who use a woman's desire and openness for love to take advantage of them. To be violent, predatory. And then the woman gets blamed for meeting up with him in the first place. Mia will not be one of those statistics.

I want to chop the man's fingers off so he can never text another woman with them. I want to remove his voice box so he can never speak to another woman. I want to slice off his feet so he can never walk to another date. I want to chop his head off so he can never think about another woman. But instead, I stay quiet. I have a feeling that's not what she needs to hear right now, even though my mind is planning it out in meticulous detail.

Mia places a hand on my arm, her touch feather-light. "Thank you for restraining yourself, Fallon. I don't need a protector fueled by vengeance. I've seen too much of that in you lately, and it's not what I need." Her gaze holds mine, deep blue eyes shimmering with emotion. "I just need my friend. Thank you for being here for me."

Whew. I made the right call there.

"There's nowhere else I would dream of being, unless it was teaching that guy a lesson. But he can wait." They all can wait.

Chapter 36

FALLON

The words of Grave and Mia echo in my head like a haunting melody, their concern for my well-being both touching and infuriating. While I don't believe they intended to double-team me, their combined words are like surround sound. And they have got me thinking, two of the people who care about me most, worrying about me like this. I sit on the edge of my bed, gripping the sheets until my knuckles turn white. They don't understand the darkness that's been eating away at me ever since Aksel betrayed me. But maybe they're right. Maybe I've let it consume me too much.

"Fuck," I mutter under my breath, feeling the weight of their concern bearing down on me. It's true—I've become a shadow of my former self, driven by vengeance and bitterness. I can't continue like this. It's not healthy.

I make a decision: I'll give Aksel another chance. Not because I trust him or because I've forgiven him—no, far from it. I still want to watch him suffer, make him pay for what he did to me. But I need to get close to him again, to find the perfect way to hurt him, just as he hurt me.

My thoughts drift to memories of our time together the other day, and the passion we shared. The way his hands felt on my body, the heat of his lips against mine. The way he felt inside me. The thought alone makes my pussy clench, a warm sensation beginning to spread through my core. It's undeniable—despite everything, I still crave him. Maybe I can use that to my advantage. I can use him sexually, keep him off-balance, and gain the upper hand. He'll let me in close, and I'll use that proximity to find his most vulnerable points. If he dares to hurt me again, I'll be ready.

I stand up, pacing my room as I plan my next move. My heart races with a mixture of excitement and fear, but I push the latter aside. Fear won't help me now. It'll only hold me back. And I refuse to be held back any longer.

"Game on, Aksel," I say, a dark smile spreading across my face. "Let's see if you can handle the fire you started. Let's see how well you can play."

Gritting my teeth, I unblock Aksel's number on my phone again. I hesitate for a moment before typing out the message, my fingers trembling with anticipation.

Fallon: Meet me at our old spot in the park tomorrow at noon.

I hit 'Send' before I can change my mind. Last time we met was about raw, primal passion. This time is about romance and rekindling old flames, at least on Aksel's part.

Fallon: I want to talk.

His response comes surprisingly fast.

Aksel: Didn't expect to hear from you, Fallon. But sure, I'll be there.

Fallon: Good.

I reply curtly, ending the conversation. I refuse to let him know how much this means to me or how desperate I am for control.

As I step into the park, the sun filters through the trees, casting dappled shadows over the lush grass. The warm air carries the scent of blooming flowers—roses, jasmine, and lavender—blending together in a dizzying fragrance. Ahead, I see the duck pond shimmering beneath the sunlight, water rippling as the ducks paddle around playfully.

"Fallon," Aksel greets me warmly, already waiting for me in the spot we used to hang out in as teenagers. His expression is guarded, but I can sense his curiosity burning just below the surface.

"Hey," I say, trying to sound casual, as if I didn't just invite him here with ulterior motives. I spread out the luxurious picnic blanket, the checkered deep red-and-white fabric contrasting against the vibrant green grass. "I brought food."

"Looks like quite the feast," he comments, eyeing the wicker basket I've packed with an assortment of meats, cheeses, fruits, and cut vegetables. There's also pâté, dips, and champagne flutes, just to make it feel a little more extravagant. If I'm going to trick this man into trusting me, this whole outing needs to seem legit. An ambience full of potential for reconnection and, one day, maybe even love. And Aksel is definitely one of those men who you can get to through his stomach, a true foodie.

"Sit down and eat," I insist, my tone leaving no room for argument.

He complies, sitting down across from me. We begin eating, exchanging small talk as we nibble on the food. It feels almost like old times, and I can't help but feel my resolve falter just a bit as I look into his eyes.

"Fallon," Aksel says softly, breaking the silence as he scrutinizes a piece of cheese. "Smoked gouda with cumin—nice. Speaking of which, this is all very pleasant and all, but why did you invite me here?"

"Can't I just want to spend time with you?" I deflect, avoiding his gaze. But that's only half the truth, and we both know it. "It didn't feel right to keep you blocked any longer. Especially after the... other night." I feel my cheeks redden.

"Maybe," he replies cautiously, clearly not convinced. "But this feels... different."

"Maybe it is," I admit, my eyes meeting his for a moment before I quickly look away again. My heart races in my chest, the familiar pull towards him growing stronger. "I just needed to see you, Aksel."

"Needed?" His eyes narrow, suspicion lacing his voice. "Or wanted?"

"Both," I confess, my voice barely audible. I hate how vulnerable I sound, but it's the truth. Despite everything, I still crave him—and maybe I'm starting to regain a crush on him, too. "Maybe it's time to move things along, to stop stagnating like we have been."

"Fallon, you know things can't go back to the way they were," he warns, looking at me with concern, and perhaps a tinge of sadness for the opportunity lost.

"Who said I want them to?" I fire back, my eyes locking onto his. The air between us crackles with tension—and something more dangerous. Desire.

"Then what do you want?" he asks, his voice low and intense.

"Right now?" I say, allowing a slow, wicked smile to spread across my lips. "I want to finish our picnic, enjoy this beautiful day, and forget about everything else—for just a little while."

As we finish the last bites of our picnic, I can't help but feel a strange mix of satisfaction and anticipation. Aksel's presence is intoxicating, and every moment spent with him only adds to the growing whirlwind of emotions I'm trying to keep in check.

"Want to go for a walk?" I suggest, as I pack away the remains of our feast.

"Sure," he replies, his voice hesitant but curious. I can tell he's wary, unsure of what I have planned.

We stand, and without thinking, I reach out and take his hand. The warmth of his touch sends a shiver down my spine, and I fight to suppress a smile as we begin to walk through the park. The lush grass feels soft beneath my feet, and the vibrant colors of the flowers lining the path seem to reflect the intensity of the emotions swirling within me.

It's exhilarating—walking with Aksel like this, hand in hand, feeling the connection between us grow despite the darkness that threatens to consume me. But I need to remind myself that this isn't just about romance, it's about revenge and protecting my heart.

"Fallon," Aksel says softly, pulling me from my thoughts. "Why did you really invite me here today?"

"I told you before," I reply, trying to sound casual. "I wanted to spend time with you."

"Right," he murmurs, clearly unconvinced. "But there's more to it than that, isn't there?"

"Maybe," I admit, unable to meet his gaze. "But right now, let's just enjoy the walk."

"Okay," he agrees, squeezing my hand gently. I can't help but focus on how comfortable my hand feels encased in his much larger palm, and how natural it feels to lazily stroll through the park together.

We continue on, passing by a serene duck pond where the water ripples with each movement of the swimming birds. I steal glances at Aksel, taking in the way the sunlight catches in his hair and the intensity of his eyes as he watches our surroundings. The desire to get closer to him, to feel his lips on mine, is overwhelming.

"Fallon," Aksel whispers, stopping in his tracks and pulling me close. I can feel his breath on my skin, and my heart races as I look up into his eyes—gorgeous gray eyes that seem to see straight through me.

"Kiss me," I whisper, unable to resist the magnetic pull between us any longer.

His lips meet mine in a tender, passionate kiss that sends shivers down my spine and sets my soul on fire. It's heady, intoxicating, and everything I've been craving since we last touched. As we break apart, panting and flushed, I know without a doubt that this moment will haunt me for days to come. The last time we met was primal, carnal lust. Just sex. But this is something way more. It's intense but gentle, tender but fierce.

"Fallon, what are we doing?" Aksel asks, his voice thick with emotion as we reach our cars, parked next to each other in the parking lot.

"I don't know," I admit, feeling more vulnerable than ever before. "But it feels right, doesn't it?"

"Maybe," he agrees hesitantly, his eyes searching mine for answers I can't provide.

With one last squeeze of our entwined hands, we part ways, both lost in a sea of confusion and unspoken desires. As I walk away from Aksel, I can't help but wonder if I'm making the biggest mistake of my life—or if I'm finally taking control of my destiny. I'm not sure where revenge factors into my relationship with Aksel, just that I want him.

Only time will tell.

Chapter 37

Fallon's touch lingers on my skin, her scent clinging to my shirt. The way her eyes pierced into mine over our picnic basket, her full lips curving into a smile that made my chest ache.

I can't stop thinking about her. About us. The push and pull between us, a dance as complicated as our history.

She wants this. I know she does. I see it in the way she looks at me, like I'm her salvation and damnation all at once. But there's something holding her back, a barrier I can't break through.

Maybe I never will.

Maybe the damage is already done. Years of resentment and heartbreak standing between us, an impenetrable wall. For all I know, she's just playing games, fucking with my head.

I slam a fist on my desk, rattling my laptop. I should focus on work, on the betrayals threatening to destroy my family's empire, but I can't concentrate. Can't stop wondering if we're doomed before we've even begun.

If Fallon will always see me as the boy who broke her heart, not the man trying to win her back, we don't stand a chance.

But if she really saw me, she'd see a man who would do anything for another chance.

I rake a hand through my hair and stare out the window into the gloom. The sky is as conflicted as my thoughts, patches of sunlight peeking through bruised clouds.

Just like Fallon lets me in before shutting me out again.

A cycle I'm desperate to break.

I stand abruptly, nearly toppling my chair. I need to see her, but first I need some advice from one of the only people I really trust... because I need to know if this can be saved before it slips through my fingers again.

Before I lose the only thing that's ever mattered. The only woman I've ever loved.

I meet Raine for lunch at our usual cafe, The Cheeky Beet, my leg jittering under the table. It's one of her favorite places in town, vegan and sustainable and various other bougie claims to fame even though she herself is quite down-to-earth. She arches a brow, reading me too well, like always.

"What's wrong?" she asks. "You look like you're about to crawl out of your skin. So it can be one of only two things. One of our siblings, or Fallon."

I take a deep breath and nod. "It's Fallon."

Understanding lights her eyes. She's the only one who knows the truth—the ugly history between me and the woman I can't stop thinking about. The one I'm desperate to win back.

"Did something happen?" Raine presses.

"We went on a date yesterday," I admit. "A picnic by the lake. It was very spontaneous and unexpected. Everything was perfect, but then..." I trail off, frustration gnawing at my insides. "We ended the date with a kiss and it was amazing. But I couldn't help waiting for her to shut down on me or pull away like I burned her. I kept waiting for her to tell me what new thing I did wrong."

"You didn't do anything wrong." Raine reaches across the table, squeezing my hand. "You can't undo the past, Aksel. No matter how much you wish you could. Fallon's hurting and it's going to take time for her to trust you again. It sounds like a romantic picnic at the park is a pretty good sign she's interested in opening back up to you."

"But what if there isn't enough time?" The question bursts out of me, laced with fear. "What if she can never get over what happened? Never forgive me? I still don't even know everything that happened from her perspective. What if she decides it's all too hard and just when I'm too far gone, she announces we're done?"

"Woah, woah, slow down there, bud," Raine smirks and puts her hand up like a stop sign. "You need to be patient with her." Her gaze is gentle but firm. "Fallon's not the same girl you knew back then. She's been through hell and it's going to take work to break down those walls she's built. But if you really care about her—if you're willing to understand where she's coming from—she will open up to you again. Guaranteed. It's human nature."

Her words hit their mark. Of course Fallon's changed. We both have, shaped by the years we spent apart. Years that hardened me and left invisible scars on the woman I love.

Scars I'm desperate to heal, if only she'll let me in.

"People are complex," Raine says softly. "The things we do, no matter how confusing, are often a reflection of our pain. Be gentle with Fallon. Listen to her. And don't give up. Not if she really matters to you."

She does. More than anything.

I meet Raine's gaze, resolve steeling my spine. "I won't give up on her. Not again."

Never again.

I return home after work, my mind spinning with Raine's advice. But as soon as I enter my study, my thoughts shift to the task at hand.

Kent and Isabella. Their connection gnaws at me, a loose thread I need to unravel.

Booting up my laptop, I dig into their backgrounds. It doesn't take long to find the connection my team somehow missed—five years ago, Kent and Isabella worked together at Storm Enterprises, a direct competitor to my family's company with strong ties to a rival local mafia organization. They left within months of each other to join King Industries.

How did we miss this? A knot forms in my gut as I consider the implications. Did they come to King Industries together with the intention to spy? Sabotage us from within?

My fingers curl into fists, rage simmering in my veins. If I find even a hint of betrayal, they'll both pay.

A chime interrupts my brooding. When I check my phone, my anger evaporates, replaced by a surge of warmth.

Fallon: Thinking of you. Hope your day's going well.

I stare at the message, reading it again and again, a smile teasing my lips. However brief, her words are a balm, easing my frayed nerves.

Before I can overthink it, I type a reply:

Me: You're always on my mind too, Fallon-y. My day is better now.

I test the waters by teasing her with the special nickname she used to hate, but that made her laugh by the time we eventually went out in high school. I want to say more, to tell her about Kent and Isabella's suspicious connection, my need to protect my family's company. But those worries can wait, and instead I keep things light and flirty. Right now, all I want is to lose myself in Fallon—in fantasies of her smile, the scent of her skin, the taste of her kiss.

A kiss I'm desperate to claim again, despite the demons lurking in our past. Demons I'll slay if it means a future with the woman who still holds my heart.

Chapter 38

FALLON

My phone beeps.

(Unknown number): Hey! Is this Fallon?

I typically ignore anonymous numbers, but something tells me I should pick this one up. After all, it could be a client referred to me by someone else.

Fallon: Yes. Who is this?

(Unknown number): Roxy! Roxy King! Remember me?

Do you remember me, she asks? Ha! As if I could forget Aksel's baby sister. We used to be fairly close back in high school, at least during the parts where Aksel and I were growing into a relationship. She's always been sweet, funny, a little rebellious. She's refreshing to my soul. But I wonder why she's reaching out to me now of all times. I haven't spoken with her in years.

Fallon: Roxy! Of course I remember you! How have you been? What's up?

Roxy: Okay, so I know this is a bit out of the blue, but, Fallon, would you like to have lunch with me?!

This is definitely unexpected. But, given I'm trying to get all the tea on Aksel and figure out what to do with him, this might be useful. And Roxy has always been super nice to me, so I figure there's no harm. Food with a fun person. I'm in.

Fallon: It's a bit of a surprise but it's great to hear from you! Sure, I'd love to catch up.

The moment I hit send, I realize I'm a little disarmed by Roxy's genuine warmth. It's a stark contrast to her rebellious nature, but I know she means it. I'm sure the connection between Aksel and me, a smoldering ember that refuses to be extinguished, has not gone unnoticed by his perceptive younger sister. And so she's reached out, offering an olive branch. Maybe she's being nosy, or perhaps protective of her brother. Or maybe he's using her as a messenger and she has something important to tell me. I just don't know. But I guess I'm about to find out.

Roxy: I haven't been to Rubio's for a while. You in?

I laugh when I read her text. Rubio's is an old school hangout from way back. A classic joint with an extensive comfort food menu and a chill vibe. It sounds like the perfect location for diffusing the tension that's building inside me at the thought of interacting with another member of the King family. Especially while everything's all up in the air with Aksel.

We figure out a time to meet that gives me just enough time to get across town.

The warmth of the restaurant embraces me, a stark contrast to the chill outside, its atmosphere pulsing with life. I take in the mingling scents of exotic spices and fresh herbs, my stomach growling in anticipation. Roxy's eyes dance with excitement as we slide into the cozy booth, our knees brushing against each other. The hum of conversation and clinking cutlery adds to my nerves, driving me into slight sensory overload.

"I thought this might be a blast from the past!" Roxy grins, her eyes twinkling. "Have you been here since you were in college?"

I shake my head, my fingers absently tracing the edge of the plastic-covered menu. "No, but it still looks amazing. Like it's finally entered the current decade but with the same nostalgic feel, if that makes sense." I laugh. "Gosh, more than half the menu is the same as it was back then. The prices have just tripled."

"Trust me, it's just the same," she assures me with a grin. "I don't know about you, but I'm starving."

As we peruse the menu, a subtle energy crackles between us, a pulsating anticipation that speaks of rekindled camaraderie. Our shared connection to Aksel serving as a foundation upon which something real can grow.

But I still don't know why she invited me here, and Aksel is still her brother. Beneath the surface, shadows linger. Memories of Aksel's past betrayals simmer within me, threatening to boil over at the slightest provocation. They're not Roxy's fault, so I push those thoughts away, determined to embrace this opportunity, hoping to find solace in the company of someone who understands the complexities of loving Aksel.

"Have you ever tried Moroccan food before?" she asks, her voice tinged with genuine curiosity. A small smile plays on her lips, making me wonder if she's already pictured my reaction to the unfamiliar cuisine. "They've added it to the menu fairly recently. They really do have everything here now."

I laugh. Rubio's is known for adding additional cuisines at an exponential rate, every time the owner takes a vacation somewhere, really, and I'm sure the food is not at all authentic, but nearly everything has always hit the spot.

"Can't say that I have," I admit, feeling the initial awkwardness begin to dissipate. "But I've been wanting to."

"Then you're in for a treat," Roxy grins, her eyes sparkling with mischief. She leans forward, her elbows resting on the table as we peruse the menu together. "Let's see... How about we start with some b'stilla and share a tagine?"

"Sounds delicious," I agree, following her lead as we place our order.

As we wait for our meal, the conversation flows easily between us. Roxy shares stories of her rebellious youth—sneaking out of the house, skipping school, and wild parties that would give any parent nightmares. I can't help but laugh at her antics, finding myself drawn in by her magnetic energy. A couple of her stories have me laughing so hard I feel happy tears forming in the corners of my eyes for the first time in a long time. It's a welcome reprieve from the darkness that has become all too familiar in recent times.

"Your turn," she says, her eyes twinkling with genuine interest. "Tell me something about yourself that no one else knows."

I hesitate for a moment, unsure of what to reveal. But then I remember her vulnerability, her willingness to share her own experiences, and decide to reciprocate with one of the more outlandish experiences I can think of. At least, one that doesn't involve her brother.

"Well, while I was in college, I accidentally became a phone sex worker. For like five minutes."

"Wait, you what?!" She cracks up laughing. "Tell me more, I need to know!"

"Well, I applied for a job and I expected it to be one of those standard telemarketing type things. It said I needed customer service skills and to be over 18 with a pleasant and professional phone manner. So I applied and got the job, and then they said 'just follow the script'. So I got on the phone and answered my first call. Sure enough, the script popped up and then I realized what I'd gotten myself into. I couldn't get through the call without blushing and laughing so hard I almost peed my pants!"

Roxy is laughing so hard she almost spits out her drink. "Oh my god. The great Fallon Dempsey, accidental teenage phone sex worker."

I laugh as well. "Right? Like nothing wrong with that profession at all. In fact, I think it could be quite fun. I just had no idea that's what I'd been hired to do. Could have used a warning. I thought I'd be asking people survey questions about cheeseburgers or appliances or something."

The conversation continues to flow easily. But as the lunch progresses, something shifts, and I feel familiar shadows clawing at the corners of my mind. I try to hide my concern, but Roxy, ever observant, seems to catch glimpses of the unsettling undercurrent that flows just beneath the surface of our conversation. When she innocently mentions a recent bad date, it strikes a chord within me and I find it hard to conceal my emotions. Yet another tale of a predatory, narcissistic man taking advantage of a woman who doesn't deserve it.

As we part ways, Roxy appears somewhat confused, her brows furrowed in concern. "Hey, sorry if I overstepped by reaching out. I just missed you and Aksel mentioned your name and I...".

As soon as she says the words, her hand flies across her mouth.

"Oh he did, did he?"

"Just something about a picnic. Said you guys had reconnected."

"Something like that," I say.

Of course, there's no problem with Aksel telling his sister stories about his life. They're close and always have been. Of course he'd mention me. I'm not sure why it makes me feel betrayed somehow, but I do. I retreat into the shadows of my thoughts, a reminder of the complexities that lie within me, hidden beneath layers of pain and vengeance.

"Are you okay, Fallon? You're great as ever. I've always loved spending time with you. But you seem a little different today."

I clear my throat and blink, trying to clear my head. "Guess I was just surprised by your invite, but it was really nice to see you. I hope we can do it again sometime."

We hug and part ways. I'm sure Roxy is just as confused by my mood as I am.

The bond forged over lunch may be fragile, but it's at least a start. An unexpected connection, born from shared experiences and a mutual care for the enigmatic man who binds us together. The difference is, I'm the only one contemplating the ticket to his downfall.

Chapter 39

AKSEL

The pulsating beat of punk music vibrates through my bones as Roxy and I slide into a corner booth at Mirabella. The trendy atmosphere wraps around us like an electric embrace, the walls adorned with abstract art that screams 'take a picture in front of me and slap me on Instagram'. Animated conversations fill the air, the vibrant energy of the bustling restaurant threatening to swallow me whole.

"Isn't Mirabella fabulous?" Roxy gushes, her pride at securing us a reservation at the newest 'it' spot evident in her wide grin. "It's the latest hot spot in town. All the movers and shakers dine here."

I raise an eyebrow, taking in the hipster crowd and chaotic ambience. I typically prefer quiet venues for our sibling meet-ups, but I can't help but crack a smile at her contagious enthusiasm. "You certainly know how to pick 'em, Roxy. I was thinking more along the lines of a cozy place, but I can see the appeal. It's fun in here."

Roxy's eyes twinkle with excitement, and she shrugs nonchalantly. "Come on, Aksel, live a little! We're in the heart of the city, and Mirabella is where everyone who's anyone hangs out. Plus, the food is supposed to be out of this world."

I chuckle, knowing full well that resistance is futile when it comes to Roxy's flair for the trendy. "Alright, I'm fine with staying here. But if I get lost in the sea of hipsters, you're navigating us out, little sister. I'll leave a trail of kale so we can remember our path."

As we peruse the eclectic menu, I can't help but feel a bit out of my element. Mirabella is a far cry from the low-key spots I'm used to, but Roxy's enthusiasm continues to propel me through the experience. The girl knows how to make a splash, and I can't deny the allure of stepping outside my comfort zone, especially with my baby sister who I adore.

"Hey, Aksel," she says, snapping me out of my thoughts. "You're not zoning out on me, are you? I know how you get when we're at home, but this is different."

I smirk, appreciating her keen perception. "Don't worry, Roxy. I'm present and accounted for." It's true—despite the sensory overload, I find myself more focused than ever, eager to make the most of our time together.

We order a couple of daring dishes, each with exotic ingredients that promise a culinary adventure. I can't help but feel a thrill as we dive into conversation, the punk music setting the perfect backdrop for our banter.

The sizzle of dishes being prepared in Mirabella's open kitchen fills my ears as I watch Roxy animatedly recount her lunchtime escapade. The scents of exotic spices and seared meats waft through the air, a tantalizing accompaniment to the restaurant's chic atmosphere.

"...and then Fallon just went all serious on me," Roxy says, spearing a bite of her quinoa salad. "Like, out of nowhere. Did I miss something?"

"She's been, um... preoccupied lately."

"Okay, so you're aware of this whole way she's acting? Tell me everything," Roxy says, leaning in conspiratorially. "What's going on with her? What kind of weird dark mission is she on?"

I pause, my fork hovering mid-air as I gather my thoughts. "I wish I knew, Roxy. All I can say is that she's become more...intense lately. Like she's got some unfinished business with certain people. Including me. It feels like there's a side of her I never knew existed, and it's unraveling right in front of me. When she'll take the time to meet with me, that is."

"Women, huh?" Roxy muses, taking a thoughtful bite of her quinoa salad. "Well, whatever it is, she's lucky to have you by her side. Just give her time. She'll open up when she's ready."

I nod, grateful for her vote of confidence. "You're right. I just hope she realizes she doesn't have to face whatever it is alone."

Roxy grins, sipping her artisanal sparkling water. "And that's where you come in, big brother. You've always been fixated on her and you always will be. It sounds like you're becoming a couple even though you're both in denial. I took her to Rubio's by the way," she grins.

"Oh my god, you take her to the best place in the city that is relaxed and the food is great and nobody is pretentious. And you bring me *here*? Gee thanks!"

"This is what big brothers are for." Roxy beams, a knowing glint in her eye, and my sense of indignation immediately dissipates.

As Mirabella hums with activity, I can't shake the feeling that there's more to Fallon's story than meets the eye. Even my sister, who hasn't seen her for years, picked up on it over only one brief meeting. But one thing remains certain: I won't let her face the darkness alone. For better or worse, I'm in this with her, and together, we'll find our way through the tangled web.

Chapter 40

AKSEL

The dim light casts shadows on the bedroom walls, creating a sinister ambiance. I watch as Fallon paces back and forth, her eyes ablaze with fury, her fists tightly clenched. My heart aches at the sight of her–this bitter, vengeful woman who's replaced the sweet, caring girl I once knew.

"Those bastards won't get away with it," she spits, her voice filled with venom. "I'll make sure they pay for what they've done."

I can't help but feel a pang of guilt for my part in driving her to this dark place. Though I know we both share the blame for the events that have transpired, I can't shake the feeling that I should have done more to protect her.

"Fallon," I say, my voice barely audible above the storm raging inside me. "We need to talk."

She stops pacing, her gaze locking onto mine. The fire in her eyes is momentarily replaced by confusion, but she says nothing, waiting for me to continue.

"Look at what's happening to us, Fallon," I plead, trying to keep my own anger in check as I confront the changing dynamics within our relationship. "We're not the people we used to be. This obsession with revenge... it's tearing us apart."

"Maybe it's the only thing keeping me together," she snaps, her jaw set in a hard line.

"Is that really what you believe?" I ask, desperately trying to reach her. "Or are you just afraid of facing the pain and moving on?"

"Fuck you, Aksel," she hisses, turning away from me. "You have no idea what I've been through."

"Neither do you," I retort, my frustration rising to the surface. "We've both suffered, Fallon. We've both lost something. But this... this isn't the way to heal. We can't keep letting our anger and our need for vengeance control us."

"Maybe you're right," she concedes, her voice barely a whisper. "But I don't know how to let it go."

"Neither do I," I confess, the weight of my own emotions threatening to crush me. "But we can try, Fallon. We can try to find a way through this darkness together."

"Can we really?" she questions, tears brimming in her eyes as she finally turns back to face me.

"I hope so," I say softly, reaching out to take her hand in mine. "Because I can't bear to lose you, Fallon Dempsey. Not like this."

The room is silent as we stand there, holding onto each other amidst the chaos consuming us both. But for now, at least, we dare to believe that maybe–just maybe–we have a chance to save not only ourselves but whatever's left of the love that once bound us together.

I wake with a start and realize I was dreaming. Of course I'd be dreaming of Fallon, that's no surprise. But despite only spending limited time with her lately, I feel inextricably connected. Like she is part of my soul. But I still don't know if I can trust her and this new edge to her. I know she blames me for things left unsaid. I still don't know what I can do to fix it. All I know is awake or asleep, I can't get her off my mind.

The dim glow of a single lamp casts long shadows across my study as I sit in contemplation. The room, adorned with shelves and walls of souvenirs collected from my travels, mostly old books and artwork, feels both comforting and stifling. My mind is heavy with the weight of uncertainty that hangs in the air.

I lean back in my worn leather chair, fingers steepled in front of me. My gaze fixes on the lamp's flickering bulb, lost in thought. The room is silent, except for the distant hum of a computer's processor. Outside, a faint drizzle begins to tap against the windowpane, mirroring my inner turmoil.

The brewing situation with Kent Farrington and Isabella Warner gnaws at me, like an insidious undercurrent threatening to pull me into treacherous waters. Espionage—a word that once felt alien in my family's tight and impenetrable circle, now whispers through the corridors of my thoughts. My mind, sharp as a dagger in most circumstances, works tirelessly to piece together the puzzle of deceit and hidden motives. We're so careful about who we hire. We do such thorough due diligence. How could we—I—have missed something so obvious, and let the enemy in so close?

All I know is I'm experiencing an increasing inability to trust those around me. My eyes, normally clear and perceptive, now bear a shadow of doubt. I'm not sure who is an ally, a pawn, or my downright enemy.

The rain outside intensifies, tapping on the window with a relentless urgency. I, however, remain still—immersed in the intricate dance of shadows playing on the walls. It's like a chess game, but I don't know who I'm playing against.

Closing my eyes as the rain continues to drum against the window, I take a deep breath, bracing myself for the challenges that lie ahead.

Chapter 41

FALLON

I step out of the Uber, smooth my dress, and stare up at the imposing Dempsey mansion. My stomach twists into familiar knots. I'd normally have driven here, but the thought of getting through tonight without whiskey or copious amounts of wine is too much to bear. Another week, another mandatory family dinner designed to shred my nerves.

I take a deep breath and climb the steps, bracing for impact. The shadows in my soul stretch longer each day, darkening my ties to this family. While I always felt like an outsider, this place still felt like a semi-friendly port in the storm for me, but no more. That ship has sailed, leaving roiling, choppy waves in its wake.

My heels click on the marble as I enter the grand foyer. Zara's piercing gaze slices into me. Before I can blink, she's sinking her claws in.

"That dress is far too revealing, Fallon. Have some modesty."

I clench my jaw and fire back. "Says the woman wearing a miniskirt. We're the same age, Zara. Remember that."

She's such a bitch. I knew I couldn't trust her when she tried to act motherly the other day. It's almost like she's replaced me in the family dynamic, and I'm the unwanted one now.

Zara's smug expression sours. One point to me. But my victory is fleeting. Surviving this dinner will require nothing short of a miracle.

I steel myself and walk into the lion's den, braced for the next attack. There's nobody I would like to see less than Link. My relationships here swing like a pendulum, shifting from stable to chaotic in a heartbeat, especially with him. But I'll be damned if I let any of them see me sweat.

Game on.

I take my seat at the long mahogany table, scanning my brothers' faces. Fenton offers me a smile, but it doesn't reach his eyes. The others barely acknowledge my presence.

Cheston clears his throat, a mischievous glint in his eyes, clearly ready to break the tension. "Folks, brace yourselves. I have an announcement." He pauses for dramatic effect. "Rayner and I are engaged!"

The room erupts into a mix of cheers and applause. But my lips stay sealed. I eye Cheston suspiciously as he grins like the cat who caught the canary.

Rayner Bellamy. Stunning, twenty years his junior, and tied to a family with shadowy secrets. She's the belle of any ball she attends, but something about her rings false to me.

Fenton raises his glass. "Well done, Cheston! It's about time. Now bring Rayner to these dinners so we can meet our future sister-in-law."

My gut twists. Fenton just gave his blessing without a second thought. But I know better than to ignore my instincts. Rayner's dazzling smile hides something dark. I can feel it in my bones. Or maybe I'm just highly suspicious of everyone these days. I make a mental note to look into her further.

For now, I'll stay silent, biding my time. But the truth has a way of rising to the surface. And when it does, no one will be cheering. Least of all Cheston. I'll be fucked if someone else enters this family and is more accepted than me.

As dinner continues, the celebrations drone on, all smiles and laughter around me. Champagne is brought out for everyone to toast Cheston and the absent Rayner. But my mood remains stormy, thoughts churning like violent waves.

A presence appears beside me. Link. The thorn in my side I can never fully remove. I sigh, making it as loud and exaggerated as possible.

He clears his throat. "Fallon, about the investigator...I'm sorry. I called them off. I didn't mean to invade your privacy like that."

Skepticism etches itself across my face. As if mere words could make up for his trespass.

"You think an apology cuts it, Link?" I quirk a brow. "I need action. Stay the hell out of my business unless you want me digging up your skeletons, too."

His eyes flash with anger, followed by maybe a flicker of concern. I wonder what he's hiding that has him slightly ruffled. "Don't threaten me, Fallon. I'm trying to make peace here."

"Peace? Is that what you call spying on me?" I retort. "Here's some advice. Don't poke your nose where it doesn't belong."

"Who I investigate is none of your concern," he snarls.

"It sure as hell is when it's me," I shoot back.

We trade verbal blows, voices rising. The others pretend not to notice, but the tension in the room is palpable.

Finally, I've had enough. I grab my purse and storm toward the door, emotions churning inside me like a hurricane.

Over my shoulder I call back, "Stay out of my life, Link. Or you'll regret it."

I slam the door behind me, cutting off his shouted reply.

Dark thoughts swirl as I tap at my phone, selecting the Uber that promises to get here fastest and drive me off into the night. "As quick as you can, please," I say to the driver as I collapse into the back seat. I grip my purse tightly as we speed down the dark road, putting distance between us and the Dempsey mansion. The further I get, the more my anger simmers.

Link's fixation on me remains a mystery, one I intend to unravel. Why can't he let me be? What drives his relentless need to dig into my life? It's like he's obsessed with me in the worst possible way. And my other brothers always take his side, no matter what.

Tonight was no different. I confronted Link about the private investigator he sicced on me again, and Fenton jumped to his defense. "He's just looking out for you," Fenton said. As if spying on me is an act of care. If I did that to any of them, they would one-hundred percent guaranteed lose their shit.

They're all blind to Link's issues. But I see the darkness in him as clearly as my own reflection. The way his eyes follow my every move, cold and calculating. How he uses my family against me, turning them to his side. He's manipulating them, even if they can't see it. Just like he manipulates everyone around him with his polished charm and easy smiles. But it's all an act. Underneath, he's twisted in a way I can't comprehend.

I fully intend on digging up his skeletons. There must be a bunch. But for now, getting distance from him is all I can do to keep my sanity.

Somehow I'll find the truth. About Link, about Rayner, about all the secrets threatening to destroy this family. I won't stop until justice is served. Until finally I feel whole and part of something. If I need to destroy other people in the process, so be it. The Dempsey family web is stretched thinner than ever, ready to rupture. But I won't be the one left dangling when it breaks.

My hands ache from clenching the armrest. I force myself to relax and take a deep breath. Getting worked up over Link will accomplish nothing right now. I need to be smart if I'm going to uncover the truth. All I know is, whatever his endgame is, I'll be ready. My days of being a pawn in his schemes are over. Now it's time to turn the tables, before his darkness consumes everything I care about.

I'm through playing defense. If it's a war Link wants, then it's war he'll get.

Chapter 42

AKSEL

Fallon looks like sin in heels when she steps through my door, all long legs and fire under those ocean eyes. She's wearing a short skirt that barely covers her butt, and a crop top that reveals a tantalizing hint of her stomach and lower back. I'm still thrilled and shocked that she accepted my invitation to come over for dinner. I'd figured there was a ninety percent chance she would decline, and an even higher chance she'd get last-minute cold feet. But here she is, looking like temptation itself.

The scent of roast chicken and garlic bread wafts around us as a smile tugs at the corner of her mouth. "Trying to convince me to fall for you with food, Aksel?"

"Just giving you a taste of the good life." I pause, and then admit the obvious. "I didn't make it myself. Trust me, it's better that way."

She smirks, and then her gaze drifts over the table, the wine, the candles. There's a story there, behind those eyes, but I don't push.

We sink into easy conversation over the meal, trading jokes and stories. For a while it's like we're the only two people in the world. Like nothing else matters but her smile, her laugh.

When silence falls it's comfortable. Familiar. She leans back in her chair, studying me. "You always know how to make a girl feel special."

Heat flares in my gut at the raw vulnerability in her tone. I reach across the table and lace my fingers through hers. "You deserve to feel special every damn day, Fallon."

Her breath catches and for a second I think she might cry. Then she's rounding the table, sliding onto my lap, and kissing me like her life depends on it.

My hands find her hips, and I grip her tight enough to leave bruises as she grinds against me. The world narrows to the taste of her mouth, the feel of her body against mine.

After a heady make-out session, she returns to her seat and smiles at me from across the table, her lipstick and eyeliner slightly smudged, and her hair mussed, in a way that makes me want to rip her clothes off and take her right there, tonight's hired waitstaff be damned.

Tonight I'm going to show her just how special she is. And if by the end of it she's too wrecked to stand, I'll consider it a job well done.

Because a woman like Fallon Dempsey deserves to be worshiped. And I plan on spending all night on my knees.

For dessert, the private chef appears with a pavlova, Fallon's ultimate weakness. I've hit the sweet spot, and Fallon's momentarily distracted from whatever's got her in a twist.

The chef sets the dessert down with a flourish, presenting it like a work of art. Meringue nests filled with fresh fruit and slightly sweetened whipped cream, and dolloped with the sour and sweet tang of passionfruit pulp.

Fallon's eyes go wide, a smile lighting up her face. "You remembered."

"How could I forget?" I pour two glasses of moscato, and hand one to her. "To new beginnings... to this..."

Her smile deepens into something tender that makes my chest ache. She clinks her glass against mine. "To this..."

We dive in, Fallon closing her eyes on the first bite, a soft sound of pleasure escaping her. Watching her enjoy it is almost better than eating it myself.

Almost.

The sweet-tart burst of berries and passionfruit, the crunchy outside and fluffy inside of the meringue, melts on my tongue. But nothing compares to the warmth in my chest seeing that look of bliss on Fallon's face.

After dessert, I suggest we switch gears. I top off our glasses and take Fallon's hand. "Come on."

She follows without question as I lead her over to the lounge area, dimly lit and cozy. A fire crackles in the fireplace, casting a warm glow over the space. The vibe is just perfect, and the connection between us goes from electric to magnetic.

"This is nice." She settles into the cushions, tucking her feet under her.

"I thought you might want to relax and unwind." I sit beside her, close enough that our thighs touch.

Her smile is soft, a little sad. She stares into the fire, the flames dancing in her eyes. "You always know just what I need."

"What can I say, I'm intuitive." I bump her shoulder playfully.

She bumps me back, the sadness fading into something lighter. "My knight in shining armor?"

"Hardly. Dented armor maybe." I curl an arm around her shoulders, pull her in against me. "But more than anything, just a guy who cares very much about you. Who wants you to be happy."

She rests her head on my shoulder with a contented sigh. "I am happy. Here. With you."

Her words ignite something warm in my chest. I tilt her chin up, gaze into those endless blue eyes. "Yeah?"

"Yeah." She wets her lips, and I'm gone. I capture her mouth in a searing kiss, all the desire I've been holding back unleashed in the span of a heartbeat.

She kisses me back hungrily, hands tangling in my hair. The sweet ache between my legs intensifies into a raging inferno. I slide my hands under her shirt, savoring the feel of her silken skin under my palms.

She arches into my touch with a soft moan that goes straight to my cock. I trail kisses along her jaw, down the pale column of her throat.

"Aksel." My name on her lips is pure sin.

I drag my mouth back to hers, kiss her deeply. She shifts to straddle my lap, and grinds against the hard ridge in my jeans.

A growl rumbles in my chest. I grip her hips and thrust up to meet her. The friction is maddening, not nearly enough. I need to feel her, skin to skin, no barriers between us.

She seems to read my mind, tugging at my shirt. "Off. Now."

I tear the shirt over my head and toss it aside. Her hands roam my chest, setting my blood on fire.

"You're overdressed," I tell her, reaching for the hem of her shirt.

She lifts her arms as I peel the shirt off. I take in the sight of her, pale skin and black lace, desire slamming into me.

"So beautiful." I trace the edge of her bra with a fingertip, along the swells of her breasts.

A shiver runs through her and she moans. "Touch me, Aksel. Please."

I unclasp her bra, bare her to my gaze. "As you wish." I cup her breasts, thumbs teasing her nipples.

She cries out, rocking against me. The ache between my legs becomes nearly unbearable. My cock is rigid, straining against my jeans.

I claim her mouth again in a searing kiss as my hands explore every inch of her. The world outside this room ceases to exist. There is only her, only this, only us.

I trail kisses down her neck, along her collarbone. Her breath comes in gasps as I close my mouth over one nipple, teasing her with my tongue.

Her fingers curl into my hair. "Oh god, Aksel."

I lavish the same attention on her other breast, savoring her sounds of pleasure. My cock throbs, impossibly hard. I've never wanted anything as much as I want her.

Sliding lower, I peel off her skirt and panties in one smooth motion. She's bare before me, flushed and needy.

"So wet for me already," I murmur, sliding a finger through her slick folds.

She whimpers. "Please, I need—"

"I know exactly what you need." I settle between her thighs and draw her clit into my mouth. "To be worshiped the way you deserve."

"Ah!" Her back arches off the couch as I feast on her. One hand fists in my hair, the other clutching at the couch cushion.

I slide two fingers inside her, crooking them just so. She shatters with a cry, inner walls clamping down. I don't stop, relentless, devouring her through the tremors of her orgasm.

Her breaths come in ragged gasps. "Oh god, Aksel, please..."

I glance up at her, a wicked grin on my lips. "I'm nowhere near done with you yet."

I grab a silk rope from the side table, swiftly binding her wrists together.

Her eyes widen, pupils blown dark with desire. "What are you—?"

"Shh." I silence her with a kiss, tangling my tongue with hers. "You're at my mercy now."

A shiver runs through her, arousal spiking. She's completely under my control, and we both know she loves it.

I trail a hand down her body, watching her squirm against her restraints. "So responsive," I murmur. "So desperate for me."

She whimpers, tugging at the rope. "Please, Aksel..."

"All in good time." I grasp her hips, flipping her onto her stomach. Her ass is lifted, an invitation I can't refuse.

I spank her once, twice, leaving faint red marks on her skin. She gasps, pushing back for more.

My cock is granite, straining for release. I can't wait any longer.

Gripping her hips, I thrust into her slick pussy. We moan in unison. She's scorching, pulsing around me.

I drive into her with quick, deep strokes. The rope must be biting into her wrists, but she only urges me on.

"Harder," she gasps. "God, yes, fuck me harder Aksel!"

I pound into her, fingers digging into her hips. The coil of heat in my gut tightens unbearably. I'm close, so close—

My release hits me like a tidal wave, wrenching a shout from my throat. I spill into her, thrusts turning erratic as I ride out the tremors.

Breathless, I collapse beside her and undo the rope with fumbling fingers. She immediately curls into my arms, gazing up at me with a soft smile.

"That was incredible," she murmurs.

I brush the hair back from her face, struck by the depth of feeling she inspires. "You're incredible."

Freed from her restraints, Fallon gazes up at me with a sweet smile. "I didn't expect this. I didn't know how this was going to go, but I'm glad I came. You're really something special, you know?"

Her words hit me like a punch to the gut, but the punch is made of butterflies. I'm not used to this—this intimacy, this bone-deep caring. It terrifies me.

For a moment, I'm worried she might run off, but she stays curled up next to me on the couch.

I tense, waiting for her to bolt. But she only nuzzles closer, draping an arm over my chest.

My heart stutters. I wrap her in my arms, pressing a kiss to her hair.

She's not leaving. The realization washes over me in a warm wave.

I don't know what this is between us or where it will lead. But for now, for tonight, she's here. And that's enough.

"Stay," I whisper.

A soft smile curves her lips. "I'm not going anywhere."

The words echo in my mind as I drift off to sleep, still holding her close. Stay. She's really staying.

I wake slowly, senses swimming back online one by one. The warmth of her body curled against mine. The soft sound of her breathing. The citrusy coconut scent of her shampoo.

My eyes blink open to find her gazing up at me, lips curving in a sleepy smile. "Morning." We seem to have made it from the couch to the bed, although I can't remember how we got here.

I glance at the clock. "Well, 2am isn't quite morning." I brush a stray lock of hair from her face, struck anew by her beauty. "How are you sleeping?"

"Best sleep I've had in ages so far." Her smile widens, turning impish. "Must have been all the exercise."

Heat floods my cheeks. "Minx."

She laughs, the sound like music to my ears. "You love it."

I catch her chin, tilting her face up to mine. "I love you."

The words slip out before I can stop them. I tense, heart pounding, as her eyes widen. Shit. Too soon. I've ruined—

Then she surges up and kisses me, effectively cutting off my panicked thoughts. I groan into her mouth, clutching her close. She kisses me with a fierce tenderness that leaves me breathless.

When she finally pulls back, her eyes are bright. "I think you're quite alright yourself, Aksel King."

Joy explodes in my chest, nearly painful in its intensity. I crush her against me, burying my face in her hair to hide the sheen of tears in my eyes. She loves me, or she's getting close.

After a long moment, she nudges me onto my back and straddles my hips, her hair tumbling around her face in a riot of curls.

"Round two?" she asks with a wicked grin.

I grip her hips, heat already pooling low in my gut. "Thought you'd never ask."

She leans down to nip at my lower lip, eyes gleaming. "Let's see if we can outdo last night, shall we?"

A laugh rumbles in my chest. "Challenge accepted."

And then she's kissing me again, and I lose myself in her once more.

Chapter 43

AKSEL

The morning sun burns through my eyelids. I stretch, a lazy smile spreading across my face. The warmth radiating from what feels like a body curled into my side tells me Fallon stayed the entire night.

My contentment evaporates when I open my eyes to find rumpled sheets and an indentation in the mattress where she should be, only a pillow remaining in her place.

What the hell?

The clock reads 7:23 AM. Too early for her to be up and about, especially after the exertions of last night and how long round two took, because that was magical. I grab my phone, but there are no messages.

A sour taste floods my mouth as I throw back the covers. She left without a word, like I'm nothing but a means to an end. I thought we had something more.

Damn it, Fallon.

Fallon

The sun peeks over the horizon, its golden rays chasing my heels as I dart down the street away from Aksel's stylish high-rise. My chest burns from the brisk pace, but I can't slow down. Can't think. Can only feel.

Feelings I have no intention of examining.

I fumble with my key in the lock of my front door, hands shaking. The lock tumblers click into place and I stumble inside, sagging against the heavy wood.

Aksel was supposed to be a distraction. A way to turn off my brain for a sweet night while I used the opportunity to find out how to take him down. Instead, he's awakened something inside me, a yawning chasm of longing and need I've kept carefully contained. It was one thing having rough sex to mirror the primal no-strings-attached interludes I've long used as a distraction and a way to numb my feelings. But last night? The way he looked at me, the way he worshiped my pussy with his mouth, his hands, his cock. That was much more than just a physical act. It was mental, spiritual. Not to mention he used the L word, although, to be fair, he seemed as taken aback by that as I was.

I shake my head and try to push the feelings away. No. I will not go down that road again. I have too much at stake.

With a frustrated growl, I shove from the door and stomp toward the shower. Time to wash away the remnants of Aksel's touch and refocus on what really matters.

Doing right by my clients, and getting back at anyone who's ever hurt me.

The spray of hot water does little to ease the turmoil in my mind. I scrub at my skin as if I can wash away the memory of Aksel's hands, his lips, and the low timbre of his voice whispering wicked promises against my ear.

It's no use. I can still feel him, branding me from the inside out.

I slam my fist into the tiled wall, relishing the spike of pain. Anything to distract from the maelstrom of emotions threatening to drown me.

When I emerge from the shower, skin raw and knuckles bruised, a single text lights up my phone.

Aksel: Everything okay? You left in a hurry. I thought maybe we could get breakfast?

My throat tightens at the casual intimacy, the unspoken expectation that there will be more between us than a single night. That's a complication I don't need.

I type a quick response, hoping to nip this in the bud before it has a chance to bloom into something messy and painful. Something that will only end in heartbreak.

Me: Sorry, work emergency. Rain check?

It's not entirely a lie. My work—the business my father is so determined to see fail—must come before anything personal. Before anyone personal. I have too much riding on my success to be distracted by a man, no matter how well he makes me forget my troubles.

Aksel: No worries, duty calls. I totally get it. Let me know if you need anything x

I read into his words, searching for some hidden meaning, but find only polite concern. Damn him for being so practical, so understanding. With a sigh, I toss the phone onto my bed and continue to get ready. I don't deserve his concern and have no intention of reciprocating.

Now dressed for the day in one of my signature work outfits—never a suit but always stylish—armor against the world, I stare at my reflection. The woman gazing back at me is a stranger, with hard edges and cool indifference masking the tempest inside.

Good. Just the image I need to project. Emotions are a liability I can ill afford.

The time for distractions is over. It's time to get back to work.

I walk into the office, steeling myself against the curious glances and whispers sure to follow. Of course, nobody knows I spent the night at Aksel's, but I know, and it's making me paranoid. Rumors spread quickly in this place, and the fact I ended up half an hour late to work despite being notoriously punctual, is only going to get tongues wagging.

Let them speculate. As long as the work gets done, their opinions matter little.

Still, unease settles in my stomach at the thought of my personal life as office fodder. The echo of laughter, mocking and cruel, resonates in my memory. A reminder of the price paid for weakness. Trust, already a fragile thread in my world, feels like it's unraveling.

Never again.

One of my junior team members, Olivia, rushes over, worry etched into her features. "Fallon, I've been trying to reach you all morning. There's been a problem with the scheduling for the upcoming advanced program, and—"

I hold up a hand, cutting her off. "Handle it. That's what I pay you for, isn't it?" I snap, my voice sharp, no effort made to hide my irritation. "To deal with these issues so I can focus on the important things?"

She swallows hard, hurt flashing in her eyes before nodding. "Of course, my apologies."

Remorse pinches at my conscience as she walks away, but I shove it aside. I can't afford remorse or apologies. Not now.

Maybe not ever.

The unsettling feeling of not knowing who I can trust settles in, making me question the motives of those around me. How deep does the rot go? Have more than just a few minor scheduling conflicts arisen in our upcoming course catalog? Can I even trust these people I surround myself with each day, or are they part of some sinister plot designed to take me down?

Paranoia begins to take root, insidious tendrils that threaten to choke out the fragile bloom of trust I've somehow managed to nurture. I can't help but wonder who else might wish to see me fail.

Chapter 44

FALLON

The office meeting room glows amber, shadows dancing across Mia's freckled face. My heart pounds. I have to tell her. About one of the times. She doesn't need to know about the first time.

I suck in a breath. "I spent the night with Aksel."

Mia's brows lift, a flicker of something dark in her eyes. Then her lips curve. "Oh, really? How was it?"

Her tone's too casual, like she's asking about the weather. My fingers curl into fists. "It was...good. Different."

I scan her face, but she's shuttered tight. My chest aches. After being friends for so long, and after so many years of closely working together, I can usually read her, but now...

"Well, that's great." She stands, grabbing her jacket. "I should get going. Early day tomorrow."

"Mia, wait." I jump up, catching her arm. "Are we okay?"

She smiles, but it doesn't reach her eyes. "Of course. Why wouldn't we be?" She pulls from my grip.

"I don't know. You're acting strange." I glance at her with concern.

"Don't be silly." She shrugs into her jacket, avoiding my gaze. "I want you to be happy, Fallon. You deserve that."

"But—"

"Congratulations." She brushes past me.

"For sleeping with my ex boyfriend?" I quirk a brow.

"No," she shakes her head. "For moving on."

My eyebrow raises even higher. She's being so cryptic.

Mia, usually an open book, now seems to have chapters I can't access. Her response is casual, almost indifferent. "Well, that's what you wanted, right? To move on."

"Um, I guess?"

"Well, then I'll be more specific. Congratulations for moving on and going back to remake the same mistakes all over again."

My throat tightens. She wrenches open the door, a blast of chill air rushing in.

I stagger after her. "Mia!"

But she's already halfway down the path, dissolving into the night. "Your life, your choices," she calls as she disappears from view.

A sob rises in my chest. She's gone. Maybe she was never really there for me at all.

After freezing in place for a moment, I chase after her. I can't have someone else important in my life just up and leave. It's too much to bear. I catch up with her right beside her car.

"Mia, are you not okay with this?"

She offers a nonchalant shrug. "Why wouldn't I be? Like I said, it's your life, your choices."

I frown. She's avoiding the question, hiding behind evasions. This isn't like her. "Come on, Mia. Talk to me."

She sighs, raking a hand through her hair. "I'm fine, really. You don't need to worry about me."

"Too late for that." I fold my arms. "Spill."

Her lips thin. She stays silent for so long I think she won't answer. Then she says quietly, "Maybe I'm not ready to move on yet."

My heart stutters. "What do you mean?"

She looks away. "Nothing. Forget I said anything."

"I can't do that." I step closer, searching her face. "Mia, please talk to me."

Her eyes shine with tears she won't shed. She whispers, "Watching you with him...it hurts, okay?"

The air feels heavy with unspoken words. I sense a distance growing between us, a wedge driven by something unsaid. I press on, "Mia, seriously, what's going on? You're acting strange."

Mia hesitates, her eyes avoiding my gaze. "It's nothing, really. Just dealing with my own stuff."

Never one to let things slide, I push further. "Mia, we don't keep secrets from each other. What's going on?"

"I told you, it's nothing." Her voice is tight. She's lying.

I step closer and place a hand on her shoulder. "Mia, please. Look at me."

She meets my eyes, hers turbulent. I read the truth in them and my chest aches.

"You're jealous," I whisper.

She jerks back. "Don't be ridiculous."

"Admit it." I grasp her hands. "Mia, please. We promised we'd always be honest with each other."

"I..." Her lower lip trembles. "Okay, fine. I'm jealous, all right? Happy now?"

She tries to pull away, but I hold on tighter. "Mia, look at me. I'm sorry. I never meant to hurt you."

"Well, you did." She swipes at her eyes. "Hearing about you with him, it feels like you're slipping away. For years, I've held you while you cried over him and how much he hurt you. I guess I'm not ready to share you with him yet. I'm scared of things going back to how they were. You've done so much work to get over your shattered heart."

My heart swells. "You don't have to be scared or worried. Things between us haven't changed. You're my best friend, Mia, always."

A fragile hope glimmers in her gaze. "Truly? You mean that?"

I cup her face, pressing my forehead to hers. "Truly. No one will ever come between us again."

She closes her eyes, a tear sliding down her cheek. But she's smiling. "Promise?"

"I promise," I whisper. "BFFs. Always have been, always will be."

She takes a shaky breath and nods. "Okay. I believe you."

I brush the tears from her cheeks. "Good. Now, how about we order some pizza, crack open a bottle of wine, and have a movie marathon like old times?"

Her smile widens. "That sounds perfect."

We head back to her place and settle onto the couch with two glasses of merlot and a pizza between us. Mia curls into my side, her head on my shoulder.

Halfway through some trashy horror romance she let me choose, she murmurs, "He's not right for you, you know."

I glance at her. "Who?" I ask, despite there only being one person she could possibly mean.

"Aksel," she rolls her eyes, the merlot giving her a boost of confidence to say what's on her mind. "He's too..." She waves a hand, searching for the word. "... self-absorbed. And polished and stuffy. He doesn't understand you like I do."

"What? You trying to date me, Mia?" I smirk.

"No," she laughs, a wistful look on her face. "I just don't want to have to pick up the pieces all over again."

Chapter 45

FALLON

I steel myself as Claudia steps into the room, her haunted eyes meeting mine. She clutches a worn notebook to her chest, knuckles white, and I know it contains horrors I can scarcely imagine. She's a tall, elegant-looking woman in her forties or potentially early fifties. Soft golden-brown layers frame her face, her angular features giving her a regal appearance.

She takes a deep breath. When she speaks, her voice wavers, but the iron in her spine holds her upright. "You need to know what I've been through."

My hands curl into fists, because I know the basics of her ordeal. I want to wrap her in my arms, tell her she's safe now, that the nightmare is over and that revenge will soon be hers. But she needs to share her story, purge the poison from her soul. I nod, a lump forming in my throat. "I'm here, Claudia. You can tell me anything."

She looks past me, her gaze distant, and begins. "The house he kept me in was both a sanctuary and a prison. We picked the home out together when we first got married. It was my dream home, with gorgeous painted shutters and a bright yellow front door. Every feature I'd wished for in a forever home." She frowns. "What I didn't realize was that once we purchased it, he had soundproof insulation installed. Doors that would lock from the outside. Shutters that couldn't be opened without a special code. And the basement...." She shivers at the room which I read earlier was some kind of depraved sex dungeon filled with implements for torture and unusual rituals. "From the day we moved in, he chose everything—what I ate, what I wore, when I slept." Her lips twist. "A puppet dancing on his strings. He told me I was nothing without him. That the outside world would devour me."

She shudders, rubbing her arms. "The windows were barriers, shutting out everything real and good. Some days, I wondered if anything existed beyond those walls."

My nails bite into my palms and I taste blood as I realize I'm chewing on my bottom lip. How dare he? How fucking dare he?

"In the basement, I found trinkets. Clothing. Souvenirs of other captives." Her eyes meet mine, haunted and bleak. "Apparently he wasn't averse to creating snuff films and distributing them among his friends. As far as kidnapping goes, I wasn't the first. But I was the one who got away."

"Jesus," I breathe. Rage burns through me, hot and swift, but I bank the flames. She needs me steady. Strong. "You're safe now, Claudia. He can't hurt you anymore."

Her lips tremble. She looks small and fragile, but steel glints beneath the surface. "I still feel trapped. The darkness follows me, its fingers around my throat." Her gaze hardens. "I want you to help me stop him. Permanently."

I take Claudia's hands, squeezing tight. "You're strong. You survived hell and came out the other side. Don't ever doubt yourself."

She inhales sharply. "Some days I can almost believe that. But then the panic comes, and I'm back in that house hearing the lock turn, knowing I'll never escape." Her fingers tighten around mine. "You have to promise you'll stop him. I can't live like this, always looking over my shoulder and waiting for him to come after me. He has to pay for what he's done."

"He will." My voice emerges flat and hard. "I swear to you, Claudia, he will suffer for every moment of pain he inflicted. You came to me for justice and I always deliver."

Her eyes shine with tears and fierce purpose. "Thank you. There's no one else I trust to do this. To make him hurt the way I did."

My heart aches for all she's endured. For now, she's safe here with me. No one will ever hurt her again.

"Alright then, Claudia. This part is going to bring up some memories, but it's time to face your demons," I say gently. "Tell me everything about Harvey Maxwell. His habits, his routines, his weaknesses. The more I know, the better I can make him suffer."

Claudia's lips curve into a slow, vicious smile, and I realize I haven't given her enough credit for her strength. "I've been waiting for this." She grips my hands tighter, her knuckles pure white. "Harvey always said I'd never escape. He was wrong." Her eyes gleam with purpose. "Now, it's his turn to face the dark."

I nod, waiting for her to continue.

"I should have killed him when I had the chance," Claudia says bitterly. "He didn't expect me to fight back that night. For once, I surprised him." A fierce smile lights her face before fading. "But I couldn't do it. As much as I hate him, I'm not a killer."

I give her hands a gentle squeeze. "You don't need to be. That's why you came to me."

She searches my face, equal parts hope and fear in her gaze. "You can do this for me? Make him suffer without..."

"Without taking a life?" I finish softly. "Yes. There are far worse things than death." My smile is slow and vicious, colored by the promise of retribution. "Harvey Maxwell will beg for death before I'm finished with him. I will systematically destroy everything he values, everything that gives his life meaning. And when he has nothing left, when he's broken and hollow, I'll leave him to rot in his own personal hell."

Claudia's eyes light up, the thought of her estranged husband getting his just desserts clearly giving her energy. "You really mean this? It's going to happen?"

My pulse thrums with purpose. "Consider it done." The demon will pay for his sins. Claudia came to me for justice and I aim to deliver. "You're free now, Claudia. And together, we're going to make sure he never hurts anyone again."

A fierce joy lights Claudia's eyes. The shadows of the past retreat, banished by the light of justice. She's no longer a victim. Today, she has reclaimed her power.

"Thank you," she whispers. "For giving me back my life."

"You're welcome. And you're welcome for what's to come."

Vengeance will be swift. And it will be sweet. Harvey Maxwell will pay for his sins. Claudia will have her justice.

And I will relish every moment.

Chapter 46

FALLON

The cold air in my basement wraps around me like a shroud, chilling me to the bone. But it's not the temperature that causes my hands to tremble, it's the plan brewing in my mind. A plan that promises vengeance and justice. I glance over at Grave, who stands at the top of the stairs, his expression unreadable.

I survey the cold, concrete basement floor, my mind racing with ideas on how to transform it into a suitable prison for Harvey Maxwell. The air is damp and stale, a fitting atmosphere for the hell he'll soon inhabit.

"Harvey Maxwell will pay for what he did to Claudia," I say, my voice as steely as my resolve. "I'm going to keep him captive down here. Deprive him of anything but the most basic of necessities."

"Fallon," Grave warns, his gravelly voice full of concern. "You know the risks of holding a volatile man like Harvey Maxwell captive. He won't go down without a fight, and he has connections that could make our lives a living hell. Plus, it's literally just really hard to keep someone captive for any length of time."

"Did you see that woman back in my office?" I snap back, my eyes blazing. "Her mind was a cage. And I'm determined to put him in one, too." My heart races, pounding against my chest. The hurt and anger that had been simmering within me comes bubbling up to the surface. I can feel it coursing through my veins, fueling my determination.

"Fallon, I understand your need for revenge," Grave says, his tone softer now. "What

Claudia's husband did to her was quite frankly terrifying and unforgivable. But you have to think this through. Is it worth risking everything?"

"Justice for Claudia is worth any risk," I declare, my jaw set stubbornly. I know there are consequences to my actions, but I refuse to let the man who destroyed Claudia's life walk away unpunished.

"Then I'll help you," Grave concedes, running a hand over his shiny bald head. "But we have to be smart about this. We can't afford any mistakes." Once again, Grave chooses his loyalty to me over fear. "Thank you, Grave," I whisper, relief washing over me. With him by my side, I know we can see this through to the end.

"Alright," I say, turning to Grave. "We need to make this place as secure as possible. Reinforce the door, install locks, soundproof the walls."

"Fallon, you're playing a dangerous game here," Grave warns, his eyes filled with concern. But I see something else in them too—a flicker of admiration for my determination. "But like I said, I'm with you. Remember, we have to be careful when getting our supplies," he adds, crossing his arms. "We can't leave a trail for anyone to follow."

"Of course," I reply, taking a deep breath. "What do you suggest?"

"First, don't buy everything at once or from the same store," Grave advises, his voice low and cautious. "Spread your purchases out over a few days, and use cash whenever possible. Don't literally create a kit that screams 'I'm buying this stuff to kidnap, hold captive and potentially murder someone'. That's never good."

"Got it," I nod, mentally cataloging his words.

"Second, wear gloves when handling anything that could be traced back to you," he continues. "And for God's sake, don't talk about this plan to anyone, even if you think you can trust them. Even Mia."

"Understood," I say, feeling a chill run down my spine. This operation requires stealth and precision, and I can't afford to slip up. The candiru fish retribution was pretty full-on, but this is next level.

"Lastly," Grave says, his voice firm, "be prepared for the worst-case scenario. If things go south, you need an exit strategy."

"Let's hope it doesn't come to that," I murmur, swallowing hard.

As we stand in the dim light of my basement, planning our dark revenge, I feel an odd sense of satisfaction. For too long, Harvey Maxwell has preyed on the vulnerable and innocent. But now, the hunter will become the hunted.

And justice, in all its merciless glory, will be served.

Over the next few days, I follow Grave's instructions to the letter. I venture out to various hardware stores, purchasing chains and padlocks, soundproofing materials, and other essential items. Each time, I pay in cash and remain as inconspicuous as possible. I even don an assortment of wigs, hats and clothing I wouldn't normally wear in order to make my clandestine movements even harder to trace.

At night, I lay awake in bed, my mind churning with a mix of anticipation and dread. Revenge courses through my veins like a drug, fueling my resolve to see this through. But kidnapping a man is a huge deal, something I never previously would have pictured myself doing. Although I could say that about a fair few things lately, the weight of the consequences presses down on me, a constant reminder of the risk we're taking.

"Fallon," Grave's voice interrupts my thoughts early one evening as we stand in the near-finished basement prison. "Are you sure you're ready for this?"

"More than ever," I reply, my voice steely. This is for Claudia, I remind myself. For justice.

"Alright then," he says, his face etched with determination. "Let's finish this."

The sun beats down on my back as I haul bags of cement mix out of the truck. Sweat drips down my face, and I can feel the strain on my muscles as I carry the heavy load into the basement. This is the price of vengeance, I tell myself, gritting my teeth as I push through the pain.

"Fallon, you should take a break," Grave calls out from across the room. His face is streaked with dust, his hands raw and blistered from hours of work.

"Can't afford to," I reply, dumping the bags onto the floor of the basement. "Maxwell's still out there, and every second we waste is another chance for him to hurt someone else."

"Fine, but don't say I didn't warn you," he grumbles, returning to his task of assembling the metal bars that will soon become Harvey Maxwell's prison cell.

In between trips to the truck, I check my phone, only to find it silent and empty of notifications. It's been some time since I last heard from Aksel, and while I know he's busy dealing with his own demons, I can't help but worry about him. What if something's happened? What if he needs me and I'm not there? Not that he's ever needed me before. I guess I'm just feeling rejected, even though I'm the one who ran away.

"Fallon, can you hand me that wrench?" Grave asks, snapping me out of my thoughts.

"Sure thing," I say, grabbing the tool from the workbench and passing it to him. As I watch him work, I can see the sweat pouring off him, the grim determination etched in the lines of his face. And yet, despite everything, there's also a sense of pride in his eyes—pride in what we're accomplishing together.

"Almost there," he mutters, tightening the last bolt on the cage. "Just need to get these chains attached and we'll be ready."

"Good," I breathe, my heart pounding in anticipation. The thought of finally exacting justice on Harvey Maxwell sends a shiver down my spine—one that's equal parts fear and excitement.

As we work together to put the final touches on our makeshift torture chamber, I can't help but feel a twisted sense of pride. Soon, Harvey Maxwell will know what it means to be trapped, to be powerless, just like Claudia was.

And in that darkness, he'll find me waiting—cold, unforgiving, and relentless. Just like the vengeance I seek.

"Alright, that should do it," Grave announces as he steps back from the cage. "What do you think?"

I survey our handiwork, taking in the cold metal bars, the heavy chains, and the concrete floor stained with sweat and effort. It's not pretty, but it doesn't need to be. It's kind of the point. This is a place for punishment—a place where monsters will come face to face with the consequences of their actions.

"It's perfect," I whisper, my voice barely audible over the pounding of my heart.

"Good," Grave says, clapping me on the shoulder. He seems a little excited, even, despite his warnings. "Now let's get cleaned up and grab some food. We've earned it."

"Sounds good," I agree, though part of me wants to stay here until the moment we bring Harvey Maxwell. But I know there's still work to be done, and I can't afford to lose focus now. Without Grave's reminder, I almost certainly would have forgotten to eat.

As we make our way upstairs, my phone buzzes in my pocket, startling me. I pull it out, expecting to see Aksel's name on the screen, maybe a text message just checking in. Instead, I find a missed call from him—one that came in hours ago, while I was lost in the depths of my vengeance.

"Shit," I mutter under my breath, guilt twisting in my gut like a knife. He needed me, and I wasn't there. Reception must be finicky down here.

"Everything okay?" Grave asks, his brow furrowed in concern.

"Yeah," I lie, forcing a smile onto my face. "Just a missed call. Nothing important."

But deep down, I know it's anything but unimportant. It's a tangible example of how my priorities have shifted, and I don't know that there's ever any going back. As I stand there, surrounded by the darkness of my own making, I can't help but wonder if I'm losing myself in this quest for revenge—and if the price of justice will be too high for any of us to bear.

Chapter 47

FALLON

The excitement surges through my veins as I envision Harvey, broken and tormented in the basement. A smirk dances on my lips, and I reach for the phone to call Aksel. I'd never tell him about the man I'm holding captive in my basement, but I sure can use this energy for our mutual enjoyment.

"Hey, it's Fallon," I say as soon as he picks up. "I'm sorry I missed your call. Is everything okay?"

"Yeah, I was just checking in and had something to ask you."

I can't wait for my turn to speak, feeling more than a little hyped up after taking another look at my gorgeous new torture basement. "I have a proposition for you," I blurt.

"Is that so?" Aksel's voice is low and seductive, igniting a fire within me. "I like the sound of that."

"Come over tonight. We're going to make some magic happen."

"Sounds like fun. I'll be there."

The anticipation builds throughout the day, and by the time Aksel arrives at my doorstep, I'm practically vibrating with energy. As soon as he steps inside, our mouths crash together in a fierce, passionate kiss. The hunger between us is palpable, a dark craving demanding to be sated.

"Are you ready for this?" Aksel whispers against my lips, his hands gripping my hips tightly.

"More than ready." My voice is breathless, and I can't suppress the wicked gleam in my eyes. If I was in another world, I'd bring Aksel down into the basement and we'd fuck in the middle of Harvey's future torture dungeon, just because we can. But I don't think that would go down well with him. Maybe I'm underestimating the guy, with his family company's well-known mob affiliations, but it's too soon to take any chances.

So I do the next best thing. I take sick pleasure in knowing what lies in the basement, and the fact Aksel is oblivious. It's a delectable, dark power imbalance.

Regardless of who knows what about my basement, we need to satisfy our own desires. Our clothes are quickly discarded, a trail leading to my bedroom. Aksel pushes me down onto the bed, his powerful body hovering above mine. His eyes pierce into me, dark and full of lust.

"Tell me what you want," he growls, his fingers trailing along my inner thighs.

"Make me feel alive," I plead, desperate for the connection only he can provide. "Make me forget everything but this moment."

"Your wish is my command," he replies, his voice raw and provocative.

His lips hungrily devour mine, his tongue teasing and taunting me. A moan escapes my throat as his hands explore every inch of my body, igniting a fire within me that only he can extinguish. Our bodies meld together, heat and passion intertwining in an erotic dance.

"God, Fallon," Aksel groans, his voice thick with desire. "You feel so damn good."

He grabs something from the nightstand, a smug smile curving his lips. It's my rose vibrator.

Aksel smirks, his spicy cologne invading my senses as he approaches the bed, his long legs eating up the space between us. "I've got you, baby." He grinds the toy against my clit, the rumbling vibrations shooting straight to my core. It's been so long since I've felt this devilish delight but already I'm dripping with need.

"Don't call me that," I bite out through gritted teeth.

He leans down, his lips brushing against my ear, his breath hot. "What would you prefer?"

"Nothing," I breathe, trying to steady myself, but it's no use. My body is ready for him, craving his touch. I can't deny it any longer.

The sheets rustle as he moves closer to me, his muscular thigh pressed against mine as he peers down at my pussy. His fingers circle my clit slowly, teasingly before plunging inside me, finding their rhythm. I gasp as the vibration combines with his skilled touch, my hips bucking off the bed. I'm putty in his hands, unable to resist the blissful torment he's dishing out.

"Feels so good, doesn't it?" he murmurs, his voice low and rough.

"Yes, so good," I moan, arching into his touch as well as the vibrator.

He increases the speed of the vibrator on my clit, sending sparks of pleasure coursing through me. I cry out, my head thrashing back and forth on the pillow. My body trembles underneath him—a mix of ecstasy and fear. I hate needing him so much, but I also love it.

"Aksel..." My voice is husky, pleading.

He smirks as I squirm beneath him, helpless against the onslaught of sensations. "Tell me you love me, Fallon."

"I hate you," I grit out between parted lips, my eyes squeezed shut.

He laughs, the sound deep and throaty. "Say it like you fucking mean it." A finger finds my ass, pressing against the tight ring of muscle while my pussy pulsates to the rhythm of the vibrator. "I want to hear you beg."

"Fuck!" I cry out, my body tensing at the intrusion. "Please...Aksel."

"Beg me."

"Please," I whisper, my voice barely audible. "Please, I love you, Aksel," I moan out, more as a plea than anything.

"Good girl," he growls, trailing his hand toward my pussy once again and pushing his fingers inside me as he searches for my G-spot.

"I'm going to make you come so hard, Fallon," he whispers against my throbbing clit, his breath warm against my skin. I whimper, my hips bucking up to meet his touch. "And then you'll be begging for more."

He speeds up the vibe, my walls convulsing around his fingers as I come undone in waves of pleasure, his face only inches from my pussy. I scream in pure bliss, my body shattering around his fingers. Tears stream down my cheeks from the overwhelming sensation. My entire body shudders in aftershocks.

Aksel pulls his fingers out, making me whimper in protest.

"Turn over," he commands, his tone cold as he sets the vibrator down on the bed beside me.

I comply and get on all fours, biting my lip as he retrieves a glass toy from the nightstand, lubes it up and slowly penetrates my ass with it.

"Oh fuck," I gasp, my body tensing at the unfamiliar sensation. But it feels...good. Filled in a different kind of way than when he's inside me. More intense, and in a pleasurable way.

"You like that?" he taunts.

"Aksel," I gasp, my voice breaking.

"Come now, Fallon," he demands, his hand on his cock. "I'm going to fuck you and you're going to take it deep. But first, hold the vibrator against your clit."

I don't know why I obey, because I'm already so sensitive from the last orgasm, but I do. The vibrations hit me with increased intensity and I gasp. Aksel slides into me from behind and thrusts his hips in rhythm, his cock slapping against my pussy alongside the pulsations of the vibrator. It's almost too much. Nearly too intense. I can feel my walls clenching, the sensations overwhelming me.

"Oh God, Aksel," I moan, my body taking over. "Please..."

"Tell me you want more," he growls, his fingers digging into my hips.

"I want more," I whimper, my voice cracking.

He smirks and increases the speed, my body spasming around him. I can feel the familiar tightness building, the pressure growing. And then it hits me–another intense orgasm. I scream Aksel's name, the sound echoing around the room.

He pulls out but instantly pulls my hips to his, his cock pressing against my ass crack. "What do you think you're doing?" I ask warily.

I close my eyes, bracing myself for what's to come. The snap of a lube bottle lid permeates the silence. The head of his cock presses against me, and he slides in ever so slightly. I moan at the slight sting combined with the cool sensation of the lube.

"You doing okay, baby girl?" he rasps.

"Mmm yes," I reply, my eyes half-closed as I relish the sensation of his cock slowly working its way into my back entrance.

He continues to slide in, slowly, carefully, until he groans as he presses in me to his hilt. He slides back, slowly at first as if testing the waters, and when I moan as a sign of encouragement and enjoyment, he surges inside me, filling me up. He starts thrusting hard and fast, slapping my ass with each powerful stroke. I gasp and arch my back toward his chest. My nails dig into the sheets as he takes me roughly, his hips smacking against my ass with each forceful push.

"So good," he pants, his hands fisting in my hair.

I grind my teeth together, trying to ignore the burning sensation between my legs. I hate how good this feels, how much I need him even though he's hurting me. He pulls out and slaps my ass, making me yelp. Then he slams back in, his heavy balls slapping against my ass cheeks.

"More," I moan, hating myself for wanting more.

"You're such a brat," he says, but he gives me what I want—faster, harder thrusts that leave me gasping for breath.

He reaches around and wraps his palm around my throat.

"Aksel!" I choke out his name in a moan.

He groans, his hips jerking forward violently.

"You like that, don't you?" he taunts. "You like being choked."

I nod, unable to speak. My head is swimming with pleasure and pain and confusion. All I know is that he feels so damn good inside me, despite everything.

He tightens his grip on my throat, choking me slightly as he picks up the pace.

"Say it," he demands harshly.

"Yes!" I cry out, gasping for breath.

"Good girl," he grits out. His grip around my throat loosens slightly as he continues to pound into me, his free hand slapping my ass in time with his hips. "Cum for me, brat," he growls, thrusting deep.

I come hard, crying out his name as my body shudders and quakes beneath him. I can feel him getting closer to his own release, and I know what comes next. I brace myself for the impending pain even as I crave the feeling of his cum shooting inside me.

I feel his body tense and he pulls out, and I scream as he covers my back with his hot seed, the sting mixing with the pleasure from our orgasms. We both pant heavily as he steps away from me, leaving me sprawled on the bed, tangled in the bedsheets, sticky and sore.

He walks to the bathroom and I hear water running. Moments later, he returns with a warm, wet washcloth that he uses to gently clean me up while he kisses me softly. Once he's finished, he slides into bed next to me and wraps his arms around me, and I settle comfortably into the nook of his armpit.

"Stay the night," I whisper against his chest, my fingers tracing lazy circles on his skin.

I lose all reason for a moment as I realize it's our family dinner the next day. "And I know this is random, but we have a weekly dinner at the estate tomorrow and I'm wondering if you might like to join me? I know it's a lot of pressure, so feel free to say no."

"I'd love to," Aksel says without hesitation. Then he frowns, but there's also a touch of excitement in his voice. "I know things might get... tense."

"Let them," I reply with determination. "It's time everyone knows exactly where we stand. Together."

"Alright," he agrees, pressing a soft kiss to my forehead. "For you, I'll face anything."

As we drift off to sleep, wrapped in each other's arms, I know that I've made the right choice. With Aksel by my side, I'm ready to confront the past and embrace whatever twisted future awaits us. And, if he does hurt me, I'll be well-positioned to hit him where it hurts the most.

At dinner, I find myself holding Aksel's hand under the table, feeling the softness of his skin against mine. The tension in the room is palpable, and I'm acutely aware of how my family is reacting to a King being in the room as well as their own sentiments about me—Fallon Dempsey, Chief Black Sheep. Still, I felt a sense of familial obligation so I came, perhaps thinking I might stir a little shit in the process.

My father glares at Aksel, while Link's eyes dart between them with a mix of confusion and anger. Cheston watches them both warily, a frown etched deep on his face as he no doubt prepares to step in and mediate. I know my brothers hate Aksel for what he's done to me over the years, but they respect me too much to protest openly. At least to begin with.

The scent of garlic and rosemary fills the air as we take our seats at the table, the chatter quieting down as we dive into our meals. The tension is palpable yet contained, like a coiled snake waiting to strike.

Zara seems unaware of the tension, gracefully sifting through the conversation like a butterfly among predators. Her eyes flicker over to Aksel every so often before landing back on her wine glass. I watch warily, knowing full well what she wants. She's an insatiable flirt, and Aksel is a very handsome man.

We sit in silence through the first part of the meal, the waitstaff moving discreetly around us. Occasional small talk breaks out but quickly fizzles. The clink of silverware on china fills the air as we slowly eat, each bite heavy with anticipation.

Even Link holds back from creating a scene until the main course arrives, and there's silence for a moment before he speaks up. "So, Aksel," he says coolly, "let's address the elephant in the room. How did you manage to worm your way back into my sister's life?"

A grin spreads across Aksel's face as he takes a bite of the expertly seasoned filet mignon. "I simply showed her what she's been missing out on all these years," he responds nonchalantly, his eyes meeting mine for just one second before returning to focus on his plate. My cheeks redden as he chews slowly, savoring every bite as if daring them to do something about it. My brothers exchange glances, knowing the intention behind Aksel's words.

I feel my stomach churn with anger but force myself not to react. I won't give them the satisfaction even though I feel all their digs are either at me or about me, and now it feels like Aksel is joining in.

As dessert is served, I clear my throat. I'm about to say something but then Zara decides to take matters into her own hands, leaning over and running her fingernail down Aksel's chest in response to something he just said. "I must agree with you there," she purrs, her cleavage on full display as dishes clink together. "I can see what you mean now."

I grit my teeth as I force down a mouthful of food, trying not to lunge across the table and rip out Zara's ugly hair extensions, or perhaps her throat, for being the entitled bitch she is. Aksel shrugs nonchalantly, his jaw ticking as he continues to answer a battery of questions from my brothers. The night is tense, and it only gets worse as they continue to prod at him.

Then, Link decides to throw fuel onto the fire. "Yeah, well... just remember we were here first and we'll be here long after you've gone again," he snaps. "You didn't seem so interested in this life when we were in high school."

Aksel takes a long sip of his wine, staring back at Link with an unyielding gaze that mirrors his own. "I've grown up a lot since then," he retorts slowly, his voice low and menacing. "And I know how to appreciate what's really important."

I want nothing more than to scream at them all right now. My heart aches for Aksel, who's trying so hard to be civil despite their hostility. I can't help but admire his restraint. I know he's not here for my family's approval, but for me.

Suddenly, out of the corner of my eye I see Zara's hand brush against Aksel's thigh under the table—a deliberate move meant to provoke him, or potentially to arouse him.

Gross. But instead of reacting in anger or surprise, Aksel places his hand over hers and gives it a gentle squeeze before removing it from his lap. "I think it's time for me to take Fallon home." He stands up, leaving the table.

Zara gasps in outrage while I look on in confusion but admiration, quickly hopping up after him. Aksel's actions were unexpected and bold yet undeniably attractive. As we walk away, he whispers in my ear, "Don't let them get to you. They don't deserve your innocence." If only he knew.

With my heart racing and body tingling with anticipation, I follow him out of the dining room and the estate, eager for our future together amidst all the chaos around us.

"Aksel, can you join me for a dance after dinner?" I lean into him, my body pressed against his side. I feel him tense slightly, but he nods stiffly.

Music begins to play softly from hidden speakers, and we rise together, swaying to the slow melody. Link's eyes narrow as we lock gazes, his jaw clenching tightly. I lead Aksel out onto the dance floor, our bodies moving in sync despite the animosity surrounding us. I see Bronson eyeing Aksel warily from across the room, but I don't let it deter me. This is my night—my moment to show them all.

As we dance closer, I whisper directly into his ear, "I want you to fuck me against that wall."

I can feel Aksel's cock harden against my thigh as he grinds his hips into me, his voice rough with desire when he responds, "You got it, sweetheart."

The taste of chocolate tart lingers on my tongue as he bends me over against the polished wood paneling, my skirt hiked up around my waist. He slams into me roughly, pushing me into the cool surface, claiming my body as his own. I moan loudly, my pleasure mingled with pain. I glance over my shoulder and see everyone watching us, my entire family. It fuels my need for revenge even more, them trying to steal this one moment of enjoyment from me.

My father's face turns crimson, Link looks away, and Colton's eyes narrow with a mix of jealousy and anger. Aksel's possessive grip on my hips pulls me even closer, our bodies slapping together in rhythm. We continue like this until I cry out, my orgasm taking me unaware.

When we finally part, we're both breathing heavily. Walking back to rejoin the family, I feel empowered by the display of dominance. My father clears his throat, trying to break the tension. "Well, that was quite the performance you two put on," he says sarcastically.

Aksel smirks and retorts, "We aim to please."

I glare at both of them but can't help the smile that plays at my lips. Despite everything, this is exactly what I wanted—to hurt them all.

I wake with a start. I'm in my room again and *thank fuck* for that! What a warped mind I have, and it's only getting worse. Clearly introducing Aksel to my family dinner was a step too far, but at least we didn't fuck in front of my father and brothers. There are many things I intend to do to embarrass him when the time is right, but that is not one of them. This whole situation is clearly getting to me, and I need to put a stop to it and fast.

Before I truly lose my mind.

Chapter 48

AKSEL

The streets slip by in shadows as I grip the steering wheel. Echoes of tension thrum in my veins, pulses of anger from watching Link bait Fallon throughout dinner. I didn't want to leave her, but we both have early starts in the morning and she insisted she had work to do late into the night.

I slam the brakes at a red light, my knuckles white. That smug bastard did it on purpose. Link. The sly digs and smirks aimed at Fallon, meant to cut her down and keep her in her place. As if he has any right to control her after all the things he's done to her over the years. And he was clearly coming for me with his barbs. And then Zara, coming onto me in front of the entire table. What a shit show. I guess it's nice to know my family isn't the only one with issues.

The light turns green, but I don't move. My breath comes fast, rage simmering in my gut. I failed Fallon tonight. I should've put Link in his place, made it clear he can't hurt her anymore. But I held back for Fallon's sake, swallowing fury for diplomacy.

I pound on the steering wheel, wincing at the sting in my knuckles. Diplomacy gets us nowhere with men like Link. He only understands force, the language I should've spoken tonight, although I bet he couldn't handle one punch from me.

With a growl, I accelerate into the empty intersection, glancing at the phone in my cupholder. A text from Fallon lights the screen:

Fallon <3 <3: Sorry that dinner was rough. Thank you for being there for me.

My anger fades, replaced by a surge of protectiveness. I failed tonight, but it won't happen again. Fallon won't face Link's abuse alone, not as long as I'm with her.

I pull up in front of my building and tap out a reply:

Me: Of course, Fallon. I'll always protect you, from Link and anyone else who dares hurt you. We're in this together.

I hit send and get out of the car, the night air cooling my flushed skin. The battle lines have been drawn. Diplomacy is dead. Link wanted a fight? He'll get one. And this time, I won't hold back. Anything for my girl.

I slam my apartment door behind me, Link's taunts still echoing in my mind. Every smug grin, every sly insult—they play on a loop, fury simmering in my gut. Driving usually calms me, but it was a quick trip and I'm just so furious at Link. And Zara too, for that matter, but I feel like I dealt with her quite effectively in the moment. From what I could tell, Fallon seemed to think so, too.

I stalk to my living room and collapse onto the sofa, rubbing my eyes. The Dempseys were hospitable enough, although it was strained all round, but Link made it clear I'll never truly belong. Not with his venom poisoning any chance at a real bond.

With a sigh, I glance at a photo of Fallon and me on the bookshelf, her smile as radiant as the day I took it. My chest tightens. She's endured so much pain because of Link, and because of the hold her dad has over her family. I can't—won't—allow that toxicity into our lives anymore.

Fallon and I are starting to build something true and real, despite the shadows of our past and even though it's still very early stages. If this works out, we will have survived betrayal and heartbreak to find each other again. I'll be damned if I let Link or any other Dempsey destroy that now.

My phone chimes and I grab it, hoping for another text from Fallon. Instead, Cheston's name flashes on the screen. I debate ignoring it, but open the message.

Cheston Dempsey: Thank you for coming to dinner. I know it wasn't easy being in Link's line of fire. Fallon is lucky to have you. You're already part of this family, no matter what Link says."

A wry smile tugs at my lips. At least someone in that house has sense. I tap out a reply:

Me: Your support means a lot, thank you Cheston. I have every intention that Fallon and I are in this for the long haul, and it'll take more than a few venomous comments from Link to tear us apart.

I set down my phone, resolve hardening within me like forged steel. Link wants a battle? He'll get a war. And when the smoke clears, there will only be one man left standing at Fallon's side. Me.

Chapter 49

FALLON

The sun filters through the windows of the spa, warmth seeping into my skin. Roxy chatters beside me as we settle into plush pedicure chairs, the scent of lavender calming my frayed nerves.

I glance at Raine who sits to my other side, and she's deep in thought. What is she thinking? Does she suspect there's more to my relationship with Aksel than I've let on?

I'm still feeling a little thrown that I'm sitting here with Aksel's sisters, invited to a girls' day out. I love Roxy and I don't know Raine that well, because she's quite a bit older than Aksel and had long-since graduated high school by the time we were together, but she seems nice and he seems to look up to her.

"So, Fallon, what's the deal with you and my brother?" Raine asks, watching me with perceptive eyes. "I know you're at the early stages of figuring things out, but I sense something beneath the surface. Spill."

Shit. I should have known she'd see right through me. I've heard Raine always could read people too well.

I swallow hard, searching for the right words. How much do I share? I could give her some superficial throwaway line, but this cuts deeper and she deserves to know the truth.

"It's complicated," I say at last.

Raine arches a brow. "With Aksel, everything is complicated. Always has been."

I give a humorless laugh. "Touché."

The nail tech buffs my nails to a shine. I stare at the deep red color we chose, like congealed blood. Fitting.

Before I know it, I'm spilling everything that happened to me after I broke up with Aksel so many years ago.

I take a deep breath and the words tumble out in a rush. "I was assaulted. After Aksel and I broke up in college. It...changed me. Hardened me."

The bad decisions and even worse company. The sexual assault. All the trauma in the wake of our breakup that I attribute to him.

I get the sense Raine has faced her own battles, and for whatever reason, I immediately trust her.

Raine's eyes glisten with tears, and she gives my hand a gentle squeeze. "I'm so sorry you went through that." Her voice is soft, laced with pain and understanding. She's been there too, in that dark place. "You didn't deserve that. No one does."

"I let it twist me up inside," I admit. "It turned me vengeful. Ruthless." I swallow hard. "Aksel was my light and when he left, the darkness took over. It consumed me."

"You're not alone," Raine says quietly. "I've fought my own demons, and our experiences aren't that different. But we're survivors. We're stronger and there is still light inside us, no matter how faint it seems."

Her words strike a chord, resonating deep within. I cling to them like a lifeline, daring to hope.

"Does Aksel know?" Raine asks softly. "About what happened to you after you broke up?"

My throat tightens. I can't bring myself to say the words to him, to speak of the demons that haunt my dreams. The assault. The betrayal. The scars that refuse to fade. But I feel comfortable in the presence of these women and the words sprang forward effortlessly.

I meet Raine's gaze, shadows flickering in her eyes. She understands without me saying a word.

"He doesn't deserve you if he can't handle your past," she says.

"Maybe no one does." The words slip out before I can stop them. I clench my jaw, annoyed at my lapse. I don't need her pity. I don't need anyone.

Raine reaches over, squeezing my hand, careful not to disturb my polish. "You deserve to be happy, Fallon. Don't forget that."

I stare at our joined hands, an ache building in my chest. When was the last time I let myself feel this—this glimmer of hope?

Maybe Raine is right. Maybe the shadows don't have to eclipse the light forever. Maybe I can beat this. Banish the shadows for good.

I lift my gaze to Raine's, a fragile smile curving my lips. "Thank you. For understanding. For giving me hope."

Raine smiles back, radiant as the sun. "That's what sisters do. We hold each other up. Remind each other of our strength and light."

Sisters. The word wraps around me in a warm embrace. I'm no longer alone in this. Raine and Roxy, they're my light in the darkness. My way out of the shadows.

Maybe with them by my side, I can finally turn my back on the darkness for good. Forgive the past and look toward the future. A future with Aksel.

I squeeze Raine's hand, taking care not to smudge her manicure, a surge of gratitude and love swelling in my chest. Today, my world grew brighter. The shadows receded.

It turns out there is still light, even within the dark.

Chapter 50

The dimly lit diner seems to swallow us whole as we walk through the door, the smell of stale cigarettes and burnt coffee invading my nostrils. Grave's towering presence at my side is a reminder of our purpose here—justice, revenge, and protection from those who prey on the vulnerable.

"Fallon," Brynn Waterford whispers, waving us over from her booth in the corner. Her designer outfit screams money, making her stand out like a peacock amongst pigeons in this dingy establishment. She keeps glancing around nervously, her conspiratorial tone evident even from a distance. Theatrics much, I smirk inwardly, while trying to keep my expression neutral.

"Ms. Waterford, I'm Fallon, and this is my associate, Grave." My greeting is firm, professional, but with a subtle edge that conveys our shared dark intentions.

"Call me Brynn, please," she insists, her manicured fingers playing with the edge of her napkin. "I didn't want to meet at your office because... well, I don't know who might be watching."

"Understandable," I reply, taking a seat across from her while Grave slides in beside me, his broad frame casting a shadow over the table. "What brings you to us?"

"Griffin Dunlop," she spits the name out as if it's poison on her tongue. "My ex-husband. He cheated on me, over and over again. But that's not why I'm here."

"Go on," I prompt, feeling Grave's gaze on me as I lean forward to hear her better.

"Recently, I found out he's been doing... horrible things. To children." Her voice trembles, but the fire in her eyes burns bright with wrath. "I tried getting the authorities involved, but he's incredibly powerful. A dangerous man. Part of what attracted me to him at first, if I'm honest. But things turned sour quickly, and danger is quite different when it turns on you." She shakes her head, a deep frown marring her otherwise stunning features. "He threatened me, my kids, anyone who would dare speak against him. He's paid off the cops, even a local judge, to keep his disgusting activities under wraps." She details names, places and specific situations.

The fury I feel at her revelations is like a red-hot iron searing my insides. Grave's hand brushes against mine in a silent but rare offer of support, but I barely register his touch as my mind churns with thoughts of vengeance. He knows crimes against children are a trigger point for me, as are wealthy families who pay off judges to forget their atrocities.

"Are you certain of this information?" Grave asks, his tone measured but hinting at the same rage I feel.

"Is there any evidence of his criminal activities?" I ask, my voice barely above a whisper. The question hangs in the air like thick fog, threatening to suffocate us all.

Brynn's eyes dart around nervously before she answers. "There was, but he destroyed it. He's meticulous, careful." She clenches her fists, her knuckles turning white with the effort. "Without a doubt," she adds, her voice low and steady. "I saw it with my own eyes, and I wish to God I hadn't. I've tried everything, Fallon. Please, you have to help me."

The desperation in her voice shakes me to my core. It's as if she's clinging to a fragile thread of hope, and we're the only ones who can keep it from snapping completely.

"That's horrific and I'm so sorry. Thank you for bringing this to our attention, Brynn. We'll handle Griffin Dunlop," I promise, my voice cold and unwavering.

Her eyes glisten with unshed tears, but her gratitude is evident. We've given her hope, something she clearly hasn't felt in a long time. And for that, we will deliver justice—swift, brutal, and merciless.

"Thank you," she breathes out, relief etched across her face.

With a nod, Brynn pushes herself to her feet, her designer heels clicking against the tattered linoleum floor. She smooths down her expensive dress, looking entirely out of place in the dingy diner. Her gaze lingers on Grave for a moment before settling back on mine.

"I'll be waiting for your call," she says, determination adding an edge to her voice.

"Expect to hear from me soon," I tell her, my own resolve echoing in my words. She offers a small, grateful smile before disappearing into the shadows beyond the diner's doors.

As the door swings shut behind her, I feel the weight of responsibility settle firmly on my shoulders. This isn't just about revenge anymore; it's about justice—for Brynn, her children, and the countless others whose lives have been shattered by Griffin Dunlop's depravity.

"Let's get to work," I say, glancing at Grave. His eyes are dark, stormy pools, reflecting the same lethal intent that surges through my veins.

"Whatever it takes," he agrees, and I know we won't rest until Griffin Dunlop is nothing but a bitter memory, swallowed by the darkness he so richly deserves.

The air grows heavier as we're left with the gravity of Brynn's story, and my blood boils with every beat of my heart. I can't help but picture Griffin Dunlop's face, a smug grin plastered on it as he takes advantage of innocent lives. The thought of what he's done to those children makes my stomach churn, and I know one thing for certain—he has to pay.

"Grave," I say, struggling to hold back the rage in my voice, "I think we both know there's only one way to deal with someone like Dunlop. He needs to die."

Grave's eyes meet mine, his expression unreadable. "Fallon, I understand your anger, and I agree that what he's done is unforgivable. But are you absolutely certain that murder is the best course of action?" His voice is low and steady, betraying no emotion.

"Of course I'm sure," I spit out, my fists clenching at my sides. "What other choice do we have? This man is a monster, Grave. He deserves nothing less."

"Look, I get it. But murder, Fallon...it changes you." He hesitates, and I see something flicker in his eyes before he continues. "I've been down that path before. More than once. And each time, it leaves its mark on you. No matter how deserved it was."

Chapter 51

FALLON

The bustling hum of the office fades as Mia and I find a rare moment of privacy in my corner suite. I love this time of year, when a new cohort of interns joins the firm for a three-month stint. They're eager to learn and bursting with creativity, providing an injection of enthusiasm during their time here. There's definitely a lot more laughter around... and TikToking.

As invigorating as their presence is, it also means the office is a lot busier and therefore noisier than usual. The glass walls that typically offer transparency, now with blinds drawn, provide us with a cocoon away from prying eyes and eager ears.

I watch Mia hesitantly playing with her curls, her freckled face revealing the weight of unspoken words as she perches on the couch where clients usually download me with their traumatic stories. She takes a deep breath and finally spills the truth that's been gnawing at her.

"Fallon," Mia begins, her voice carrying the weight of a confession, "I need to tell you something." She pauses, looking conflicted about whether she can end the conversation and go sprinting out of my office or not. But then an expression of determination sets in and she blurts what's been bottled up inside: "I was offered another job, and I'm seriously considering taking it."

My heart skips a beat as I look at her with a mix of surprise and hurt. "Another job? Why would you even consider another offer—we've built this company together, Mia. You're not happy here now all of a sudden?" I question, trying to make sense of her revelation.

She doesn't immediately respond, and I search her face for answers. "Is it the pay, Mia? Because we can revisit that. And benefits are top-of-the-line, I don't think anyone could find better elsewhere." I frown as I try to consider what other impetus Mia might have to leave my side. "Or is it something else?"

Mia's gaze softens, her eyes searching mine for understanding. "I've just been thinking that, maybe, if we weren't constantly in this high-stakes environment, we could focus on our friendship more. It feels like we've become workmates more than friends, and I don't want to lose what we had." Her words hang in the air, vulnerable and pregnant with meaning. "So when the recruiter reached out, I took their call and...this new opportunity could be a really good one for me, Fall."

I clench my jaw, struggling not to let my emotions betray me. This is not how I imagined our partnership would evolve. We were supposed to be in this together, thick as thieves, loyal to the bitter end. Mia was there with me in the early days, part of some of the first concept meetings where we figured out the types of programs we would run, and even the types of work we would and wouldn't do. She was there for the financing conversations, the branding and the hiring. All of it. She was meant to grow with me, and be part of the evolution of this company as it expands first nationally and then globally. But now she's pulling away? It seems like weird timing, especially when she has a whole career path wrapped up in this plan.

My mind goes wild with possibilities.

However, before I can fully grasp the intention behind Mia's decision, she adds another layer to her confession. "And, Fallon, I don't like the dark side of this business. The... revenge operations."

I immediately feel very defensive. "You mean the 'dark' side where we actually make a real impact? The part where victims become survivors, and where justice is properly served?"

She pauses as if carefully considering her words. "I know it's well-intentioned on your part, Fallon. I can see that. But, nevertheless, it's been getting to me, and I thought a change might be good for both of us."

"Good for both of us?" I repeat, my voice barely concealing the bitterness seeping through. Mia's always been the kind-hearted one, but I never imagined she would back out when things got tough. I sneer, "You really think we can sustain a business on the back of informative lectures about derelict fuckboys? You think that charging women to fill out spreadsheets about their love language and their propensity to withstand shitty behavior from mediocre men is what pays the bills?"

"Fallon, please understand. I just want us both to be happy and safe," Mia pleads, her eyes glistening with unshed tears. "Physically, psychologically... all the ways."

I struggle to swallow the lump in my throat, my heart aching from the raw honesty of her words. I can see she genuinely believes it's for the best, but the thought of losing her, of facing this formidable mountain, is almost too much to bear.

"Is that what you really want, Mia?" I ask quietly, trying to steady my voice.

She nods reluctantly, her hand reaching out to grasp mine. "I think it's what we both need, Fallon."

As her words sink in, I realize that Mia's consideration of this new role isn't an act of betrayal, but rather one of love and loyalty. She wants to protect our bond, even if it means walking away. She wants Fallon... her friend, above Fallon, CEO and covert Revenge Seeker, Enactor of Vengeance, Avenger of the Screwed Over. I just wonder if it's too late, and if we'll just simply continue to drift away from each other, like I suddenly realize we already have been.

"Alright, Mia," I whisper, my hand on hers. It stings, but I know what I have to do. "Thank you for putting our friendship first. I'll be here to support you however I can."

Chapter 52

FALLON

I step out into the morning light, the sun's rays piercing my eyes. Aksel's arms wrap around me from behind, his lips finding the nape of my neck, causing goosebumps to trail their way from my chest up to the base of my ear. I melt into him despite the unease churning within.

"I missed you last night," he murmurs, his breath warm on my skin.

Guilt twists my gut. I turn in his arms, forcing a smile. "Early client meeting. You know how busy it gets."

The lie burns my tongue. If he knew where I really was, who I was with...

Aksel cups my face, his thumb tracing my cheek. "I know the hours you put in. Just don't forget about me." His words pierce my conscience, his gaze emanating unconditional trust in me, which makes my stomach drop.

I kiss him, desperate to drown the deception, if only for a moment. We cling to each other, passion rising.

He has no idea of the darkness I harbor, or the revenge that drives me. I compartmentalize, justifying my actions. This is for my clients, for justice.

But with Aksel, I find light. A refuge from the shadows, even after all he did to me. He's a good distraction, one that has me thinking differently, getting my mind off the dark thoughts that he doesn't even know torment my brain as I ruminate and seek out numbness. I crave these stolen moments with him, even as my secrets eat me away inside.

I'm split in two—the lover and the avenger, bound by a delicate thread. I fear the day he learns the truth, shattering the world we've built.

For now, I sink into his kiss, savoring the eye of the storm. The duplicity may destroy me, but I'm powerless to stop the swirling chaos within. I can't just cease my revenge operations because I met a man who wouldn't approve of it. That would mean letting so many people down who need my help.

The dim basement light casts my face in shadows as I descend the stairs. The captive man's eyes widen, his breath quickening in ragged gasps. He scrambles back against the cold concrete wall.

"Please," he rasps, his voice hoarse. "I'll give you anything. Just let me go."

I circle slowly, relishing his panic. "Anything?" I quirk a brow. "You took everything from her, Harvey. Her freedom, her self-worth, her future."

Grave looms behind me, his face obscured by darkness. Harvey Maxwell's gaze darts between us, terror rising.

I crouch down, getting close, just out of reach at the very end of the man's shackles. "You don't get to bargain, Harvey. You're going to feel the full weight of what you did."

He whimpers, shrinking away toward the wall. Pathetic. This shell of a man bears no resemblance to the monster who ruined my client's life.

"Look at you," I hiss. "You're nothing now. Just like you made her feel. A silly man in a serious cage."

Tears stream down his face. He starts babbling apologies, pleas for mercy. The words blur together, falling on deaf ears.

I straighten up, glancing at Grave. One nod and he grabs the man, wrenching his shackled arm back. A cry of pain pierces the stale air.

"Please stop!" Harvey shrieks. Music to my ears. "I'll never hurt anyone again! I promise!"

I force myself to turn away, to leave him with Grave. His anguished screams follow me up the stairs.

Justice is brutal, but necessary. I steel myself, ready to deliver more. My clients deserve retribution, and I'm more than happy to serve as their instrument of vengeance.

I emerge from the basement, Harvey's screams fading behind me. Upstairs, silence greets me—a stark contrast to the dark deeds taking place below. I figure having Grave knock some sense into Harvey will be a good way to set the tone for our captive. And, I also figure Grave could use a little fun. I know this isn't his first kidnapping-torture-basement-type scenario. He definitely knows what he's doing.

I move through the condo in a daze, adrenaline still coursing through my veins. In the kitchen, I catch my reflection in the window and pause. There's a wildness in my eyes, an intensity I barely recognize. This quest for vengeance has awakened something primal within me.

Shaking my head, I grab a glass of water, willing my pulse to settle. I can't lose control, especially right now. There are more battles to be won for my clients, more justice to be meted out. I need to remain clear-headed. Still, there's something about taking a grown man—a grown *bad* man—that has me excited. Like when you spend all day summoning the courage to go on the biggest, scariest water slide imaginable, and then you finally do it, and immediately want to go back and do it again. That's me. Let's kidnap another fucker right away!

My phone buzzes with a new message. It's from Aksel, checking in, asking about my day. I stare at the screen, a knot forming in my stomach. The sweet, gentle Aksel of today. If he knew what I was capable of, would he still look at me the same way?

I think back to our last date, how his smile soothed my soul, and how his laugh filled me with light. He sees the best in me, even when I can't see it in myself. I crave his warmth, his goodness. It makes me feel human again.

But the basement still calls to me, its icy darkness a lure I cannot resist. My clients need me to embrace that darkness so I can drag their tormentors into the light. I try to picture his face if he accidentally stumbled on the torture basement. What he'd think of me. How quickly he'd run away from me and into some other woman's arms... Carissa's, maybe. I shudder at the thought.

I close my eyes, tension gripping my shoulders. Two sides war within me—the woman seeking connection with someone who may be my soulmate, versus the avenger stalking the shadows. I have a revenge business to run, and Aksel isn't entirely off the hook yet. I'm still collecting information to decide what happens to him. I want to be both, a lover and an avenger, but I'm worried the universe is going to make me choose.

For now, I'll continue to keep these worlds separate. Aksel, despite the turbulence he caused me years ago, is my current refuge from the storm, and it's vital that he doesn't find out what's going on with Harvey or any other client targets. I tap out a vague reply, warmed by his affection yet chilled by my deceit. I'm balanced on a knife's edge.

All I can do is move forward, one act of vengeance at a time, hoping I don't lose myself—or those I care for—along the way.

My boots thud against the cold concrete as I descend into the shadows of the basement. The man's eyes follow me, wide with fear, as he watches me descend the stairs. Good. Let him taste what Claudia tasted for two long years trapped in his clutches. He's acquired a couple of bruises since I last saw him—a black eye, a fat lip. His nose perhaps looks a little more crooked than last time I set eyes on it.

I slam the tray down, the sharp clatter echoing through the confined space. "Eat up," I snarl. "It's more than you gave her."

He reaches tentatively for the food, but I swat his hand away. "Not yet, actually. First, you listen."

I lean in close, the faint basement light flickering across my face. "You took everything from her. Her hopes, her freedom, her spirit." My voice drips with contempt. "She was your lover, and you crushed her."

He cowers under my accusing words. "I didn't mean to," he whimpers. "I just wanted to protect her—"

"Protect her?!" I slap him hard across the face. The sound ricochets off the cold walls. "You isolated her from the world and called it love. You broke her and called it concern."

I grab his bearded chin, forcing his watery eyes to meet my fiery gaze. "She trusted you. And you betrayed that trust. Just like he did."

Bitter memories flood through me as I see Aksel's face in this sniveling man's. The one who claimed to love me but left scars far deeper than this brute's.

"He?" the man quirks a bloodied brow, looking confused.

"Nevermind," I shake my head as my fingers dig into the man's jaw. "Men like you take what isn't yours to take. You destroy beauty and call it correction." My words drip with venom. "It's an unhealthy, misogynistic form of control. It's abuse. And you, Harvey Maxwell, don't get to play God with people's lives."

I fling his head back and stand tall, every muscle taut. His neck is tucked into his shoulders, eyes bulging with fear and discomfort. "You're in my world now, and I *will* teach you the meaning of helplessness. I'll show you what it means to be at the mercy of someone else." My voice echoes with righteous fury. "Justice will be done here. No matter how long it takes. So don't even bother to think about escaping, or that you can bribe me to let you go. You'll be allowed to go once you've learned your lesson and made things as right as can be."

I turn sharply and climb the stairs, not waiting for a response. The darkness clings to me as I return to the light, my soul wrapped tight in vengeance's embrace. I haven't had the opportunity to hold a target captive in my home before, and I have to say, I'm starting to quite like it. It's like therapy with a captive audience who thinks you're a complete lunatic, who is on edge because they think you might murder them, and I can't recommend it highly enough.

I emerge from the basement, the lingering adrenaline from my confrontation still coursing through my veins. As I step back into the normalcy of my condo, the two worlds feel strangely disconnected.

I move to the window and stare blankly outside, the image of Aksel invading my thoughts. I see his smile, feel his touch, hear his laugh. The man who makes me feel treasured, desired. Who looks at me like I alone command the stars, the stock market, and of course, his cock.

Yet now there's yet another gaping chasm between us, and this time it's my fault. A secret darkness he can't know, because I fear that if he glimpsed even a fraction of the rage within me, and if he even got wind of my revenge ops business, it would repel him. We'd be over just as quickly as we began this time around.

I rest my palm on the cool glass. No, I rationalize, my business isn't about base vengeance, or pettiness for the sake of it. It's about justice. Righting serious, life-changing wrongs the law cannot or will not. My clients deserve someone to fight for them, to be their champion. Without me, they'd never get the justice they deserve.

Still, the duplicity eats at me. I hate lying to a partner, and compartmentalizing this clandestine work from my time with Aksel feels wrong. The more I justify it, the more hollow the words sound, even to me.

I close my eyes, tension gripping my shoulders. I can't stop now. Too many current and potential clients need my help. Their pain fuels my purpose, even as it threatens all I'm starting to build with Aksel.

I let out a shaky breath. He may never understand my crusade, but I can't sacrifice it. Not even for him. I'll carry this weight alone, and if one day he happens to find out about it, we'll address any of his concerns then. Even if it means the end of us.

The world needs more justice, and I will be the one to deliver it. For my clients, and for myself. No matter what it may cost.

Chapter 53

FALLON

I can't believe I'm actually holding this invitation to the charity gala of the year in my hands. The Dempsey name has always been synonymous with high society, so I wasn't surprised to receive it. It's just the fact Aksel's name is right there on the invitation too, next to mine. We're invited together—as a couple, which is both thrilling and terrifying.

"Are you sure you want to do this?" I ask Aksel, my voice shaking only slightly. "Go to the gala together, as an official couple?"

"Absolutely," he replies confidently, wrapping an arm around my waist. "It's about time we showed the world who we belong to."

I nod, swallowing hard. This could either be a dream come true or the complete opposite.

The days leading up to the event are filled with excitement and anxiety. I spend hours poring over fashion magazines and browsing online for the perfect gown. My heart races at the thought of attending the gala on Aksel's arm, showcasing our blooming relationship and unity for everyone to see. It's almost as if by publicly showcasing our relationship at an event like this, I'm also confirming it to myself. That Aksel and I are serious, that we're in a legitimate adult relationship. Maybe showing everyone else we're a real couple will help break through the surrealness for me, also.

Finally, I find it: a stunning, floor-length silk gown in deep midnight blue. The cut is elegant and sophisticated, hugging my curves while draping gracefully to the floor. The cowl neckline adds a touch of sensuality, and, although I don't normally like busy detailing, the intricate beadwork along the waist shimmers like the night sky. This is the dress—the one that will make me feel invincible, untouchable by the whispers and stares that are bound to follow us at the event.

"Wow, Fallon," Aksel breathes as I carefully step my way down the staircase in a delicate pair of strappy, silver-studded heels. "You look incredible."

"Thank you," I reply, blushing under his gaze. "As soon as I tried this on, I knew it was the one." I soak in his appearance, nearly drooling at the sight of him dressed in an immaculate tuxedo replete with bow tie. I can't wait to yank every piece of it off him later, even if every button on his meticulously starched shirt pops off in the process.

"Definitely." He smiles, reaching for my hand. "You're going to knock everyone dead at the gala."

I can't help but smile back, feeling a surge of confidence. Together, we'll make a statement—a declaration of our emerging love, and defiance against those who've tried to tear us apart in the past. Including ourselves.

"Let's show them what they're up against," I say, entwining my fingers with his.

"Absolutely," he agrees, his eyes filled with determination. "Together."

Aksel

The moment I lay eyes on Fallon, my breath catches in my throat. She stands at the top of the staircase, her midnight blue gown shimmering under the soft lighting, and she looks like a goddess descending from the heavens.

She's absolutely breathtaking.

She gives me a shy smile as she glides down the stairs, her cheeks tinted with a rosy blush. "Thank you, Aksel. You look quite dashing yourself."

My heart swells with pride and desire, knowing that this stunning woman has chosen to stand by my side. We've been together for a while now, but it's not something we've shared beyond close family and friends, and there's been no public announcement.

Time seems to slow as we share a tender kiss, our lips barely grazing before we reluctantly part.

"Ready?" I ask, offering her my arm.

"More than ever," she replies, slipping her hand into the crook of my elbow.

But as we head for the door, the urge to touch her, to feel her body against mine, becomes too strong to resist. With a growl, I pull her to me, our lips crashing together in a fiery kiss that sends shivers down my spine.

"Wait," I whisper hoarsely, my voice thick with want. "I need you, Fallon. Now."

"Here?" she asks, her eyes wide with surprise and excitement.

"Here," I confirm, leading her toward the living room. We can't wait any longer, and the gala can damn well wait.

In the middle of the living room, I strip off my suit jacket and bow tie, leaving them crumpled on the floor. Fallon follows suit, allowing her exquisite gown to pool at her feet, followed by her sheer lace bra and panties. Good god, I can't wait to remove those with my teeth later.

We both hop onto the leather couch. The sight of her naked body, glowing under the soft light of the lamp, is almost more than I can bear. My erection is rock hard, eager for her.

"God, Fallon," I groan, pulling her close and kissing her deeply. "You're irresistible. There's no way I could wait until later on tonight."

"Then don't resist," she breathes against my lips, wrapping her arms around my neck and pulling me closer.

We lose ourselves in each other, our bodies tangled together as we give in to our passion. The glowing light in the living room surrounds us like a protective cocoon, inside of which nothing outside matters.

When we finally rise from the couch, we're both flushed, giddy, and utterly satisfied. Fallon's eyes sparkle like the stars themselves, and I can't help but feel like the luckiest man alive.

"Come on," I say, helping her back into her gown before slipping into my suit once more. "Let's do this. Let's introduce the world to the future Mrs. Aksel King."

Fallon's eyes fly wide open and she glances at me sideways.

"Just checking to see if you were listening," I smirk.

She playfully punches me in the arm, and although she tries to play it cool, I can't help but notice the little red flush developing on her cheeks.

The limousine pulls up to the dazzling venue, and the night air buzzes with anticipation. Reporters and photographers swarm the car, eager to capture the glamorous Dempsey-King duo as we make our grand entrance.

"Ready?" I ask, tightening my grip on Fallon's hand.

"Ready," she confirms, her eyes shining with determination.

As we step out of the limo, a flurry of camera flashes greet us, their staccato bursts blinding and relentless. We walk arm-in-arm towards the entrance, ignoring the shouted questions and intrusive lenses, our focus solely on each other.

"Remember," I whisper into her ear as we reach the doors. "No matter what happens tonight, we're in this together."

"Always," she replies, squeezing my hand. And with that, we stride into the gala, ready to face the world.

Inside, the gala is a dazzling display of wealth and influence. Crystal chandeliers drip from the ceilings, champagne flows freely, and the room thrums with conversation and laughter. Many eyes turn to us as we enter, whispers and murmurs trailing in our wake.

I feel Fallon's grip on my arm tighten, her unease palpable. Public scrutiny has never been easy for her, unless she's running one of her programs and speaking to her clients in the intimate environment of her own lecture theater, whereas I'm used to being under the microscope in the boardroom. Still, a boardroom is a much more intimate venue, and without less paparazzi, than a star-studded ballroom. I make an effort to appear relaxed and confident as we navigate the sea of scrutinizing faces.

"Just ignore them," I murmur. "This night is about us."

Fallon nods, a brave smile fixed on her flawlessly painted lips. But as we make small talk with various socialites and tycoons, her discomfort visibly grows. I overhear snippets of crude speculation about our relationship, including accusations of it being a publicity stunt.

"Did you hear about the cheese factory explosion?" I squeeze Fallon's waist gently as I point over at a tray of charcuterie including a busy spread of cheeses.

Fallon glances at me like I've lost my mind. "Huh?"

"There was nothing left but de-brie." I smirk. "Sorry, I couldn't resist."

She rolls her eyes but her laughter, while strained, seems to help settle her nerves. We continue mingling, and the night progresses smoothly. Between us, we know several attendees who run in our respective circles, and we introduce each other. "This is my partner, Aksel," she says to one group, and "Aksel here is my boyfriend," she says to another, as if testing out the way the words feel in public. And to be honest, I don't care what she calls me, as long as she calls me hers. I'm just grateful to be firmly in her orbit once again.

When lively music fills the hall, I seize the opportunity. "Dance with me," I say, leading Fallon to the floor before she can protest. I pull her close as we sway and twirl, our bodies pressed together intimately.

As expected, our dance attracts even more prying eyes. But Fallon seems to relax in my arms, momentarily forgetting the judging stares and letting herself enjoy the moment. Other than the recent charity event, it's been a long time since I've danced in a formal setting like this, the last time probably back with Fallon at prom. And it somehow feels like that was just yesterday as we once again entwine our limbs on the dance floor.

Although I'm feeling more than satisfied by our earlier encounter, it still turns me on to have Fallon in my arms, guiding her across the dance floor and spinning her around at my will.

The song ends, and I dip her low, her hair brushing the floor. "Was that so bad?" I ask playfully as I draw her back up.

"Not at all," she says, a genuine smile on her flushed face. No matter what rumors swirl around us, we sure can dance.

Fallon's smile falters as she spots Carissa sauntering towards us, a calculating glint in her eyes.

"Oh god," she frowns. "I forgot she was going to be here. It feels like she's everywhere we turn."

"Mind if I cut in?" Carissa asks sweetly, already wedging herself between Fallon and I.

I tense, old memories threatening to resurface. But Fallon beats me to a response.

"Actually, we do mind, Carissa," she says sharply. "Why don't you slither back to whatever hole you crawled out of?"

Carissa recoils as if struck, clearly not expecting such a biting retort from Fallon. The surrounding guests pretend not to have heard, but I catch more than a few poorly concealed smirks.

She looks at me for some type of support and I just shrug, not a shred of empathy on my face or in my mind.

With as much dignity as she can summon, Carissa turns on her heel and stalks away. Her heel wobbles, and she stumbles, almost losing her balance and taking a spill on the dance floor. I feel a swell of pride for Fallon, along with a pang of nostalgia.

"Just like old times," I say with a rueful chuckle. "Carissa never could take a hint."

Fallon nods, the fire in her eyes fading to lingering uncertainty as we sway gently to the music. I know she's thinking of the disastrous misunderstandings from our school days, when Carissa's scheming very nearly tore us apart for good. Her presence has once again stirred up old wounds and painful memories Fallon and I both would rather leave buried. But the time has come to set the record straight. She deserves to know the truth.

"Fallon," I begin gently, "about what happened back in high school..."

She tenses in my arms, eyes flashing in warning. "Don't," she says sharply. "I don't want to rehash ancient history. Especially not tonight, here, in front of all these people. We've already drawn enough attention just by being here."

"Please—."

"No, Aksel," she hisses. "The last thing we need is for me to have a breakdown in the middle of the dance floor." She holds up her thumb and forefinger, roughly an inch apart. "And I'm this close to falling apart as it is, so please..."

"Please, just hear me out," I press on. "Carissa didn't tell you the whole story that night. She deliberately misled you, made you think..."

I trail off as Fallon pulls back, shaking her head. "It doesn't matter now," she says, but there's a waver in her voice belying her words.

"It does matter," I insist, tipping her chin up to meet my earnest gaze. "You thought I betrayed you, but I never would have. Carissa lied to drive us apart."

Fallon searches my face, hesitation and longing warring in her eyes. In this moment, she looks as vulnerable as the heartbroken girl I once knew, still nursing those old wounds.

"You have to trust me," I implore her. "One day, you'll understand the full truth. But know this—you're the only one for me. You always have been."

She blinks back tears, then nods slowly. The band strikes up a new song, and I pull her close once more as we continue to sway.

The past can't touch us here.

Chapter 54

AKSEL

(Unknown number): Is this Aksel?

Me: Yes. Who's this?

(Unknown number): Oh hi Aksel. This is Fenton Dempsey, and I'm here with Bronson.

My gut clenches as I read their names, which sound like the old money and privilege associated with the men that bear them. Of all of Fallon's brothers, it's Fenton and Bronson that I know the least.

Why now? After all these months, what do they want?

Me: Oh, hey guys. What's up?

Fenton: We'd like to meet with you at the cigar lounge on 4th. Have some whiskey and a chat.

Fallon's brothers want to meet with me for a chat? I'm guessing it's about their sister, of course. But what couldn't wait until the next family dinner? I guess this means they're either going to interrogate me, or they want to talk about Fallon without her overhearing. I guess I'll find out soon.

It's intimidating, the thought of going into the lion's den alone, although at least it sounds like Link won't be there. But neither will Cheston, and he's the one who always makes everything okay for everyone. Whatever the agenda, I'm happy to go. Because for Fallon, I'll walk through fire.

The lounge is dimly lit, all dark wood and leather. My boots thud on the plush rugs that cover the dark wood floor, the sound muffled by conversation and tinkling glasses.

Fenton spots me first. "Aksel, glad you could make it." His smile is friendly, guarded.

Bronson nods. "Been a while." His gaze is sharp, assessing.

My smile is a baring of teeth. "It has been a minute."

We exchange meaningless pleasantries, sizing each other up. Beneath the civility, tension hums.

Finally, Fenton leans forward, whiskey in hand. "That family dinner you attended, that was a bit of a doozy."

I smirk. "I wasn't sure if that's how they normally go or... Fallon hinted it might not have been a typical family dinner, but I thought maybe she was just making sure I'd come back a second time."

Bronson snorts. "Nah, you really picked an epic dinner. Her and Link going at it like that."

Fenton takes the opportunity to segue into the reason the three of us are really here. "How is she, really?"

The question I've been dreading. My chest tightens. "Fallon is..." How to answer? Not fine. Struggling. Drowning in darkness. "She's coping."

Bronson's stare intensifies. "We've noticed things aren't right. She's... different."

I swallow hard. "You've seen it too."

Bronson sighs. "Stubborn as hell, which is typical for her. But this black mood..."

"She won't accept help." I rub the back of my neck, rage and fear twisting inside. "But she needs it."

"She's always been stubborn," Fenton says, swirling his whiskey. "Never listens to reason. Charges ahead without thinking of consequences."

As serious as the topic is, it's amusing hearing someone else so close to Fallon describe her using almost the exact same words I would.

"That fierce independence is what I love about her," Bronson adds. "But it's going to get her into trouble one day."

I grip my glass, the urge to defend Fallon warring with the truth in their words. "She's resilient. Determined. She always fights her way through," I say, unable to hold back. "Some of that can come across as stubbornness, but I think those qualities are important and positive."

Fenton studies me. "You really care for her, don't you?"

Heat creeps up my neck. I look away, unable to lie.

"Well, shit," Bronson breathes. "Fallon finally found someone as stubborn as she is." He pauses. "But you're right. She's always been so damned independent." Affection softens his gruff tone, but then he frowns. "But this goes deeper. There's something wrong."

The truth spills out in a rush. "She's haunted by something she hasn't shared with me yet. Something that happened after we broke up back in high school, maybe something that happened in college. Whatever it is, it's destroying her."

Clouds seem to pass over both men's faces, their eyes growing dark with memory.

"She made some questionable choices back then, and ended up running with a bad crowd. Some of them... they... hurt her," Fenton growls.

"They hurt Fallon? How?" Ice slides through my veins and I freeze, my whiskey glass partway to my mouth.

They exchange a look, coming to some unspoken agreement. Fenton leans forward, his expression grave. "If you truly care for our sister, then there's something you should know."

I sit up straighter, heart pounding. "What is it?"

"There's a darkness in Fallon. Has been since she was a teenager, since soon after you broke up. It only got worse in college. We've always tried to protect her, but..." Fenton trails off, brow furrowing.

"She has enemies," Bronson says bluntly. "Dangerous enemies. And if they discover how much Fallon means to you..."

I meet Fenton's gaze, jaw set. "Tell me everything."

They exchange another look, then begin.

"She didn't tell you? Yeah, she was physically hurt by some guys that attended the same school. They were never brought to justice because of some legal technicalities, and because their daddies hired a great defense lawyer who made her look like the villain. But it's her story to tell you if and when she's ready. I can't say more than that."

"They can't get away with hurting her," I frown. "Whatever it is, it happened a while ago, but they can't just wander around free for the rest of their lives."

Bronson's eyes meet mine, hard as flint. "Oh, we know. And they won't. We're just biding our time."

In this moment, I see the truth: they love Fallon as fiercely as I do. Intimidating at first, but now my allies. Our bond forged in fear for the woman who holds our hearts.

"So how do we help her to get through it in the meantime?" Bronson asks.

Fenton slams his glass on the table, amber liquid sloshing over the rim. "We have to do something. Before it's too late."

"I know." A dull ache builds behind my eyes. "But Fallon won't accept help. And if we push too hard, she'll shut us out completely. Things between her and me are still... fragile, developing."

"So we help without her knowing." Bronson cracks his knuckles, a habit when he's thinking hard. "Be there for her. Watch out for her. Make sure she's safe."

"And plot our revenge." Fenton's smile is sharp as a knife. "We destroy those guys, together. They'll never see it coming."

The ache in my head intensifies, fueled by rage. "They won't know what hit them."

Our drinks sit forgotten as we make plans. Every word, every idea, brings me closer to the vengeance I crave.

"I do know she's at least safe at work," I confess.

"How so?" Fenton looks skeptical. "Because based on what Link's private investigator found, it sounds like she's into some pretty dangerous shit."

"Well, her work associate, Grave... I kind of planted him there. I needed someone I could trust to watch over her, and I knew Grave was the best for the job."

Fenton and Bronson exchange glances, a mixture of surprise and understanding passing between them. The atmosphere is charged with unspoken questions, the weight of my confession hanging in the air.

"So...you manipulated the situation so Fallon would hire this Grave guy without knowing you knew him?" Fenton quirks a brow.

"And you did that for Fallon? You weren't doing it to like, stalk her or anything, right?" Bronson eyes me suspiciously. "You did it because you care about her safety like we do?"

"Yeah," I rake my hand through my hair. "I've been extremely concerned for Fallon's safety. I did want to keep tabs on her, but more in the sense that I just needed to know she was okay. I wasn't trying to be intrusive."

Fenton and Bronson both seem to take me at face value, and their expressions soften.

"I needed her to have the best protection, even if it meant bending the truth a bit."

Bronson nods. "We get it. We also look out for family and others who are close to us, no matter what."

Feeling touched by the camaraderie of the evening, and the unspoken pact we've made to keep Fallon safe and support her through the challenges ahead, I raise my glass. "To family, and to ensuring Fallon's safety. We're in this together."

By the time we part ways, our pact is sealed. We'll stand by Fallon's side through the darkness. And we'll make her attackers regret the day they decided to fuck with her.

The war has begun. There will be blood.

I stride into the night, purpose steeling my spine. Fallon isn't alone anymore. At least two of her brothers are with her now.

And so am I.

Chapter 55

As I step onto the boat, Aksel's hand on the small of my back guiding me, I can't help but roll my eyes. A romantic dinner cruise? Seriously? It sounds like something my parents did decades ago when they were still together.

The yacht glides smoothly across the water under the moonlit sky, casting a mesmerizing glow on the rippling waves. Lights on the shore twinkle like pretty strings of diamond bracelets. And although I want to brush it off as cheesy, I have to admit, there's something utterly enchanting about it.

"Really, Aksel? A dinner cruise?" I tease him, arching an eyebrow and smirking. "What are you, eighty years old?"

He feigns offense, placing a hand over his heart and pretending to sulk. "Ouch, Fallon. That one cut deep," he says, his faux old-man voice dripping with sarcasm. "I thought you'd appreciate a little romance. Something a little bit special."

"Romance?" I snort, unable to suppress the laughter bubbling up inside me. "This is so cliché." But despite my words, I feel a warm, fuzzy sensation spreading through my chest as we take our seats at a private candlelit table, set intimately for two.

"Fine, next time I'll just order pizza and we'll watch Netflix," Aksel retorts playfully, shooting me a sidelong glance that makes my stomach flutter. "But you'd be missing out on some top-notch food here, Fallon."

"Okay, okay, I'll give you that," I concede, my gaze wandering over the beautifully plated dishes set before us. Aksel has always been a man of exquisite taste, and tonight is no exception. As we dig into our meal, exchanging playful banter and teasing each other mercilessly, I realize that the setting, as cliché as it may be, holds a certain charm that I can't deny. And as much as I hate to admit it, I'm falling for it—and for Aksel—more than I ever thought possible.

As the evening wears on, our conversation takes a more serious turn. Aksel asks about my work and my family, seeming genuinely interested in getting to know me on a deeper level. So much time has passed since he was thoroughly intertwined in my teenage years that we have a lot to catch up on. His thoughtfulness catches me off guard, and I find myself opening up to him in a way I rarely do with anyone. It's like we're back in his room again, each wearing one headphone from his music player, sharing our innermost secrets and feelings.

When the waiter brings out dessert, I slide a small gift bag across the table to Aksel. He looks at me quizzically, eyebrows raising in surprise. "What's this? A gift for me? Tonight I'm meant to spoil *you*."

I shrug, feigning nonchalance despite the nerves twisting in my stomach. "Just a little something. You know, since you went to so much trouble planning this evening."

Aksel pulls the tissue paper out of the bag, and for a moment he just stares at the contents, silent. My anxiety spikes, and I rush to fill the silence. "It's, uh, just a first edition of one of your favorite childhood books. I know how much you loved the Hardy Boys, and how hard it can be to find, so I thought—"

But before I can finish, Aksel looks up at me, eyes shining with emotion. "Fallon, this is...amazing. Perfect, really. How did you know? This is the one book I've been missing, and now I have the complete set."

A flush creeps up my neck at the awe in his voice. I glance away, embarrassed by the intensity of his gaze. "I pay attention," I say softly. "And it always used to be your favorite. I remember you showing me your collection back when you had that special shelving system in your room."

Aksel reaches across the table, grasping my hand in his. I meet his eyes again and see depths of tenderness there that make my breath catch. "You always surprise me," he says, his thumb grazing slow circles over my knuckles, his touch sending electric shivers up my arm. "There are so many layers to you, Fallon, and I find myself discovering new ones every day. I knew you were complex, my Fallon-y, but I never realized the extent. I have a feeling that even if I lived forever, I'd still be learning new things about you every day."

A warmth blossoms in my chest at his words, which are way more meaningful than any physical intimacy we've yet shared, as wonderful as those moments have been. In this moment, I realize that what we have between us is far deeper than I ever thought it could be. And as Aksel lifts my hand to his lips, pressing a gentle kiss to my fingers, I know with certainty that I'm falling irrevocably, terrifyingly in love with this man.

We stumble through the front door of my condo, lips fused together, hands roaming and grasping. Aksel kicks the door shut behind us and backs me up against the wall, pinning me there with the hard length of his body.

I moan into his mouth as his hands slide under my shirt, callused fingers splaying over the sensitive skin of my stomach. Need rises up within me, hot and urgent, fueled by the memory of our earlier encounters and the new depths of intimacy we've reached tonight.

When Aksel's hands reach for the clasp of my bra, an idea sparks in my mind. I place my hands on his chest and push him back, breathless. "Wait here," I say, and slip away into my bedroom closet.

Aksel is obedient, waiting by the entrance to my bedroom, curiosity etched into the lines of his face. I emerge a moment later with a length of soft rope and a pair of handcuffs dangling from one finger.

His eyes widen, then darken with lust as understanding dawns. "Fallon," he growls, stalking toward me, "you're full of surprises."

I grin up at him, anticipation thrumming through my veins. "I told you I like to play rough."

Aksel takes the rope and cuffs from my hands, securing my wrists behind my back with the rope with a skill that sends heat pooling between my thighs. "And I like to indulge you," he purrs against my ear, nipping at the tender lobe.

"How did you get so good at that? Have you been tying lots of people up or something?" I feel a twinge of jealousy at the thought of him learning to expertly bind rope by practicing on any other woman.

"Yacht club," he smirks, and I feel a wave of relief wash over me. Wow, I never considered myself a jealous person but he's sure bringing it out in me.

He guides me to the bedroom, where the only light comes from the moon outside the window, and proceeds to lavish my body with touches both rough and reverent.

Heat radiates off Aksel's skin like a furnace, each of his touches like lightning strikes. He loosens the bindings behind my back and pulls my hands to my sides, and now ties my wrists to the headboard of the bed with the rope, binding them just enough to leave me vulnerable but not tight enough to hurt me. He bites his lip as his eyes trace over every inch of me, hungrily taking in the sight of my bare body. I whimper when he runs his fingers down my stomach, tracing the delicate lines of my ribcage and hips. His breath is hot against my skin as he kisses my neck and down my throat, leaving a trail of goosebumps in his wake. I shudder under his touch. He pinches my nipples hard, making me cry out, and then trails hot kisses down my stomach. His teeth graze my hipbone before he nips at the skin there. I arch my back, wanting more.

His hands grip my thighs, lifting me up to position me on the edge of the bed. I gasp as he roughly slides into me. I'm writhing and incoherent, awash in a sea of sensation. He claims me with each thrust, filling me up completely. I bite my lip to stifle my moans, feeling the pain and pleasure intertwine in a way that sends shivers down my spine. He's rough and demanding, his eyes never leaving mine as he takes what's his. Our lovemaking is frenzied, almost desperate, carrying echoes of our first time but underscored by a new tenderness.

Our bodies move together in a violent dance, the sound of flesh slapping against flesh echoing in the silence of the room. Every word is a groan, every touch a caress tinged with anger and desire.

I feel the anger and lust rising within me, fueling our connection. We're two broken pieces finding solace in each other's pain. He pushes deeper, his hand finding its way between us, teasing at my clit as he thrusts harder. I cry out his name, begging for release. The world around us melts away as we become lost in this twisted union.

It's not love making; it's a battle for control. A power struggle where we both know who holds the upper hand. But there's something about it that frightens me—how much I crave this kind of attention from him. How much I need him to own me, even if only for this moment. My body is on fire with his touch, my mind foggy with desire.

He growls low in his throat when he feels me tighten around him. "That's it," he murmurs, his words sending shivers down my spine. "Give it to me."

I do.

He gazes at me intensely as my pussy clenches around him, my back arching against the mattress as sparks fly in my peripheral vision. He doesn't let up, continuing to thrust as my legs shudder uncontrollably and I cry out his name.

And then, suddenly, he stops, not seeking his own release. His hand grips my chin harshly, forcing me to look into his eyes. "Remember this," he says, his voice low and dangerous. "This is what you did to me."

A single tear escapes as I nod, my heart pounding in my chest. He releases me slowly, withdrawing and watching as I collapse onto the bed, trembling. For a moment, we stare at each other—two enemies caught in a passionate dance—before he turns and walks away, leaving me alone with my thoughts and the tangled sheets.

We take a brief break, rehydrating with tall glasses of ice water. It's an easy companionship as we sip our cool drinks. We're both naked and glowing, eager to play some more.

"What do you want to do for the rest of the day?" he quirks a brow, a knowing smirk on his face.

"Oh, I think you know," I say back, sipping my drink before grabbing his hand and pulling him back into the bedroom.

"I want you again," I say, my voice rough like sandpaper over his skin.

He licks his lips, his eyes locked on mine. "Then have me."

He doesn't realize I have plans of my own to apply a little control and restraint.

I handcuff Aksel to the bedpost so he's unable to move his arms this time, his wrists bound tightly as they bulge against the steel cuffs. He tries to pull away but it's no use. I step back, taking in his restrained form.

He's aroused from eyeing him up, his chest heaving, his cock jutting out from his jeans, trying to escape.

"Fallon—"

I shush him, my mind spinning with thoughts of how much pain he caused me, and how much pleasure he can bring me.

"This is mine," I whisper, running a finger down his chest.

I know that my touch sends shivers down his spine, just as I intended. It's just another weapon in my arsenal.

I kneel before him and admire his hard length.

It twitches as I wrap my lips around the head, tasting him for the first time today. He cries out, his long, deep groan filling the room. I take him deeper, sucking and licking until he's panting and thrusting his hips.

"Fuck," he curses under his breath.

I continue to suck and lick, taking his cock deep into my throat and only releasing when

I feel my gag reflex kick in.

"My fucking god," he moans, each lick and suck taking him closer to the edge. "Suck my fat cock, baby."

But I'm not letting him come quite yet. I have other plans.

I mount him, grinding slowly at first, relishing the way he gasps for air as my pussy slides over his length.

This time when I ride his cock, it's on my terms. He can't move his arms or guide me by my waist the way he has before. Instead, the pace and rhythm are largely up to me. He just has to lay there and take what I'm giving him.

I lean forward, kissing his collarbone. "You like this?"

His hands grip the bed, and he tries to meet my gaze, but I won't let him.

"You fucking tease," he growls.

"You're mine now," I murmur as I ride him even harder, taking control of our dance.

My nails dig into his shoulders. "Say it."

"I'm yours," he gasps out.

I bite down on his neck, and he hisses.

"And you're mine," he says through gritted teeth.

"That's better."

Our bodies grind together in a rhythm that feels primal, desperate. His skin tastes salty where I've kissed him, and his scent is all musk and lust. It's intoxicating.

"Fallon," he whispers, his voice raw. "Please."

I lean forward and whisper in his ear, "Why so much talking?"

"Fallon—"

I grind down on him, savoring the feel of him inside me. "Shut up and enjoy it."

And that's when I start moving faster, my body slamming against his, our hips meeting in a frenzy.

"You're mine," I repeat, arching my back and crying out as I climax around him.

He follows quickly, his body shuddering underneath mine. His warmth fills me, and I hiss as I ride out his orgasm.

We stay like this for long moments, his heavy breathing mixing with mine, hearts racing as we try to catch our breath.

Finally, I release him from the cuffs and roll off, feeling turned on and satisfied in a way I never have before. He watches me, his eyes dark and full of so many emotions.

"Fallon... I'm not going anywhere."

"What do you mean?"

"I don't want to leave you," he clarifies. "I want to sleep here tonight."

I hesitate but nod finally. I curl up next to him, our bodies touching from hip to shoulder.

I allow myself a slight smile, content for the first time in years.

"You're going to stay?" I have to make sure I didn't mishear him.

"Yes," he replies, his hand trailing down my side. "I'm going to stay."

We drift off to sleep, holding each other tightly, our twisted love story continuing into the night.

Early the next morning, I wake to find Aksel watching me, a pensive look on his face.

"What is it?" I ask, stretching languidly. My body thrums with echoes of pleasure that I long to recreate over and over again.

He shakes his head. "Nothing's wrong. I was just thinking...there's so much about you I never suspected. Layers upon layers." His gaze turns inward. "Part of me worries there are sides to you I won't like as much. That I've created this perfect illusion of you in my head, that I've built you up to be something impossible."

"Oh great, so keeping expectations low then. A nice, achievable bar." I glare at him.

He shakes his head. "But that's the thing. I want to know all of you, Fallon. The good and the bad and everything in between."

I sit up, ignoring the protest of sore muscles, and cup his cheek. "You already do. Last night...that was me. All of me."

Aksel clasps my hand, pressing a kiss to my palm. "I know. And I wouldn't change a thing." His smile is tinged with vulnerability in a way that makes my chest ache. "You're it for me, Fallon. However long this lasts, you've ruined me for anyone else. You already did back in high school, and now you've done it all over again."

Joy and fear mingle inside me, a heady blend. I want nothing more than to lose myself in Aksel, consequences be damned—but I know all too well how fragile happiness can be. How easily it can slip through your fingers. How many times I've flip-flopped between the promises of love and revenge.

Still, when he kisses me, slow and deep, I push aside my doubts. I'll deal with the future when it comes. For now, I have this moment, and this man in my arms, and that's enough.

More than enough.

Suddenly he pulls back, brushing a lock of hair from my eyes as his face takes on a serious expression. "I should let you get some rest. We both have an early start."

I pout. "Stay. I can work from home today. Move some appointments around. We can sleep in for a bit."

"As tempting as that is, I don't think either of us will get much sleep." His gaze dips to my mouth. "And we both know where that will lead."

Heat unfurls in my belly at the promise in his voice. Even exhausted, my body stirs for his. But Aksel is right. We need our rest.

I sigh. "Fine. But you owe me a breakfast."

Aksel chuckles. "Yes, ma'am." He kisses me once more, a fleeting press of lips, and rises from the bed. I admire the play of muscle under skin as he dresses, desire flickering despite my fatigue.

"Keep looking at me like that and you'll be taking the whole day off." Aksel's voice is rough with want, his gaze simmering.

"Can't help it," I say, my voice husky. "You're delicious."

Aksel groans. "Cheeky minx. Get some beauty sleep, not that you need it." He crosses to my side of the bed, bending to drop a kiss on my forehead. "Dream of me."

"Always."

Aksel's smile is soft and pleased. "Sweet dreams, Fallon."

"Mmm, I'll be dreaming of you." I watch him go, warmth blooming in my chest. However complicated things become, I'll always have memories like this, of last night and this morning, to sustain me.

Aksel is nearly to the door when he pauses, glancing over his shoulder. "You really are it for me, you know. Always."

Joy steals my breath as Aksel slips out the door. Always.

The word echoes in my mind as I drift back to sleep for a few more hours, a smile on my lips.

Chapter 56

The scream pierces my eardrums. I tighten the rope, watching Harvey's face turn an alarming yet satisfying shade of crimson. He writhes in yet another futile attempt to free his hands, but the bonds securely fasten them behind his back. He's unable to use them to loosen the rope that restricts his ability to breathe.

The same way he strangled Claudia on so many occasions, it's now his turn to have his life flash before his eyes over and over again. I just have to make sure I don't go too far, and that I keep pulling him back from the brink so he can suffer adequately. At least for now.

My phone buzzes in my pocket. Mia. Again.

I ignore it. She's been calling all morning, worried I'll miss our meeting about the charity ball. But this is far more important than some pretentious event where people in designer outfits splash money around in an attempt to make themselves look good. Sure, I'll attend, because it will help to raise the profile of the company further, but for now, my priority is making Harvey Maxwell pay. Revenge trumps ostentatious charity events, always.

I loosen the rope slightly and Harvey gasps for breath, eyes bulging, his skin a disgusting, blotchy, mottled mess. I lean close. "How does it feel to be powerless, you sick fuck?"

He whimpers. I sneer, fist clenching. It's nowhere near enough. The damage he caused can't be undone so easily. I'm not surprised to hear him whimper. From experience, these types of guys can't handle a fraction of what they've been dishing out to women for years. They cry like little baby monsters at the first hint of discomfort.

My phone buzzes insistently. Mia leaves another voicemail, her tone increasingly shrill. But she doesn't understand. She can't. She knows I have something going on with the dark ops side of our business and that it's been keeping me occupied, but I've spared her the details. Nothing good can come from having too many people in the loop on the specifics. Grave told me not to share any details with her. And she's made it very clear she doesn't support this part of the business, anyway.

I pull the rope tighter around Harvey's neck again, cutting off his air supply once more. When he goes limp, I drop him. He crumples to the floor, his chest heaving. Not dead yet. Pity. I nudge at his large frame with my steel-capped toe. "Shut the fuck up, you monster."

I stride to the door, pausing to glance back at my prisoner. "By the way, we're nowhere near done here. This is just the beginning."

The phone buzzes again as I climb into my car. It's not Mia this time. It's Aksel. I glance at the car's clock.

Shit. Our coffee date. I completely forgot.

I debate not answering, but I can't do that to him. Not again.

"Hey," I say, trying to sound normal despite my ragged breath. "I'm so sorry I missed our date."

"Fallon, what's going on with you?" Aksel's concern comes through clearly. "This isn't like you. Talk to me."

I grip the steering wheel, torn between the truth and the lies. But of course, I can't tell him about Harvey. He wouldn't understand.

"I'm fine," I say softly. "Just...dealing with some personal things. And got distracted by work. Fully absorbed in a high-priority... spreadsheet."

Aksel sighs, clearly not believing my excuse. "You know you can tell me anything, right?"

"I know." I swallow hard. "I'm sorry again for missing our coffee date. I have to go."

Before he can protest, I end the call. My knuckles pale against the steering wheel as I take a deep breath. No one can know the truth except for Grave. By the time we're done, not even Claudia will know the full extent we've gone to on her behalf. She will just know that revenge has been done. She's been through enough already, and now this is our burden to bear.

Aksel

It was a surprise when Fallon didn't show up for our coffee date. She's usually irritatingly prompt and, given her line of work, has zero tolerance for ghosting.

But after twenty minutes passed with no sign of her, I started to worry. When I did manage to get in touch, her excuse about being distracted by a spreadsheet didn't really fly. She's supremely organized with her work, with alarms and appointment reminders set up for everything. There's no way she would have missed our coffee date if she was really in front of her computer like she claimed to be.

So it feels like she's pulling away once again, like she always has when I've gotten too close. But it feels like more than that this time. Is she hiding something from me? Is there someone else in her life? Worry gnaws at my gut. Something is wrong with Fallon, and for the life of me, I can't figure out what. But she could have at least called. My day is also busy.

I leave the coffee shop, my temporary annoyance fading into concern. Whether I have a business to run or not, I'd happily wait around forever just for one more chance to spend time with her. But Fallon's behavior has been increasingly erratic lately. She's distracted, prone to mood swings, and more secretive than usual.

I've tried to get her to open up to me, but she always pulls away with a vague explanation. Whatever she's dealing with, she insists on handling it alone.

Usually, I'd respect her privacy and just let things blow over, but this feels different and it seems to be escalating. The Fallon I know isn't flaky or unpredictable. She doesn't blow off commitments or go incommunicado for hours at a time. Yet these new behaviors feel like they're fast becoming a pattern.

Something is wrong. Really, truly wrong. And if she won't tell me what it is, I'll have to find out for myself.

I think of the voicemail she left me last week, frazzled and nearly in tears.

I can't do this anymore, Aksel. I don't know how much longer I can keep this up, she had said.

Keep what up? What has her so distressed?

Worry builds in my chest as I start my car and pull into traffic. I have to see her, have to make sure she's okay. And this time, I won't let her brush me off so easily. I'm going to get answers, one way or another. But I need to pick the right timing, because I don't want to risk driving her out of my life forever.

Fallon needs help, whether she wants to admit it or not. And I intend to give it, because when you love someone, you don't give up on them.

Not even if they push you away.

Chapter 57

AKSEL

I can't quite shake the uneasy feeling creeping up my spine when Mia reaches out to me. It's been ages since we last spoke—as in back in high school—and I can tell from the urgency in her message that something's wrong.

Mia: Hey Aksel, this is Mia.

Me: Hey Mia. Nice to hear from you. What's up?

Mia: It's Fallon. I'm worried about her. Can we meet? I know it's a strange request but I know you care about her too.

My gut reaction is to decline her request for a discreet meeting, but there's a raw vulnerability in her tone that makes me reconsider. It feels like I'm going behind Fallon's back, but then again, this is for her own good, and it doesn't appear Fallon is going to open up to me about what's going on any time soon.

I remember Mia being fairly shy and reserved back in school, so it's even more surprising that she's reaching out to me—whatever it is, this must be serious. I text her hesitantly.

Me: Alright, Mia. Let's meet.

We decide on her house as the location for our rendezvous—private and far away from prying eyes given the sensitive topic matter. The entire drive over, I can feel the weight of guilt pressing down on me. I'm betraying Fallon by meeting with Mia behind her back, but it's clear that something's going on that I need to know about. And I can only help her if I have more information.

When I arrive at the door, Mia ushers me inside hurriedly. Her eyes are filled with worry, and she looks like she hasn't slept in days. I've never seen her like this before, and it only heightens my concern for Fallon. But, despite her concern, she seems fresh—her house bears the scent of a recent shower combined with the familiar scent of freshly-applied cosmetics.

"Thank you for coming, Aksel," she says, her voice strained. "I didn't know who else to turn to."

"Of course," I reply, trying to sound reassuring. "What's going on?"

Mia takes a deep breath before diving into her story. "Look," she places her hand on my arm. "Fallon's changed," she says. "She's not herself anymore. She's more... " she pauses and looks upward, as if she's hoping the heavens will drop the words she's looking for, "...ruthless, vindictive. I know those are harsh words, but to say anything softer wouldn't do justice to the changes I've seen in her. I'm worried about her, Aksel. Really worried."

Her words hit me like a punch to the gut. I've noticed the subtle changes in Fallon too, but I've been trying to downplay them, thinking they were just a result of stress. Or at least compartmentalize them to her struggles with her family, Link in particular. But hearing Mia's observations forces me to face the truth: something's seriously wrong with Fallon and it's extending to her work and other parts of her life.

"I've noticed it too," I admit, my voice barely above a whisper. "But I thought it was just... I don't know, the pressure of running the firm getting to her. Family drama with Link and the constant pressure from her dad."

"Believe me, I wish it were that simple," Mia says, her eyes filling with tears as she shakes her head. "But it's not. It's so much more than that."

She goes on to explain the rising tension between her and Fallon, how their relationship has become strained and filled with unspoken resentments. She tells me about Fallon feeling betrayed by Mia letting her know that she's considering leaving the company.

As she speaks, it's clear Fallon and Mia's bond is much stronger than I was aware. I didn't even know they were that close, just that they'd known each other since school and they work together now. But Mia seems to have real insight into Fallon's psyche, even moreso than her brothers whose worries were far more generalized. So this conversation has me more alarmed than ever about Fallon's rapidly disintegrating state of mind.

"God, I had no idea it was this bad," I murmur, guilt gnawing away at me. "I wish I could do something more to help."

"Maybe you can," Mia says quietly. "Lately, you've become closer to her than anyone else." A shadow passes across her face and she frowns. "Maybe you can get through to her."

The responsibility weighs heavily on my shoulders, but she's right. I have to try, for Fallon's sake.

"Fenton and Bronson confided in me about Fallon getting in with a bad crowd after I broke up with her," I frown. "I haven't raised it with her yet, though. They didn't get into the specifics, only that she was hurt. I want her to feel like she can tell me on her own time. And not feel like everyone was talking about her behind her back. I was really worried about meeting you now for the same reason... I know she can't bear it when she feels like her friends and family are conspiring against her."

"I understand. I feel a bit cloak and dagger about the whole thing, too. But I didn't know where else to turn. It didn't seem right to reach out to her family with all the conflict going on at the moment. What happened back in school has definitely affected her a lot. And she's certainly developed a healthy fascination with getting revenge on men who behave badly. But I think there's more to it than that. What happened back in school may be part of it, but there's a bigger picture."

"Alright," I say, determination setting in. "I'll do whatever it takes to help her."

Mia breathes a sigh of relief. "Thank you, Aksel. I knew I could count on you."

We sit in silence for a moment, the weight of our conversation settling over us. I know this won't be easy, but Fallon's well-being is worth any sacrifice.

"There's something else you should know," Mia says hesitantly. "Fallon's been keeping some dangerous company lately. I've seen her with some shady characters, people rumored to be involved in...various criminal activities. I'm worried she's getting tangled up in something she can't get out of."

My stomach drops at her words. Fallon, mixed up with criminals? That seems far more plausible for her family's business, which I know she avoids involvement with as much as possible, or King Enterprises for that matter. For Fallon's personal empowerment business it seems impossible and unlikely, yet the grim look on Mia's face tells me she's dead serious.

"Why would she get involved with people like that?" I ask, dread pooling in my gut.

"I don't know for sure," Mia says. "But I have a theory. After what happened to her, after she was raped by those four guys...I think maybe she's looking for a way to take back control. And power over others is an easy way to do that, so she's become obsessed with getting revenge on other people who have been wronged. And I think it frees her to help others who are unable to help themselves. Being involved in things like that sometimes takes you into dark places with dangerous people."

The words hit me like a fist to the chest. My mind reels, *rape* echoing through my head.

"She was—raped?" I choke out, barely able to utter the nasty word, ice once against sliding through my veins at the thought of anyone hurting my love. "When? How?"

"Back in school," Mia says softly. "By four guys she thought she could trust. She hasn't been the same since."

I stare at Mia, stunned into silence.

"I'm so sorry," she says. "I didn't intend to tell you here, like this. When you said you knew she'd been hurt back in school, I thought you knew the whole story."

How did I not know this? Her brothers mentioned her being hurt somehow, and it sounded like some type of violence, but I didn't realize how bad it was. They were using euphemisms that hid the fact she was raped. Perhaps being protective brothers who were uncomfortable with using the raw, unfiltered word. How could I have let this happen to Fallon, the woman I've loved for as long as I can remember?

Guilt and sorrow wash over me in waves as the truth sinks in, that I've failed her, in the worst possible way. But no more. I'll do whatever it takes to make this right, to save Fallon from the darkness threatening to consume her. No matter the cost, I will make her whole again.

Mia watches me with knowing eyes, as if she can read the fierce determination rising within me.

"I'm going to help her," I say, my voice rough with emotion. "Whatever she needs, whatever it takes. I won't fail her again."

Mia nods. "I knew I could count on you." Her gaze turns inward for a moment. "There's one more thing you should know...." She hesitates and squeezes my arm before letting go. "After the assault back then, Fallon started drinking heavily. She did better for a while, but she seems to be heading down that path again. And I think she's maybe been mixing pills with the alcohol. I'm worried she's using it to cope with her trauma. We had a conversation the other day and she seemed giddy... unhinged, even."

The air leaves my lungs in a sharp exhale. Mixing alcohol with pills? Fuck. This just keeps getting worse.

I rake a hand through my hair, struggling to process this avalanche of revelations. How did we get here, to this point where the woman I love is in so much pain she's turned to drugs and dangerous people to numb herself? And that I had to find this all out by going behind her back and having a secret meeting with her best friend?

Guilt stabs at me again, more vicious than before. If I hadn't let my pride get in the way all those years ago, if I'd fought for Fallon instead of walking away...none of this would be happening.

I swallow hard against the lump in my throat. "I'm going to fix this, Mia. I'm going to save her, even if it means saving her from herself."

My hands curl into fists, knuckles turning white. "And anyone who tries to hurt her again will have to go through me first."

Mia's eyes shine with emotion. She reaches out and grasps my arm. "I know you will fix this."

I'm going to help Fallon defeat her demons once and for all—no matter what the cost.

This is a promise I fully intend to keep.

A surge of gratitude and affection for Mia sweeps through me. She leads me out onto her home's front steps, and I impulsively wrap her in an empathetic hug, our bond tied together by our mutual love for Fallon. As we embrace, I hear a rustling from the nearby bushes that surround Mia's property and hear the distinctive click of a camera shutter. Mia and I look toward the noise, and there's a loud click followed by a bright flash.

I glimpse a shadowy male figure capturing our embrace on camera. As soon as he sees us looking in his direction, he breaks free from the bushes and sprints away. Propelled by instinct, I chase after the strange man. Despite him being in sneakers, and me in dress shoes, I almost catch up to him, but at the last second he ducks down a side street, just before a garbage truck rolls slowly past, blocking the alley.

"God damn it!" I smack the truck with my palm as the man disappears into the shadows.

As I stand in the middle of the street panting, I reflect on what just happened. I'm not sure what that was about, but it can't be good.

Chapter 58

AKSEL

The sun caresses my face, offering a momentary escape from the suffocating urban jungle. I sit on a riverside bench, stomach aching with hunger, and watch the strong current of the river pulling along debris and the odd kayak. I forgot to bring lunch again, and I have back-to-back meetings all afternoon, too. Fuck.

"Hey, Aksel," Raine's voice cuts through the air like a sharp breeze. Her apricot labradoodle, Alfred aka Alfie, dances around her feet, tail wagging in sync with the sunshine. She grins, handing me something that smells like heaven.

As Raine hands me the familiar package, my stomach clenches in anticipation. My eyes light up at the sight of the sandwich shop logo, and I can't help but grin like a child.

"Damn, you know me too well," I mutter, tearing into the wrapping with enthusiasm. The aroma of my favorite muffuletta sandwich hits my nostrils, and my mouth waters at the familiar scent. As I take a bite, I marvel at how Raine always seems to have my back, providing what I need when I need it most.

The sun's rays dance on the water, reflecting a golden warmth that brings life to the riverside bench. I can't help but let out a small chuckle as Alfie, sensing our lighthearted conversation, begins to engage in his own playful antics. He leaps and bounds around us, his tail wagging to the beat of our banter.

Raine's laughter rings out like the tinkle of wind chimes. "I do know you too well. You always forget to eat, especially when you're investigating allegations of corporate espionage. Did you think I'd let you starve?" she teases, her voice full of affection. A playful smile curls her lips as she bites into her own sandwich. Sitting under the sunlit sky, I feel grateful for her presence, anchoring me in a world that threatens to pull me apart.

"Never," I affirm between bites of the layered sandwich, savoring the complex flavors of the curious combination of sesame-crusted bread, olive salad and cold cuts dancing on my tongue. One trip to New Orleans and I've never found a better sandwich since. "You're my rock, Raine."

Her expression softens, and there's an unspoken understanding that passes between us. We've endured so much together, and in this moment, our shared history weaves its way through our conversation.

I take a huge bite of the sandwich, delighting in its exquisite, multi-layered taste. "But don't worry, I'll make sure to enjoy every damn morsel now."

"Good. You need your strength," she says, brushing a strand of hair away from her face. The sun highlights the fierce determination in her eyes—a trait we both share, but she wields it with more grace.

"Did you find anything new?" I ask between bites, quirking an eyebrow over my sandwich.

"Nothing concrete yet, but we're getting closer," she assures me, a fire burning behind her eyes. My sister is relentless, just like me. And she's hot on the trail of Kent and Isabella. While my older sister has largely extracted herself from the day-to-day runnings of King Enterprises, preferring to focus on more artistic pursuits, she's whip-smart with investigative skills and is happy to come on board for high-risk, discreet projects where we prefer not to get external parties involved. This is definitely one of those cases. So far, she's been researching the shit out of Kent and Isabella in order to try and figure out their exact plan to take the company down.

"Good. They won't know what hit them," I respond, clenching my free hand into a fist. The sandwich satisfies my hunger, but it can't quell the rage simmering beneath the surface. The thought of two people inserting themselves in power positions within our family company, with the primary goal of taking it down from the inside, blows my mind and makes me intensely uncomfortable. And very, very angry.

"Remember, Aksel," Raine warns as she places a hand on my arm and squeezes, her voice softer now. "We're doing this for justice, not just revenge."

I nod, chewing thoughtfully. Her words echo in my mind, mingling with the taste of my favorite sandwich. It's a potent cocktail of wisdom and sustenance, fueling my resolve as I prepare for the battle ahead.

"Justice is what's driving me here, and of course protecting our family name," I insist, swallowing the last bite of my sandwich. "But a little bit of personal satisfaction doesn't hurt either. They'll pay for what they did to us."

"Agreed." She gives me a knowing smile, and I feel the bond between us strengthen. I often feel like we're two sides of the same coin, having both grown up with a sense of familial responsibility throughout our lives that extends far beyond being a sibling and is much more like being a parent. "Just don't let your anger consume you," she cautions, swallowing the last morsel of her sandwich.

I nod, absorbing her wisdom as I watch her dog chase after a butterfly, its innocent joy momentarily distracting me from the heavy weight of our mission. A sudden gust of wind sends a shiver down my spine, and I'm reminded of how quickly things can change.

"Come on, let's get back to work," I say, standing up and brushing crumbs off my shirt. Raine nods, Alfie following at her heels. "Thanks again for lunch. I feel like I'm going to have a productive afternoon now that I'm no longer hangry."

"Right behind you," she replies, standing up and brushing crumbs off her lap and following my lead.

As we walk away from the riverside bench, the taste of my favorite sandwich still lingers on my tongue, a reminder of Raine's unwavering support. And with her by my side, I know we'll achieve the justice we seek. Together, we'll make those who wronged us pay. As I walk alongside Raine, I'm reminded that our bond is stronger than any darkness that threatens to engulf us. And as the sun casts its warm rays upon us, I'm reminded that even in the darkest moments, there is light.

Chapter 59

FALLON

The scent of freshly roasted coffee beans assaults my senses as I push open the door of Flicking the Bean Cafe. What kind of name is that for a coffee shop? I smirk at the neon sign that simulates, well... a coffee bean being flicked, of course.

A burst of laughter escapes my lips before I can stifle it. The warmth of the cafe seeps into my skin, a welcome respite from the biting wind outside.

A blonde in an oversized sweater glances up from her book and offers a hesitant smile. Wren.

I take a deep breath and head to her table, hyperaware of the tremor in my hands. What am I doing here?

"Fallon, hi." Wren stands, knocking over the contents of her paper cup. Coffee streams across the table. "Shit, I'm so clumsy. Let me clean this up."

"Don't worry about it." I grab a wad of napkins from the nearby condiment stand and help mop up the mess. "So this is the place, huh?" I glance at her combat boots with boot socks that stick out over the top. "I love your footwear, by the way! Perfect for this weather and so cute!"

Wren flushes, still embarrassed from the spill, avoiding my gaze. "Thanks, they're new. And yeah, Bronson and I spent a lot of time here in the early days of our relationship. I guess the name has sentimental value."

"Nothing like a smutty pun to set the mood." I arch a brow, waiting to see how she'll respond.

After a beat of silence, Wren bursts into laughter. "You got me there." She shakes her head, tucking a stray lock of hair behind one ear, suddenly looking like a huge weight has been lifted off her chest. I guess she's remembered I don't bite. "I'm glad you suggested meeting. It's nice to finally connect outside of formal family time."

The tension in my shoulders eases. Maybe this won't be as awkward as I feared. She was nice enough when I met her with my brother, but one-on-one time with someone you barely know always creates a unique type of pressure to carry a conversation.

I settle into a chair across from Wren, the aroma of fresh coffee permeating the space between us. "The coffee here better be as good as the name implies."

"One sip and you'll be hooked." Wren's lips quirk into a smile as she waves over a barista who quickly returns with two fresh mugs of their famous house coffee. The scent of possibility lingers, as rich as the dark roast in my cup. I take a sip, savoring the bold flavor on my tongue.

Maybe Wren's right. Maybe I will get hooked.

Over steaming cups, Wren shares anecdotes about her own journey with Bronson.

"Bronson was so nervous when he asked me out for the first time. He spilled his coffee all over the table, then tripped over his own feet on the way to grab napkins." Wren's eyes soften at the memory. "But his awkwardness was endearing. Underneath it all, I could see how much heart he had."

I trace my finger along the rim of my cup, warmth blooming in my chest. Wren's story hits closer to home than I care to admit.

"Aksel was nervous too, when we first got together. He—" I clamp my lips shut, unsure of how much to reveal.

Wren's gaze is knowing. "You can talk to me, you know. I understand what it's like to care for someone who's been through hell. Although I have a feeling you've been through your own version of hell. Maybe you're still in it?"

The walls I've constructed, brick by brick, begin to crumble. I swallow hard against the lump forming in my throat as I remember back to the angsty days of high school when Aksel was starting to feel the brunt of familial, academic and athletic pressure. "He tried so damn hard to push me away. But I saw the good in him, even when he couldn't see it himself."

"And now?" Wren prompts gently.

The rawness rises, impossible to contain. "I don't know where we stand. I love him with everything in me, but I'm afraid..." My voice trails off as a single tear escapes, betraying my vulnerability.

Wren reaches across the table, squeezing my hand. "Love is risky. But if you love him, and he loves you—really loves you—then it's worth fighting for. From what Bronson's told me, it sounds like Aksel's got it for you pretty bad..." Her smile is soft, sisterly. "Take it from someone who's been there. Follow your heart, Fallon. You won't regret it."

Her words resonate, echoing what I already know deep down. I blink away the remainder of my tears, gratitude swelling within.

"Thank you. I needed to hear that."

"Anytime." Wren gives my hand another quick squeeze before pulling away. "That's what friends are for."

Friends. The word settles over me with a comforting warmth rivaling that of the coffee. I've found more than an ally here. I've found yet another sister I never had. It makes me wonder how much more of a community I could already have established around me if I hadn't been so dead-set against letting anyone in.

Our conversation lapses into silence. But it's not an awkward quiet—it's the type of comfortable companionship that exists between two people who don't need words to understand one another.

Wren checks her watch with a startled laugh. "Wow, we've been here for hours. I should let you get going—I'm sure you have other things to do today other than listen to me prattle on."

I shake my head, a smile tugging at my lips. "Nothing that can't wait. I'm enjoying this."

"Me too." Wren's eyes glimmer with humor. "But as much as I'd love to stay, I should head home. Bronson's making dinner tonight, and I don't want to be late." She pauses, glancing out the window at the deepening dusk. "He cooks once in a blue moon, so when he does I like to encourage it!" She grins. "Do you have plans with Aksel this evening?"

At the mention of his name, my chest clenches. I shake my head again, slower this time. "We haven't talked since..." I trail off, the ache intensifying. I should call him. I know I should. But fear roots me in place, and the risk of more rejection looms. I still feel guilty about missing our coffee date. I could picture him sitting there, anxiously looking at his watch, waiting for me. But having Harvey Maxwell captive in my basement has me preoccupied.

Wren studies me, her gaze both knowing and gentle. "You can't avoid him forever, Fallon. And you know as well as I do that you'll regret it if you do."

I sigh, raking a hand through my hair. She's right, of course. But that doesn't make facing him any easier.

"Start with a call, maybe," Wren suggests. "Keep it light. Rebuild that connection, and the rest will follow. You just have to take the first step."

Her advice is a lifeline, pulling me from the churning sea of indecision. I cling to it, mustering a shaky smile. "Thank you, Wren. Again."

"You're welcome." Wren stands, shrugging into her jacket. "Call me in the next couple of days and let me know how it goes. But I have a feeling everything will work out exactly as it's meant to."

Hope flickers, lighting the shadows. I stand as well, wrapping Wren in a fierce hug. "I'm glad I met with you today. It's just what I needed."

"Me too." She hugs me back just as tightly. "Now go get your man."

We part with smiles and waves, the aroma of coffee and newfound courage trailing me out the door. Tonight, I'll call Aksel. And this time, I'll follow my heart.

The night air is crisp, scented with possibility. I walk with purpose, renewed determination fueling my strides.

By the time I reach my building, a plan has taken shape. I'll call Aksel once I'm inside, keeping the conversation light and casual.

We'll make plans to meet, and when I see him again, I'll lay my heart bare. No more hiding, no more running. It's time to stop letting fear dictate my choices. And it's important to me that we have the deeper discussion in person rather than over the phone. It seems more transparent, more real and raw that way.

Heart pounding, I unlock my front door and step inside. My phone weighs heavily in my pocket, but I don't hesitate. Not this time.

I find Aksel's name in my contacts and press Call before doubt can creep in. The phone rings once, then twice, and panic flares. What if he doesn't answer? What if—

"Fallon?" Aksel's voice is gravelly with sleep, and warmth floods me. "Is everything okay?"

"Yeah, everything's fine. I just..." I take a deep breath, steadying my nerves. You can do this. "I realized we haven't talked in a while. I thought maybe we could get coffee tomorrow? If you're free, that is. I promise I won't stand you up this time."

There's a beat of silence. Then, "I'd like that. A lot. As long as you promise not to stand me up again?"

Relief and joy mingle, loosening the knot in my stomach. "Great. How about noon at Flicking the Bean?"

Aksel chuckles, a low, intimate sound that makes my pulse leap. "That's a real thing? Oh yeah, that's right, it's the place Bronson and Wren used to meet up. I remember him telling me about that. It's a date. I'll see you then, Fallon."

"See you then," I echo softly.

The call ends, but I stand there smiling at my phone. Tomorrow, everything will change. Tomorrow, I'll show Aksel the truth of my heart.

And this time, there will be no turning back.

Chapter 60

FALLON

The intercom buzzes, jerking me from my daze. I tap into the app on my phone and see a familiar face: Link. Why the hell is he here? My brother hasn't visited since I first moved in and the family dinner was moved here for a one-off housewarming. That evening was a complete disaster, so I wouldn't expect him to come rushing back. And it's not as if we're exactly on friendly terms.

I punch the button, annoyance prickling under my skin. "What do you want?"

"Just let me up. It's important." For once, there's no hint of malice in his voice. He sounds serious and tired. Still, I'm skeptical.

I reluctantly buzz him in and soon hear footsteps approaching in the hallway. I open the front door in anticipation of his arrival.

He strides through the door, eyes shadowed. The cocky grin I'm accustomed to is nowhere to be found.

Unease curls in my gut. Link is never serious.

"We need to talk." His voice is rough gravel, not the typical polished tone.

I fold my arms, struggling to ignore the dread gathering in my chest. "Spit it out."

He sighs. "Look, I'm really sorry, but I haven't been entirely honest with you."

I narrow my eyes at him. What could he possibly have been hiding from me? After all, he's fairly transparent about the fact he's a complete jerk.

"I know I said I called the private investigator off, but I didn't," he frowns. "Before you get upset, let me explain. I had a niggling feeling that maybe all wasn't as it seemed with Aksel, and my protective big brother instincts kicked in. I know we have our problems, but deep down I care about you very much."

I stare at him, emotions churning. Anger at his intrusion wars with gratitude that he cares enough to look out for me. "And what did you find out?" I attempt to keep my voice calm, measured, but I hear myself waver.

He holds up a photo. My heart stutters. No. Please no.

I snatch it from his hands. Aksel and Mia, wrapped around each other in an intimate hug. I recognize the house in the background as Mia's home.

What the hell? This can't be. They barely know each other, just ghosts that walked past each other now and then back in high school. And here they are, in photo evidence, in an intimate embrace outside her place.

The photo slips through numb fingers, drifting to the floor.

Betrayal rips through me, savage and burning. I trusted him. Believed his lies and empty promises. And I trusted her as well.

How could I be so stupid?

My eyes narrow as I turn to face Link. "You had no right," I say tightly. "You're probably enjoying the shit out of this schadenfreude moment."

"No, I'm not." He frowns, his mouth set in a thin line that conceals the plump lips his little girlie fans go crazy for. "But I can assure you I'm getting no satisfaction from this. I just wasn't going to stand by while he played you for a fool." Link's jaw clenches. "You deserve the truth, even if it hurts."

"The truth." I laugh harshly. "You've never cared about the truth before."

"I care about you," he says softly. "Aksel's charming act may have fooled you, but I saw through it from the start. He's all wrong for you, Fallon. Always has been."

His words bring out my defensiveness. They make me feel like he was watching, judging from afar. "You don't get to decide that." I'm trembling, torn between lashing out and clinging to him. Paralyzed with indecision, instead I laugh, the sound jagged. "Don't pretend you care. This is what you wanted, isn't it? To prove you were right about him."

"I never wanted this for you." He reaches for my arm. I jerk away.

"Don't touch me, Link!" I scream. "Haven't you ruined enough?"

"I'm trying to protect you, sister." His eyes are turbulent, full of emotions I can't unravel. "I won't apologize for giving a damn."

"I never asked you to give a damn!" I shove at his chest but he doesn't budge.

I stalk to the other side of the room and grab the nearest thing, a glass vase, and hurl it at him. It shatters against the wall, shards raining onto the floor behind him.

Link flinches but stands his ground. Stubborn bastard.

I grab another missile but he lunges forward and catches my wrist. "Enough, Fallon. I'm not the enemy here."

"Like hell you're not." I try to twist free but his grip is unyielding.

"You did this!" I shove Link away, rage blinding me. "If you hadn't stuck your nose in my business, I'd still be happy. None of this would have happened!"

Hurt flickers in his eyes before his expression hardens. "Don't blame me for Aksel's mistakes. I was trying to protect you, even if you're too stubborn to see it. I had to tell you, Fallon. You deserve to know the truth." Link's gaze holds a quiet intensity. "No lies. No hiding things to protect you. And the same goes for you. That's not how we work."

His words strike a chord. We've always been brutally honest with each other, for better or worse. Link has never been one to sugarcoat the truth, even when the truth is painful.

"I didn't want you wasting another second on that bastard," Link continues. "You're worth more than his lies and excuses. I'm so sorry, Fallon. I really am." His voice cracks.

I stare at the photograph again, bile rising in my throat. The image of Aksel and Mia burns into my mind, searing away the last remnants of my denial. They look so intimate, wrapped up in their own world. As if I never existed. And to think I helped Mia pick out her home, to unpack and set everything up, even throw a housewarming for her. Only to have her take my boyfriend there, my soulmate, stealing him away for herself.

"He doesn't deserve you," Link says, guessing the direction of my thoughts. "He never did."

Anger flares, white-hot and venomous. How could I have been so stupid? I ignored all the red and pink flags. I believed Aksel's lies because the truth was too painful to face.

"I'm going to kill him," I whisper. The words emerge on a dangerous edge, laced with a thirst for vengeance.

"Whoa." Link's hand closes over my arm. "Let's not do anything you might regret." His gaze searches my face. "Revenge won't undo the damage. It won't take away the hurt."

I know Link is right, but right now, vengeance is calling to me. "He destroyed me... twice now," I say through clenched teeth. "He doesn't get to walk away from this unscathed."

I slump onto the couch, emotions churning like a whirlpool. The photograph burns into my mind, a betrayal captured in still motion.

Aksel and Mia together.

Happy. Carefree. Intimate.

The image shreds my heart into ribbons. I gave Aksel everything, and in return he gave his heart to Mia. My best fucking friend.

How could I have been so stupid?

All the signs were there, but I was too blind to see. Consumed by my love for Aksel, by my wish to feel whole and no longer lonely, I missed the lies and deception. While I was busy building a future with him, he was busy screwing my best friend behind my back. No wonder she's been so distant lately. And it explains why she's considering leaving the firm, too. She must have a shred of a conscience, not wanting to face me every day while she's fucking my boyfriend and playing happy families.

"You say you did this to protect me?" I scoff at Link. "You destroyed me. My life was finally coming together, and you tore it all apart."

"Your life was a lie," Link snaps. "But you were too blinded by your precious Aksel to see the truth. At least now you have to face reality so you can take action, and stop putting your head in the sand."

His words cut deep, piercing my anger. I know Link is right, but it's easier to lash out at him than face the reality of my own foolishness. I frown and blink back tears.

"Look, sorry I just spoke so harshly. But I hate seeing you hurt." His eyes are dark and turbulent. "You deserve so much better than that piece of shit."

"You hate seeing me happy," I spit. "This is what you wanted all along."

"That's not true." He pulls me into his arms. I struggle but it's useless. Link is a solid wall of muscle.

I pound at his chest, screaming curses. He takes the abuse, holding on.

Finally, I sag against him, the fight draining out of me. Sobs wrack my body.

He strokes my hair, murmuring comfort. I cling to him, the only steady thing left in my crumbling world. Ironic, given it's Link of all people. Link has never been my shelter in the storm. But right now, with everything in ruins around me, I need my brother. The one person who knows me inside out, flaws and all, and loves me anyway.

I glance at him. "I hate you sometimes."

"I know." He kisses the top of my head. "But you love me, too."

And that's the damn truth. Against all odds, I do.

Link holds me while I cry, ragged sobs that shake my entire body. His embrace is my anchor in a sea of chaos and uncertainty. He sighs, running a hand through his hair.

"Revenge won't undo the damage, Fallon. It won't take away the hurt."

"Maybe not." I slam the empty glass on the table, relishing the spike of pain in my palm. "But it will sure as hell make me feel better. What Aksel did..." My voice cracks, betraying the anguish writhing beneath my rage. "He destroyed me, Link. Shattered me into a million pieces. I'll never trust anyone again."

"Your heart will heal, Fallon. It's just going to take some time. Not all men are like him." Link's voice softens with understanding.

"Enough of them are." I stand abruptly, the room tilting around me. The whiskey burns through my veins, fueling my anger.

When the storm of tears finally subsides, I pull away and wipe at my eyes. "I'm sorry." My throat is raw, my words hoarse.

"Don't apologize." Link's eyes soften. "You have nothing to be sorry for."

"I shouldn't have lashed out at you." I swallow hard. "You were just trying to protect me."

"Yeah, well, that's what big brothers do." He shrugs, aiming for casual and missing the mark. "Even when their sisters don't want them to."

I give him a watery smile. "I guess I'm stuck with you, aren't I?"

"Like glue." He nudges my shoulder, a quiet reassurance. "What do you want to do now?"

The question hangs between us, weighted with unspoken fears. I don't know how to move forward from here. How do I rebuild when the ground has shifted beneath my feet?

I stare into the amber depths of my glass, watching the light dance across the rippling surface. "What any self-respecting woman would do after finding out she's been made a fool of." I down the whiskey in one burning gulp. "Make them pay."

"Fallon, don't do something you'll regret." Link's warning falls on deaf ears.

Regret is for the weak. I've already shed enough tears for Aksel's betrayal. Now it's time to make him bleed. The thought slices through my fragile composure, sharp as a knife. I struggle to breathe, overcome by a fresh wave of anguish. The pain of being able to block things out for a moment is that you need to re-remember them all over again.

I scream, my voice raw and primal, and hurl a framed picture of Aksel and I across the room. The crash of exploding glass mirrors the fragments of my broken trust.

"I can't believe he did this to me," I whisper. Tears burn my eyes, trailing down my cheeks in hot streams. I gave Aksel the power to break me, and he shattered me into a million pieces. I feel like such an idiot, ashamed, for making the same mistake twice.

Link's hand closes over mine, grounding me. "We'll figure this out together, Fallon. Whatever you decide to do, I'm here for you."

His quiet vow resonates within me. We have our differences, but Link has always been there when I needed him most. For better or worse, our bond is unbreakable.

I cling to him like a lifeline. "I don't know what comes next. But as long as I have you, I know I'll be okay."

"Damn straight." Link pulls me close again, fierce and protective. "Aksel's going to regret the day he ever hurt you. And if he thinks he's getting away with this, he has another thing coming. Just don't kill the guy, please, as much as you might want to right now. I don't want to have to visit you in prison, although you know that I would."

"Stay out of my way, brother." I stalk to the door, ready to show him out. "You're either with me or against me. Choose carefully." As the words leave my mouth I realize that, for once, it feels like Link is on my side. And it feels really nice.

Aksel will soon learn that destroying my heart for the second time was a bad idea. Because I'm about to unleash all of my rage on his lying, cheating ass.

Chapter 61

The air crackles as I storm into the meeting room where Mia sits in front of a stack of papers, one of my hands balled into a fist, the other grasping a blown-up version of the photo that crushed my heart. I can feel the rage etched into the lines of my face, my lips pulled back in an uncontrollable snarl. I try to neutralize my expression, but it's like my face is frozen, my emotions setting it in an immovable mask.

"Did you think I wouldn't find out?" My accusation slices through her, sharp as a knife, and she looks up at me with surprise.

She jerks back as if struck, glancing at my hand that's holding the photo. "Find out what? I have no idea what you're talking about. What is that you're holding?"

I scoff, disgust twisting my lips. "Don't play dumb with me, Mia. I know you've been undermining me here at the office. And I know what else you've been doing as well! Screwing Aksel behind my back, you home wrecking snake bitch!"

Her eyes grow wide and her jaw drops. "What? No, that's ridiculous!" I can see the outrage and hurt war within her. "How could you think so little of me, Fallon? I've been nothing but loyal to you. I would never do something like that."

"Oh, really?" I slam the photo on the boardroom table in front of her.

Mia grabs it from the table and her face pales, her eyes large and her hand trembling. "I didn't do this. I didn't do any of what you're saying," she rasps. "You have to believe me."

"I don't believe a word you say," I yell. "You've always been jealous of me, Mia, waiting to stab me in the back at the first opportunity. So now you're coming for my business and my man."

"That's not true!" Mia cries out, desperation cracking her voice. "Fallon, please listen to me. I don't know what you're talking about. I would never do anything to hurt you or your business. And as for Aksel, I promise I never—"

"Save your lies for someone who hasn't known you as long as I have." I jab a finger at her, accusation dripping from every word. "You're doing your best to destroy me, but your pathetic attempt at sabotage won't work. Everyone knows you're just riding on my coattails, and that without me you're nothing."

I pause, my eyes narrowing.

Mia looks like she's been slapped.

"I don't believe anything that comes out of your lying mouth." I lean over the table, eyes burning with fury. "You're a snake, waiting to strike when people least expect it. You'll do anything for your fifteen minutes of fame and a fat paycheck. Isn't that right? Next thing I know, you'll be selling stories about your 'relationship' with Aksel to the tabloids. You make me sick!"

Mia staggers back as if struck. "Fame? And losing our friendship over money? After everything I've done for you, Fallon, really?! How dare you?!"

"If I hadn't given you a job when you were desperate, you'd have nothing. No career, no success, no life. I made you, Mia, and I can destroy you just as easily."

The words taste bitter on my tongue, but I can't stop them from spilling out in a toxic flood. Our friendship is shattered beyond repair, and if hurting Mia is the only way I can find closure, so be it. She deserves this.

Rage replaces the hurt on Mia's face, white-hot and venomous. "How dare you say such hateful, untrue things? I've sacrificed everything for you, Fallon. I've devoted years of my life to helping you achieve your dreams, and this is the thanks I get?" She surges forward until we're toe to toe, uncharacteristically aggressive, our harsh breaths mingling. "The only one destroying things here is you, Fallon. But go ahead, keep telling yourself I'm the villain if it makes you feel better about throwing our friendship away over baseless rumors."

My eyes narrow, a muscle in my jaw twitching. "Get out of my sight before I do something we'll both regret."

Mia gives a bitter laugh, the sound jagged in her throat. "You've already done that, Fallon. And when your little empire comes crumbling down around you with no one left to pick up the pieces, I hope the knowledge of what you lost today brings you comfort."

With that parting shot, she turns on her heel.

"Get out," I spit, even though she's already on her way out. "Get out of my building right now. And you are fired." Our friendship is over, the future we've planned for so long torn to shreds, but Mia will come to regret the day she turned against me.

I glare at her, chest heaving, and she looks over her shoulder at me. For a long moment we remain locked in confrontation, the air between us simmering with tension.

Finally Mia straightens, smoothing a hand over her jacket. "With pleasure," she sneers. "I never want to see your face again."

The door slams behind her with a note of finality, sealing the end of our friendship forever.

Returning to my office, I sink into my chair, head in my hands. How did it come to this? Mia and I have been through so much together, a partnership forged in the fires of childhood dreams, and adult ambition and grit. Now everything lies in ruins, destroyed by mistrust and betrayal.

On her way out, Mia stops by my office, her belongings in hand. Her voice is low and sad. "The worst part is, I didn't do anything bad behind your back. I would never do something underhanded to sabotage the reputation of the company you've worked so hard to build. And I certainly didn't cheat with Aksel. But I guess you'll never believe me now."

She's right. Our friendship is shattered beyond repair, the damage done. Her true colors are shining loud and unmissable, professionally and personally.

Anger simmers in my gut, bile and regret churning into a toxic mix. I trusted Mia with my life, stood by her side through failures and triumphs, and this is how she repays my loyalty? Betraying me like this?

"Spare me the lies, Mia."

"I'm done, Fallon, I mean it. I stayed because I cared about you, but now..." She trails off with a shake of her head. "You've shown me what I really mean to you. It's time I moved on to bigger and better things. You can say you fired me, or you can say that I quit. I honestly don't care anymore, as long as I don't have to be here any longer. With you."

With that, she turns and walks out the door.

As her heels click down the hallway and out of the building, I bury my head in my hands again. I'm trembling, rage and grief warring for dominance. How am I supposed to move on from this? Mia has been my anchor for as long as I can remember, her presence a constant in my tumultuous world. Now she's gone, our relationship left in ruins, and the future looms before me, empty and uncertain. Clearly, she's not the person I thought she was. And clearly, neither was Aksel.

Her loss. His loss. *Their* loss.

Oh god, I hate that there's a *them*.

Chapter 62

AKSEL

My phone buzzes. Heart racing, I grab it, expecting a message from Fallon confirming coffee and checking to see how my day is going.

There it is. A text, short and sharp as a blade. But not the one I expected.

Fallon: We're done.

The words slice into me, cold and merciless. My chest seizes as I read them again and again, trying to comprehend how two simple words can sever what we had.

How did we get here? Weeks ago, we were tangled in each other's arms, whispering promises of forever. Now this—a death knell delivered via text. Fallon has been acting strange, but this seems extra cold. I was trying to give her space, not anticipating her completely eliminating me out of her life via a text message.

Fingers numb, I call her. Each ring ratchets my panic higher. Voicemail. I call again. And again. Nothing.

She's gone. Vanished from my life as swiftly as she entered it. I'm adrift, unmoored from the one thing anchoring me to solid ground lately.

My condo feels empty, echoes of laughter that once filled these rooms now mocking me. I wander aimlessly, searching for clues, any scrap of her remaining. But like Fallon herself, all traces have disappeared.

I find one of her shirts in my laundry hamper and hold it against my face. Her scent lingers on the fabric, a ghostly reminder of embraces that will never come again. I breathe it in, clinging to the fading wisps of her essence.

In the closet, a flash of red catches my eye—the dress she wore on our dinner cruise date. I snatch it and crush the silk in my fist, ripping it to shreds. Needing to destroy something, anything, as my world crumbles around me.

Shreds of scarlet flutter to the floor. But no amount of ruin can fill the void within, or erase the memory of how she looked in that dress. How she made me feel. Whole. Alive. Loved.

I sink down amid the ruins, clutching at scraps that can't be pieced back together. The thin, ragged edges dig into my palm, almost drawing blood, and I welcome the pain—a distraction from the ache in my chest.

The sting fades quickly, but the hollow remains.

Panic sets in, and I dial Fallon's number again, desperation evident in my rapid keystrokes. The phone rings, but each unanswered tone amplifies the growing void within.

"Fallon, please...don't do this. We can work it out. Just talk to me." My voice cracks, emotions warring inside me. Anger, sorrow, disbelief—they surge and collide, riptides that threaten to drag me under.

The call goes to voicemail. I dial again. And again. Hoping against hope that she'll answer, and this will all turn out to be some sick joke or a simple misunderstanding. But there is only silence. An impenetrable wall of quiet where her laughter once flowed.

Message after message, I beg and plead. Demand answers. Question what went wrong. Apologize for mistakes I'm not even sure I made.

Each voicemail and text message lays my heart bare, stripping away layers of pride until only raw need remains. The need to hear her voice again. To look into eyes that once gazed at me with tenderness, but I imagine are now only cold and distant.

But there are no replies. No explanations. No mercy. Just the steady march of time carrying her further away with each unanswered call. I almost wish she'd block me again so I couldn't keep leaving messages. Because I'm compelled to reach out to any and all lifelines that connect us, and might put me in her path once more.

The void expands, threatening to swallow me whole. But I cling to the fraying edges of our bond, unwilling to surrender so easily.

Unwilling to believe she could dismiss me this way, as if I never mattered at all.

Love leaves us in the end. But not like this. Anything but this.

Fallon's silence is deafening. A condemnation without trial, a sentence carried out with ruthless efficiency. She has made her judgment, and I am found wanting. For what? I'm clueless.

The calls continue to go unanswered. But I keep dialing. Hoping in vain that she will show me mercy and end this torture. Grant me closure, if nothing else, and release me from this limbo of unknowing.

Each ring echoes mockingly in the emptiness she left behind. A reminder of joy now turned to ashes. Of a heart offered up and so callously crushed. Maybe I deserve this, karma for my immature actions in high school and college.

But deserved or not, I can't bear this. I need answers.

I pound on Fallon's door with a fury born of desperation, panic rising as the seconds tick by without response.

"Fallon! Open the damn door!" I shout, rattling the handle in vain. No sound emerges from within. No sign of life.

The apartment is as silent as her phone, as unyielding as her heart.

I lean against the door, chest heaving. How did we come to this? When did the laughter fade, warmth leaching from her eyes, replaced by something hard and cold? Or was it there all along and I was just too happy to be back with her that I refused to see it?

A dull ache settles behind my eyes. I never saw the end coming. Never imagined a day where I'd be shut out so completely, barred from the life we were just starting to build together.

"Fallon, please," I whisper, forehead pressed to the wood that keeps me from her. That may always keep me from her now.

"Don't do this. We can work through it. Whatever it is, we can—"

The door gives beneath my weight, creaking open. I stumble forward into the condo, pulse racing at the thought of seeing her combined with the heady, disconcerting thrill of breaking into someone's home. I make a mental note that if I can ever possibly salvage this relationship, we need to improve her condo's security immediately.

But it's empty. No signs of disturbance, no clues to her abrupt disappearance. Just the hollow echoes of happier times mocking me in my grief.

I pace the length of her condo, anger and panic warring for dominance. She can't just disappear. Can't leave me with nothing but the shredded remains of my heart on her floor.

There has to be an explanation. Some reason she's cut ties so abruptly, sealing me out of her life. Out of her heart.

My hands clench at my sides, nails biting into my flesh. I need to know. Even if the truth is my undoing, I have to understand why she left me, why she betrayed me like this.

With trembling fingers, I dial Mia's number. If anyone has answers, it's her.

One ring. Two. The line clicks. "Aksel, I can't—"

"Where is she?" I demand, pulse pounding behind my eyes. "What the hell is going on?"

Silence. Then, softly, "I'm sorry, Aksel. I can't tell you anything. You should talk to Fallon yourself."

The line goes dead. I stare at the phone in disbelief, rage burning through my veins. No one seems willing to give me the answers I deserve.

I picture the phone shattering against the wall in a burst of glass and sparks, fragments raining down around me. My chest heaves with the force of my anger, vision hazy with red. But I know that although it would give me a moment's satisfaction, I need to keep my phone intact in case she calls me back.

There's only one way to get the truth, then. I won't stop until I have the answers I need. I won't rest until Fallon's before me, telling me why she destroyed us.

I'm not letting her go that easily. She owes me more than fading into the shadows. She owes me the truth.

And I'll tear this whole damn city apart to find it.

My phone nearly slips from numb fingers as I dial her work number, dread pooling in my gut. She hasn't been in for days, they tell me. An unexpected leave of absence, with no notice given. Courses postponed indefinitely.

The phone slips from my grasp, clattering to the floor. She's erased herself from my life as neatly as ripping a page from a book.

No loose ends remaining. No mercy given.

Gone. She's just gone.

Chapter 63

FALLON

The phone buzzes again, rattling against the table.

Another call to ignore. Another voicemail I won't hear. The hollow ache in my chest flares to life, fueled by memories of Aksel's voice. Of whispered promises and laughter that once filled these empty spaces.

My fingers curl into fists, nails biting into skin. Pain helps ground me in the present, a reminder of the path I've chosen. Of the shields I've erected to protect a heart too broken to risk again.

Aksel has now twice filled my world with light and love, only to bring everything crashing down around me. Now there is only darkness, and anger that fuels my quest for vengeance.

The phone buzzes again and I snatch it up, thumb hovering over the answer button. Half of me craves the sound of his voice. The other knows it's a weakness I can't afford. A trap, an unnecessary distraction. My kryptonite.

With a growl, I hurl the phone against the wall. It shatters on impact, pieces scattering across the floor. Silence descends, thick and cloying. The echo of Aksel's name fades, leaving me adrift in a sea of purpose. Of revenge. The knowledge nobody can get in touch with me right now is exhilarating. I'll be left alone to plan, to plot, to exact the vengeance I seek and deserve.

My gaze lands on the files strewn across the table. Details of Harvey's sordid affairs. Of the offshore accounts funding his corruption. Of the lives he's ruined clawing his way to power, and the people he's stomped on, used and abused along the way. Rage surges, red-hot and pure. Harvey's destruction will be my salvation. I flip open another file, scanning the contents. There, another weakness to exploit—more scams, more shady business practices. More secrets to lay bare.

The buzz of purpose returns, dulling the ache of Aksel's loss. I have a new lifeline now. One threaded with vengeance and justice. Harvey's ruin will be my redemption. We'll be releasing him from captivity soon, but Claudia's retribution won't end there. No, it'll follow him for the rest of his life. I'll make sure of it.

A knock sounds at my office door, startling me from my focus. I glance up to find Raine peering through the frosted glass, worry etched into her features.

My fingers curl into fists, nails biting into flesh. Her concern is a distraction I can't afford. Not now. Not when I'm so close to bringing Harvey to his knees. I'd told my reception staff to tell anyone calling for me that I was unavailable, but I didn't expect anyone to show up to my physical office. At least, I knew Aksel wouldn't. Even he wouldn't cross that line.

Raine raps at the door again. "Fallon, please open up. We haven't heard from you in days." Her voice is muffled, but the strain in it comes through loud and clear. "Aksel is worried sick. We all are."

The sound of his name strikes like a blow, cracking my composure. Aksel. My breath hitches, heart clenching with a pain so acute it steals the air from my lungs.

I shake my head, dragging my gaze from Raine to the files on the table. Harvey. I have to focus on Harvey.

When I glance up again, Raine's eyes meet mine through the glass. Determination shines in their depths. She isn't leaving. Not without answers.

With a resigned sigh, I push to my feet and cross to the door. Shields in place, I remind myself. I have work to do. Raine and Aksel are a distraction I can't afford. But I can't be mad at Raine. She's a consistent voice of reason, so wise, with her own dark history that she doesn't talk about, but you can just see.

I click the lock. The door creaks open and Raine surges forward, pulling me into her arms. "Thank God you're okay." Her hug is fierce, her voice muffled against my hair. "We've been so worried."

Guilt flickers, a spark I hastily smother. I harden my heart and pull away. "I'm fine. Just busy."

Raine searches my face, her frown deepening. "That's not true. I can see how much this is hurting you." Her hand closes over my wrist, her grip gentle. "Talk to me, Fallon. Please."

I stare at her hand, willing myself to remain detached. To feel nothing. "There's nothing to say. I have work to do, Raine."

"This isn't healthy." Her fingers tighten. "Bottling it all up and throwing yourself into your work. You're going to break if you keep punishing yourself like this."

Irritation flickers to life. A spark to stoke the fires of purpose. My gaze lifts to hers, hard as flint. "My work is none of your business. Now, if you'll excuse me, I have things to do."

"Fallon, you and I both know this isn't just about work. You and Aksel really need to figure things out. You can't keep going on like this, either of you."

"I'll do it on my own time. Now can you please leave? Respect my privacy." I wrench my wrist from her grip.

She looks hurt, but she heads out the door with one last look over her shoulder. I slam the door as she heads toward the reception area. The echo of it closing is final. My path is set, and I won't be deterred. Not by Raine. Not by anyone.

Harvey will pay for what he's done. Justice will be served. No Kings are going to get in the way of justice for Claudia. I return to the table, to the details of Harvey's destruction. The ache for Aksel, and the guilt at the way I just treated Raine, fades beneath the buzz of purpose.

A few hours later

One of my junior assistants, Jeremy, pokes his head into the office. He's essentially taken over Mia's role since she quit, although he still has a lot to learn. Still, he's bright and I've always respected his bluntness.

"You look like shit." His gaze rakes over me, judgment etched into the lines of his face. "When was the last time you slept? Or ate?"

I shrug, gaze already shifting back to the files. "I'm fine."

"Like hell." He snatches the folder from my hands. "Everyone can see how twisted up you are over this Mia stuff, whatever it is. We're worried about you."

Irritation flares, my fingers curling into fists. I straighten, meeting his gaze with a hardness that makes him take a step back. "I don't need your worry or your pity. And you're overstepping. Now give me the file."

"Not until you go home and take care of yourself." His jaw sets, his eyes narrowing. "Whatever happened between you, Mia wouldn't want to see you like this." He hunches over conspiratorially. "And you really don't want Aksel to see you like this. I'm thinking full-blown glow-up. Make him regret the day he ever crossed you." His eyes light up at the thought.

Rage ignites, a flash fire fueled by grief and loss. "Don't you dare speak either of their names to me." My voice emerges in a venomous hiss. "You have no right."

Silence falls, thick and cloying. I hold out a hand, rage simmering in my veins.

He hesitates only a moment before surrendering the file, his voice softening. "Sorry, Fallon. I didn't mean to make you more upset." He pauses and places a comforting hand on mine. "For what it's worth, we're here for you. All of us."

I don't grace him with a response, my attention already consumed by the details within the folder. He lingers a moment before retreating.

For the rest of the afternoon, I feel his gaze heavy on my back.

Shadows of the past linger in moments of solitude. Aksel's name, though unspoken, echoes in the quiet corners of my mind.

The ache of missing him is a hollow void, an endless chasm stretching between the woman I was and the one I've become. Our last conversation plays on a loop, the memory an open wound refusing to heal. The one commonality between then and now: Aksel's propensity to hurt me, to callously shatter my heart.

I loved you, Aksel. God, I loved you so much. And you betrayed me… trampled on my heart—twice. Shame on me.

Aksel King broke me in ways I'm still discovering. But he also made me. Molded me into something hard and sharp, a weapon honed for a single purpose.

Vengeance.

As the days and then weeks go by, my work becomes my everything. Details of cases, the intricacies of revenge, and the web of connections I navigate become all-consuming. Victim after victim shares their story with me, mirroring the complexities of my own shattered world. Grave is growing distant, I can feel it, but I don't have the emotional bandwidth to worry about that right now. All of my energy is focused on my work.

I won't allow myself to miss Mia, her betrayal clawing at my spine just another catalyst for me to focus on my clients. She's no better than the ones we seek revenge against, after all. And as for my budding relationships with Raine, Roxy and Wren, well, they were always conditional, attached to my being with Aksel. Fuck it. I don't need them, anyway.

But in the quiet of night, darkness wraps around me like a familiar but uncomfortable cloak. It's in these moments the past emerges to haunt; specters of what might have been. A life of love and laughter with a man who held my heart.

Aksel thinks he's won, humiliating me with my own best friend and trampling my heart a second time. He probably thinks that when they're over, I'll crawl back to him, broken and begging for forgiveness.

He has no idea what's coming.

Chapter 64

FALLON

The silence between us stretches endlessly, broken only by the scrape of Grave's knife against the cutting board. His eyes stay fixed on the task at hand, slicing vegetables with sharp, efficient movements. I watch him from across the kitchen, studying the set of his jaw and the tension in his shoulders.

Something has shifted between us. The air feels heavy, laden with unspoken words that neither of us dare give voice. We dance around each other, careful not to make contact, afraid that a single touch might ignite the fuse on this ticking time bomb we call a partnership.

I scrub a hand over my face, exhaustion seeping into my bones. The revenge business was supposed to be straightforward—an eye for an eye, a life for a life. Now the lines have blurred. "Grave, thank you for coming over. I figured we both needed to eat, and of course, Henry's right down there." I nod my head in the direction of the basement stairs.

"Yep," Grave nods, monotone. His knife pauses for a fraction of a second before resuming its rhythmic slicing. I wonder if he's thinking about the man chained in my basement, contemplating his fate.

Guilt twists in my gut at the thought of what I've become, this monster capable of unspeakable violence. I cling to the memory of why we're here, the events that set our path on this collision course. Anger flares, hot and familiar, chasing away the shadows of doubt.

It's not like we're out there attacking innocent women and children. We're hunting people who destroy innocent lives. And we explore every legal avenue first. We're the backstop for those who can't otherwise be helped. If it weren't for us, these people would be lost souls who'd never get retribution. We'd be letting the fuckboys win.

I harden my resolve. Justice will be served, no matter the cost.

When Grave finally meets my gaze, his eyes are troubled. "Fallon," he starts, his voice rough with uncertainty. I brace myself for the confrontation I know is coming, steeling my nerves against the battle of wills ahead.

The knife slips from Grave's fingers, clattering against the cutting board. In the silence that follows, I glimpse the truth reflected in his stare—that our partnership is fracturing beneath the weight of impossible choices. The foundation we built on vengeance and justice is crumbling, and I'm not sure if there's anything left to salvage. Hell, if I'm going to blow my life up I may as well do it all at once.

A muscle ticks in Grave's jaw. He clenches his hands at his sides, his knuckles whitening. I stare back at him, unflinching, and wait. The next move is his.

Grave drags a hand through his hair, his eyes flickering shut for a brief moment. When he opens them again, resolve hardens his gaze. "We can't do this, Fallon. Keeping Harvey captive, contemplating murder—this isn't justice. It's vengeance, and it's gone too far."

Anger flares in my chest, white-hot and blistering. "You don't get to make that choice, Grave. Not after everything they did." My hands curl into fists, my nails biting into my palms. The familiar ache is grounding, anchoring me against the maelstrom of emotions threatening to overtake me.

"I won't be party to another murder." Grave's tone leaves no room for argument. "I've been involved in enough of that sort of a thing. We always said an eye for an eye, and now we're starting to cross the line."

Betrayal cuts deep, a jagged wound torn into the fabric of our partnership. The foundation of trust we built lies in ruins, crumbled beneath the weight of Grave's doubt. This man, willing to murder and torture countless others, but won't do it for our cause. Won't do it for me. What a hypocrite. They say when someone shows you who they are, believe them, and maybe this is Grave showing me who he really is for the very first time.

I straighten, squaring my shoulders. "Then that's all I need to know. Get out." My voice is flat, emotionless. I cling to the anger burning in my veins, using it to cauterize the rawness of loss. "I thought you believed in what we're doing."

Grave's jaw clenches. For a long moment, he simply stands there staring at me. I see the internal struggle reflected in his eyes, the warring factions of loyalty and doubt. When he turns on his heel and strides from the room without another word, I'm not surprised.

I'm alone in the silence that follows, standing amidst the wreckage of broken promises and shattered trust. The knife gleams on the counter, a reminder of justice not yet served.

Steeling my resolve, I make for the basement and the man chained within. The path ahead is clear, even if I have to walk it alone.

The stairs creak under my feet, a discordant melody announcing my descent into darkness. Shadows cling to the walls, shrouding the basement in shades of gray.

A rusty pipe drips in the corner, the only sound breaking the heavy silence. The rhythmic tapping does little to soothe my frayed nerves or calm the storm of emotion raging inside me.

Anger and betrayal war with loss, the conflicting currents threatening to drown me in their depths. I cling to my purpose, using it as a lifeline to pull me from the abyss.

Justice will be served tonight.

My captive stirs at the sound of my approach, metal rattling against metal. He blinks against the dim light filtering from above, confusion etched into the lines of his face at the absence of Grave.

"Back for more, sweetheart?" His tone is mocking, though there's an edge of something else beneath it. Fear, perhaps. He's smart if it's fear. Maybe he can tell I should be more feared than Grave. After all, he's only a dangerous traitor, whereas I'm a rageful scorned woman with nothing to lose.

The knife feels heavy in my grip as I stride forward. He flinches away instinctively, the chains binding him to the wall clanging.

"Where's your partner in crime?" His gaze darts around the basement, as if expecting Grave to materialize from the shadows. "Didn't want to get his hands dirty?"

"We're not partners anymore." I keep my tone flat, refusing to betray the maelstrom of emotion churning inside me. "He couldn't stomach what needed to be done."

Understanding dawns, his eyes widening. The implications of being at my mercy alone seem to sink in, his fear spiking. He struggles against his bindings, metal groaning. Whoever thought someone would be more scared of me than Grave?

I step closer, close enough to see the sheen of sweat on his brow and smell the sour tang of terror clinging to his skin. The knife rises, glinting in the low light.

"Now, it's just you and me." My smile is slow, sharp. "And we have unfinished business."

His gaze darts to the knife, his Adam's apple bobbing as he swallows hard. "You don't have the guts."

The words are a challenge, meant to provoke me into action. I tighten my grip on the hilt, knuckles whitening as I wonder if I can replicate Grave's apple peeling on the soft, delicate skin of Harvey Maxwell's throat.

"Don't I?" My tone is deceptively soft, belying the tumult churning inside me. The desire for vengeance wars with the memory of Grave's disapproving gaze, his unspoken judgment hanging between us.

The captive's eyes narrow, a glint of cunning surfacing. "You need me alive. What will you do once I'm gone? That hardly seems like fitting revenge." His lips twist into a mocking smile. "Seems you've lost more than your partner today."

The barb strikes deep, resonating in a place raw and aching. I stiffen, the urge to wipe that smug expression from his face nearly overpowering my restraint.

The knife wavers, then steadies in my grip. I step closer and grasp his jaw, my fingers digging into bone and flesh.

"I don't need anything from you," I hiss. "Least of all, your worthless life."

I slam his head back against the wall and press the knife to his throat, the sharp edge nicking his skin. A thin rivulet of blood trickles down his neck, crimson against pale flesh.

His breath comes in ragged gasps, his chest heaving against my arm. The mocking expression has bled from his eyes, replaced by stark terror at the revelation that I am not of sound mind.

"Please," he rasps. "I'll give you anything. Just let me go."

The knife wavers against his throat. Indecision wars within me, the desire to end him vying with Grave's disapproving stare. His unspoken judgment echoes through my mind, a refrain of *you promised you wouldn't kill him.*

I grit my teeth against the unwelcome thoughts, tightening my grip. The knife digs deeper into his flesh, a vivid red line welling against silver metal.

"Please," he gasps again. "Have mercy."

Mercy.

The word resonates, Grave's voice echoing in my memory. *We can't cross this line, Fallon. If we do, there's no going back.*

My hand trembles against his throat. The knife slips, just for a moment, and he sucks in a sharp breath.

In this instant, I glimpse the shadow of the woman I once was. The one who didn't resort to murder for vengeance. The one Grave believed in.

The one who committed to an eye for an eye. And nobody has been killed by Harvey Maxwell, to my knowledge.

The knife clatters to the floor, released from my trembling fingers. I stumble back a step, staring at the crimson-stained silver metal.

"You're going to regret this," the captive rasps, a triumphant gleam in his eyes. "Should've killed me while you had the chance." Arrogant and cocky despite the power imbalance, exuding the expected and misplaced confidence of a mediocre white man.

My gaze lifts to his, defiance etched into every line of my face. "No," I say softly. "I won't."

And I know, with stark certainty, that I've made the right choice. My revenge remains incomplete, but perhaps I've salvaged one of the parts of myself worth saving.

The woman Grave once admired isn't gone, after all.

I find Grave in the dim light of the quiet dive bar I know he frequents, a tumbler of whiskey clutched in one hand, his brow furrowed. He glances up at the creak of the door, startling when he sees me on the threshold.

For a long moment, we stare at one another, the silence thick with unspoken questions. The knife, cleaned but not yet sheathed, feels heavy in my pocket.

Finally, Grave rasps, "Did you—?"

"No," I say softly. "I didn't."

Relief flickers in his gaze, quickly replaced by wariness. "What now, then? We can't keep him forever."

"I agree, it's time to let him go." I meet Grave's startled look with steady resolve. "He's suffered enough, and I believe we've got what we need from him. What Claudia needs from him. It's time to move on."

"Just like that?" Disbelief colors his tone. "After everything we did to get to this point, you're really just going to let him walk away? I thought you were going to try to keep him as a forever pet or something."

"We went too far," I say quietly. "*I* went too far, and I nearly crossed a line I can't come back from. I won't do that to myself, and I won't ask that of you."

Silence falls between us again, heavy with uncertainty. At last, Grave sets his glass on the bar and rises in a rustle of movement.

He stops before me, conflict etched into the lines of his face. For a long moment, he hesitates, and I wonder if this will be the end of us. If the Harvey situation will prove too much to move past even though I pulled back before ending his life.

Then he reaches out, his large hand squeezing my forearm, the height of him expressing physical affection. "Come on," he says roughly. "Let's go and figure out how best to let him go."

Relief floods me, and I lean into his touch. He awkwardly embraces me in a side hug, his body dwarfing my much smaller frame. The foundation of our partnership may be scarred, but apparently it remains intact.

We walk out of the bar together into the shadows of night. A reset, hard-won and imperfect, but ours all the same.

Chapter 65

AKSEL

I walk into my condo, each step an echo of happier times. Memories of Fallon assault me from every corner. Laughter we once shared. Intimacy we once craved and enjoyed. Love we once nurtured within these walls, now shattered into a million pieces.

My fingers instinctively reach for the light switch. The light flickers on, casting shadows in the empty space that was once filled with her presence.

The silence is deafening.

Music, television, the hum of the city—none of it fills the void she left behind. Her absence resonates in the walls, a constant reminder of the love we once shared in this place.

Seeing it usually works, I try to lose myself in a workout, in the burn of each rep and the ache of strained muscles. But her face haunts me. Her eyes stare back at me, reflected in the sheen of sweat on my skin. My heart races with the memory of her touch, her kiss, the feel of her body pressed against mine.

The silence persists.

My fingers hover over a couple of dating apps in a futile attempt at connection. But betrayal simmers beneath the surface. It doesn't feel right to activate my profile and start the dance of swiping left and right on women I don't care about and never will. The ghost of her lingers, a barrier I can't bring myself to cross. Fallon is the only person I ever want to swipe right on again. To do anything else would be a lie. An empty act.

The walls close in around me, suffocating in their emptiness. I'm drowning in the silence. In the memories. In the love I can't escape.

I sit on the edge of the bed we once shared, head in hands. It's been weeks and despite many loads of laundry, the faint scent of her perfume clings to the walls, a cruel reminder of the intimacy we've lost.

And in the silence, I ache for her.

Crave her.

Need her.

The way I always will.

I lose myself online instead, navigating to a couple of my favorite sites where anonymity is a comfort. But her face finds me even here, in the pornographic images and scenes meant to distract, to numb. Her eyes stare back at me in every actress, reflected in moments we once shared.

There is no escape. Not here. Not anywhere.

My heart races and breaks all at once, torn between the memory of her touch and the knowledge I may never feel it again. I cling to the fading scent of her on my skin, the softness of her voice in my ear, the warmth of her in my arms.

And I wonder if I'll ever be free of this. Of her.

If I even want to be.

Because the truth is, she owns me. Heart, body, and soul. She always has. For god's sake, I can't even jerk off to porn without her image pervading my senses.

Instead of relieving myself, I draft messages I'll never send, pouring my heart out to her in the darkness. I tell her I'm sorry. That I miss her. That I'm lost without her. That she's the best and worst thing that's ever happened to me.

The words remain unsent. Lingering in the silence that stretches between us. A reminder of all that will never be.

In the end, she's left me with nothing but the ache of her absence. An emptiness that can't be filled. A heartbreak with no end in sight.

I'm haunted by the ghost of her. Shackled to the memory of us. And I wonder if this is what love does to you—if it leaves you with nothing at all.

I wake with her name on my lips, the fading whisper of a dream already slipping through my fingers. For a moment, I can almost feel the warmth of her in my arms again. Taste the softness of her kiss. Hear the sound of her laughter, bright and carefree in my ear.

And then I open my eyes.

The room is empty. Silent. Cold.

Reality crashes over me, harsh and unforgiving. She's gone. She left me. And she's never coming back.

I rise and shuffle to the kitchen, craving the burn of whiskey down my throat. Needing anything to dull the ache inside. My phone chimes with a message, and for a fleeting second, hope flares.

But it's not her. Of course it's not. It's just my assistant reminding me about a presentation that needs to be finalized by the end of the week.

I pour a drink with shaking hands, the amber liquid sloshing over the rim of the glass. I welcome the sting as it slides down my throat, igniting a fire in my chest.

Anything to feel something other than this.

Other than the broken, gaping hole where my heart used to be.

But the whiskey does nothing to dull the pain. If anything, it amplifies the memory of Fallon, as if her ghost has come to haunt me. I see her face everywhere I look. Hear her voice in the silence. Feel the ghost of her touch in the empty spaces between us.

She's always there. And she's always out of reach.

I stand at the window, watching the city below. A surge of anger rises, sharp and sudden, clawing at my insides. I hurl my glass at the wall, shards of glass raining down as the amber liquid slides to the floor, puddling on my luxe Persian rug.

The flare of rage is fleeting. In its wake comes a surge of remorse, and I'm left with only the ruin I've made.

Just like I ruined us.

The glass lies shattered at my feet, a reflection of the wreckage inside. And I wonder if I'll ever be able to piece myself back together again. Or if I'm broken beyond repair.

Chapter 66

AKSEL

The thump of an ax embedding itself in wood greets me as I walk through the door. My gaze sweeps the dimly lit room, taking in the mismatched furniture and buckets of axes lining one wall. Punk music pumps in the background, and I smell the distinctive scent of cheeseburgers and spilled beer.

Carson waves me over from one of the makeshift throwing lanes. "You're late." Of course he'd pick this place. It's just so... *him*. Colorful, trendy and a little bit hipster-ish. A little jock-y, a little dorky. Carson, in the form of a venue.

"Traffic." The excuse falls flat. I was stalling, the idea of socializing in public about as appetizing as a chocolate-covered fish with cheese sprinkles.

He hands me an ax. "Well, hi to you too, brother. Also, we're not leaving until you can at least hit the outer ring."

I grip the ax, feeling the weight of it, and step up to the line. With a practiced motion, Carson sends his ax flying. It hits the bullseye dead center.

Show-off. "What'd you want to talk about?" I ask, stalling again.

Carson gives me a look that says he knows exactly what I'm doing. "Just throw the ax, Aksel."

I throw. The ax glances off the edge of the target and clatters to the floor.

"Pathetic," he scoffs.

"I have other skills." I waggle my eyebrows at him. There's something about my younger brother that always cheers me up, even when I'm in my darkest of moods. There's little that brings me more joy than being able to make him laugh. Tonight is no exception.

"Ew. Shut up and throw." But there's laughter in his voice. The sound eases some of the tension coiling in my gut.

I pick up another ax and throw again. This time it sinks into the second ring. Not bullseye, but at least I hit the damn target.

"Better." Satisfaction colors Carson's tone. He throws another ax, the rhythmic thunk of metal on wood keeping time with my thoughts.

As fun as this is, something's off here. The texts, the choice of meeting place...Carson's stalling as much as I am. My concern ratchets higher. This isn't just brotherly bonding. Whatever Carson has to say, I have a feeling I'm not going to like it.

The next ax flies from my fingers, finding its mark in the center ring. But my mind isn't on the game. It's on Carson, and the sinking suspicion that this night is going to take a turn. Still, if he's reaching out to anyone for advice, I'm glad it's me.

Carson lines up his final throw, muscles flexing under his t-shirt. But his hands hesitate on the ax handle.

"Spit it out." I cross my arms, axes forgotten. "You're very good at this, but I know you didn't drag me out here for a round of lumberjack. What's going on?"

He meets my gaze, his blue eyes troubled. "I got into something, Aksel. Something... bad."

Everything in me goes still. "What did you do?" My voice emerges flat, hard as the ax handles.

Carson looks away, dragging a hand through his hair. "Not me. Them. Some guys.. .they want me in on their operation. High stakes poker games, cybercrimes. Big money shit."

The words land like a blow to the chest, stealing my breath. "Cybercrimes? Are you insane?"

"I turned them down," he says quickly. "But they're not taking no for an answer."

"Who are they?" I demand. "Give me names, Carson. Now."

He rakes a hand down his face. When it emerges, his expression is bleak. "The Marcello brothers. Word is they're tied up with the Italian mafia."

My heart stutters. The Marcellos. This is worse than I feared. "You can't get mixed up with them. They're dangerous. We've had beef with them in the past and it was rough."

"You think I don't know that?" Carson snaps. He hurls his ax at the target, and it strikes the bullseye with a violence that makes me flinch.

"Then why didn't you come to me sooner?" I stride over and grip his shoulder, hard. "I could've helped you. Protected you."

"I didn't want to drag you into this mess," he says quietly. "But I'm scared, Aksel. They threatened me. Threatened Amy and our family. I don't know what else to do."

Rage and fear curdle in my gut as I pull Carson close. "You listen to me. I won't let anyone hurt you or anyone else in our family, you understand? That includes Amy. You're out of this. We're going to cut ties with these bastards once and for all."

I feel him nod against my shoulder. Around us, the axes stick in their targets like a ring of silent sentinels. But new enemies have emerged tonight.

And if the Marcellos think they'll get their hooks in my brother, they have another thing coming.

I release Carson and stride over to retrieve my ax. My hands clench around the handle, slick with sweat, as I turn to face him.

"Tell me everything. Names, dates, details of the threats. I need to know what we're up against."

Carson drags a hand through his hair. "About a month ago, I got into a high-stakes poker game. Won big. That's when they approached me. Said I had a gift, wanted to bring me in on some of their 'business opportunities.'"

He swallows hard. "I told them no, but then they started showing up wherever I went. Said if I didn't play ball, they'd go after Amy and everyone else I ever cared about. Even showed me photos of her leaving work."

The thought of dangerous men like them being anywhere near my sisters or Carson's girlfriend makes my blood run cold.

My ax trembles in my grip. I hurl it at the target, and it splits the wood with a crack like a gunshot.

"Bastards," I snarl. "They didn't touch her, did they?"

"No, but they made sure I knew they could. Aksel, I don't care what happens to me, but if anything happened to Amy or Roxy or Raine because of my stupidity—"

"Nothing will happen to her." I stride over and grip the back of Carson's neck, our foreheads pressing together. "We end this now. I'll help keep Amy safe, you hear me?"

Carson retrieves another axe, weighing it in his hand. "I don't want you involved in this, Aksel. It's my mess to clean up."

"Too late for that. You're my brother. We're in this together. Just promise me you won't do anything stupid," I say. "No more secret meetings or risky bets. Stay away from the Marcellos and their goons. Let me handle this."

Carson opens his mouth to argue, then closes it with a snap. He knows I'm right. Getting tangled up further will only make things worse.

"I promise," he says softly.

He drags a hand through his hair. "I never should've gotten involved with them in the first place. I just...I got drawn into it before I really understood who I was dealing with and what the stakes were. But now—"

"Hey." I grip his shoulder. "We all make mistakes. What matters is making this right."

"But how? If I don't give the Marcellos what they want, they could destroy everything. And if I do, I'm basically signing on to be their puppet for life." Carson's eyes meet mine, bleak with despair. "There's no way out of this, Aksel. I've really fucked things up this time."

"We'll find a way out, Carson. We always do." I squeeze his shoulder and summon a smile. "Remember when we were kids and got lost in the woods overnight during that camping trip? Everybody else panicked, but we stayed calm, worked together, and made it out alive. This is no different. The Marcellos are just another problem to solve."

Carson huffs a mirthless laugh. "Somehow I don't think they'll be as easy to outsmart as a couple of hungry raccoons, bro."

I release Carson's shoulder and step back, surveying the axes embedded in the target. Each weapon represents a threat, shadows gathering on the horizon.

"Maybe not." I pluck the ax from his hands and add it to the target, where it lodges deep in the wood. "But they're messing with the wrong family. And by the time we're done with them, the Marcellos are going to realize they should've left us the hell alone."

Chapter 67

FALLON

Something's not right. Grave's instincts were correct about Brynn Waterford. The emails I found on the clone I made of her laptop don't add up. The timeline of events she described to us, the sequence of how things went down with Griffin—it's all fucked.

I slam the laptop shut, bile rising in my throat. That bitch tried to play us. This whole damn time.

Meticulously organized files, providing receipts to back up accusations. On closer look, each piece of evidence seeming slightly off, as if created by the same person on the same computer.

My hands shake as I pace the dimly lit room. Griffin isn't guilty of the atrocities Brynn claimed. It was all in her mind, and seems to be an elaborate scam to get him killed so she can take the insurance money and run off with her newfound beau. She's been manipulating me, using my thirst for revenge to get what she wants. A big fat undeserved paycheck.

I sigh and shake my head. How could I have been so stupid? All the signs were there, but I was too blinded by anger to see through her lies. Buying into her story like a gullible minion.

My hands clench into fists, fingernails biting into my palms. I should never have doubted Grave. We were played, both of us, in Brynn's twisted game, although he saw the signs well before I did.

The realization hits me like a punch to the gut. I wanted vengeance so badly, I didn't care who suffered. I would have killed Griffin based on Brynn's lies and doctored evidence, all to satisfy my personal thirst for revenge. It was only Grave's insistence we trust but verify that resulted in me seeing the truth before it was too late.

Shit. What have I become? So ready to exact revenge. So ready to kill.

I drop my head in my hands, overcome by the gravity of it all. The foundation of my convictions has crumbled into dust. I don't know what's right or wrong anymore, who's guilty or innocent.

All I know is that I can't continue down this path. The darkness has consumed me, and I'm losing myself in the quest for revenge.

Life has turned me into a monster, but I let it. I embraced the darkness willingly.

I slump down in my chair, at a crossroads, torn between the truth and lies, justice and vengeance. The path ahead is shrouded in shadows, but I know one thing for sure—I have to stop this. Before it's too late.

My fingers tremble as I reach for my phone. There's only one thing left to do.

Grave answers on the second ring. "Fallon." His voice is rough, wary. I don't blame him. After all I've put him through recently...

"We need to talk." The words stick in my throat, but I force them out. "I know the truth. About Brynn. About the evidence."

A sharp intake of breath. "What?"

"It was doctored. Manipulated. Brynn set us up, tried to play us. Tried to get us to—" I swallow hard. "I'm so sorry, Grave. For everything."

Silence. Then, "Fallon, I don't understand. How did you—"

"It doesn't matter." I cut him off, the ache in my chest intensifying. "You have to believe me. Brynn has been pulling the strings this whole time. I was blinded by vengeance, but now I see the truth. She was trying to get insurance money to fund her affair, and get rid of her husband in the process. He doesn't seem like a very good man by any means, but there's no evidence of him doing the most terrible things she claims."

"I don't know what to say." Grave's voice softens, the wariness fading. "After everything that's happened, why should I not assume you're going to want to murder the next alleged betrayer? Do you get how serious this is? We almost murdered an innocent man, Fall..."

"Because..." My eyes sting. "Because you once trusted me. And I'm asking you to believe in me, just this once. Please, Grave." I take a shaky breath. "End this madness with me. It's gone too far."

Another stretch of silence. Then, "Okay."

Relief washes over me in a dizzying wave. "Okay?"

"I believe you." Grave lets out a harsh breath. "May the universe help me, but I do."

Tears spill down my cheeks as a sob rises in my throat. We were broken, shattered into a million pieces, but maybe now we can start to heal.

Maybe this is one relationship I can actually salvage.

"It's over," I whisper. "This ends now."

No more lies. No more vengeance. No more darkness.

As the hours go by and I dig further into Brynn's web of deception, the revelation hits me like a punch to the gut.

I was this close to murdering Griffin, to obliterating any chance of happiness in my life. How could I have been so blind? So hellbent on vengeance that I ignored the truth staring me in the face?

Shame and self-loathing rise in a bitter wave, threatening to drown me. I screwed up, almost past the point of no return, and now the knowledge of what I almost did will haunt me forever.

But Grave forgave me. Just like that. Against all odds, he chose to believe in me. To help me end this madness and find our way back to the light.

I cling to that lifeline as my doubts and regrets intensify, shredding my fragile hopes. How can he ever trust me again after everything I've done? I turned on him and was ready to kill a man to satisfy my quest for revenge.

I grapple with questions I'm not sure I'm ready to face. Have I gone too far to turn back? Am I capable of redemption after embracing the darkness for so long? Or will the thirst for vengeance always lurk inside me, waiting to be unleashed again? Will I ever be able to stick to my boundaries?

I don't know. All I know is that I have a chance to make this right. To take back control of my life and choose a different path, one where the light outweighs the dark.

Grave is willing to walk that path with me, despite everything. I cling to that truth, to him, as the only way to save myself from the abyss threatening to consume me.

<h1 style="text-align:center">Chapter 68</h1>

AKSEL

The familiar scent of cinnamon and sandalwood wafts over me as I step into my formidable grandmother's study. She sits in a high-backed velvet chair by the fireplace, a glass of brandy in one hand and a worn leather book in the other.

She glances up, her steel-gray eyes peering at me over the rim of her glasses. "What troubles you, dear one?"

I sink into the chair opposite her with a sigh, raking a hand through my hair. "It's Fallon. I don't trust her anymore, and I feel like an idiot for letting her in again."

Grandmother closes her book, giving me her full attention. "What's happening with Fallon?"

"She's been sneaking around, and her behavior was becoming increasingly erratic and unpredictable," I clench my jaw, rage simmering in my gut. "She reeled me back in and then stopped talking to me cold turkey."

"I see." Grandmother takes a slow sip of brandy, gazing into the fire. "I can't say I'm surprised. Women like Fallon are dangerous creatures, Aksel. Venomous snakes waiting to strike when you least expect it." Her eyes harden. "Forget about her, Aksel. She's not worth your time nor affection."

My grandmother seems to further process what I've just shared and then sets her mouth in a grim line, her sharp eyes narrowing. She stays silent for a long moment, her gaze distant as if she's seeing some long ago memory play out.

When she speaks again, her tone is hard as granite. "She has always been jealous of what she cannot have. Even as a child, Fallon coveted the lives of those more fortunate, resenting them for what she lacked. You should have seen the way she used to look at you and your siblings. And if you had another girl within twenty feet of you... well, all hell broke loose."

She looks at me, worry and anger warring in her expression. "You shouldn't have trusted her. I warned you, but you refused to listen."

I clench my jaw, old guilt rising. Even back in high school, she told me Fallon was trouble, but I was too blind to see it. Too blinded by lust and desire to heed the wisdom of my elders. Still, the thought of her getting jealous over me even being in the same room as another girl gets me a little hot under the collar.

"I know," I say quietly. "You were right. I should have listened."

The admission does little to soften the grim set of her mouth, but she reaches out a gnarled hand to clasp my own. "You're not the first to be fooled by a pretty face and honeyed words, Aksel dear. But we are family, and we protect our own." Her fingers tighten around mine, as hard and unyielding as the vow in her voice. "She will not threaten to weaken our family again."

I rake a hand through my hair again, torn between my love for Fallon and the wisdom in Grandmother's words. She has decades more experience in these matters. If she says Fallon can't be trusted, she's probably right. But then she always has had a mistrust of the Dempseys.

"You're distracted," Grandmother says, "and we can't afford distractions right now. Not with the Farringtons circling like vultures, waiting to pick our bones clean." She sets her glass down with a sharp click. "You need to focus on the business. Matters of the heart can wait."

I nod, guilt and relief warring in my chest. Fallon has betrayed me, but I don't wish her harm. The family business must come first. Grandmother is right, as always.

"Thank you," I say quietly.

She smiles, reaching over to pat my hand. "You're welcome, dear one. Now, tell me what else is on your mind."

The warmth of her touch and, despite the hardness she usually exposes to people, the comfort of her presence, eases the turmoil in my soul. I take a deep breath and begin to speak.

I tell Grandmother everything—my suspicions about Kent and Isabella's ulterior motives, as well as Carson's bad choices and the details of the threats against Amy and my sisters from the Marcellos. She listens without interruption, her sharp eyes peering into my soul. By the time I finish, dusk has fallen and shadows fill the room.

"This is troubling about Kent and Isabella," Grandmother says at last, "but not unexpected. The Farringtons have always been ruthless opportunists, and Kent is no different. He aims to destroy us, and will use any means necessary to achieve his objectives. It sounds like he's found an ally in his goals." She sighs, weariness etching fine lines around her mouth. "And as for the Marcellos, we must be careful. Increase security, especially around Raine and the children, as well as Roxy and Amy. I do not trust that following Amy and threatening her was an isolated incident, and we need to be on high alert."

I nod in agreement. "Will do."

"Leave Kent and Isabella to me," Grandmother repeats. "I'll get a full download from Raine and ensure neither of them cause any more trouble for this family." A steely glint enters her eyes, and a shiver runs down my spine. My grandmother doesn't fuck around when it comes to protecting our family business.

"If there's nothing else, I should be going," I say, standing. I have plans to make and measures to take.

Grandmother smiles, sharp and cold. "Yes, go. Take care of our family, Aksel, and I will handle the rest."

I bend to kiss her cheek. "Thank you," I whisper, preparing to leave. Darkness has fully fallen, shadows lurking in every corner, but I refuse to be afraid. With my formidable Grandmother by my side, as well as Raine and her incredible inner strength, together we will destroy our enemies. The King family will prevail.

My grandmother releases my hand, the iron glint in her eyes signaling she means business.

"Promise me you'll be careful," I urge. "The men Isabella and Kent are working with are dangerous."

A grim smile touches her lips. "So am I." She pats my cheek, a gentle reprimand. "Don't worry about me. I've lived a long life and faced far greater threats. This is but a minor blip."

Her confidence does little to assuage my concerns, but I know further protests will be in vain. Once my grandmother sets her mind on something, nothing short of divine intervention will deter her.

Kent and Isabella have also severely miscalculated. The vipers I unwittingly took into my sanctuary will soon feel the sting of vengeance.

I find Fallon waiting in my office, perched on the edge of my desk with one long, lean leg crossed over the other. She's wearing another one of those little black dresses that cling to her curves, her red lips curved in a smirk.

"Miss me?" she purrs, sliding off the desk, as if she hadn't just peaced out of my life for months. Her heels click on the marble floor as she saunters toward me, her hips swaying. I harden at the sight, heat pooling low in my gut. She always affects me like this, no matter my mood or intentions.

"What are you doing here?" I ask roughly, clenching my jaw in disbelief at her audacity, but also thrilled at the sight of her. I need to stay strong, and remember why I can't give in to her or the desires she stirs.

"I wanted to see you. Is that wrong?" She reaches up, trailing clever fingers along my collar. I grab her wrist before she can go any further, my grip tightening when she tries to pull away.

"Enough games," I growl. "You can't keep ducking in and out of my life like this."

All traces of seduction flee her expression, her eyes widening. "You're one to talk. After what you did."

"Enough lies," I repeat coldly. "You are no longer welcome here. If I see you near my family again, you will regret it."

I release her wrist and step back, steeling myself against the hurt in her eyes. She has no one to blame but herself. I gave her a chance, opened myself up to her despite everything, and she betrayed me.

Lesson learned. I will never trust so easily again.

I wake with a start, still hard at the thought of Fallon and her unexpected attempt to seduce me. As my eyes adjust to the light, I realize it was only a dream. I'm partially relieved, because I don't know how I could have reconciled her behavior with how much she's hurt me. But I'm mostly disappointed. What I'd give to have her in my arms again, her lips on mine, if only for a moment.

Chapter 69

FALLON

The air in the dive bar is thick with the smell of stale beer and smoke. Neon signs flicker outside advertising the budget beer and whiskey that form the signature combo of this venue, casting an eerie red glow through the grimy windows.

I sit alone in a shadowed booth, nursing my third whiskey. The burn in my throat barely registers through the haze in my mind. I can't stop thinking about him. Aksel.

I force the image of his face from my thoughts, focusing instead on the mission ahead. My clients are counting on me. The revenge business has consumed my life, and I can't afford distractions. It almost turned me into a murderer, for fuck's sake. I need to be on my game.

Grave slides into the booth across from me, his perceptive gaze taking in my disheveled appearance. He knows me too well.

"You look like hell," he says bluntly. Always straight to the point with him.

I shrug, avoiding his eyes. "Just tired. It's been a long week."

He shakes his head, leaning forward intently. "There's more to it. I can tell."

Damn him. I take a long sip of my drink, debating how much to reveal. But the words spill out before I can stop them.

"I can't get Aksel out of my head," I confess bitterly. "On top of everything else going on. Releasing Harvey, the new information about Griffin and Brynn. Mia. It's just a lot."

Grave's expression softens with understanding. We've been partners for years. He gets me in a way few others do.

"Feelings make things complicated," he says. "That's why I avoid them. But you can't let it distract you from the job. This is a critical point, and if we make a misstep the company could crumble. And both of us could spend the rest of our lives in prison. Or we could wind up dead."

I nod, knowing he's right, and a shiver runs down my spine at the thought. With effort, I force Aksel from my mind again, focusing on why we're here.

"You're right," I say firmly. "I won't let him get in the way anymore."

Grave studies me a moment longer before leaning back and nodding, seemingly satisfied with my reassurance, though I can tell a sliver of doubt lingers behind his eyes. He knows me too well.

I take a deep breath, steadying myself. Time to get back to business.

Grave steers the conversation to the thing he's most concerned about—my boundaries. "Things keep spiraling," he says, his voice gruff as ever, the dim light casting shadows across his face, giving him an enigmatic aura. "When I joined you, I knew I was going to get my hands dirty, which I'm more than fine with, but I wasn't intending on you going down a murderous path."

I meet his gaze. "That was never my intention, Grave. I always said our revenge would be eye for an eye. And none of our clients have come to us from beyond the grave. Yet at least. I agree, murder is an overstep for our current business model."

He smirks.

I feel my defenses slowly crumbling, my vulnerability making a rare appearance in front of one of my most trusted humans. "To be honest, I'm not sure where the line is, Grave. It keeps shifting. I feel comfortable about holding Harvey Maxwell captive and making him feel pain. After all, he did that to Claudia. But did I go too far? Keep him too long? Inflict too much physical damage? I'm not sure."

I don't add what's really on my mind—how much I've let my work be clouded by my personal situation. My own feelings of betrayal and darkness driving my desire to avenge my clients. Aksel's actions long ago being the reason I started this part of my business in the first place.

"You know I don't judge you, right?" Grave asks, his voice unusually soft. "Anything a person could ever have done to inflict pain, I've probably done it. And as for taking lives? There have been more than I'd care to count. And each time, it leaves a mark on your soul. It's unfixable, even with time. So you have to know when to stop. I wish I'd known that back then." Ghosts of his past dance in his eyes under the dim bar lighting.

"I know I don't know the details, Grave, but please believe me when I tell you that I trust you implicitly. That you're one of, if not the, most trusted advisors I have in my life. So if you had to go to those levels, I know it was out of necessity."

An unspoken bond of trust permeates between us, leaving the air electric. I've never felt so strongly about a man I haven't been interested in a relationship with.

Clearly, he feels it too. Always awkward about a show of feelings, to the point he claims not to have them at all, Grave breaks eye contact and takes another sip of his drink.

The discussion shifts to the future. "We still have to figure out how to deal with Harvey so he doesn't come back to bite us. And then there's the matter of dealing with Brynn," he says, both situations raising chilling questions that linger in the air.

"I still can't believe Brynn tried to use us as pawns. I'm so glad I eventually listened to you, even though I should have from the outset. I'm so sorry for not looking into your concerns sooner, Grave. I was so dismissive, so hellbent on what felt like righteous vigilante justice that I almost had us kill an innocent man in cold blood."

"Listen, people make mistakes," says Grave. "I'm just glad you came to your senses before it was too late."

"So, what are we going to do about her? Any ideas?" I quirk a brow.

"I have a few things in mind. Let me look into it further."

I nod, relieved we were able to at least begin resolving issues in our professional relationship.

"So, where do we go from here?" I ask quietly. The next steps seem murky, but I know Grave and I will navigate them together.

He meets my gaze, determination etched on his face. "Wherever this path takes us. But we walk it side by side."

I reach across the table and squeeze his hand, a silent pact sealing our partnership. He shifts awkwardly, but doesn't pull his hand away. We may dwell in darkness, but within it we've found trust—and purpose.

Chapter 70

AKSEL

The familiar scent of bergamot and sandalwood envelops me as I step into Raine's living room. Soft lamplight washes over mismatched furniture and threadbare rugs, a soothing balm after the day I've had.

Raine smiles, lines crinkling around eyes that hold wisdom beyond her years as she hands me a cup of hot ginger tea. I eagerly take the steaming mug from her. She's always had an uncanny knack for knowing exactly what I need.

Motioning for me to sit, she settles into the armchair across from mine. The quiet grows heavy with anticipation until she breaks it, her gaze steady on mine.

"Life's complex, little brother, but you're strong. Stronger than you know."

Her words hit their mark, a lump forming in my throat. I drag in a breath, fisting my hands in an attempt to keep them still. "If you saw what I did today—"

"I don't need to see." She leans forward, clasping my wrist. "I know you always keep family top of mind, and sometimes that means you need to do things you're not proud of."

I jerk my head in a sharp nod, my throat too tight to speak. She knows me too well.

After increasing security on Amy, Roxy, Raine, Carson, Grandmother, myself—and even Fallon, although she's not aware my men are trailing her twenty-four seven—I took matters into my own hands with the help of a couple of my most trusted men. The Marcello brothers are out of commission, one dead and two severely wounded after what police and news media will come to describe as a randomized drive-by shooting in one of the city's worst neighborhoods. I took the kill shot myself, savoring the smell of gun smoke and the red dot that slowly started bleeding between the oldest Marcello brothers' eyes. Nobody fucks with my family.

"As for Kent and Isabella, they betrayed you because you trusted them, and now you want revenge." Her gaze sharpens. "I won't tell you not to go after them. But remember who you are. Don't lose yourself in the darkness. Let Grandmother take care of it like she offered to. She's reached out to me and I've told her everything I've been able to dig up."

"How can I not be more involved in taking them down?" The words scrape from my chest. "They tried to destroy everything. We would have had nothing left. They almost obliterated us from the inside out. I feel like I'm not doing enough."

"Just remember, you're not alone. You have me." Raine squeezes my wrist. "And you have Roxy, Carson and Grandmother. Don't forget that. Don't feel like you need to carry the weight of the world on your shoulders all by yourself either, okay?"

I drag in a shaky breath and clasp her hand, clinging to the anchor she offers.

She's right. They may have almost taken everything else, including my ability to trust, but they can't have us. As long as we have each other, there's still light to be found. Even in the darkest of nights.

As Raine's words linger in the room, a renewed sense of purpose rises within me. Our bond has always been a source of strength. Raine has walked through her own storms, emerging with wisdom and scars in equal measure, and she uses both to guide me through mine.

I rise from the armchair, movements slow but steady. The path ahead is uncertain, the future unclear, but I have my compass in hand, and I know what I need to do.

Raine studies me, her gaze sharp yet soft with understanding. She knows I've found my footing again, at least for now. The demons will return to haunt my dreams, but I'll have her voice to echo in my mind. A light in the darkness. A star to navigate by.

I pull her into a fierce hug, hoping it conveys what words can't. She returns it without hesitation, a silent promise that she'll be there whenever I falter. We have each other. They can't take that away.

When I step outside, the night air is cool against my skin. The storm has passed, leaving a clear sky in its wake. The stars shine bright, illumination to guide my path.

I roll my shoulders back and stride into the night, purpose in my step. The heart may not always lead me on a straight path, but it will guide me to where I need to be.

To Fallon.

Always to Fallon.

Chapter 71

FALLON

I stalk down the stairs, my footsteps echoing. The man I've trapped in this confined space shrinks at my approach, rattling his chains. The dim light in my basement casts long shadows, creating an eerie atmosphere as I stand before him. The air is thick with tension, and the only sound is the distant hum of the ventilation.

"Please," he whispers hoarsely. "No more."

My lips curl into a sneer. "You don't get to plead for mercy, Harvey Maxwell. Not after everything you've done."

My stoic expression gives nothing away as I slam a tray of food onto the floor, just out of his reach—another simple meal and a glass of water. He lunges for it, starving and desperate, but the chains hold him back.

"Filthy animal," I spit. "Although that's an insult to animals."

He glares up at me, defiance flickering in his eyes. "You're the monster here, not me."

Rage bubbles up inside me, hot and caustic. I backhand him across the face, splitting his lip. "Don't you dare speak to me like that. I'm not the villain in *this* story."

"Aren't you?" he rasps, blood dripping down his chin. "Look at what you're doing to me. How long are you going to keep me here like this?"

I slap him again, harder this time. He collapses onto his side with a pained groan, too weak to fight back.

"You've had it easy, considering what you did," I declare, my voice devoid of any warmth. "Basic meals and a toilet—that's more than scum like you deserve."

The man, a representation of all the men who have wronged others, looks up at me with a mix of fear and defiance. He's become a canvas onto which I project my anger and frustrations, and every interaction with him fuels the resentment that simmers within me.

"You thought you could control someone's life," I continue, my words cutting through the stagnant air. "Tell them what to wear, what to eat. Keeping them locked inside a cage and fucking with their mind. But here, you get the bare fucking minimum. Just like you did to all those women you hurt. Especially Claudia."

He opens his mouth, but I cut him off with a glare. "Don't you dare speak. You have no right to utter a single goddamn word."

I take a step closer, relishing the panic that flickers in his eyes. He tries to shrink away, but the chains keep him bound in place. In this moment, his fear is intoxicating.

Good. Let the fear sink in, you pathetic waste of space. Let it crawl into your veins the way you crept into the lives of your victims. My hands curl into fists, every muscle in my body tense with rage. Rage at the injustice of it all. Rage at a system that failed to protect the vulnerable. But most of all, rage at the fact that men like him always get away with it.

Not this time.

Shame and anger war within me, twisting my insides into knots. I squeeze my eyes shut, willing the voices in my head to be silent. The man's taunts scrape against wounds that have never truly healed, ripping them open anew.

I'm not like them. I'm not.

When I open my eyes, the man is watching me with a knowing look. Like he can see the rot that festers in my soul.

With a snarl, I grab his hair and slam his head into the concrete floor. He goes limp, unconsciousness claiming him at last.

I stand over his broken form, my chest heaving. The voices quiet, receding into the shadows. In their wake comes a bone-deep exhaustion and a dull ache between my legs.

Shame threatens to overwhelm me as I recognize the signs of arousal. I've become no better than the monsters I hunt. But there's no turning back now.

"You will pay for everything you did," I vow, my voice low and trembling with anger. "And when I'm done with you, you'll beg for the mercy of death."

I turn on my heel and stride out of the basement, slamming the door behind me. The lines between revenge and personal vendettas blur, but I can't bring myself to care. Not when justice is finally within my grasp.

I take the stairs two at a time on unsteady legs, gripping the railing until my knuckles turn white, eager to escape the suffocating confines of that room. With each step, the voices gain strength again, whispering that I'm no better than him. No better than any of them.

But even upstairs, I can't seem to catch my breath. By the time I reach the top, their accusations have risen to a fever pitch. I slam the door behind me, in an attempt to trap the echoes of my sins in the cellar along with the man. The walls seem to close in around me, echoes of the past threatening to drown me in a sea of anguish and despair. I know I need to let this man go, that I've already held him captive for too long. But I don't know how. And part of me still thinks he needs to pay more than he already has.

In the kitchen, I scrub the blood from my hands until my skin is raw and stinging. But no amount of soap and water can wash away the stain on my soul.

Aksel's face swims before my eyes, his smile as charming as it is deceitful. Like all the others, he wore a mask to hide the monster that lurked beneath. I was a fool to believe his lies, to think that he could be different. That any of them could be different.

My hands curl into fists, my nails biting into my palms. The pain barely registers through the haze of anger and bitterness. I want to scream, to rage against the unfairness of it all. I want to burn away the remnants of my naïveté and wash away the taint of their touches.

But I can't. I can never be clean again. All I have left is this anger, this thirst for vengeance that threatens to consume me whole. It's what fuels me, what gives me purpose when all else is lost. I cling to it with every fiber of my being because, without it, there is nothing left.

The man downstairs, Harvey, is just a means to an end, a vessel for my wrath. But with every defiant glare, he becomes the face of my tormentors. Aksel, my father, every man who dared to lay claim to my body and my soul. Their sins are carved into his flesh, bleeding and raw under my ministrations.

Let him scream. Let him beg for mercy as I've done. He will find none here. Not as long as there is breath in my body and blood on my hands. I swore to make him pay for everything he's done, and I always keep my promises.

Just like I promised to make them all burn.

Exhaustion drags at my limbs as I make my way to the living room. My gaze lands on a photo of Aksel and I, one I haven't yet damaged, a relic of happier times. Before everything went to hell. Before I became this twisted, unrecognizable version of myself.

Anger surges, hot and bitter, chasing away my shame. Aksel may have broken me, but I won't break for him. I won't give him the satisfaction.

I snatch the photo from the shelf, my fingers tightening around the frame. I haven't been quite ready to take it down, but the time has come. With a snarl, I hurl it at the wall. The glass shatters on impact, our smiling faces fracturing into a thousand pieces. At this rate, I should invest in a glass business. But I really don't care. It makes me feel better seeing the tiny shards of glass coating my condo floor.

Breath rasping in my chest, I stare at the ruined photo. The voices fall silent at last, their accusations fading into the darkness. In their place comes a cold, ruthless calm.

Chapter 72

FALLON

The call comes out of the blue, Roxy's name flashing on my phone. My stomach knots—what now? Did Aksel put her up to this?

I almost don't answer, but some masochistic part of me wants to rip the bandaid off. And if I'm honest, she's a lifeline to Aksel. "Yeah?"

"Fallon, it's not what you think." Roxy's voice is urgent, tense. "The whole situation with Aksel and Mia? There's nothing going on. There are two possibilities. Mia either set Aksel up and manipulated everything to make it look like he was cheating when he wasn't. Or she's also innocent and was just trying to help, but through a catastrophic sequence of events, everything looks so, so bad."

"What?" The word comes out sharp as a knife. "How...why would she do that? The first thing?"

"Well, I have a feeling she's always been jealous of you and Aksel," Roxy says. "She wanted him for herself, and when he wouldn't give her the time of day, she decided to destroy you to get back at him. Or maybe she wanted *you* for herself. Did you ever think about that? It seems like maybe you were spending much more time between work and Aksel that maybe she was feeling neglected. I don't know... but either way, Aksel and Mia are not—and never were—having an affair behind your back. Did they meet without you? Yes. Was that shitty? They probably could have handled things differently. But from where I'm sitting, I can't speak for Mia, but Aksel's actions were one hundred percent out of concern for you."

"But she—." I don't even know what to say, so my words trail off.

"I didn't want to believe it either," Roxy says softly. "But I saw messages between them discussing their plan. She played us all, Fallon. Including Aksel. She told him that she wanted to meet with him to talk about *you*. She preyed on the fact she knows how much he cares about you, and that he was worried about how you'd been acting. And then your brother had the private investigator on Aksel's trail, and the photo opportunity presented itself, and then..."

The floor drops out from under me. My stomach churns with anger and regret—so much regret. I accused Aksel of the worst things, said such hateful words I can never take back. Ruined the best thing in my life over a venomous lie.

My head spins. It can't be true. Mia is—was—my best friend, she would never—but then I think of how distant she's been lately. The way she reacted when I told her Aksel and I had spent the night together.

"Where is he?" I whisper.

"Fallon—"

"Where is he, Roxy?" My voice breaks.

She sighs. "At his place. He's...he's a mess, Fallon. He thinks he lost you for good."

I close my eyes against the sting of tears. "I have to see him. I have to make this right."

"Go to him," Roxy says. "Just...be careful with his heart, okay? He loves you so damn much, and he doesn't deserve any more pain."

"I love him too," I say thickly. "I never stopped."

I hang up and grab my keys with a shaking hand. As I head out to my car, a wild hope blooms in my chest.

This isn't over.

I speed to Aksel's place, my heart pounding so hard I feel dizzy. What will I say to him? How can I possibly make up for the things I said?

When I pull up outside his condo, the lights are on, but his parking space is empty. My stomach drops—what if he's not here? What if he's gone somewhere to drown his sorrows, lost in a haze of alcohol and heartbreak—or even sex—because of me?

I race to the front door and pound on it with both fists. "Aksel! Aksel, please open the door!"

No response. Panic rises in my chest. I've already lost so much time with him, so many moments we'll never get back. I can't lose him completely. Not now, not when we have a second chance. I pound on his door one more time.

As tears blur my vision and I prepare to leave, defeated, the door creaks open. Aksel stands there, pale and glassy-eyed, in a pair of gray sweatpants and a wrinkled t-shirt. Even this disheveled, he's the hottest man I've ever seen. At the sight of me, a flicker of pain crosses his face before it smooths into a blank mask. His eyes are guarded, wary, but then I see a flicker of longing he can't hide.

"Fallon," he says tonelessly. "What are you doing here?"

The hope inside me ignites into a flame. We're not over. Not by a long shot. I give him a tremulous smile and say the words that will change everything: "We need to talk."

Aksel stares at me for a long moment, emotions flickering across his face too quickly to read. Then he steps back, opening the door wider in silent invitation.

I slip past him into the familiar space, hyper-aware of his presence behind me. The tension is so thick I could cut it with a knife, but there's something else too—a spark of possibility. Of new beginnings.

Aksel closes the door and turns to face me. His eyes are wary, guarded, but I see the longing he can't hide. "Well?" he asks, his voice rough. "You're here. Talk."

"Aksel, I'm so sorry," I blurt out. "Roxy told me the truth. She found proof that it was all a lie, a trick by Mia to break us apart. Or maybe something totally innocent that just looked really bad. I never should have believed Link and the private investigator over you. I'm so stupid, and stubborn, and I ruined everything because I didn't trust you enough. And I just felt so betrayed by two of the people closest to me, and—"

"Is this true?" He searches my face intently, as if looking for any hint of deception. "Do you mean it?"

"With all my heart." I reach for his hands, barely daring to hope when he doesn't pull away. "I love you, Aksel. I never stopped. And I want another chance...if you'll have me. I'm so sorry." My voice breaks on the last word. I've made so many mistakes, but this one cuts the deepest.

His eyes shine with tears as a smile slowly spreads across his face. "You infuriating, ridiculous woman," he says huskily. "How could I not?"

And then his arms are around me and I'm home, sobbing against his chest as he holds me close. We have a long road ahead to rebuild what was broken, but in this moment, it's enough to know that we'll walk it together.

"Fallon," he whispers in my ear. "I'm the one who should apologize. I should have fought for you, instead of letting you go so easily. I was a fool."

"We both were," I whisper. "But we can be fools together, if you'll have me." I close the distance between us, laying my hand on his chest, over his heart. It's racing as fast as mine, proof this means as much to him as it does to me.

Aksel cups my face in his hands, his gaze burning into mine. "Always," he murmurs, and then his lips are on mine, and we're lost in a kiss that feels like coming home.

Chapter 73

AKSEL

Roxy and I step into Tanoshī, and my senses come alive. The aroma of grilled chicken skewers and garlic assaults my nose. Lively chatter and laughter fill the space. Dim lighting, wood accents, and minimal decor create an intimate vibe. It took every ounce of resolve to tear myself away from Fallon's naked form earlier, but she convinced me she had some evening work to do and insisted I meet my sister for dinner as scheduled.

We're led to a cozy booth in the corner. As Roxy peruses the menu, the glow from the paper lanterns cast shadows across her face. My gaze lingers on her soft features, and I can't help but picture her as a bubbly child running around our house, squealing with glee at the smallest things.

Guilt rises in my chest at the thought of how I've been digging into what she's spending her time doing these days. I know what I have to do, but the timing has to be right. I didn't intend on nosing around in her business, but when I upped the security detail in response to the threat from the Marcellos, additional information came to light, clear as day. Roxy has created an online adult content streaming profile, and while she hasn't posted on it yet, negotiations are in the works for her to pose in some provocative pictures and star in videos that, once on the internet, will be impossible to erase. The worst part? Carlo Marcello is the person pressing her to take this next step.

A waitress delivers two glasses of chilled sake. The crisp, clean taste does little to soothe my nerves. I watch Roxy take a sip of hers, mesmerized by the movement of her throat as she swallows.

"You're being quiet tonight," Roxy says. She sets down her glass and reaches for my hand. Her fingers are soft and warm as they entwine with mine. "Is everything okay? How are you and Fallon doing?"

Her touch ignites a maelstrom of emotions. I swallow hard, grappling for the right words. How do I tell my little sister I have concerns about her life choices, and that I feel she's putting herself in danger on a daily basis through her work? How do I warn her against ending up with the same type of dark regrets that I do?

"We're doing okay, better than before, thanks to you," I say. "But that's not why I wanted to meet you today."

The words lodge in my throat as I meet her gaze. Those bright blue eyes that have always held me captive since she was a baby, all I want to do is protect her. In this moment, I realize I can't go through with it. I can't bear to see the hurt and betrayal that will surely dawn in those eyes once I confess the truth.

So I do the only thing I can. I lie.

"Everything's fine," I say, forcing a smile. "Just tired from work, that's all."

Roxy squeezes my hand and smiles back, the warmth in her expression piercing me to the core.

The aroma of yakitori skewers mingles with my guilt, churning my stomach. I scan the menu without seeing the options, my mind replaying Roxy's radiant smile over and over.

How can I destroy that smile by coming across as a judgmental older brother? When she's just doing what we've all wished we could—strike out on our own, away from the weight of familial pressure. The last thing she needs is her dreams being crushed by what probably looks like some self-appointed morality police. But that's not what it's about. I worry for her safety.

Roxy glances up from her menu, a crease forming between her brows. "You've barely said a word since we got here. I know you said you're tired from work, but I feel like there's something else going on. Is something wrong? Are you and Fallon really doing better now?"

I swallow against the lump in my throat and force a smile. "Just enjoying your company."

The crease in her brow deepens, and she sets down her menu to give me her full attention. Her eyes are luminous in the soft glow of lantern light, searching mine for answers I can't bring myself to give.

I reach across the table to take Roxy's hand in mine, the warmth of her skin searing my conscience. "Okay, look Roxy. There's something I've been meaning to talk to you about."

Roxy stiffens at my words, her eyes widening with apprehension. She knows me too well, knows I'm holding something back.

I give her hand a gentle squeeze, scrambling to find the right words. "You've seemed distracted lately. Unfocused. I'm worried you're not taking life seriously enough. And I'm worried that you're making some choices that put you at risk. That you're hanging out with the wrong people, and you're not setting yourself up for long-term success. I'm here to support you, but I think you need more structure, more boundaries with the people you spend time with. And I need you to know I know about the, uh... online work you've been contemplating. Just remember, what happens online is almost impossible to erase once it's out there. It might seem like a short-term quick fix, but it could have lasting impacts."

There. I've said it. As much as I can without pushing it too far. My heart pounds against my ribs, waiting for her reaction.

Roxy blinks at me, confusion clouding her expression. She opens her mouth but no words come out. The clinking of glasses and distant chatter seem oddly muted in the wake of my words, as if the world is holding its breath along with me in anticipation of her response.

She looks down at the sake cup that she grasps tightly with both hands. "I haven't decided whether I'm doing it or not. And why are you spying on me, anyway?"

"I'm not. I just—." I sigh. "Listen, I didn't want to alarm you, but Carson has got himself caught up in a tricky situation with the Marcello brothers. I've been helping him with it, and have taken care of it at least for now, but in the meantime we thought it wise to ramp up security on the whole family. And as you know, our security team is very thorough. They reported that you've been doing the, uh, online stuff... and it's got me very concerned."

Roxy withdraws her hand from my grasp, averting her gaze. A rosy flush stains her cheeks as she fidgets with the edge of her napkin.

When she finally speaks, her words come out in a rush. "Look, I don't think there's anything wrong with it. If I choose to do it, it's up to me. I'm an adult. And if you're referring to Carlo, sure, he's dangerous. But not to me. To me, he's the sweetest guy. We have a special bond and he's trying to help me with my career." She sticks her nose up and clenches her jaw in typical indignant Roxy fashion. I know I can't push too much further or it will just engage her rebellious streak and then there'll be no stopping her.

"Okay, well, don't say I didn't warn you. But our family has enough dangerous influences in our circle without voluntarily adding more. Especially ones who have threatened to harm us." I push away from the table, the wooden legs of my chair scraping against the floor with a violence that makes Roxy flinch.

"Don't go," she puts her hand out in a stop gesture. "I need to head out, anyway. I'm swapping someone in for your last course. So you can keep your lecture to yourself. Enjoy your dessert."

I glance around in confusion and glimpse a familiar figure walking toward us. Fallon, looking more stunning than ever if that was possible, slips into the booth beside me.

Chapter 74

AKSEL

Roxy slides out of the booth with a sly smirk, leaving me alone with Fallon. My heart slams against my ribs at the sight of her. She's a vision in red, her fiery hair tumbling over her shoulders, green eyes glowing.

"Hi there." Fallon fidgets under my stare, color blooming on her pale cheeks. "Roxy said you wanted to talk."

The tension evaporates, replaced by a surge of hope. She came. Despite everything, she came.

"Thank you for coming." The words sound inadequate, but it's all I can manage.

Her lips curve. "You're welcome."

We descend into silence. The space between us feels charged, alive, vibrating with things unsaid.

Dessert is dropped in front of us, and I'm suddenly ravenous. Silence is replaced by the clinking of utensils against china. But as beautifully as the dessert has been plated, I can't take my eyes of Fallon.

Minutes later, I drag my gaze from her face to the remains of our dessert. Two empty plates, two pairs of chopsticks, and a single mochi left untouched in the center.

Heat floods my face as I meet her gaze. Does she know she's always been my heart's desire? That she's the reason I'm sitting here, the reason my limo waits outside to whisk her away to my penthouse if she'll have me?

"Fallon—" The word emerges hoarse and ragged. I clear my throat and try again. "There are things I want to say to you, things I should have said a long time ago."

Her eyes soften. "I'm listening."

It's all the encouragement I need. The words come in a rush—my regret, my longing, my hope for a second chance. By the time I finish, my heart feels scraped raw and vulnerable.

Silence falls between us as Fallon processes my confession. Then she reaches across the table and takes my hand, her fingers twining with mine.

"We have a lot to work through," she says quietly. "But I want to try again, too."

Joy and relief flood through me in equal measure. I squeeze her hand, unwilling to let go. "Thank you. You won't regret this, Fallon. I promise you."

She gifts me with a soft smile. "I know."

The air between us has shifted, and grown warm and intimate. Desire flickers to life, heating my blood. I want nothing more than to get her alone, to show her how much she means to me.

I raise her hand to my lips, brushing a kiss over her knuckles. "Are you ready to go?"

Her cheeks flush, but she nods.

The limo ride to my penthouse passes in a blur. As soon as the partition slides shut, sealing us in privacy, she's in my arms. Our kisses are hungry, devouring, full of pent-up longing.

By the time we stumble through my front door, we've shed half our clothes. Fallon's hands roam my bare chest as I back her toward the bedroom, desire burning white-hot.

After tonight, there will be no going back. Fallon will be mine again, the way she was always meant to be. My heart swells at the thought.

At last, we've found our way home.

Inside my bedroom, the lights flicker on automatically, casting an amber glow over the plush sheets. A soft sound escapes from her throat as she takes in the sensual scene. Shadowy light dances across her skin, highlighting every curve.

I can't wait to taste her again.

"I missed this," I confess. "Missed you."

She moans softly, cupping my face. "Me too."

With that, I lower my mouth to hers, kissing her deeply, pushing her against the wall. The rough textured paint scraping her back doesn't seem to bother her as she throws her leg over my hips, grinding against me. Her breath hitches when her pussy meets my erection.

We fall onto the bed together, our weight muffled by the plush duvet. Our bodies move in perfect sync, and we're in a dance of lust and need.

Moans escape us as we find our rhythm once more. She tastes sweet, like cinnamon and honey, and every gasp sends a shiver down my spine. Her nails dig into my shoulders in the quiet of the room as I bite her bottom lip, drawing blood. The metallic taste sends a jolt of desire through me.

As we climax, our cries echo off the walls, filling the room with a satisfying symphony of pleasure.

I roll off of her, panting hard, staring at the ceiling. This is what we needed.

I wrap a towel around my waist and zip to the kitchen, returning with a slice of fluffy cheesecake and a small fork. "Here, have some."

She laughs weakly, her body still trembling from our earth-shattering release. "Thank you, but I think I've had enough sweetness for tonight." I take a bite, the rich flavor exploding on my tongue as I watch her watch me.

"What's your grandmother going to say when she finds out we're back together?" Fallon sighs, crawling closer to me, her skin slick with sweat. "You know she's going to be pissed when she finds out about us."

I smirk, running my finger through the small pool of sweat that's gathered between us. "Let her be."

"What the hell is wrong with you?" She slaps my chest playfully. "You used to care about what people thought. Especially her."

I chuckle, kissing her neck. "Only one person's opinion matters to me these days."

Her breath hitches, and she playfully hits my arm. "You're such an asshole."

I lean in, capturing her lips with mine once more. Our tongues dance as we savor each other like a fine wine.

When we break apart, she lays her head on my chest. "Dinner with the Dempseys tomorrow?"

"I know," I say, stroking her hair. I'm prepared this time."

She smiles up at me, her eyes shining. I know it means a lot to her when I attend her family dinners, as tense and uncomfortable as they can be.

"Forgive me?" I ask.

She nestles closer, her breath hot against my skin. "For what?"

"For making you mine again."

She tilts her head up, her eyes meeting mine. "You didn't make me yours again. I've always been yours."

Her words hit me like a ton of bricks, nearly knocking the air from my lungs. How could I have been so blind? So stupid?

I cup her face, my thumb caressing her cheek. "I'm so sorry, Fallon. For everything. For letting you push me away, for pushing you away back then, for not fighting for us."

A single tear slips down her cheek as she places her hand over mine. "We're both here now. That's all that matters."

"It's not all that matters," I say firmly. "You deserve so much more than this—than me. You deserve the world, Fallon. And I'm going to spend the rest of my life making sure you get it."

Her lips curl up in a soft smile as she wipes the tear from her cheek. "You're all I want, Aksel. You always have been."

I swallow the lump in my throat, blinking back the sting in my eyes. "I don't deserve you."

She shakes her head, her smile never fading. "That's where you're wrong. We deserve each other. We always have."

I crush my lips to hers, pouring every ounce of love I have for this woman into the kiss. She is my heart, my soul, the very air I breathe. And I'll be damned if I ever let her go again.

When we break apart, I rest my forehead against hers. "I love you, Fallon. So damn much."

"I love you too," she whispers. "Always have. Always will."

My heart swells at her words, bursting with love and joy and hope for our future.

We stay there for a long while, basking in the comfort of each other's arms and the knowledge that we're finally home.

The next day

The limousine glides through the city's bustling streets as Fallon and I continue to kiss, our tongues tangling in a slow, sensual rhythm.

Her hands slide beneath my shirt, her fingertips tracing the muscles of my abdomen. I groan into her mouth, my cock already straining against the zipper of my pants.

She smiles against my lips, her hands drifting lower until she's palming my erection through the fabric. "Someone's eager," she teases, giving me a firm squeeze.

I growl, grabbing her wrists and pinning them above her head. "Tease me again and I'll have you bent over the seat of this limo with your skirt around your waist and my cock buried to the hilt in your sweet pussy before you can blink."

Her eyes darken, pupils dilating with lust. "Promises, promises."

"Try me," I dare, grinding my hardness against the apex of her thighs.

She whimpers, her hips lifting to meet my thrusts. "Please."

The single word is my undoing. I crush my mouth to hers once more before trailing a path of hot, open-mouthed kisses down her neck. Her pulse thrums wildly beneath my lips as I lick and nibble my way to the swells of her breasts peeking out from the top of her dress.

"So beautiful," I murmur, palming one full globe in my hand and teasing the nipple to a stiff peak. "So perfect."

"Aksel," she moans, arching into my touch. "Please, I need—"

"I know exactly what you need, baby." I smile against her skin before sliding to my knees on the floor of the limo. "Just sit back and enjoy the ride."

I yank her panties down her legs and off, tossing them aside. The scent of her arousal fills my senses, my cock twitching in response.

"So wet for me already," I growl, nudging her thighs apart. I blow a stream of cool air over her soaked pussy, chuckling when she squirms. "Patience, love."

"I swear to God, if you don't—ah!" Her threat cuts off on a sharp cry as I plunge my tongue deep inside her pussy.

I lap at her greedily, fueled by her moans and the slick heat of her cunt. She fists her hands in my hair, riding my face as I tongue-fuck her. I can feel her walls start to flutter, her orgasm building.

"Come for me, Fallon," I order, sealing my mouth over her clit and sucking hard.

Her back bows, a strangled shout tearing from her throat as her release crashes over her. I lap up her juices hungrily, my cock straining against the confines of my pants.

When her tremors subside, I stand and hastily undo my belt and fly. My erection springs free, swollen and leaking.

Fallon's eyes widen. "Fuck, every time I see your cock I can't believe it's mine."

"All for you," I growl, fisting myself. "On your knees. Now."

She scrambles to obey, sinking to the floor of the limo. I grab a fistful of her hair, guiding my cock between her parted lips.

"That's it, take it all," I groan, sliding into the wet heat of her mouth. Her tongue swirls around the head, teasing the sensitive underside. "Just like that, baby. So good."

My hips jerk forward, fucking her mouth in earnest. The sight of her lips stretched around my girth, her eyes glazed with lust, pushes me rapidly towards the edge.

"I'm getting close," I warn, giving her a chance to pull away. Instead, she takes me deeper, swallowing around my length.

With a shout, I come undone, spilling down her throat in hot, salty spurts. She milks me dry, only releasing me once I've stopped pulsing in her mouth.

"Come here," I say hoarsely, pulling her into my arms. I cradle her against my chest, stroking her hair as we catch our breath.

"That was..." she trails off, smiling up at me coyly.

"Amazing," I finish for her, brushing a kiss over her swollen lips. "You're amazing."

Her smile widens into a grin. "Round two at your place?"

I chuckle, nipping at her jaw playfully. "Don't threaten me with a good time, woman."

She laughs, the sound music to my ears. In this moment, tangled up together, the world feels right again. Fallon is here, in my arms, and this time I'm not letting her go.

Back at my condo, we don't waste any time. I lead her into the bedroom where I yank down her panties once again and slide a finger into her wet heat, groaning at how ready she is for me. "So wet, baby. You want this fat cock in your ass, don't you?"

She whimpers, pushing back against my hand. "Yes, please Aksel. I need you."

"Good girl," I praise, withdrawing my finger. Wasting no time, I snatch a container of lube from the nightstand drawer. Snapping it open, I squeeze out an ample amount of the clear gel and apply it to my hard cock. I grip her hips, lining myself up with her entrance. "Relax for me."

I push in slowly, gritting my teeth at the tightness. She's panting, hands fisting in the sheets. I pause, rubbing a soothing hand over her lower back. "Breathe, Fallon. You can take it."

With a sharp inhale, she forces her body to relax. I sink in further, growling at the sensation. "That's it, good girl. You're doing so well."

When I'm fully seated, I stop again, waiting for her signal. After a few moments, she nods, rolling her hips experimentally.

"Move," she gasps, clenching around me.

I pull back slowly before snapping my hips forward, burying myself to the hilt. She cries out, her back arching in pleasure.

"Yes!" she shouts, rocking back to meet my thrusts. "Harder!"

I set a brutal pace, fingers digging into her hips as I pound into her tight ass. The sensations rocket through me, intense and overwhelming.

Fallon's hands twist in the sheets, her cries muffled in the pillow. I lean over her, hooking an arm under her chest and pulling her up against me. She turns her head, capturing my mouth in a sloppy kiss.

I snake a hand between her legs, circling her clit roughly. Her inner walls clamp down around me as she comes with a wail, throwing her head back against my shoulder.

The pressure around my cock sends me tumbling over the edge after her. I bury myself deep, warmth flooding her as I empty myself inside her with a shout.

We collapse forward onto the bed, limbs tangling together in a sweaty heap. I gather her close, pressing soft kisses over her face and neck.

"I love you," I whisper, my heart overflowing.

Her answering smile is radiant. "I love you too."

I carry Fallon into my bathroom, cradling her against my chest. She nuzzles into my neck with a content sigh, her fingers tracing idle patterns over my chest.

I set her on the counter in the bathroom, turning on the faucet and adjusting the temperature. Steam rises around us as I wet a washcloth and gently wipe between her legs.

Fallon watches me through half-lidded eyes, a soft smile on her lips. "You're so good to me," she murmurs.

I press a kiss to the inside of her thigh. "You deserve nothing less."

When she's clean, I help her into the shower, following her in. We take our time exploring each other's bodies, hands and mouths roaming slick skin as the water cascades over us.

By the time we make it to bed, exhaustion has settled into my bones. I pull Fallon against me, her back to my chest, and drape an arm over her waist.

"I'll never forget this night," she whispers.

"Neither will I, baby." I kiss the top of her head, breathing in the scent of her shampoo.

"Get some rest. I'll be here when you wake up."

Fallon laces our fingers together over her stomach, giving my hand a gentle squeeze. Within minutes, her breathing evens out, deep and steady in sleep.

I close my eyes, drifting off to the sound of her heartbeat and the feel of her in my arms. Tonight has been a new beginning, a chance to rebuild what we once had.

And this time, I'm never letting her go.

Chapter 75

FALLON

The clinking of silverware on fine china plates fills the elegant dining room. I glance around at my polished family gathered around the long mahogany table. Cheston and Link chat about work while Bronson loses himself in thought, no doubt pondering a case. Colton whispers something to Fenton, eliciting a chuckle from my brother. Probably a golf joke, I roll my eyes.

Zara emerges from the kitchen, her face flushed from pretending to cook, and from the couple of martinis she sucked down when she thought nobody was looking, her arms laden with a succulent pot roast. It was no doubt lovingly prepared by an underpaid staff member at the local bougie grocery store, but let's let stepmother dearest take the credit. Despite the questionable origins of the meal, I have to admit that the savory aroma makes my mouth water. As she sets the platter down, my father stands to carve.

"Let's give thanks," he rumbles in his deep voice. Heads bow. The scrape of chair legs fills the silence as we sit and begin passing dishes.

At first, it seems like a typical Dempsey family dinner. The conversation flows as freely as the wine Link pours. But when talk turns to ancestors, an undercurrent of weird tension and tomfoolery simmers beneath the surface.

Bronson's fork clatters onto his plate. "Remember Great-Aunt Mathilde?"

Cheston nearly chokes on his mouthful of pot roast. "The burlesque dancer?"

Awkward glances bounce around the table and Aksel looks at me with a bemused expression. Leave it to Bronson to dredge up random family secrets.

"Well, she certainly was...adventurous," Dad says delicately, sipping his wine.

"Adventurous? She was a badass!" Bronson exclaims. "Shaking her tassels in Paris nightclubs. Makes our family tree a little more interesting, eh?"

I stifle a laugh at the thought of our conservative lineage having a risqué burlesque dancer in its ranks. Bronson has a knack for challenging propriety and making self-deprecating yet zinging-ly accurate jokes about our family.

Link cracks up, and everyone turns to him in anticipation. "Well, if you think that's something... it turns out our mild-mannered cousin Rodney isn't just an accountant..."

He pauses, glancing around the table. "He also moonlights as a kinky ventriloquist."

A stunned silence settles over the room. Then the laughter starts, slowly at first, but soon becoming raucous.

"A kinky ventriloquist?" Fenton guffaws. "Are you serious? What does that even mean?"

Link laughs and nods, taking a giant gulp of his wine. "Yeah, so he told me all about it at cousin Deb's birthday last year. I guess it started as a silly hobby, but he's actually gotten quite good. He performs at adult clubs on the weekends."

"Does he bring his dummy on dates, too?" Fenton jokes.

"As a matter of fact, yes, he does. Apparently, Mr. Wiggles is very popular with the ladies. At least the way cousin Rodney tells it," Link says with a perfectly straight face.

The family erupts into renewed laughter. I study their reactions—Dad shaking his head in amusement, Zara covering her mouth to hide her shocked grin.

Link makes a show of shrugging nonchalantly. "I know it's a bit weird, but he says it's quite fun and lucrative. Much more interesting than crunching numbers."

The juxtaposition of our cousin's buttoned-up exterior and his risqué double life adds an absurd humor to the situation. But underneath the laughter, there's a growing sense of acceptance, of embracing the quirks that make each of us unique.

As the family continues excavating our past, I glance at Aksel, wondering how he's processing these revelations. His own family, so notorious, so mysterious.

"Well, I may as well come clean too," he says suddenly, an impish grin spreading across his face. "Did I ever tell you my great-uncle was a mob boss in Sicily?"

Gasps erupt around the table. Of course, there had always been speculation, but I never imagined the day would come where he'd come straight out and say it.

"Oh yes, the Morettis were quite the infamous crime family back in the day," Aksel continues breezily. "Uncle Salvatore ran all the rackets on the island. Gambling, bootlegging, you name it. I know there have always been whispers, so I figured I might as well just come out and say it seeing we're among family and friends here."

I glance around to see my family's reactions, and I'm not sure whether it's the wine or something more, but everyone is smiling and nodding, and there's the occasional shrug as if to say 'hey, we're not surprised, but thanks for sharing.'

He takes a swig of wine. "And, on perhaps a far lighter note, my grandparents were quite the progressives. They were founding members of a very avant-garde sex club in the 70s. I don't like to think about it in too much detail, but our family's skeletons extend far beyond the bounds of King Industries. Let's just say the estate wasn't just known for stuffy white tie events..."

Raucous laughter fills the room. Trust Aksel to match our eccentric tales with his own outrageous family secrets.

Under the candlelight, faces flush with amusement. The food sits almost forgotten as stories flow late into the night.

The laughter eventually dies down, leaving a slightly awkward silence hanging in the air. I glance around at the familiar faces of my family, all of us processing these surprising revelations.

Next to me, Aksel catches my eye and places his hand on mine. As the newest member of this eccentric clan, I wonder how he's taking it all in.

"Well," he says, clearing his throat, "I have to say, you Dempseys really know how to liven up a family dinner."

His wry tone makes me smile. Trust Aksel to diffuse the tension with humor.

As I look around the table, I'm struck by how even the strangest quirks and secrets can bring people together.

We're bonded by the realization that no family history is without its spice, its rebels, its rule-breakers. Our roots may not be spotless or genteel, but they are ours, flaws and all. And as we raise our glasses in a final toast for the evening, acceptance links us more meaningfully than blood.

No matter what surprises lurk in our pasts, this family has built a home where everyone belongs. Aksel is no longer an outsider, as of tonight, but one of our own.

And nothing, not even Uncle Sal's and King Industries' mafia connections, can change that.

Chapter 76

FALLON

The city streets stretch before me, empty and endless in the pale glow of streetlights. Aksel's voice echoes in my head, urging me to let his driver take me home, but I shrug it off. I need to walk. To feel the chill of night on my skin and sort through the mess of emotions swirling inside.

Satisfaction. Guilt. Lust. Anger. They war within me, shadows dancing at the edge of light.

I shove my hands into my pockets and pick up the pace, my boots striking the pavement with a sharp crack. The rhythmic beat matches the pulse pounding in my veins. I have a playlist of songs that are in sync with my fastest walking speed, and I love nothing more than to charge around the city at lunchtime, headphones blaring, to get my steps in. But there will be no headphones tonight. It's dark out, and I need my wits about me.

In the distance, a dark figure emerges from an alleyway. It turns to face me, and despite the distance between us, I think his face twists into a terrifying smile. I tense, my senses alert, and drop into a fighting stance as the figure, much larger than me, hurtles toward me and lunges at me with a snarl. The figure reeks of madness and desperation. Instinct takes over as adrenaline floods my system. I pivot, snapping out my arm and propelling it right into my assailant's face..

I follow up with a punch, my knuckles connecting with flesh and bone. A single blow that sends my attacker crashing to the ground with a groan.

Breathing hard, I stare down at his body, his features slack in unconsciousness, and his clothes tattered and grimy. Blood trickles from his nose, a vivid red against his pale skin. I have a strong urge to kick the motionless figure, to continue to punish him, but I quell it. I've rendered him immobile, so he can't hurt anyone else, and there are people much more deserving of my time.

I frown, shaking out my hand. What was that about, anyway? A mugging gone wrong? My gaze narrows, scrutinizing his prone form. No, there's something not quite right here. A madness lurked behind those eyes, a cunning sort of madness. Not the unhinged look of a man who randomly steps from an alley to assault a stranger. The madness of a man hired to kill someone known to be tricky to catch. As if—my breath catches. What if this attack wasn't random, and only made to look that way? I can feel the weight of eyes upon me, watching from the shadows. The hairs on the back of my neck prickle.

Whoever's out there isn't very good at subtlety. I scoff, rolling my shoulders and tilting my chin up in challenge. If this display was meant to intimidate me, they chose the wrong woman.

I move on through the dim streets, leaving the figure behind. As I get further away, I begin to doubt myself. Whoever that guy was, the attack was clearly just random. I'm just paranoid, thinking it was anything more than a coincidence that I happened to be walking past when he stepped out on the road.

The city embraces me in its solitude, bearing witness to the storm within. My pace is quick, and my heart pounds as if trying to break free of my chest. I draw a sharp breath, the cool night air scraping my raw throat. Everything feels amplified in the stillness before sunrise—each sensation, every conflicting thought.

Far away from my attacker, I once again consider the emotions battling in my head. Can love and the desire for revenge exist together? Can I ever truly love Aksel despite what he did back then? I don't know. But for now, I walk alone. I know I need to choose when the time comes. And I will.

The sky lightens to dove gray as the first golden rays of sunrise peek over the horizon. I pause in the middle of an intersection, alone at the center of converging streets. Around me, shadows recede. But within me, they remain. Darkness and light, coexisting yet separate. I stand at the crossroads, unsure of which path to take.

I continue walking, hands shoved in my pockets, boots striking a steady beat. The city surrounds me, silent and empty, mine alone.

My mind replays the night, images flickering through my thoughts like a movie reel.

The way Aksel made an effort to get through family dinner smoothly, even sharing self-deprecating stories about his own family in an attempt to fit in. I flash back further, to the multiple times recently that I've gotten to experience Aksel's hands, his mouth, the feel of his body against mine. The satisfaction, the pleasure.

As amazing as those moments were, though, they're now soured by the bitterness clinging to its edges. Because the longer I spend away from Aksel, I've come to learn, the less I believe we're meant to be.

Why did I go to him so many times, especially that first time over at his condo? I knew it was a mistake, and knew I shouldn't give in to the hunger that had been building between us. But in that moment, I couldn't help myself. I wanted to lose myself in sensation, to bury the anger and doubt beneath a rush of endorphins. I wanted it to be him, because I knew my mind would wander to him, anyway.

But my attempt to bury things didn't work. If anything, the conflicting emotions have intensified, twisting my insides into knots. I'm torn between the desire for retribution and this aching need to connect—not just physically, but emotionally. To find solace in another's arms. Aksel's arms.

Chapter 77

AKSEL

Fallon sits across from me at my condo's massive kitchen island, hands clutching her coffee mug. Her knuckles are white. Something's wrong.

"We need to talk," she says.

My stomach clenches. Those four words are never good, especially when said by a stubborn, irresistible woman haunted by darkness. "About what?"

She looks away, jaw tight. She takes a breath. "I can't do this anymore, Aksel."

"Do what?" But I already know. Fear and anger surge through me, a toxic mix.

"Us." Her eyes meet mine, stormy gray. "I just can't."

"Please, Fallon." My voice is steady despite the chaos in my chest. "We're so close to things being perfect between us."

"More like closer to destroying each other." She shakes her head, frowning, then tilts her gaze upward to meet mine. "I don't want that life anymore. I want to move on."

"With someone else?" The words taste bitter. But it would explain why she's so eager to end things with me.

"No, Aksel," she shakes her head. "There is nobody else. But I need some time apart while I figure out what's right for me. I can't keep putting my heart on the line like this. Every time I'm with you, I think this is it, that we're meant to be together. But then I spend some time away from you, and my head clears and I realize it would be easier, safer, to go on without you."

I can't tell if she's bluffing or not, and in the absence of real information, my mind concocts a slide show of visuals. Fallon with a group of guys fawning over her, like some type of reverse harem. Fallon at a family dining table with a husband out of a Nordstrom catalog laughing with their children as he serves grilled meats. Hot surfer man bringing Fallon breakfast in bed, offering himself as dessert. Tormented by these images, I shake myself back to reality.

"I won't let this happen." I slam my fist on the table, rattling the dishes. Coffee sloshes over the rim of her mug and she flinches.The thought of her going about her life without me as if I was a passing fling stings me. Fallon making her own coffee, pouring a cereal for one. Fallon texting her friends about the latest news, the latest reality show. "You're mine, Fallon. I'm not letting you go."

"I'm not a possession." Her voice is soft but steely. "I'm not yours to let go of. But you do need to be okay with me going. To be clear, this isn't the end of our relationship. I just think we both need some time apart. Things have been so confusing lately, and I think it's necessary for our growth as individuals and for the longevity of our connection. If we want something that lasts the distance, rather than this constant back and forth that's destroying us emotionally, we need to come back with clear heads."

I stare at her, emotions warring within me. Anger that she's leaving, fear that she won't come back, sorrow at how much this hurts. But beneath it all is a grudging acceptance. Fallon has never lied to me. If she says this is for the best... and if this will get us onto a good track where my emotions aren't in a constant state of whiplash... it's got to be worth it.

I swallow hard. "How long?"

She bites her lip. "I don't know. However long it takes. It could be days, it could be months." Her eyes are bright with unshed tears. "But this isn't goodbye, Aksel. I just need to find myself again, to recenter. And I want you to do the same."

I pull her into my arms, breathing in her scent. How did we end up here, in this mess of tangled emotions? But Fallon is right. The darkness that lingers inside both of us will only poison us if we don't face it.

I stare at her, this infuriating, intoxicating woman. The one person I'd burn the world for. And now she wants to leave, before we've even really started again?

My heart twists, the back and forth of our love like an unstoppable pendulum. But beneath the hurt and anger, I know she's right. If I really love her, I have to set her free.

Even if it shreds me to pieces.

"Go then," I say roughly. "If that's what you really want." I close my eyes, steeling myself. Then I place a soft kiss on her forehead and release her. "Do what you need to do. I'll be here waiting when you come back."

A tear slides down Fallon's cheek. But there's gratitude in her smile. Grasping my hand, she gives it a squeeze.

She hesitates as if second-guessing her decision, as if disappointed at my immediate acceptance of her suggestion, and for a second, I think she might stay. But then she nods once, as if convincing herself, and walks away. And then she's gone, the door closing behind her with a soft click.

I close my eyes, alone in the silence. Waiting for the pain to hit.

Initially, it comes in waves, crashing over me until I'm drowning in it. I stagger to the couch and drop my head in my hands, struggling to breathe.

I get why she's doing this.

Fallon's right that we were toxic. I see that now. But letting her go... it's the hardest thing I've ever done. She says it's not permanent, but maybe the time apart will change her mind. Maybe that's the whole point.

I straighten, scrubbing my hands over my face. She wanted me to change, to become a better man than the one who has now broken her heart twice. I need to honor that, even if she refuses to see me. I owe her at least that much.

But instead of the old anger and rage I'd expect to feel in a situation like this, there is only peace. Fallon has given me a gift beyond price—the chance at redemption.

I'll give her as long as she needs to process the parts of her that are holding her back. And in the meantime, it's up to me to become the man she deserves. No matter how long it takes.

The first step is dealing with the mess I've made. I pick up my phone and dial a familiar number.

"We need to talk," I say when she answers.

My older sister is silent for a long moment on the other end. On the outside, it looks like Raine and I are so close and tell each other everything. But in reality, there's so much I've hidden from her and the others over the years. Things I'm not proud of that I needed to do in order to keep the family business afloat. Only my grandmother knows the half of it, and most of it was at her direction.

"I've been waiting to hear those words for a long time," she says at last. "I'm here. Talk."

The words spill out of me in a torrent. Everything I've done, the lies, the violence—she listens without judgment. And when I'm finished, wrung out and empty, she speaks. Not with anger, but with love.

"You were protecting our family," she says gently. "And the past is gone. All you can do is decide the man you want to become, and start walking that path. I'll walk with you. It's never too late."

Tears burn my eyes. After everything, she's still here for me. Still willing to forgive.

"Thank you. Raine," I whisper. "For not judging me, ever, even though some of my actions were pure evil."

"That's what family is for." I can hear her smile through the phone. "Welcome back, little brother. It's felt like you've only partially been here for a long time, but now I see the whole you again. I'm so relieved. I hope you feel the huge weight off your shoulders."

I end the call and sit in silence, letting peace fill the spaces where darkness once dwelled. The road ahead won't be easy. But for the first time, I feel hope. Maybe Fallon was right after all. Maybe our ending—temporary or not—was a beginning.

Chapter 78

FALLON

After days of silence, the urge to reach out gnaws at me. I wasn't sure how much time apart I needed—days, weeks or months—but I miss Aksel dearly. I rummage through memories of him, searching for something to breach the chasm between us. A flash of his smile when showing off a rare comic sparks an idea.

I rifle through dusty boxes in the attic until my fingers close around smooth cardboard, and I pull out the package encased by familiar plastic wrapping. A first edition Footrot Flats comic. The companion book to Aksel's prize possession, the one I gave him for his seventeenth birthday. I'd had this ready to go for his nineteenth birthday, naïvely assuming we'd always be together, so it's been collecting dust for quite some time.

As I wrap the comic in decorative tissue bearing a pretty pattern, a pang squeezes my chest, a vivid reminder of simpler times. I slip it into a gift box and scribble a note, the words tumbling out in a rush: *See you soon, trouble.*

I remember Aksel's delight at discovering a rare issue, the way his eyes would light up like the sky on Fourth of July. Late nights camped out on his bedroom floor, our hushed voices and laughter muffled by shadows as we got lost in other worlds.

The comic is a relic of what we once shared, untarnished by the ugliness that came later. For a moment I let myself pretend that the rift between us never formed, that we're still the people we were as teenagers with our whole lives stretched out before us.

But time marches on, and there's no going back. We're strangers now, bound by a history that feels like something from another lifetime. Still, I cling to the hope that this small piece of our past might pave the way to reconciliation.

That we can find our way back to each other, even though we can never again be those kids with stars in our eyes, dreaming of forever.

My finger hovers over the button that will summon a courier to my house to drop the gift off at Aksel's, my heart jackhammering. Sending this is a leap of faith, a white flag in our private war. With a deep breath, I hit send.

Aksel

A package arrives on my doorstep, Fallon's familiar scrawl on the brown paper wrapping. I nearly pitch it in the trash, the urge to punish her flaring hot and bright. I hate being ignored, and being ignored by the woman I'd put my life on the line for is agony. But curiosity gets the better of me.

I tear into the package and stare. A first edition Footrot Flats comic, edges in pristine condition, slips into my hands. A wave of nostalgia washes over me as I trace the familiar cover, transporting me to the aftermath of my seventeenth birthday. Fallon had shyly presented this comic's companion issue, her cheeks pink as though she was both excited and nervous to present it to me. "It's your white whale, thought you'd like to finally catch it."

For a long moment I can only stare at the cover, an undertow of memories threatening to drag me under.

Fallon remembers.

After everything that's passed between us, she remembers the things that mattered most, that still matter most now. The little details that shaped our history, moments worn soft around the edges with time.

I trace a finger across the comic's cover, transported to the past. To the joy of uncovering a new issue together, Fallon's delighted laughter as we pored over each page. I knew she didn't love the comics, but she did it for me. The simplicity of those early days, before life conspired to pull us apart.

The gift is an olive branch, a fragile bridge to what we once shared. A reminder that despite the distance between us, our history remains—and with it, the possibility of finding our way home.

That maybe we can be those kids again, if only for a little while. The ones who still had a lifetime of adventures ahead, whose future was filled with promise.

Tonight I'll lose myself in the comic's pages, remembering how it felt to be us. Tomorrow the real work begins, but for now, I'll cling to the hope Fallon's gift represents.

The hope that we might yet have a new story to tell.

I find her note tucked into the pages, the scrawl as familiar as my own name. My breath catches at the closing. *See you soon, trouble.* A white flag if there ever was one. A way of saying the break is over as far as she's concerned.

As excited as I am to see her again soon, I'm conflicted. It's only been a few days. Is that enough time for her to have truly found herself and figured out what she wants? How do I know she won't just turn around and say she needs time apart again?

I pick up my phone, her name lighting the screen. My thumb hovers for a single breath before connecting the call.

"Trouble." My lips quirk at the old nickname. "You always did know the way to my heart."

A soft laugh, more sob than chuckle. "Took me long enough to remember."

The ragged note in her voice slices through my defenses, and I surrender to the lure of her words. We have a long road ahead but, for now, this is enough.

"Come over?" The question is out before I can stop it.

"Already on my way." The line goes dead.

I sit in silence, Footrot Flats open on my lap, and wait, sipping on a cold, crisp glass of sauvignon blanc.

Every minute drags until a knock rattles my door. I'm on my feet and across the room before I realize I've moved.

Fallon stands on the threshold, her eyes wary. "Hi."

"Hi." I step back. "Come in."

She brushes past me, a ghost of her usual stride. The door clicks shut behind us, sealing us in a silence thick with things unsaid.

I clear my throat. "Thank you for the comic."

A flush stains her cheeks. "You're welcome. I thought—" Her gaze drops to the floor. "I'm glad you like it."

"It's perfect." I take a step forward, my hand finding hers. "Just like old times." I lean closer, my voice a rough whisper. "Seeing this again brought back so many memories.

Simpler times, before everything got so damn complicated." I run a hand through my hair.

"I miss those days," she admits quietly. "We had something special once. Something worth fighting for."

Her eyes bore into mine, and I reciprocate with raw intensity in my gaze. "Do you really believe we could find our way back?" I ask. "After everything?"

Her breath catches at the vulnerability in my words. This is a side of myself very few are allowed to see, the side I only reveal in unguarded moments with the people I trust most.

"I have to hope we can," she whispers. She reaches out almost automatically and brushes her fingers along my jaw.

I inhale sharply, leaning into her touch. The years between us seem to melt away as we share this tender moment. "We have a lot to talk about..."

Her fingers tighten around mine, a fragile lifeline in a sea of uncertainty. "Yeah." Her eyes meet mine, shadows lurking in their depths. "About that..."

I lift her hand and brush my lips across her knuckles. "We have things to work through, I know." My thumb traces circles against her wrist. "But for now can we pretend?"

The corners of her mouth quirk up. "Pretend?"

"That we're seventeen again. No broken hearts or bitter words between us." I tug her closer, her warmth seeping into my bones. "Just you and me and a stack of comics."

"I'd like that." Her other hand comes to rest against my chest. "Even if it's only for a little while."

"A little while is all we need." I wrap my arms around her, the familiar shape of her body slotting against mine.

Tonight we'll lose ourselves in nostalgia's embrace. Tomorrow we'll face the wreckage of the past, but for now this is enough.

Fallon

Aksel lifts his hand to cover mine, pressing my palm against his cheek. His eyes flutter closed for a moment as he turns his face into my touch. When they open again, his gaze is soft, almost vulnerable.

"I've missed this," he murmurs. "Missed us."

My heart clenches. "Me too."

I trail my thumb along his stubbled jaw. The years between us feel like they're falling away, leaving only this charged moment stretching between us.

Slowly, giving him time to pull back, I lean in. Aksel meets me halfway, his mouth finding mine in a kiss that starts off tentative but quickly ignites into heat and hunger.

My fingers twist into his shirt, holding him close as our lips move together urgently. He walks me backwards until my shoulders hit the wall, his body pressing flush against mine.

"Fallon," he groans, breath hot against my lips. "Are you sure about this? If we go down this road again..."

"Shh." I silence him with another searing kiss. "I've never been more sure of anything."

At my words, his restraint seems to snap.

We stare at each other, suspended in this charged moment. The comic lies forgotten on the floor, its message received. Then he leans in closer.

His hand slides down my back, cupping my ass, squeezing it hard. My dress hikes up, revealing the lacy black thong I have on underneath. He spanks my ass once, making a loud smacking sound that echoes in the empty hallway. I gasp as pain and pleasure mix together. His fingers trace the edge of the fabric, tracing my pussy lips. I feel him smirk against my neck as he rubs me teasingly.

"You're so fucking wet," he whispers against my ear, his breath tickling my lobe. "I can feel your wetness through your panties. You're soaking for me."

I groan, unable to resist him anymore. "Aksel," I moan, arching into his touch.

His hands slip under my thighs as he lifts me, urging me to wrap my legs around his waist. My thighs straddle him, his cock pressed tight against my center. I gasp at the sensation, feeling him pulsing against me. My hands grasp his shoulders, digging into the muscles beneath his suit jacket. His free hand grasps my breast roughly, pinching my nipple hard through my dress. He groans into my neck, kissing and sucking it.

He places me on the ground, my back still against the wall, and kisses me hard, pushing his tongue in deeper, bruising my lips with his teeth. I can taste wine on him and it makes me shiver. He grabs my hair, pulling my head back roughly, exposing my neck. He bites down gently before growling against my skin.

"You like that, don't you?" he asks, his voice a low growl.

"Yes," I pant, unable to form a coherent thought. My body is on fire for him. He wraps his other arm around my waist, pulling me even tighter against him. His erection rubs against my clit, and I buck my hips up into it.

"You're finally mine again, Fallon," he whispers, his voice dark and threatening.

I close my eyes, feeling the wall at my back and him beneath me, longing for him to be inside me. "I'm fine with that," I admit, my voice breathless. I never thought I would ever feel like this about anyone, but Aksel has a way of making me lose control.

He thrusts his hips forward, rubbing his cock against my aching center. "You will care when I'm done with you."

I whimper, my body craving him. "Do it," I beg, needing him to claim me, needing him to make me forget everything else.

He growls low, kissing his way down my neck and collarbone before looking up at me with a predatory grin. "Say it again."

"Please," I whisper, my lips trembling.

He chuckles darkly before pressing his lips to mine roughly again. His tongue invades my mouth, ravishing it as he pushes against my thong. My mind goes blank as he thrusts against me, rubbing my clit with his hard cock. All I can feel is him and the need building inside of me.

"You're so fucking hot when you beg," Aksel mutters, his hand gripping my hair tightly as he pulls my head back.

I moan into his mouth, feeling his rough hand against my scalp sending shivers down my spine. "Am I? What else do you want to hear me say?" My words come out breathy and needy.

His eyes flash with lust. "Tell me what you want."

I swallow hard, unable to believe I'm saying these words. But they're true. "I want you to fuck me raw."

He groans, throwing my head back against the wall. "Oh, princess," he says before pushing two fingers inside me, stretching me. I gasp as he continues to rub against my clit, sending shockwaves of pleasure through my body.

"Aksel," I whimper, arching into him.

He kisses my neck again, hard and possessive. "Tell me you're mine."

I dig my nails into his shoulders, feeling the muscles ripple beneath his skin. "I'm yours."

"Say it," he demands, slamming his hips against me.

"I'm yours," I pant, feeling him filling me up.

"That's my good girl," he whispers. Then, he pulls his fingers out, making me gasp at the loss. He leads me to the bed, throws me down on my back, and positions his thick cock at my entrance.

He pushes in, filling me slowly, watching my face as he buries himself inside me. I try to act nonchalant to tease him, but my body betrays me as it clenches around him, needing him despite everything. He growls low in his throat, his eyes darken with hunger. "You're mine now, Fallon."

I bite my bottom lip, my body aching to be claimed. "Yes," I whisper. "Yours."

Aksel's hands tighten on my hips, holding me still as he begins to move. I gasp at the sensation—this brutal, unyielding possession. He's rough and demanding, his hips slamming against me over and over again. I can't help but cry out with each thrust, the friction causing my thighs to burn. But it feels so good.

He groans against my neck, his body shuddering as he starts to pick up speed. "You feel so fucking tight," he mutters, teeth grinding together. "My beautiful queen."

I close my eyes, focusing on the sensation of him inside me. The way he fills me up completely, taking what has always really been his.

His hands roam lower, cupping my ass cheeks, pulling me harder against his hips. "Look at me," he commands.

I open my eyes, meeting his gaze. His eyes are wild, his mouth twisted into a grimace of pleasure.

"Fallon," he groans, his voice ragged. "You're so fucking tight."

I moan, unable to contain myself as I feel him pulsing inside me. "Aksel..."

He picks up the pace, driving deeper and harder, each thrust sending shockwaves of pleasure through me. "You're all mine now," he growls, his lips brushing against my ear. "My sweet lover."

I can't help but arch my back, meeting his intensity. My nails dig into his shoulders, leaving red marks as he thrusts harder still. The bed creaks under us, the sound punctuating the air.

Aksel's hips buck against me, driving himself deeper than before, claiming me completely. I cry out, feeling the warmth seep between us. He's filled me, marked me, taken me as his own.

He pulls out, both of us panting heavily.

"Turn around," he commands, his tone low and deadly.

I swallow hard and do as he says, turning to face the headboard. The cool, smooth wood feels good against my flushed skin.

Aksel spanks my ass. "Good girl," he murmurs before he pulls me back into his embrace, his cock sliding into my soaking pussy once again. He begins to move again, slowly at first, then faster. His hands roam over my body, exploring every inch.

I gasp, feeling the sting of the slap on my ass cheek. "That's it, baby girl," he whispers. "Feel it."

I moan, my body responsive to his touch. Aksel's lips trail hot fire over my shoulder, down my spine. "You belong to me, Fallon. My pet."

I shudder at his words, part of me hating them but another part loving the domination.

"Yes, Aksel," I whisper breathlessly.

His hips slam into me, driving home his point. His thick cock hits my g-spot over and over, claiming it as his. Groans escape him, mingling with my own moans.

"You like that, don't you?" he demands, his voice rough.

"Yes," I whimper.

His hand finds my clit, rubbing slowly at first, then more roughly as he thrusts harder. I bite my lip to keep from screaming out. My hips buck of their own accord, demanding more.

"Say it," he orders, his fingers relentless.

"I'm yours."

He curses, his hand moving to my neck, holding it still. His thumb brushes across my pulse point, making me shiver.

"Good girl," he whispers, thrusting faster. "Mine."

I nod, unable to form words.

"Say it," he demands again.

I gasp, "I'm yours," as he sucks my earlobe.

He smirks against my skin, "Yes, you are. Now take what you've been given."

I squeeze my muscles around him, milking his cock as he plunges deeper still. We both groan, lost in the heat between us.

"Come for me, baby girl," he whispers, biting my neck gently.

I'm falling apart, my body spiraling out of control. "I'm coming," I moan, my orgasm hitting me hard.

He groans, thrusts one final time, and fills me with his warmth.

"Aksel," I whimper, as he pulls out, unable to hold back a sob.

He chuckles darkly, "That's my good girl."

He guides me to the shower, turning on the water to cool. I kneel on the slippery floor, the ceramic cold under my knees, as he steps in behind me, his hands on my hips.

"Open your mouth," he demands softly. From the expression on his face, his eyes dark with lust, I can tell we're not close to being done. And I'm totally okay with that.

I obey his command, my lips parting. He steps closer, his hard cock brushing my lips. I close my lips around the head, tasting him, exploring his flavor. My tongue swirls around him, and I take him deep, loving the feel of him in my mouth.

He gasps, "Fuck." His hands slide into my hair, holding me still with my lips wrapped around his shaft.

I suck him gently, savoring the taste of his essence, wanting it to linger. His hands on my head guide his cock deeper into my throat, and I choke a little, but I don't pull away.

"That's it, baby girl," he praises.

I look up at him through my eyelashes, unable to hide my need. He smirks, lifting me to my feet, taking my chin in his hand and pulling my face to his. Our lips meet in a fiery kiss. I motion toward the bed, and he pulls back with a groan. "Not yet."

His fingers disappear, and I whimper in protest. He grabs my hips roughly, turning me around, and pulling me back onto his cock in one swift motion. It feels amazing—so full, stretching me, claiming me. His hands fist in my hair, holding me in place as he takes me hard from behind. My head falls back against his chest, and I feel his other hand slide down my stomach to find my clit once more. This time, he doesn't tease but rubs in tight little circles, finding that spot that sends me over the edge.

My vision blurs as he pounds into me, our bodies slapping together, the water torrenting down on us. He grabs my hair, using it to pull my head back, exposing my neck. His teeth graze my skin, and I shudder. I'm at his mercy, vulnerable.

"Do you really want to be mine, Fallon?" he growls.

I nod, unable to form words, feeling his cock slide in and out of me, hitting my sweet spot with each thrust.

"Say it," he commands.

"I want to be yours," I whisper.

He smirks and kisses my neck, sucking a mark onto my skin. "Good girl."

His hips speed up, fucking me harder against the tile wall. I feel his thighs brace against my ass, holding me still. Our passionate moans fill the small bathroom. The water crashes around us, echoing off the tiles. He curses under his breath, his breath hot against my neck. His grip in my hair tightens, pulling slightly.

I arch my back, needing more, wanting to feel him. He slides his hand between my legs, finding my soaking wet folds. He teases me, circling his finger around my clit, making me gasp. Then he adds a second, stretching me wider.

"Aksel!" I cry out, needing him to fill that ache.

He laughs darkly, "You're so fucking mine."

He turns me around and hoists me up, my back against the wet, cold wall and my thighs wrapped around his slick body. With one quick movement he slides back into me.

I'm panting, "Fuck, Aksel!"

He growls, "That's it, baby girl," as he thrusts harder. Our skin slaps together, water splashes, and his rough hands hold me hostage as he takes my mind, my body, my soul. My walls start to pulse around him, and I feel him stop moving, holding still.

"Come for me again, baby," he commands.

I do, my voice cracking, my knees weak. He follows, filling me with his hot seed.

We stay like that for a moment, panting, before he lowers me down to the tiles gently.

He leans down to kiss my shoulder, our chests heaving. "You're fucking unbelievable."

I smile against his chest, "Speak for yourself."

He climbs out of the shower, grabbing two fluffy oversized towels, and I watch as his toned ass disappears behind the curtain. When he's done, he hands me one, and I wrap it around my body.

Our fingers intertwine, and we head out into the bedroom.

"You look so fucking pretty like this," he whispers, his voice gruff as he gazes at me. He hooks a finger around the top of my towel and yanks it so that the towel crumples to the floor.

I blush. "Thanks."

He gently lays me out on the bed then crawls on top of me, kissing my neck, my jaw, my chin. Desire smolders in his eyes.

"You want more of this?" he asks.

My heart races, "Yes."

His smirk reflects the hunger in his eyes, "Good. 'Cause I'm not done."

He steps back, nudging my legs apart, and I spread for him. He dives in, his tongue tracing my slit, tasting my juices. My legs shake at the sensation, my back arching off the mattress.

"Aksel," I moan.

He grins against my clit, looking up at me. "You like that?"

I nod frantically. His tongue swirls again, sucking my clit into his mouth. My hips jerk up, and he holds me down.

"Oh my god," I moan as he flattens his tongue and laps at my swollen clit.

"Mmm," he hums, sending vibrations throughout my pussy.

"Stop," I gasp.

He pulls back slightly, "Why?"

"I want you inside me again," I say between pants.

He smirks against me, "Always the bossy one."

"Always." I agree, biting my lip.

He licks his way up my inner thighs, teasing, until he's at my entrance. His fingers slide inside, filling me, and I can feel that I'm soaking. I groan, "More."

He chuckles lowly, "More? You're insatiable."

My breath hitches as he lines himself up. "Yes."

Slowly, he slides in, filling me completely. I gasp, still tender from the last time we fucked.

"Fucking hell," I exclaim as he thrusts in and out, dragging against my tender walls.

"Am I too much for you?" he growls.

"Almost," I rasp. "But also never. You're never too much. You're perfect."

His expression intensifies as he continues to thrust, his pace quickening.

He plows into my pussy, smashing into my cervix. It's an unusual sensation, but at the same time I never want it to stop.

"I'm going to come," he pants.

"Good. Come for me baby," I say, relieved this isn't going to be an all-night session. I need time to recover, my pussy tender from the way he's been destroying it.

His pace increases again and I feel his body go still. He groans, yanking my hips so my pussy slams down onto his cock to its hilt. "Fuck, you're amazing, Fallon-y," he grits, his cock pulsing, releasing inside me. "You're the best."

I grin and plant a kiss on his sexy lips. "Likewise," I say.

Chapter 79

AKSEL

The bouncy castle looms before me, an obscene shade of neon pink against the carefully curated greenery in the large amenity space behind my condo. How did I let Fallon talk me into this? Or rather, how did she get me so captivated that I remember a throwaway comment she made over a decade ago and wanted to make her belated dreams come true.

Despite the inconvenience, when she gasped, her eyes lighting up, I knew it was worth it. It was worth the strange looks from the delivery men when I admitted I didn't have a toddler, as well as the ache in my back from helping set up the monstrosity.

"You remembered!" Fallon throws her arms around me, nearly knocking me off my feet. "How did you know I always wanted one of these?"

"You mentioned it once, I believe after a particularly tortuous algebra exam." An offhand comment from years ago that she probably doesn't even recall. "I wanted to do something special for you."

"It's perfect." She grins, already kicking off her shoes and bouncing towards the entrance. The childlike joy on her face makes everything worth it.

Running ahead and clambering inside, Fallon pokes her head out of the entrance, her hair mussed and smile wide. "Well? Are you coming in or what?"

With a dramatic sigh, I follow her in. The floor gives beneath my feet and for a moment panic rises in my chest at the thought of making a fool of myself.

Then Fallon grabs my hands, pulling me into the chaos of the bouncy castle. We crash into each other, bounce off the walls and dissolve into laughter.

The worries and responsibilities of everyday life fade away, leaving only the present moment. Me and Fallon and a secret childhood dream brought to life.

Fallon's shrieks of delight are infectious, and the laughter bubbles up before I can stop it. We collide in a tangle of limbs on the squishy floor of the bouncy castle, the cares that had weighed us down evaporating in this moment.

For now, the past is forgotten. The betrayal, the heartbreak—none of it matters here. There is only the joy we find in each other's arms, the lightness of being together with no agenda other than bouncing the shit out of this castle.

I pull Fallon into my lap in a corner of the castle, her hair a wild tangle, cheeks flushed. She's stunning like this, carefree and happy. The woman I fell in love with, not the vengeful creature she's become. Although, I really do love her in any shape or form.

Her eyes meet mine, laughter fading to something deeper. A warmth and tenderness that loosens the knots in my chest.

"Thank you for this," she whispers. "For reminding me it's okay to feel joy again. A little dose of happiness I haven't felt in a while."

I brush a stray lock of hair from her cheek, wonder and love swelling within me. "Anytime, baby. Anytime."

After what seems like hours of laughter, we collapse against the netting, our limbs entangled and breaths coming hard.

Fallon rests her head on my chest, her fingers playing with the buttons of my shirt. "Thank you for this. For understanding me so well."

I press a kiss to the top of her head, breathing in the familiar and intoxicating scent of her shampoo. "You're welcome. I'd do anything for you."

It's the truth. To see her this happy, I would move mountains. And if a bouncy castle is what it takes, so be it. I tighten my arms around Fallon, unwilling to let go of this perfect moment. Some things are worth any cost.

We stumble out of the bouncy castle, dizzy and breathless. I pull her close, the solid warmth of my body chasing away the chill. My fingers lace with hers, a familiarity that still has the power to make my heart stutter.

Fallon smooths her dress, cheeks flushed. "I can't believe you did this for me."

"Believe it." I tuck a stray curl behind her ear. "Because I'd do anything for you."

Her eyes soften, and she blinks back tears. "I know you would."

Her words settle over me, a promise I cling to. We've weathered betrayal and heartbreak to find our way back here, to a place of understanding. I will be here for her, and I will do anything she wants or needs.

I take Fallon's hand and lead her to the car. Our next stop is one of my hidden secrets—a hole-in-the-wall, family-run Italian restaurant that not many people know about. I made a call earlier to ensure we have their most private table, candlelit and ready.

As we walk through the door, a cheer goes up from the workers bustling around the kitchen and dining room. Fallon blinks in surprise as the older couple who own the restaurant hurry over, enveloping me in warm, familiar hugs.

"You're back, Aksel darling! And with a beautiful woman, no less." The older woman pinches my cheek, her eyes twinkling. "You'll do," she grins. She leans in to expect Fallon more closely. "Sì, sì. You really are very pretty." I look on with alarm, but thankfully Nonna Giulia leaves Fallon's cheeks unscathed.

Heat rises on the back of my neck at their warm welcome. I've been coming here for years, but never with a woman on my arm. Fallon is the first, and if I have any say, the last.

Our table in the corner is just as I requested. Fallon sits across from me, curiosity in her gaze. "You've obviously been here before, everyone knows you." A statement, not a question. "You're like the restaurant's celebrity or something."

I nod, pouring champagne into her glass. "I've been here many times. The food is amazing. But tonight's company is even better."

A soft flush stains her cheeks at the compliment. She opens her mouth to speak, but is interrupted by the young grandson of the owners who toddles over to our table carrying an ornate black box which he solemnly presents to Fallon.

"A gift from the gentleman." He says in toddler voice, stumbling endearingly over the word gentleman, his chubby finger pointing in my direction before he dashes off.

Fallon stares at the box in disbelief, glancing between it and me. I lift one shoulder, unable to keep the smile from my lips. "Aren't you going to open it?"

With trembling fingers, Fallon lifts the lid. Her breath catches at the sight of the sparkling diamond tennis bracelet nestled inside.

"Aksel, it's too much." Eyes shining, she looks up at me, lifting the bracelet out of its box and turning it over in her hands, admiring it.

"Nothing is too much for you." I take the bracelet and fasten it around her wrist, the diamonds winking in the candlelight. "Perfect."

Just like this moment. Just like us.

The conversation flows easily, like the wine, and servers shuffle back and forth with complimentary tastings from the chef and his team. Every bite is more delicious than the last.

Amidst the accordion music and clattering of a busy Italian kitchen, cheeks flushed from the wine, Fallon leans back with a contented sigh. "I can't remember the last time I laughed like I have today."

"Too long." I capture her hand, brushing my lips over her knuckles. "You deserve to be happy, Fallon. To have someone who puts a smile on your face every damn day."

"And you think you're that someone?" Fallon arches a brow but doesn't pull away.

"I know I am." I lace our fingers together, staring into eyes that hold a lifetime of memories. "We have a history, you and I. One that transcends all the bullshit we went through. What we had—it was real. And it's still there, waiting for us to claim it."

Fallon looks away, but not before I glimpse the sheen of tears in her eyes. "I'm afraid, Aksel. Afraid to believe that this time will be different."

"I know." I lift her hand to my lips again, grazing her skin with feather-light kisses. "But I'm here to catch you if you fall. I'm here, and I'm never leaving you again. My role is to protect your heart now."

Against all odds, it feels like we might have just found our way back to each other. Back to love.

Fallon

"You saved the restaurant." I say in a hushed whisper. I glance around at the cozy interior, the tables filled with chatting customers. "All of these people, their jobs..."

Over the course of the seriously exquisite Italian meal, it emerged that a couple of years back the restaurant was days away from going out of business. Rising property prices were making it unprofitable and driving it out of the neighborhood. But Aksel heard about the owners' plight, and invested to ensure it could stay open. Another revelation about this complex man.

"We all have to eat," he shrugs, spearing another forkful of pasta. "And where would I take my dates if not here?"

A swift kick impacts his shin under the table. He winces, catching the glint of humor in my eyes. "I'm not just another date, Aksel King."

"No, you're not." He reaches across the table to capture my hand, rubbing my thumb over her knuckles. "You never were. And, for the record, I've never brought anyone else here. It's been my special hideaway, a precious place just for me."

"Well, then I'm honored," I feel my cheeks heating at the thought of being the only person Aksel's ever brought to this gorgeous little retreat.

To my surprise, the restaurant features a special menu item with my name—the 'Fallon pavlova' covered in my favorite passionfruit pulp and fresh fruit toppings.

"My favorite dessert!" I gasp, staring at the plate set before me, a trembling smile curving my lips. How flattering, how special. "How did you know?"

"I know everything about you, Fallon." He brushes a stray curl behind my ear, lingering to cup my cheek. "I never forgot."

Tonight is like nothing I never could have dreamed of. It's as if Aksel has given me a glimpse into the life we could have together. A life filled with laughter and love. Thoughtfulness, and genuine appreciation, care and adoration for one another. One where the past remains in the past, and the future is ours to write.

Of course, I'm still wary, still hurting from old wounds. But I feel a flicker of hope. A candle in the darkness, guiding us home.

To each other.

Aksel

The laughter we shared, the secrets whispered over candlelight—they bound us together in a way I've craved for so long.

Fallon came back to me tonight. And this time it's for keeps.

She pauses on the sidewalk outside the restaurant, a soft smile curving her lips. "Thank you for tonight. I—I had a really nice time. You were so thoughtful, and..." she glances at her tennis bracelet, "this was all very unexpected but appreciated."

"The pleasure was all mine." I tuck a stray curl behind her ear, lingering to caress her cheek. "Can we do this again really soon?"

Fallon hesitates, but in her eyes, I glimpse a flicker of warmth. Of possibility. "I'd like that."

My heart kicks into overdrive as I stare down at this woman who still holds the missing pieces of my soul. "Tomorrow night. I'm taking you out for Thai food, your favorite."

Fallon laughs, the sound like music to my ears. "Trying to butter me up with more delicious food? What's your angle, King?"

I grin, pulling her into my arms. "Maybe. Is it working?"

"Maybe." Fallon tilts her chin up, and I close the distance between us—

Tonight changed everything.

Fallon came back to me, and this time, for real, I'm never letting her go.

Chapter 80

AKSEL

I sit across from Fallon's father, the imposing figure of Colton Dempsey, in his lavish living room. The air is thick with tension as he lays down his demand: "Aksel, you need to propose to my daughter."

His words hit me like a freight train. Thank goodness Fallon isn't here to see the expression on my face. Not that I don't intend on proposing to her one day. One day soon, even. But right now, while it's early days and we still have so much to figure out?

Just this morning, we had an all-out spat about the virtues of granola versus muesli, and I'd really like to get those communication issues ironed out before we walk down the aisle and commit for life.

"Sir, don't you think that's a bit... hasty?" I ask, trying to keep my voice steady. But deep down, I can feel the pressure bearing down on me, threatening to crush our relationship. I was already feeling guilt pressing down on me for the white lie I told Fallon, that I needed to work late.

Telling her that I'd been summoned here by her father for a mysterious meeting would have pissed her off, and he'd sworn me to secrecy. But now, a mandatory marriage proposal? That introduces a whole new level of pressure.

"Tradition demands it, and it's good for business," he states firmly, not an ounce of compromise in his tone. I focus on his steely gaze, searching for any sign of empathy, but find none. Tradition. Reputation. Social status. Old money might try to present itself as modern, but these entrenched value systems have their hooks in deep beneath the surface. They're all anyone in those circles worries about, other than money of course.

"Surely, Fallon should have a say in this," I argue, desperate to fight against the suffocating expectations placed on me.

"Don't question me, Aksel. We do not need her input. She's impetuous, unpredictable. She doesn't know what's best for the Dempseys and the Kings," Colton commands, his voice booming. "You know the stakes, Aksel. I expect your answer soon." He dismisses me with a wave of his hand, leaving me to stew in my own thoughts.

As I walk out of the room, my mind races. Is this what Fallon wants? Is this what I want? Our fragile bond feels like it's teetering on the edge, ready to shatter with the slightest push. A proposal might be one step too far, and might send her scurrying far away.

It's later that night when I find myself sitting alone in the dark, nursing a glass of whiskey. Colton's demand weighs heavily on my chest, making it hard to breathe. My thoughts drift to Fallon and the challenges we've faced together. It's undeniable that our love has blossomed through adversity, but this ultimatum feels different, more sinister.

"Is this about love, or just an attempt to save face?" I mutter into the empty room. The pressure to propose feels less like a romantic gesture and more like a business transaction to augment our respective families and their business endeavors.

What has always been naturally, organically, shared between Fallon and me seems to be slipping through my fingers, replaced by the cold reality of expectations and appearances. I don't want an empty shell of a relationship, I want the genuine, authentic connection I've always felt towards her.

As I take another sip of whiskey, the burning sensation does little to soothe the turmoil raging inside me. I know that what Colton asks of me could change everything, but for better or worse, I can't be certain.

My heart aches as I grapple with whether to follow his demand or trust my gut and propose to Fallon on my own time. If I get this wrong, I could lose her. And the thought of keeping her, but having to endure Colton Dempsey being a hateful father-in-law, also sends a shiver down my spine.

The future of my relationship with Fallon hangs in the balance, and the weight of it all threatens to crush me.

Fallon

I stand over the man tied to a chair in my basement, his face bruised and swollen. Sweat drips down his forehead as he whimpers in pain. My heart races with adrenaline, but I can't deny the satisfaction I feel watching him suffer. He deserves it—every ounce of torment I inflict upon him.

"Please," Harvey begs, his voice barely audible. "No more."

"Did you show any mercy when you hurt Claudia and those other innocent women?" I snarl, gripping the handle of the whip tightly. The darkness within me rises, blurring the lines between my personal vendettas and this twisted business I've become entangled in. "And what about the people you swindled through your business? They were innocent, too, Harvey, you piece of shit. And they trusted you, just like Claudia did," I hiss.

Grave watches from the shadows, his eyes filled with conflict. Despite our recent conversation, and his willingness to come back and help me with the Harvey situation, there's still an unspoken tension that lingers between us. Like he's judging me. Like he still doesn't agree with what I'm doing these days.

"Fallon," Grave says cautiously, taking a step forward. "Maybe we should take a break."

"Stay out of this," I snap, my anger flaring at his interference. I lash out with the whip, striking the man once more. His screams echo through the room, chilling me to the core even as they fuel my rage.

"Enough!" Grave shouts, rushing forward and grabbing my arm. His eyes lock onto mine, and for the first time, I see something more than just loyalty and friendship. There's a raw, vulnerable affection lurking beneath the surface, one that he's tried so hard to conceal.

"Let me go," I hiss, yanking my arm free from his grasp. The intensity of his gaze unnerves me, stirring something deep within that I'm not ready to confront.

"Fallon, please," Grave pleads, his voice cracking. "This isn't you. This darkness, it's consuming you. We said we were going to let him go. And now you're just using him as your human pin cushion, your punching bag, your proxy for every man you've ever wanted to punish."

"Who are you to tell me who I am?" I spit out, eyes narrowed, my heart pounding in my chest. "You're just as much a part of this business as I am."

"Maybe I am," he admits, his voice heavy with sorrow. "But I never wanted you to lose yourself in it. What we do, it's dangerous—but I can't stand to see you like this."

His words hit me like a ton of bricks, the truth of them cutting through my anger and pride. As I look at Grave, once again torn between doing what he believes is right and loyalty to me, I realize that I'm not only still pushing him away, but continuing to losing myself in the process.

"Grave," I whisper, my voice trembling. "I don't know if I can stop. This darkness... it's become a part of me. I don't know who I'd be without it anymore."

"Then let me help you find your way back," he says softly, reaching for my hand. "Together, we can face whatever comes our way."

The choice lies before me, the path of continued vengeance or the chance at redemption. But as I stare into Grave's eyes, filled with hope and unwavering devotion, I know that I've already made my decision. And for once, I choose love. Love of my loyal friends, and love of Aksel.

Chapter 81

FALLON

The old abandoned warehouse comes into view, rusted metal and crumbling brick under the orange glow of the setting sun. My heart races at the sight, a flood of memories crashing over me. Just a short barefoot walk through the sand dunes, the salty shoreline, waves gently crashing onto the beach leaving froth and scattered shells.

This is where Aksel and I first kissed. Where we first made love. Where we first fought, and first made up.

So much history in these walls. Still coated in graffiti, although different patterns and colors than when we last visited, a relic of our tumultuous past but with a modern update.

Aksel stands in the center of the vast empty room, hands in his pockets, staring at a spot on the floor. The place where he first told me he loved me.

The place where he told me cryptically to meet him today.

I almost didn't want to come, the memories of this structure almost too much to bear. The hope our moments here held, the anticipation, the unabashed adoration for each other. And then the crushing hurt and betrayal. But I've shoved my emotions as far down as they'll go today. Whatever this is, whatever Aksel has planned, I want to go in open-minded, no longer shackled by memories of past betrayals. I'm fresh, reset, ready to consider things neutrally.

I step through the doorway and his head jerks up, eyes locking onto mine. Piercing gray, filled with a storm of emotion. Nerves. Hope. Fear.

Love.

"Fallon." My name on his lips is a caress, rough with longing.

I stay silent, drinking in the sight of him. Familiar yet different. The sharp cut of his jaw shadowed by stubble, a worn T-shirt clinging to his muscular frame. I long to run my fingers over him, but I settle for my eyes soaking in every angle.

He takes a step forward and stops, jaw clenching. "I asked you to meet me here, because this location carries so much meaning, for me, for both of us. It's where we first kissed, where we first called each other boyfriend and girlfriend. One of the first places we made love, when we had absolutely no idea what we were doing but it was amazing all the same, because it was with you."

I smirk.

"I also know this is where you used to run when you were sad, in pain, tormented by dark memories but also just the regular shit that comes with being a teenager and a young adult. This was your sanctuary, your sacred, secret place that you let me into. And I'm grateful to you for sharing It with me."

I nod. He knows the meaning this place carries.

"I know...I know I don't deserve this. Another chance. But Fallon, you're it for me, I meant what I said the other day. You always have been. I love you, and I want to spend the rest of my life proving that to you. If you'll let me."

His words hit me like a punch to the gut, knocking the breath from my lungs. A part of me wants nothing more than to run to him and lose myself in his embrace.

But the shadows of our past loom, waiting to swallow us whole once more.

I steel myself, meeting his gaze. "And how do I know this isn't just another lie? That you're not just manipulating my feelings by bringing me here. That you're not just luring me in so you can hurt me again."

Our past is littered with broken promises and shattered dreams. Aksel betrayed me in the worst possible way, shattering my heart into a million pieces. I swore I would never give him another chance to hurt me. When I thought he'd done it again, the pain of a second betrayal seared through my soul. Thankfully, that was a misunderstanding, but if that pain was real I don't know if I could have survived it.

Yet here we are. And despite everything, a part of me still loves him with a fierceness that steals my breath. That part of me wants to believe he's changed. That this time will be different. He's an adult now, not a teenage boy who isn't sure what he wants. That said, a bouncy castle and a diamond bracelet aren't nearly enough to make up for the pain he's caused, or to dispel my fears.

I wet my lips, a thousand emotions swirling in my chest. "I don't know if I can ever fully trust you again." My voice trembles, laced with old hurts and new hope. "I want to, I really want to. But I don't know if I can."

"I know." Regret flickers in his eyes before determination takes over. "But I will spend every day proving to you that you can. Fallon, you're the love of my life. My past, present and future. I can't imagine this world without you in it. Please." His voice breaks on a whisper. "Take a chance on me. On us. One more time."

The rawness in his words resonates in my soul. How many times have I longed to hear him say those very words? A single tear slides down my cheek as I stare at the man who still holds my heart.

Aksel pulls back to gaze down at me, his eyes soft with affection. "There's something else." He reaches into his pocket and withdraws a small velvet box. "I was going to wait, but—"

My heart leaps as he flips open the lid to reveal a diamond solitaire ring nestled inside. Simple yet stunning. My breath leaves me in a rush.

"Fallon Dempsey, will you marry me?"

The world narrows to just the two of us. His gaze locks on mine, hope and fear warring in his eyes. My heart pounds as I stare between Aksel and the ring, stunned into silence. Is this truly happening? After everything we've endured, all the heartbreak and pain, is he really asking me to be his wife? I figured he might ask one day, dreamed about it, but already?

Do I dare commit to forever with anyone, let alone this man? And so quickly?

"I know it's fast, probably *too* fast," he continues, nerves evident in his voice. "But when you realize you want to spend the rest of your life with someone, you want the rest of your life to start as soon as possible. I love you with everything in me. You're it for me, Fallon. Always have been, always will be."

Tears blur my vision as I meet his gaze. The depth of love and commitment I find there steals my breath. How could I ever doubt this man? Doubt us?

The answer comes without overthinking. Slipping into place like the missing piece of a puzzle.

"Yes," I whisper, a smile breaking across my face. "Yes, I'll marry you Aksel King."

Joy lights Aksel's eyes as a smile curves his lips. He surges to his feet and crushes me in his arms, the familiar scent of him surrounding me.

"Thank you," he breathes against my hair. "You won't regret this. I promise you, Fallon. I love you," he says fiercely, cupping my face in his hands. "Always and forever."

"I love you too." I reach up, tangling my fingers in his hair to pull his mouth down to mine.

The kiss is sweet yet passionate, sealing our promise to one another. When we break apart, Aksel rests his forehead against mine, his eyes closed.

I cling to him, emotions overwhelming me. There is no going back now. For better or worse, our fate is sealed.

Interlaced together, the way it always should have been.

Aksel stands, pulling me up with him. Our joined hands swing between us as we walk back along the beach, the setting sun casting an orange glow over the rippling waves.

Sand squishes between my toes with every step. The cool breeze carries the briny scent of the sea, fresh and clean.

After a few minutes of comfortable silence, Aksel glances over at me. "Have you given any thought to when you'd like to have the wedding? I know it's soon, but we could do a small ceremony now and plan a bigger one for later."

I laugh. "Jeez, Aksel. You only asked me a few minutes ago. I'm still trying to process the fact we're engaged!" I shrug, turning to face the water. "But I do know that I don't need anything fancy. As long as I have you, that's all that matters."

"You're all that matters to me, too." Aksel stops walking, tilting my chin up to meet his gaze. "But you deserve the wedding of your dreams, Fallon. We have all the time in the world, so take as long as you need to plan it."

"You're too good to me." I wrap my arms around his waist, pressing my face into his chest. Strong arms come around me in return, holding me close.

"Impossible. I will spend the rest of my life proving I'm worthy of you, Fallon Dempsey."

I smile against his shirt, breathing in his familiar scent. "You already have."

The moment stretches, comfortable and content.

A loud buzz from my phone shatters the peace. I pull away with a sigh, digging the device from my pocket.

One new text from an unknown number.

(Anonymous number): Remember me?

My blood turns to ice. Aksel peers over my shoulder, his frown deepening at the cryptic message.

"Who is that from?" His voice is deceptively calm, but I can feel the tension in his frame.

"I don't know." Dread pools in my gut as the implications of those two words sink in.

Someone from my past has come calling. And nothing good ever follows from that.

My hands start to shake as I stare at the text. Aksel pulls me close again, rubbing my arms.

"It's probably just a wrong number," he says softly. But the look on his face tells me he doesn't believe that.

"No." I swallow hard. "It's not."

Memories I've tried to bury for years come flooding back. The blood. The pain. The rage. I push them away, clutching at Aksel like he's the only thing keeping me afloat.

"Whoever it is, we'll deal with them together." His voice is steady and strong. "No one will hurt you again. I promise."

I nod against his chest, drawing in a shaky breath. We stand there for a long moment, his warmth and solid presence chasing away the ghosts of the past.

When my phone buzzes again, I steel myself before looking at the new message.

(Anonymous number): I'm coming for what's mine. I've had it before and I want it again.

Bile rises in my throat. I know now, without a doubt, who this is. One of the four people who have collectively haunted my nightmares for years, slipping in and out of shadows, always watching and waiting. My torment didn't stop at my attack. Each year, they reach out again. Stalking, keeping tabs on me. I can never prove it, though. They're always one step ahead. An item moved. A funny noise. A rustle in the shadows. And it's not in my head.

My rapists are back. And they want more.

"We have to leave. Now." I grab Aksel's hand, panic clawing at my chest. "They're coming for me. We're not safe here anymore."

Recognition dawns on his face.

"They're still coming after you? Even after all this time?" His eyes darken with rage, but his voice remains calm. "We're not running from these bastards. I won't let them terrorize you anymore."

"Please," I beg. "I can't lose you too. We have to go!"

He pulls me into a fierce embrace, one hand tangling in my hair. "I'm not going anywhere. And neither are you. We'll face this threat together, and I'll destroy anyone who tries to hurt you. You're mine now, Fallon, and I protect what's mine."

Maybe his words should scare me. But all I feel is love, and gratitude, and the safest I've felt in years.

The terror in me suddenly dissipates, Aksel's support for me galvanizing my fears into an opposite set of emotions. Strength and courage and the desire to right the course. It's time to take back what's mine.

My rapists have no idea what's coming for them. And this time, I won't stop until all four of them are dead. Just like I tell my most secret of clients, sometimes the justice system just isn't set up to help the victims, and you have to take matters into your own hands.

As we leave the beach, our hands entwined, the diamond on my ring finger catches the dim light and sparkles like a promise. The same beach where we used to spend lazy afternoons together as seniors. Where Aksel saved me from drowning and breathed life back into my broken body, right at the heart of our intense rivalry in junior year. Just like he's doing now, sheltering my battered soul and putting the missing pieces back together with his love.

Aksel's grip on my hand is iron-clad, unwilling to let go even for a second. I cling to him just as tightly, drawing strength and comfort from his presence. We stand in the semi-darkness of the beach at night, the only illumination coming from a pale sliver of moon and the distant glow of city lights.

"We'll get through this," he murmurs against my hair. "I won't let anyone hurt you, Fallon. Never again."

I lift my head from the sanctuary of his chest to meet his gaze. The steely determination in his eyes steals my breath. "Together," I say softly. "We'll face this together."

He smiles and presses a tender kiss to my forehead. "Together. Always."

The moment is shattered by a gunshot in the distance, followed by a startled scream. Aksel's arm tightens around me as we both peer into the gloom. Waiting. Watching.

My rapists are out there. Coming for me. And when they see Aksel, they'll be coming for both of us.

And we'll be ready. I no longer have to do this alone.

Chapter 82

FALLON

The heavy scent of roast beef and potatoes fills my nostrils as I slide into my seat at the head of the table. My family's familiar voices chatter around me, a deceptive veneer of normalcy that does little to mask the tension simmering beneath.

Cheston's gaze flickers to mine, stormy gray eyes narrowing for a fraction of a second before his attention shifts back to his plate. The jagged scar running along his jawline seems more pronounced tonight, a reminder of secrets we've buried in the past.

Fenton stabs at his meal with more force than necessary, his knuckles whitening around the knife clutched in his fist. The wounds I inflicted on him years ago have left more than physical scars, fracturing a bond that I'm not sure can ever be mended.

Bronson's laugh cuts through the tension, too loud and abrupt to be genuine. He tries too hard to lighten the mood, a pathetic attempt at obscuring his own role in the events that tore this family apart.

The ghosts of our past hang over this table, vengeful specters that refuse to be silenced. With each strained laugh and cutting glance, they grow more vocal, screaming accusations and ugly truths in a language only we can understand.

This meal is a farce. Beneath the civilized trappings of silverware and small talk, we are beasts circling each other, waiting to draw first blood. The Dempsey men have always had a taste for violence, a dark legacy passed from father to son. But as I've come to realize, the bloodlust, the taste for vengeance, did not escape the female side. I, too, am fascinated by *death and darkness.*

Tonight, that violence simmers just below the surface, threatening to erupt in a storm that will shake the very foundations of this house. The secrets we've kept for so long demand to be unleashed, and none of us will escape unscathed.

After all, in this family, we've always settled our debts in blood.

Cheston's eyes meet mine across the table, a silent warning. He knows what demons stalk my thoughts, recognizes that dangerous glint in my gaze. As always, he hopes to curb my reckless impulses, and contain the damage before it spirals out of control.

Too late for that. The bloodlust is upon me, sharpening my senses until I can taste the metallic tang of violence on my tongue.

Bronson opens his mouth again, spouting some inane comment I don't care to acknowledge. With deliberate slowness, I curl my fingers around the handle of my knife, relishing the cool press of metal against my palm.

He sees the threat in my casual grip, his words faltering as comprehension dawns. The color drains from his face, leaving his eyes stark and wounded.

Good. Fear becomes him.

"Did you really think I'd forgotten?" My voice emerges as a growl, rage giving the words an ugly twist. "That I'd forgive what you did? You betrayed me. Betrayed all of us."

"Fallon, don't—" Cheston's warning comes too late. I surge to my feet, my chair crashing behind me, and lunge across the table.

The knife finds its mark with ease, slicing through cloth and flesh. A cry of pain and shock rings out, cut short by my hand closing around a throat.

Bronson struggles beneath me, bucking and clawing at my arm. My brother's blood wells between my fingers, as crimson as the haze clouding my vision.

"You will pay for your sins," I hiss. "And when I'm done with you, you'll beg for the mercy of death."

Bronson's eyes bulge, his lips turning an alarming shade of blue. I ease my grip just enough for a rasping breath, not yet ready to end this.

"Fallon, stop!" Fenton shouts, his hands closing around my shoulders. I shrug him off with a snarl, my knife flashing out to discourage any further interference.

He stumbles back, betrayal etched deep in the lines of his face. But he stays silent, unwilling to risk his brother's life by provoking me further.

Coward. Just like Bronson. Like all of them.

My gaze drops to the ruin of Bronson's shirt, soaked through with crimson. The wounds aren't deep, but they'll scar, a permanent reminder of his sins.

A fitting punishment.

The knife nearly slips from my nerveless fingers as I stare at the ruin I've wrought. Horror and satisfaction war within me, the haze of rage receding to leave a bitter taste in my mouth.

What have I done?

I've stabbed my brother in cold blood. It felt good. And he's not even the most annoying one.

Bronson sucks in a desperate breath as I release him, collapsing to the floor in a limp tangle of limbs. His eyes find mine, clouded with pain and fear—but beneath it lingers the shadow of understanding.

We're all more alike than I care to admit, my brothers and me. Bound by blood and secrets too ugly to bear the light of day.

I scrub a hand over my face. The metallic tang of violence is gone, replaced by the acrid burn of self-loathing.

What kind of monster have I become?

Cheston steps forward, his hands raised in a placating gesture. His eyes flicker between Bronson's crumpled form and the knife still grasped in my hand, reading the violence etched into the scene.

"Fallon, what have you done?" The words emerge as a hoarse whisper, disbelief warring with resignation. "You stabbed our brother?"

I open my mouth, but no words come. What can I say to undo this?

Anger flickers in his gaze before fading beneath a veil of weariness. He kneels beside Bronson, his hands gentle as they probe the wounds.

Bronson sucks in a sharp breath but doesn't pull away. Trust, even now. Or perhaps resignation to the demons that haunt this family.

"It's not deep," Cheston says after a moment. "But it will scar."

His eyes find mine, judgment and understanding warring in their depths. I drop my gaze, unable to bear the turmoil reflected there.

"We're broken, all of us," he continues softly. "Twisted up inside until we turn on each other." A bitter smile quirks across his lips. "But we're all we have left. So we should perhaps not run around stabbing each other."

I flinch, as though struck. He's not wrong, but the truth of it cuts deep, exposing vulnerabilities I'd rather not face.

"So when things like this happen, we don't spend months—or weeks even—pointing

fingers." He shakes his head. "We pick up the pieces and move on." Cheston's hand closes over the knife, prising it from my unresisting fingers. The weight of it leaves an ache inside, a hollow yearning filled with echoes of violence.

"Because that's what families do."

Shame washes over me, sudden and suffocating in its intensity. I'm drowning in sins of my own making, unable to find purchase beneath the roiling tide of emotions.

"I'm sorry." The words emerge as a strangled sob. "Bronson, I—"

"Hush." A warm hand closes over my wrist, grounding me. I glance up to find Bronson watching me, a wry twist to his lips. "No apologies between monsters, remember?" His voice is a little ragged, sweat beading on his forehead, but he's regained a little color.

A laugh spills out, jagged around the edges but filled with the promise of absolution. The demons haven't left us, but for now they sleep, exorcized by the ties that bind.

Broken yet whole. Monsters, but together.

This is what families do.

I wake with a start, glancing over to see Aksel rubbing my arm and staring at me with concern. "Fallon, you were screaming in your sleep. Are you okay?"

"Yep," I reply, sighing. "Just stabbing my brothers at a family dinner."

He smirks. "Wow, and I thought the first one I went to was pretty tense!"

"Yep, they're always pretty exhausting. But this one took the cake," I shake my head. "Thankfully, I didn't actually commit fratricide. And Link is very lucky he didn't make an appearance in my dream. Poor Brons on the other hand," I shake my head.

Clearly, it's not just Aksel and I who have some healing to do. My subconscious is telling me my family is just as fucked. We all need help. But, if we all put the work in, I'm confident we can get there.

Chapter 83

AKSEL

My blood boils as I storm through the warehouse, my fists clenched. The familiar metallic scent of blood and fear cling to the damp air—remnants of my family's latest 'business transaction', a hostile acquisition on the other side of town.

How did I get here? When did the darkness overtake the light in my soul? I've been dragged down into the abyss of dodgy deals and organized crime, and it feels like I may never make it up for air. It provides a good life for me and my future family, from a financial perspective, but I often find myself wondering whether it's worth the psychological toll it takes. Or the damage it does to my soul.

I pause outside the door of my office and drag a hand through my hair. The familiar weight of the 9mm pistol in my jacket pocket serves as a grim reminder of the path I've chosen. Of the lives I've destroyed to protect what's mine. To protect her.

Fallon. Her name slices through my chest like a knife, sharp and swift. I told myself I was protecting her, but with each business risk I take, I'm pulling her further into the shadows. When I'm a target, she's now a target. And I don't think she appreciates what being with me entails now, and what it is she'd be getting into as a result.

The door creaks open behind me. "Boss? We got a problem."

I turn to face my lieutenant, schooling my features into cool indifference. "What is it?"

He shifts on his feet, eyes flickering away from mine. "Word on the street is the Delacortes are planning a hit. Tonight."

My fingers curl into fists at the mention of that family. They've been nipping at our heels for months, trying to take what's ours.

Tonight they'll learn their lesson.

I meet my lieutenant's gaze, allowing a slow, menacing smile to spread across my face. "Very interesting. It seems we have some unfinished business with the Delacortes, and so perhaps tonight is the night we should have that conversation with them. Move our business interests along in a mutually beneficial way."

He nods sharply. "I'll rally the men."

"Oh, and Baroni?"

"Yeah, boss?"

"If they don't come to the party, shoot them on sight. We need to send a message that we haven't suddenly become pushovers."

As he leaves to carry out my orders, I glance out the window into the inky darkness beyond. Somewhere out there, Fallon is waiting for me. Waiting for the man I used to be.

The man I can never be again. And I need some advice to get me through from the person I trust most with my heart.

I find Raine in her art studio, a paint-splattered smock covering her clothes as she studies the half-finished canvas before her. Her hair is wild, free, the auburn waves cascading wildly around her shoulders and down her back. Adorable little speckles of paint fleck her hair.

She glances up at the sound of my footsteps, brows drawing together in concern as she takes in my expression. "What's wrong?"

I lean against the doorframe, scrubbing a hand over my face. "I don't know who I am anymore."

Her paintbrush stills. "Well, hello to you too, Aksel. I see we're starting with light small talk today! What do you mean, you don't know who you are? You're a grown adult man and a successful businessman, a wonderful brother and uncle... should I continue?"

"This life, I mean," I say, my voice rough. "The family business. Being a King. I thought I could balance everything and live a somewhat normal life, but—" I break off with a harsh laugh. "There's nothing normal about this. About me."

Raine sets down her brush and crosses the room to grip my shoulders. "You're still the same person you've always been. You have a good heart, Aksel."

I stare at her, wanting so badly to believe that. "How can you say that? After everything I've done."

"You did what you had to do in order to protect us." Her eyes soften. She's one of the few people who knows the full extent of what I've been through, and she's never judged me for it. "But now you have a chance at a different life. With Fallon."

Fallon. Again that sharp twist in my chest at the thought of her. My fierce, beautiful girl. The one light in all this darkness. My fiancé.

"Do you think she could ever accept me for who I really am?" I ask quietly. "Not the person she believes me to be, but the monster I've become?"

"You're not a monster." Raine squeezes my shoulders. "Fallon loves you. But you have to be honest with her about the life you lead—and decide if you're willing to leave that life behind for a chance at real happiness. Because I'm pretty sure you can't have both, and I'm even more certain you don't want both."

"I just feel like she accepted my proposal without knowing the full story, without realizing what she's actually getting herself into. She's accepted a proposal based on a shell version of me. The person who I put on for show to get her to do what I needed her to do. Not the dark version of myself, the one haunted by demons. The criminal. The murderer. She wouldn't want a bar of that guy."

"Let her be the judge of that, Aksel. But either way, she needs to know. You need her to know."

I bow my head, a war raging inside me. Raine's right. Fallon deserves the truth. She deserves better than the shadows I've dragged her into.

I just don't know if I'm strong enough to step out of those shadows. Out of the darkness and into the light.

I hug Raine tight, taking strength from her as I always have. "Thank you," I whisper.

She hugs me back just as fiercely. "You're welcome. Now go get your girl."

I leave Raine's place with her words ringing in my ears. *Go get your girl.* Easier said than done, when Fallon has every reason not to trust me anymore. When I've done nothing to deserve her love or her forgiveness. It would be much easier to hold onto the fragile scaffolding we've recently developed and pretend everything is okay.

But as I climb into my car and start the engine, staring out at the road ahead, I make a decision. Raine's right—Fallon deserves the truth. She deserves to know exactly who I am and the life I lead, so she can make her own choice.

I won't drag her any further into my shadows without letting her know the risks. And I'll step into the light for her. Even if it means sacrificing everything I've ever known, I have to try for a chance at real happiness, at a life with the woman I love.

My hands tighten around the steering wheel as I point my car toward Fallon's place. It's time to end the lies. To bare my soul to her and accept whatever comes after.

Loss or redemption. Darkness or light.

As long as she's there to meet me on the other side.

I pull up outside Fallon's house, my heart pounding so hard I can feel it in my throat. Every instinct is screaming at me to turn around, to protect her from the ugly truth of who I really am.

But I can't live this lie anymore. Can't look into those sea-green eyes and spew one more fabrication to keep her by my side. She deserves better than that. Deserves better than me.

Still, my feet feel leaden as I walk up the path to her front door. My knuckles hover over the wood, trembling. Summoning my courage, I knock twice.

The door swings open, and there she is. Fallon, with her fiery hair tumbling over her shoulders and a smile lighting up her face at the sight of me. My breath catches at her beauty, at the warmth in her eyes. Warmth I'm about to extinguish.

"Aksel." She steps forward, her hands coming up to grasp my arms. "I'm so glad you're here."

I close my eyes against the surge of bittersweet joy her touch ignites. When I open them again, I know she sees the shadows lurking there. The secrets I can no longer contain.

"We need to talk," I say quietly. Hoarsely. "There are things you need to know. About me, and my past. Things I should have told you a long time ago. Things you definitely had a right to know when considering whether or not you want to marry me."

Fallon searches my face, her brows furrowing. But she steps back and opens the door wider in silent invitation.

I walk through, and she closes the door behind us. The click of the lock sounds like a death knell, sealing my fate.

I face her in the dimly lit foyer, heart in my throat, and begin to speak the truth.

Chapter 84

FALLON

My fingers tremble as I type out the message.

Me: Mia, I'm sorry. I understand now why you met with Aksel. You were worried about me, like always. I shouldn't have lashed out. I felt betrayed, like the two people I trusted most in this world were conspiring against me. But I was wrong.

Me: I don't expect you to forgive me. I just wanted you to know that I get it now. And I'm sorry.

Me: More than sorry. I'm gutted that I hurt you.

I hit send and stare at the screen, my heart jackhammering. She'll never speak to me again. I've lost her, like I lose everything that matters.

The phone buzzes almost immediately. A text from Mia.

Mia: Don't be ridiculous. I forgive you. I've been having a hard time too. We both said things we didn't mean.

Mia: I miss you, Fal. Can we get coffee tomorrow? I have news I want to share in person.

Relief floods through me, warm and bright. She's giving me another chance. I text back immediately.

Me: Yes, coffee would be great. I miss you too. Tomorrow works. Same place, same time as we used to?

Her reply comes seconds later.

Mia: Perfect. See you then.

Mia: Love you xox

Those two words loosen the knot in my chest. She still loves me, despite everything. We'll work through this rough patch like we always do.

Tomorrow, over coffee and pastries, our friendship will be mended. She's one of the few good things I have left. I won't screw this up again.

The next morning, I get to the cafe early and snag our usual table by the window. Mia walks in a few minutes later, looking casually chic in cropped jeans and a flowy top, her hair in a messy bun.

When she sees me, her face lights up. She hurries over and wraps me in a hug. "I'm so glad we're doing this."

"Me too." I hug her back tightly. "I've missed you. I love your outfit, by the way!"

We order lattés and muffins over small talk, then settle in. An awkward silence falls as we both try to figure out where to start.

Mia clears her throat. "So, I want to let you know that I met someone."

My stomach drops. Of course she did. Not that I'm not happy for her. Hearing this just hits home that I've missed hearing about her day-to-day experiences. While I was wallowing in self-pity, she was out living her life. "Oh?" I force a smile. "That's great. What's he like?"

"His name is Liam. He's charming, smart, ambitious. We have a lot in common." She grins, then sobers. "But there's something you should know. He recently took a job at Montgomery Enterprises. In the acquisitions department. I guess he's peripherally related to the family... like second cousins or something."

The floor tilts under me. Liam works for my family's biggest rival, the company trying to stage a hostile takeover of one of my family's biggest assets. The news cuts deep, reopening the wounds from the other night. My best friend, dating one of my family's biggest competitors, doesn't sit right.

Mia's gaze turns pleading. "Fal, I didn't know, I swear. When I found out, I almost ended it with him, even though we haven't been talking. But he's not like the rest of them. He doesn't care about the feud or the competition. He just wants to be with me. And we agreed not to talk about work because neither of us wants to confuse things."

I stare at her, the hurt and anger warring inside me. How could she do this? After everything we've been through, she chooses some guy she just met over our friendship... why not just leave things as they were? Why reach out on the pretense of trying to mend things, only to go straight out and pick the one person with a dick attached who can compromise my family's business if sensitive information gets into the wrong hands?

When I don't reply, her eyes fill with tears. "Please say something, Fallon. I don't want to lose you again over this. I want to rekindle our friendship, and that includes being transparent with you. About everything, including Liam and the Montgomerys."

My hands curl into fists under the table. But looking at her now, her gaze pleading, I can see how much I mean to her. How much she means to me. If I can't forgive her for finding happiness, even if there seem to be strings attached, what kind of friend does that make me?

I take a deep breath and let it out slowly. "It's okay," I say quietly. "I want you to be happy. Even if it's with someone from the dark side. Just please don't tell them any of our secrets."

Relief floods her face. She grabs my hand, her grip almost painful. "Thank you. You don't know what this means to me. I love you, Fal. You're my person, no matter what. I promise."

"I know," I say, giving her hand a squeeze. "You're my person, too. No matter what."

Our friendship has weathered worse than this. It'll survive a doomed romance with this Liam guy. Mia and I are forever besties, no matter the forces trying to tear us apart.

Mia smiles, the tears spilling over onto her cheeks. She stands and pulls me into a hug. I hug her back fiercely, breathing in the familiar and comforting scent of her Jean Paul Gaultier perfume with its notes of orange blossom and rose. She's worn it as her signature for so long it instantly reminds me of her whenever I notice someone wearing it, and it always makes me instantly feel at ease.

When we pull apart, she wipes at her eyes. "So, do you want to meet him?"

I make a face. "Do I have to?"

She laughs, the tension easing from her shoulders. "No, not yet. I just thought I'd ask."

"Maybe someday," I say. "When I've wrapped my head around my best friend dating the enemy."

"He's not the enemy," she protests. "His company is in competition with yours, sure, but Liam himself is a really great guy."

"If you say so." I try to keep the skepticism from my tone and apparently fail.

Mia narrows her eyes at me. "You'll see. I'm going to invite you both over for dinner and you'll love him. I know it."

"Good luck with that," I say wryly. While I want to support Mia's happiness, I can't make any promises about befriending this Liam. My loyalty is to my family's company, not some pretty-boy rival my best friend has fallen for.

Mia just shakes her head, a rueful smile tugging at her lips. "You're impossible, you know that?"

"So you keep telling me." I stand, grabbing my jacket. "Ready to head out? I'm craving a burger and am going to pick up ingredients on the way home."

"A burger sounds delicious. I might do the same." Mia loops her arm through mine as we head outside. "Thanks for giving him a chance. It means a lot."

"What are best friends for?" I say lightly.

Mia squeezes my arm, understanding in her gaze. She knows I'm skeptical about giving her new boyfriend the benefit of the doubt. But for her sake, I'll try.

Because that's what best friends do.

The next day, Mia texts me about dinner plans with Liam. My stomach churns at the thought of sitting across from my family's biggest rival, pretending to make nice. But I text back:

Me: Sure, what time?

Anything for Mia. Even if it kills me.

I show up at her place that evening in dark jeans and a silky top, hair styled to perfection. Mia opens the door, greeting me with a hug, and the scent of garlic and herbs wafts from inside.

A man who must be Liam stands in the entryway behind her, all tousled blonde hair and blue eyes and charm. He looks like he grew up on corn, whole milk and football. "Fallon, great to finally meet you. Mia's told me so much about you."

He holds out a hand. I take it, grip firm. "Likewise."

Over dinner, Liam regales us with funny work stories and compliments Mia with casual touches and adoring looks. The pasta primavera is delicious but sticks in my throat. I force myself to make conversation, asking Liam questions about his hobbies and family. He seems perfectly nice and like a decent guy, which is perfectly infuriating. I wanted to hate him on sight.

"I have to ask," Liam says with a rueful grin, addressing the elephant in the room, "how do you feel about your family's biggest competitor dating your best friend?"

Mia shoots him a warning look. "Liam..."

I spear a tomato with more force than necessary. "As long as Mia's happy, that's all that matters to me."

"Glad to hear it." Liam's eyes glint with challenge. "May the best company win, then. We'll see who keeps Dart Technologies after this week's depositions..."

I can't believe he's blatantly mentioning the asset his family's company is trying to seize from mine.

"Liam!" Mia scolds. "Be nice!"

My jaw clenches. The gauntlet has been thrown. "May the best company win," I echo coolly.

Oh, it's on. And Liam has no idea who he's up against. No one challenges me or my family and gets away with it.

Not even Mia's precious boyfriend.

Chapter 85

AKSEL

I'm sautéing mushrooms in garlic and butter when a loud bang reverberates through Fallon's condo. My heart kicks. What the hell was that?

Fallon's out picking up wine. I'm alone, or I thought I was.

Another thud. A muffled cry. The sounds are coming from below.

The basement. An intruder. Thank goodness Fallon isn't here so I can take care of this situation without endangering her.

I grab a knife from the block and creep toward the basement door. At the bottom of the stairs, my breath catches.

A man is trapped in a cage, clutching the bars. Bruises mottle his face and there are crusty incisions on his torso and arms. His eyes widen at the sight of me.

It's Harvey Maxwell, a man I recognize as the owner of one of the companies King Enterprises works with closely. An unscrupulous man known for his underhanded business dealings, but who has a monopoly on the supplies he brings into the city.

"Help me," he rasps.

My grip tightens on the knife as I stride toward the cage. "Harvey Maxwell? What on earth are you doing here?"

"You tell me," the man grits, the spit at the corners of his mouth indicating dehydration.

The door slams upstairs. "Aksel?" Fallon calls.

Shit. I stash the knife in my jacket and quietly but quickly make my way back up the stairs and gently close the basement door behind me. I make it into the kitchen just before she reaches the room, grabbing the spatula as if I'm laser-focused on cooking, and none the wiser that she has a goddamn man trapped in her basement.

"Sorry that took so long," she says breezily. "Did I miss anything?" She glances over at the frying pan where the mushrooms are getting a little golden and crispy. "Mmm, that looks divine." Whew, she changed the subject herself.

My heart hammers. How am I going to hide this from her while I figure out how to question her about it? "Yep, just cooking the mushrooms," I say, hoping my voice sounds normal. "They're basically done, so we can just keep them warm while we finish the rest of it."

Fallon glances at the basement door and narrows her eyes. "Why is that door open?"

Shit. It's slightly ajar. I must not have closed it properly, or it clicked back open.

"Oh yeah, uh—" *Think fast, Aksel.* "I, uh, made the mushrooms steam up too much so I was trying to get more free air through here."

"Fresh air..." She arches a brow. "From the windowless basement?"

Shit. She's too smart for excuses. I'll have to tell her the truth—that I've seen what's happening down there. I have so many questions, but I'm willing to hear her out.

But if I do, it could destroy everything we've built. The trust. The love. The new life we're trying to forge together.

I stare at Fallon, the woman I was ready to marry, but who I just found out is holding a man captive in her basement. A dangerous man at that.

"He knows I'm down here, Fallon!" screams Harvey, slashing any possibility she'd believe my story about air circulation. Fallon's mouth drops open and she narrows her eyes at me.

"So you're lying to me already? You went down to the basement and lied about it?" She folds her arms tightly, pissed, waiting for an explanation. I scramble for something—anything—to say, but my mind is blank.

But then I realize the hypocrisy. "Fal, you have an actual man trapped in a cage in your basement. You have some explaining to do yourself."

She examines my face for a moment, trying to read my intentions, and then sighs. "Fine. Come back down, with me this time. I may as well tell you everything."

We descend the stairs together, and once again I'm face to face with my fiancée's captive. But this time she's here with me, and she really does owe me an explanation.

Fallon

Harvey grins at both of us from the cage. I feel defeated, confused. I was worried enough about letting him out. My fiancé being here is just adding another layer to the mix.

I ball my hands into fists, rage and frustration warring inside me. Then I make my choice.

"Aksel" I say quietly. "There's something I have to tell you."

His eyes widen. He can sense this is something big. The large man chained to the basement wall covered in bruises and lacerations is probably a giveaway.

I take a deep breath. "This man here, Harvey Maxwell, has been in my basement for the past several weeks."

All the color drains from his face. "What? For *weeks*?"

"Yes, weeks. And I'm sorry," I say, my brow knotting together. "I should have told you the truth from the start. But I couldn't risk you turning me in for kidnapping him."

"Turning you in?" His voice rises. "Fallon, this is insane! You can't keep someone prisoner in your condo."

"I had no choice!" I shout. "He destroyed his wife's life, Aksel. He took everything from her. He deserved to suffer for what he did, and I have an obligation to help her!"

"So you were just going to keep him here forever?" He looks at me like I'm completely insane. "On someone else's behalf? Like some sick pet?"

I tuck a strand of hair behind my ear and frown. "I don't know, okay? I wasn't thinking straight. I was figuring it out, how to let him go. All I could see was my chance for revenge, and this seemed most equitable given the awful things he's done."

He stares at me with a mix of horror and disbelief. I've really done it now. I've lost him for good.

The thought makes my chest ache, but I don't regret my choice. At least now he sees me for who I really am, although I'm sure he doesn't understand the full picture yet: a woman haunted by the need to exact revenge for the good of others.

"He had it coming to him, Aksel. He kept his wife a prisoner in their home and completely brainwashed her. He was abusive, narcissistic, and completely controlling."

"That's awful, truly!" he sputters. "But what you did is perhaps just as insane. Kidnapping him in return! There are ways to deal with people like him like, you know... the legal system?!"

"Men like you," I look him up and down and narrow my eyes, my voice ice cold, "are naïve to think the justice system works in the favor of most victims, especially when they're female."

He quirks his brow. "So what, then? You're like some vigilante justice system? And you kept this from me this whole time?"

Harvey's eyes shuttle between us, enjoying what's undoubtedly the most exciting interaction he's witnessed in weeks.

"Well I can't exactly go around telling everyone about this part of my business, can I?" I roll my eyes.

"It's an actual branch of your business? No wonder Grave has been working out so well for you, given his background."

My blood turns to ice in my veins. "Excuse me? You know Grave?"

"I, uh—." He fumbles his words and looks down.

"Aksel? How do you know Grave?"

"I, um... I kind of made sure he was hired by your company."

"You what?" I shriek. "You made sure he what?!" I'm beside myself. The betrayal, the deceit. So he's been keeping tabs on me all this time, since well before we got back together. If Grave has been reporting back to him about me, it will be such a betrayal of trust, and obviously a massive breach of the NDA he signed. I'll destroy him. I'll destroy Aksel. Nobody will be safe.

He clears his throat and shifts awkwardly. "Only to protect you."

"So you've been spying on me through Grave?"

"No, no," he shakes his head. He's adamant, earnest, and for a moment I almost believe him. "I just wanted to make sure someone was keeping an eye on you. That you were safe."

"You know what? This is absurd," I frown, my voice rising. "I can't trust anything you do or say anymore, clearly. Never should have in the first place."

He sighs and tilts his head toward the sky, and rubs his eyes with his fingers. "I knew I shouldn't have listened to Colton. I should have taken my time."

As soon as the words are out of his mouth, I can tell he realizes he's made another mistake. His hand flies across his mouth. "I mean—".

I narrow my eyes at him. "What do you mean, you shouldn't have 'listened to Colton'?

What did my father ask you to do?"

"He, uh—. He brought forward the proposal."

I feel heat building in my chest and my body starts to shake as his words sink in. "Excuse me? Are you saying you proposed to me because *my father told you to?*"

He hesitates, and that's enough for me.

"You have to be fucking kidding me," I cry. "Get out of my condo! Get out! Get out!"

"I swear, Fallon—I was close to doing it anyway! It was just a matter of timing."

"If there's one thing you know I hate, Aksel King, it's people talking behind my back, especially with my family."

His face falls, but then he reddens as if emboldened by some revelation in his head. His mouth curls into a cruel smirk.

"Fallon, for fuck's sake, you've been harboring a fugitive in your basement, and by the looks of it, you've been torturing the shit out of him. So I hardly think you're in a position to lecture people about keeping secrets!"

His words slash at me. He wasn't meant to know the true extent of my darkness. He wasn't meant to come face to face with Harvey fucking Maxwell.

And I don't intend on stopping. So this isn't going to work. It can't work.

"You know what, Aksel? Fuck you and fuck your stupid proposal." I yank off the ring and throw it at his feet. It bounces awkwardly and then settles against his shoe. He bends down and picks up the sparkling diamond ring that I know he picked out so carefully for me. Part of me feels like an asshole, discarding it cruelly at his feet, knowing that action would hurt him, but it also makes me feel good. A moment to inflict emotions onto someone else, even if they're painful. Just because I can.

How dare he and my father think they can control me? Control my life? I'll show them both. I'll show them all.

"Fallon, please—".

"Get out! The engagement is off. And believe me, if you speak to anyone about what you've seen down here, I'll make it my life's mission to destroy you."

He shrugs and shakes his head. "I don't know what to say," he says as he makes his way up the basement stairs, leaving me alone in the basement with my captive. "But I hope you find whatever it is you're searching for."

Aksel

A week after our fight, Fallon's father corners me outside my office. "What the hell did you do to my daughter?" he demands. Given his palatial commercial space is on the other side of the city, it's pretty obvious he made a special trip out of his way just to see me and deliver his message.

I eye him coolly. "I'm afraid that's between Fallon and myself. And if you'd let me know you were coming, I'd have arranged lunch."

He grabs my arm, rage etched into the lines of his face. "She won't stop crying. She's a mess over you. Now you're going to tell me exactly what happened, or I'll—"

"You'll what?" I ask softly. "Assault me? I wouldn't recommend that. I have my attorneys on speed dial. In fact, I suggest you let go of my arm right now."

His face purples, but he releases me, pushing my arm away and clearing his throat. I straighten my sleeve, unruffled. "If you must know, Fallon broke off our engagement. It wasn't my choice, and I'd give anything to still be engaged to her. But I also realize I hurt her, and I respect your daughter's wishes. Now if you'll excuse me, I have work to do."

I start to walk away, but he calls after me, "This is your fault, you bastard! I never should have pushed her to marry you. My little girl deserves so much better than the likes of you! I was settling, thinking you were anywhere near good enough for my princess!"

I pause, anger simmering under my skin. He's right—Fallon deserves better. Better than the man I am, better than the life I can offer her. If she knew half the things I've done in the course of my work, she'd probably want nothing to do with me. Although her recent kidnapping escapade gives me pause. Maybe there's even more to her than meets the eye, which is saying a lot. Either way, she deserves perfection and I ain't it.

But regardless of how hopeless things feel right now, nothing changes the fact that she is mine. A better man might let her go, release her in the knowledge there's someone out there better for her. But I'm not a better man. And I don't give up what's mine without a fight.

The ring sits in its box in my condo, glinting under the dim light like a promise broken.

I told myself it was for the best. Then I told myself that Fallon would come to her senses and realize we're meant to be together. But it's been weeks now, and with each passing day, she slips further out of my reach.

I can't lose her. I won't.

Maybe this was her plan all along. To break my heart as revenge for when I broke hers.

Maybe she thinks she's won, that she's broken me. But she has no idea what I'm capable of. No idea the lengths I'll go to in order to claim what's mine.

Always and forever, for better or for worse. Even if I have to drag her kicking and screaming to the altar to make it so.

Chapter 86

FALLON

Aksel's first call comes an hour after I tell him it's over. I stare at his name flashing on my phone, heart pounding, fingers itching to answer. But I can't. I won't.

I call Mom instead. I'm not sure why, because she's not exactly reliable, but for whatever reason she's the one I reach out to in the most fraught moments.

She picks up on the first ring. "Fallon? What's wrong?"

Her voice is ragged, scratchy from years of chain smoking. I picture her in her dim living room, curled up on the moth-eaten sofa with a cigarette dangling from her lips, her signature floral mu'umu'u wrapped around her bony frame. She's scrawny, subsisting on a life-long diet of mixed candy, strong coffee, and a nightly dessert of vodka, valium and orange juice.

"It's over with Aksel." My throat tightens around the words.

Silence. Then a long exhale of smoke. "Come right over. I'll be waiting for you."

She hangs up. I pace the length of my bedroom, anger and grief warring inside me. Aksel destroyed us, and shattered my heart into a million pieces. I should hate him.

But I can't. I love him too much.

I quickly grab some things and get to her place within the hour. Her hug smells of nicotine and Chanel No. 5, a discordant combination that is uniquely her. Her apartment smells like mothballs and spilled vodka. But I'm not here to judge, I'm here for my mommy.

I cling to her, tears burning my eyes. She smoothes my hair and murmurs soothing words.

When my sobs quiet, she pulls back. "I'm sorry, hon. I know how much you loved him." Her eyes are soft with sympathy.

I stare at her, stunned. She isn't gloating. Isn't saying I told you so. Who is this woman? "You—I didn't realize you even knew how much I—."

She smiles gently. "I may not have approved of Aksel since all the way back in high school, but I know he made you happy. And that's all I ever wanted for you, Fallon. It sounded like you two were really working things out this time around."

Fresh tears fill my eyes. She wipes them away with her calloused, bony thumbs.

"You're going to be okay," she says. "This hurts now, but the pain will fade. You're strong, Fallon. Stronger than any man. And there will be others who will love you for who you are. People in Aksel's world come with conditions, and sometimes you need to cut your losses, like I did. But I'll be here for you either way. You've got this, my strong girl."

I cling to her words like a lifeline, hoping with all my heart that she's right.

Aksel

Carson stares at me, his eyes wide behind his glasses, disbelief etched into every line of his face. Our hands are covered in flour and dough, in an attempt to create our own homemade pizzas from scratch. Not that I'm in the mood for tomfoolery, but my siblings insisted, a transparent attempt to get me out of this funk. And they don't know the half of it, and just think Fallon and I had one of our usual tiffs. Flour is smeared across Carson's face, the aftermath of a minor food fight between him and his sister.

"You did what?" My siblings pause, freeze-frame, swiveling in my direction, mouths agape.

I rake a hand through my hair, the familiar gesture doing nothing to ease my frustration.

"I broke off the engagement with Fallon. Well, technically she did, but it was mutual in the circumstances."

"But why?" Roxy demands. "You two were so happy together!"

"We weren't happy," I snap. "Not really. Our relationship was built on lies. I should have been honest with Fallon from the start. We're both just as guilty, it turns out she was keeping a whole lot from me. Important stuff, and when I found out I realized she's not even close to being the person I thought she was. The woman I thought I was in love with. Real love can't be built on a fake foundation, and fake love never lasts."

"Oh, Aksel." Roxy's eyes soften with sympathy. She reaches for my hand but I pull away.

"Don't. I don't deserve your pity." I glance at the abomination she's creating, jalapeños and pineapple and mushrooms and a ton of garlic. "Unlike your pizza." I try to joke my way out of the serious conversation.

"That's not pity," Raine says quietly. "That's love and support for our brother who's going through a difficult time." She giggles, "although I agree with you about Roxy's pizza!"

"Hey!" Roxy places her hands on her hips and juts out her bottom lip, giving me flashbacks of when she used to pull exactly the same expression back in elementary school.

I stare at my siblings, gratitude and sorrow twisting in my chest. They may drive me crazy, but they're here for me when I need them most.

"I'm beyond sorry for how I treated Fallon, just so you know," I say softly. "I'm not some kind of asshole, or monster, like others would have you believe. The truth is, she deserved so much better than that, both back in high school and more recently. I shouldn't have kept so many secrets from her. But then she was keeping some really dark things from me, too."

"Yeah, she did deserve better, for you to be transparent." Carson's gaze is stern. "You really screwed up, big bro. Back then, which is more forgivable because you were young, and then more recently you went and screwed up all over again, which is less easily explained. But the important thing is you've realized that. Now follow your own advice and, like you've always taught me, do what you need to do to make things right."

I nod. But a gnawing feeling in my gut tells me I think this time we're really done for good. That this time it's too late.

Fallon

Zara is waiting in the foyer when I arrive at the Dempsey estate, worry creasing her forehead.

"Fallon, I'm so sorry to hear about you and Aksel." Her eyes gleam with sympathy, not malice.

I gape at her, stunned. She's never missed an opportunity to get a dig in, yet here she is offering what appears to be genuine comfort.

"Thank you," I say cautiously. I was surprised when she invited me over, out of sync with our typical weekly family dinner cadence. I suspected she wanted me to spill the tea on the breakup so she can share the details with her gossipy friends. But from the way she's speaking, it sounds like authentic concern. Talk about disconcerting.

She smiles and squeezes my arm. "I know we've had our differences in the past, but I care about you, Fallon. You're family, and family supports each other through heartbreak and pain."

Tears prick my eyes at her unexpected kindness.

"Aksel made a huge mistake," she continues, "but this says more about him than it does about you. You're strong, smart, and caring. Any man would be lucky to have you."

I blink back tears, overwhelmed by her words. Maybe Zara and I can move past our differences. Maybe we can even become friends.

"I will warn you though... your father is a little heated right now. And he's expecting to see you in his study the moment you arrive."

Zara has never ever given me a heads up about my dad and his volatile temperament. In fact, at times I think she's enjoyed sending me, unwitting, into the lion's den with an ill-timed cup of coffee or tumbler of whiskey. But today, she's choosing to warn me. Interesting. I'll take it, any shred of potential kindness is both welcome and needed.

"Thank you," I whisper. "That means a lot."

She pulls me into a hug, and for the first time, despite the noxious fumes of her vanilla and apricot body spray that everyone else stopped wearing back in high school, I don't feel like pushing her away.

My father's study door is closed when I walk by, angry shouts filtering through the thick oak. I pause outside, dread curling in my gut. This won't be pleasant.

I knock softly and push the door open. "Dad?"

He whirls around, his face contorted with rage. "I have to go, my daughter is finally here." He clicks off his phone call and he lifts his gaze to meet mine. His eyes are flashing. "How dare you ruin this for our family? For the company? Do you have any idea how much damage you've caused?"

Anger and hurt swell inside me. "I didn't do anything wrong, Dad. Aksel broke up with me, not the other way around." Not entirely true, but he played a major part in it.

"Don't give me that bullshit," he growls. "Spin it however you want, but this is your fault, Fallon. If you weren't so goddamn selfish and irresponsible—and *impulsive*, the Kings wouldn't have backed out of this deal I was trying to do with them. They're using you as an excuse to pull the escape hatch. Now get out of my sight before I say something I regret."

I stare at him, stunned into silence. He can't seriously blame me for this. I did everything he asked to secure this merger, compromising my values and aspirations in the process. It took time and effort and regret. And for what? To have him tear me down at every opportunity?

The hurt and anger curdle into something harder and colder. Something that tastes a lot like vengeance. Because I know, deep inside, that no matter what I do, it will never be enough for my father.

My body suddenly radiates with shivers. I try to still the trembling. I'm hot and cold at the same time as I realize I haven't addressed the biggest issue. And yet my father has the audacity to play things off as if they're all my fault.

"I can't believe you told him to propose to me, Dad! That I was just some business transaction to you."

He's unruffled, as if he was expecting me to come to him with this realization. "It was the right thing to do for both of our families, Fallon. I'm sure it would have happened at some point, anyway." He frowns. "That is, if you hadn't gone ahead and fucked it up the same way you fuck up everything else."

"There we go, any opportunity to call your only daughter a fuckup. I didn't have to wait very long for that old chestnut to come out."

"Well, I call things like I see them," he shrugs. "And in this case, you've once again put your selfish wants over what's best for the family, Fallon. Why am I not surprised?" He looks down his nose at me like I just flunked a minor high school quiz. Not as if I just found out my fiancé was a lying, cheating betrayer of my trust.

"Well, Dad, I hope your precious company was worth sacrificing your daughter for," I say softly. "Because you've lost me for good this time."

I turn on my heel and stalk out, ignoring his shouted curses behind me. He's not the only one who can storm out of conversations to prove a point. Our family is broken, but for the first time, I feel free, and like I truly have nothing to lose.

Chapter 87

FALLON

I take a deep breath and walk into the dining room. The chatter dies as eight pairs of eyes turn to me. I grip the back of the empty chair, my knuckles turning white. Despite my argument with my father, I still feel obligated to show up at this god-awful recurring event. It's not all about him, anyway.

Cheston clears his throat. "Fallon, come sit. Dinner's ready."

I avoid Link's glare and sink into the chair. The tension makes the room suffocating.

Zara passes the mashed potatoes. "So, Fallon, how's work?"

"Fine." I stab a potato, imagining it's Link's smug face.

"Fallon's too busy with her new boyfriend to work," Link says.

My hand clenches around the fork. "That's not true. I do not have a new boyfriend." I know he's trying to goad me, and it's working.

"Oh, really?" Link leans forward. "Then why haven't you been home until midnight all week?"

"Because I've been working. Not that it's any of your business. How would you know that, anyway? Did you hire another private investigator?"

"It is my business when that bastard is taking advantage of my sister."

"The last person I was with was Aksel, and he's not like that! And I broke up with him. You know that." I shout, throwing my fork down, instantly protective of Aksel, which surprises even myself. It clatters across the table and comes to a stop near Link.

Cheston's hand closes over my wrist. "Calm down." His warning tone does nothing to soothe my anger.

"Good one, Cheston," I growl, even though he's only trying to help. "That expression has never calmed anyone down. Like ever."

Link points his knife at me. "I don't want that lowlife anywhere near you."

I yank my arm from Cheston's grip and stand. "You don't control me or who I date!"

"Sit down, both of you," my father snaps. "And put down your knife, Link. Stop being ridiculous."

I glare at Link. "You need to accept that I was with Aksel, and that maybe this isn't the end of us." Again, my words surprise me. "If you can't, then stay the hell away from me."

Tensions rise again over dessert, the bitterness of the espresso in the decadent tiramisu aligned with the expression on my brothers' faces. Link's gaze bores into me, his jealousy palpable.

"So, did you have a good time with Aksel the other night?" His tone is biting, meant to provoke.

I clench my fork, heat flooding my cheeks. "That's none of your business."

"Oh, come on, sis. We're family. We share everything, remember?"

"Not this." I stare at my plate, my appetite gone. I can feel the others' eyes on me, judging. Pitying.

"Why so secretive?" Link presses. "What are you hiding?"

"Leave her alone." Rayner's sharp voice cuts in. She and Wren are the only ones at the table on my side. The rest stay silent, not wanting to draw Link's anger.

Link scoffs. "This is ridiculous. She can't date that guy and expect me to be okay with it."

"You don't get a say in who Fallon sees." Wren levels Link with a stern look.

Link slams his fist on the table, rattling the dishes. "The hell I don't! Jesus, it feels like all you females are ganging up on me! And you, Cheston." He narrows his eyes at our brother.

"That's enough." My father stands, his shoulders back in a rare show of authority that he reserves for the most serious of situations. "Leave Fallon's relationship status alone. Change the subject or get out."

Shock ripples through the room. No one speaks to Link like that except his father. His face reddens, rage in his eyes. But he stays silent, accepting the reprimand. For now.

The rest of the meal passes in stiff silence. But I feel a spark of hope. Not all is lost. I still have allies in this family, including two new ones. And I'm no longer alone in the fight against Link.

I push away from the table as chairs scrape back. I need air, space, away from the tension and judgment.

Without waiting for a response, I race out of the room, ignoring the calls for me to come back. My family is suffocating me, but this whole interaction has made me realize I haven't really given up on Aksel. And I'm beginning to think that maybe I never will. Not for them. Not for anyone.

Fenton catches up to me and grabs my arm as I step out onto the balcony, the night air bringing a refreshing reprieve from the stifling atmosphere of the dining room. "You okay?" His gaze holds concern and something more, a silent offer of support.

I nod, throat tight. "Just need some air."

He squeezes my arm and lets go. "I'm here if you want to talk."

His quiet promise nearly undoes me. I blink back tears and escape further outside.

The cool night air caresses my face, soothing my frayed nerves. In the shadows of the yard, I draw a shaky breath.

Footsteps crunch on the gravel behind me. I stiffen, preparing for another round with Link.

"It's just me." Wren comes to stand beside me, slipping an arm around my waist. "I'm worried about you."

I sigh, leaning into my newish friend. "I'll be okay. It's just Link..."

"He's out of line." Wren's arm tightens. "Don't let him get to you. You deserve to be happy. I'm here for you, Fallon. Whatever you need."

I blink against the sting in my eyes. "Thank you. I don't know what I'd do without you."

"You'll never have to find out. We're sisters now." Wren gives me a gentle squeeze. "Are you coming back in?"

I shake my head. "I should get home."

Wren nods. "Call me if you want to talk more."

"I will." I force a smile, grateful for the unwavering support. Not all is lost, as long as I have Wren and Rayner on my side. And maybe Fenton, if I'm reading him right. Maybe it won't be Fallon against the world anymore, at least not at these family dinners.

I drive home through the dark, heart lighter than before. The battle isn't over, but I'm no longer fighting alone. My family might be broken, but I've found the tribe that can help me pull it back together in a new form.

Chapter 88

AKSEL

I pace outside my grandmother's expansive estate, my boots crunching on the gravel. The demands of my family, of Fallon, they're suffocating me. I need to breathe. I need someone to tell me what the hell I'm supposed to do.

I knock once and let myself in. The scent of cinnamon and nutmeg wafts from the kitchen. "Grandmother?"

"In here, Aksel dear." Her voice is gentle, soothing, a far cry from the deeper voice that manifests itself during ruthless boardroom meetings. I find her stirring a pot at the stove, her silver hair pinned neatly at the nape of her neck. As usual, she's wearing a custom-tailored suit, but this time it's underneath a frilly gingham apron. The juxtaposition of my formidable Grandmother in the underground world where she made a name for herself in a city full of ruthless men, and the traditional grandmother who bakes pies and roasts dinners and knits the occasional scarf for her great-grandchildren, is jarring and amusing.

"I didn't know you were cooking." Guilt washes over me. I should have offered to help.

She waves me off, her bracelets jangling. "You have enough on your mind. Besides, it's been a nice distraction. Allowed me to think about some really serious business problems. Now, tell me what's troubling you. And take a seat. Your hovering is making me uncomfortable."

I slump into a chair at the table, dropping my head into my hands. "Fallon. My family. They all want something from me. I can't give Fallon what she needs, and I don't think you'll ever accept her."

Grandmother sits across from me, her eyes soft with understanding. "You're torn in too many directions. But this is not like you, Aksel. You've always done what needed to be done, no matter the cost, for the good of the family. And you should go back to doing things from that perspective. By the same token, if you really love this girl—and I'm beginning to think you do—you should be making decisions that are the best for both of you."

Her words strike deep. She's right. I've been selfish, only thinking of my own needs.

"Fallon is a good woman, Aksel. Strong, smart, caring. Don't let your family's prejudices ruin what you have found. Including my own." She reaches across the table, squeezing my hand. "Do what's right, not what's easy. Apologize to her. Take responsibility for your actions. If she's the right lady for you, she *will* understand."

"But you told me to watch out for her, and not to trust her."

"That's before I realized how happy she makes you, Aksel. If I'm honest with myself, I was holding her responsible for things that happened before her time." Her eyes soften. "And you're a different person when she's around. You come alive. That has to be saying something." She squeezes both my hands together, making me feel like a little boy going to collect her fresh baking from her bustling kitchen.

Of course. Fallon has always understood me in a way no one else could. My grandmother is right. I need to make this right. I stand, filled with purpose. "Thank you, Grandmother. You've given me clarity." I kiss her cheek.

"You're welcome, Aksel dear. Now go, before she slips through your fingers."

A smile tugs at my lips as I head for the door. Fallon won't be slipping through my fingers again.

Chapter 89

FALLON

Raine pulls me into her arms, and I collapse against her, tears spilling onto her shoulder. There's something so comforting about this woman, even though Aksel is her brother.

"Shh," she whispers, stroking my hair. "It's going to be okay."

Her warmth seeps into my skin, thawing the ice in my veins. I take a shuddering breath, breathing in the scent of vanilla and cinnamon.

"I'm so sorry about everything," she says softly.

I swallow the lump in my throat and pull back, wiping my eyes. "It's not your fault."

Raine pulls back, smoothing a lock of hair from my face. "Aksel only brought Grave into your life to protect you, Fallon. Because he loves you so much, even when he thought you hated him."

I frown, the mention of Grave's name bringing a bitter taste to my mouth. "He had no right to make that decision for me. To put a hitman in my path without my consent."

"No, he didn't," Raine agrees. "But you have to understand, Aksel has always been an overprotective fool when it comes to you. He saw Grave as a way to guarantee your safety when he couldn't be there himself." A wry smile twists her lips. "Not that it excuses him lying to you. Or manipulating you. He definitely has a lot to make up for."

My chest clenches at the sound of his name. "By betraying me and spying on me? It's like he found the opportunity to get closer to me than basically anyone else. How do I know he wasn't manipulating me the whole time? Do I even love the guy, or has he just used Grave to find out what he needed to weasel his way back into my life?"

She shakes her head. "I know Aksel's heart. He's a good man. He cares about you so much, he really just wanted to keep you safe."

I stare at our joined hands, remembering the warmth in Aksel's eyes when he looked at me, and the gentleness in his touch. Could it really have been borne of love and not manipulation?

"And what about conspiring with my dad behind my back? Of following my dad's instructions to propose to me? He knows how much I detest the obligations I already have to my family, and then he takes this thing—this one very personal thing that is meant to be *mine—ours*—and he takes that thing and gives all the power to *my father*! The man who already controls everything in my life."

Raine squeezes my hands. "I know that hurt you deeply, and I understand how it must have felt." She pauses and her gaze locks onto mine. "You once told me love comes in many forms, some of them dark and twisted. But at its heart, real love is about caring for another person and wanting what's best for them." Her lips curve into a soft smile. "Aksel has always wanted that for you. He just went about it the wrong way."

Her words sink in, and I realize she's right. As much as Aksel's actions infuriate me, they were motivated by love and a desire to protect me—however misguided. And if our positions were reversed, wouldn't I have done the same to keep him safe?

And as for colluding with my father? I can see that he probably wanted to impress his father-in-law, and get in his good graces before marrying his one and only daughter. I have no doubt in my mind that Aksel meant what he said, that he intended to propose to me and that I wouldn't have had to wait long. If I'm going to be mad at someone, it really should be my interfering dad.

I sigh, pinching the bridge of my nose. "I don't know if I can forgive him. Not yet. But..." I meet Raine's gaze, a fragile hope blooming in my chest. "Perhaps in time, we can find our way back to each other. If he's willing to earn my trust again."

Raine's answering smile is bright enough to chase away the lingering darkness. "I know Aksel would walk through fire itself for another chance with you." She stands, pulling me into a quick hug.

As the anger and hurt begin to fade, they leave behind a bone-deep exhaustion. But beneath it lingers a spark of hope. If what Raine says is true, perhaps Aksel and I can get back on track. Perhaps love can overcome even the darkest of places.

I meet Raine's gaze again, a smile tugging at my lips. "Thank you. For helping me see the truth."

"That's what sisters are for." She pulls me into another hug, and this time, I cling to her just as tightly.

"Now, how about some tea?" She pauses, a cheeky grin forming. "And in the back of my mind, I wonder if once again soon we might have a wedding to plan!"

Laughing, I let her pull me to my feet, the future suddenly seeming brighter than before. There may be a long road ahead, full of pain and obstacles to overcome—but as long as I have Raine's sisterly support, and Aksel's love to guide me, I know we'll make it through to the other side.

Chapter 90

AKSEL

My gaze drifts to the yellowed newspaper clippings plastered across my office wall, remnants of my family's shady dealings. We've always straddled the line of the law, never hesitating to get our hands dirty. As far as the articles are concerned, there's a perverse family tradition of slapping any mention of our family name up on the wall right after it's published. Good, bad, it doesn't matter—any publicity is good publicity really should be the King family motto.

My stomach churns with guilt. How could I judge Fallon for seeking her own brand of justice when I've benefited from the same darkness? Trafficking of drugs, human organs, entire humans. Violence, assaults, abuse. Extortion, espionage, fraud. And murder, when necessary. Sometimes even when not necessary. They're all standard parts of the King family business, and those we have dealings with, so who am I to judge?

My revelations about my own hypocrisy roil my stomach. Whether it's because Fallon is a woman, or because she struck out on her own, something rubbed me the wrong way when I heard about her dark pursuits. But they're not any different from what takes place every day under my leadership, except done with better intentions.

Jumping to my feet, I gather a few things and race over to Fallon's place, my heart pounding. She opens the door, her eyes more wary than shocked by my arrival. "What do you want?"

"Fallon, I'm so sorry. I had no right to judge you." The words tumble out in a rush. "My family's done terrible things too, including me personally. I was blinded by my anger and jealousy. I never should've turned my back on you. I never should have let you break off the engagement."

Her eyes narrow, but she doesn't slam the door in my face. A good sign. I plunge ahead. "You're the only light in my dark world. Losing you was the biggest mistake of my life. I don't deserve your forgiveness, but I'm begging for another chance. And I know it's not the first chance I'm asking for, but it will be the last chance, I swear."

Silence. Then, "You really hurt me, Aksel." Her voice wavers. "How do I know you won't throw me away again? How do I know you won't let me throw myself away? Us?"

"I was an idiot." My voice is pleading. "Please, Fallon, I love you with all my heart. I'll spend the rest of my life making it up to you, if you give me the chance." I reach for her hands, relief flooding me when she doesn't pull away. "There's so much darkness in both our lives, but together, we can beat it. You're my redemption, Fallon. My salvation. You always have been."

A tear slides down her cheek. She whispers, "I never stopped loving you."

My heart soars. I envelop her in my arms, clinging to her like she's my lifeline. We have a long road ahead, full of demons to face, but as long as we face them together, I know we'll make it out the other side.

Fallon

I cling to Aksel, emotions warring inside me. Part of me wants to believe he's changed, that we can have another chance at happiness. But the other part fears he'll break my heart again. And I know that I wouldn't survive.

Aksel pulls back to gaze into my eyes. "Talk to me, Fallon. I can see the doubts in your eyes."

I swallow hard. "How do I know you won't leave me again when things get tough? When your family causes trouble or my past comes back to haunt us?"

"I'm not going anywhere." He cups my face, his thumb brushing over my cheek. "We've both made mistakes. We both have darkness inside us. But, as long as we're brutally honest with each other about everything, we can beat our demons together. I'm ready to face any challenge, as long as you're by my side. We just need to tell each other the truth."

His words melt the ice around my heart. He's right—we've both struggled and stumbled. I can't blame him for my past, just as he can't blame me for his family's sins. If we want to move forward, we have to let go of the bitterness and forgive. And we do have to be honest.

"I'm tired of living in darkness," I whisper. "I want to change. To be better. For you, and for us."

"You're already the light that guides me home." Aksel kisses me then, a sweet, tender kiss full of promise. "Together, we'll find the light again. I know it."

A spark of hope ignites inside me. We have a long road ahead, full of obstacles and shadows. But Aksel's right—if we face them together, hand in hand, we can embrace the best parts of our darkness while also finding the light.

We drive north along the coast into the night, stopping whenever the mood strikes us. The farther we get from the city, the more the tension eases from Aksel's shoulders. He smiles and laughs, winding his fingers through mine as we walk along secluded beaches. At night, we make love with the windows open, the crash of the waves outside mingling with our sighs. We wake up to the sunrise, wrapped in each other's arms.

It's a side of Aksel I've never seen before, carefree and playful, and not a work phone or laptop in sight. The shadows seem to lift from his eyes a little more each time we laugh. I find myself opening up too, sharing stories from my past I've never told anyone. The secrets that once seemed too dark and ugly to voice don't seem so terrible when Aksel listens without judgment, wrapping me in his arms and pressing soft kisses to my hair.

We spend our day exploring little coastal towns, browsing kitschy shops and trying every flavor of saltwater taffy. Aksel wins me a stuffed bear at an arcade, popping quarters into rigged carnival games until he finally emerges victorious. I suspect he bribed the pimply teenager in charge of the game, but I don't press him on it. I drag him onto a rickety Ferris wheel as the sun sinks below the horizon, kissing him at the top of the wheel with the sea and sky stretching endlessly before us.

It's strange and wonderful, getting to discover each other all over again. The Aksel I once knew, and the Fallon he remembered, seem like different people. We're older now, a lot wiser, a lot more scarred. But underneath it all, our connection remains. Stronger, even, tempered by time and loss and heartbreak. Like the tide, it pulls us back together, as inevitable and endless as the rolling sea.

We drive back, a fantasy date over, ready to confront our day-to-day lives. The same, but different. This time, the two of us, together. Unbreakable.

Chapter 91

FALLON

The ache in my chest is almost unbearable as I watch Aksel walk towards me. It's hard to believe that now I'm officially his, and, despite how fucked up it is, there's nowhere else I'd rather be. We've had busy weeks with work, so it's been seven long days since I've been in his arms, since I've felt his lips on mine.

He stops in front of me, his eyes piercing through my soul as he searches for something. Whatever it is, he sees it because he smirks, a mix of lust and something darker that makes my stomach twist. I revel in that smile, the one that could light up a room and break hearts. But the heart-breaking stage of his life is over, or so he claims. And I really want nothing more than to believe him.

"You look beautiful," he says, taking in my little black dress that hugs my curves, and my heels that make me taller than him for once. "And I've missed you."

I roll my eyes. "Yeah, well, you look hot too." I swallow hard. "Shouldn't we be getting inside?"

He nods and takes my hand, leading me to the car. The touch sends shockwaves through my body—it's both comforting and terrifying.

Inside the car, Aksel starts the engine and turns up the music, complementing the hum of the city around us. The leather seats squeak under my bare legs as I shift closer to him, trying to ignore how good his body feels pressed against mine.

He pulls the car into traffic, his free hand brushing against my knee. I stifle a gasp at the electric shock that runs up my spine, but I let him feel it. I want him to feel it.

At the club, the neon lights hit us hard, and I squint against the harshness of it all. People stare as we walk in, heads turning to check out Aksel King. They don't know what we've been through, what secrets we share. It all seems so surreal, like a movie playing out too fast.

Once inside, he leads me to a VIP room with a bottle of whiskey waiting. He hands me a glass, his fingers grazing my knuckles as he does so. I take a sip—it burns going down but cools my nerves somewhat. He watches me intently, making me feel both wanted and scared shitless.

I take another sip of the burning liquid, feeling my nerves melt away under its influence just as he leans in closer—our bodies barely touching yet it's like we're already tangled up in bed together.

"I knew you'd want to do this with me. Our story isn't over yet," he murmurs against my skin, sending shivers down my spine. And then he kisses me—hard and hungry on the mouth. His tongue dives deep, wrestling with mine, as if he's been waiting for this moment just as much as I have. A groan escapes from his throat when I open up for him.

His hands move up my thighs and under my dress, teasingly skimming my lace-covered panties as we break for air. "You're still the only one who can handle all of me, Fallon," he whispers hoarsely, gripping my hips tightly.

His fingers slip inside me, pushing through my pussy lips, seeking more of my juices. It feels so good to be touched by him again that all rational thought leaves my mind. I press closer, moaning into his mouth when he finds my g-spot and starts to rub in circles. "Aksel," I breathe out, arching my back—wanting more.

"We should go... we should go... home," I pant, grinding against his palm. Jesus, at this rate I'm going to come right here in the VIP booth. The music is good, but all I can think about is Aksel being inside me.

He laughs darkly against my lips before pulling away. "Too easy," he taunts, his voice rough with lust.

He yanks his phone out of his pocket and presses a button. Over a brief, muffled call he requests the driver pull his car around as soon as possible.

The driver meets us out front in less than two minutes, and he expertly drops us at a trendy boutique hotel less than an hour later. Faster than getting to Aksel's or my place. We rush inside, Aksel pulling me behind him and depositing me on a very comfortable couch.

And then he's unbuttoning my dress, kissing his way down my collarbone and chest, stopping at my breasts. His teeth graze my nipple softly, making me gasp. My back arches off the couch in response. He pulls at my panties, tossing them aside before taking my aching clit into his mouth. I cry out loudly, hands fisting in his hair as he sucks and tugs gently.

"Fuck, Aksel!" I gasp, throwing my head back. He plunges two fingers inside me, filling me up, and I come on his tongue with a scream.

When he stands up, I'm left panting and needy, staring at him through heavy-lidded eyes. He smirks wickedly, undoing his pants and revealing his hard cock straining against his boxer briefs. He steps in close, pushing me back onto the couch so I'm lying down. "Take off your dress," he demands roughly.

I shake my head slightly, not wanting to comply but unable to resist. My fingers fumble with the buttons and zipper until my dress falls to the floor, leaving me in just my bra. He kneels between my legs again, kissing my stomach and teasing my inner thighs with his hot breath. I whimper, needing more.

Finally, he positions his cock at my entrance and pushes inside me slowly, groaning as he slides in, inch by delicious inch. I gasp again at the fullness, arching my back to beg for more. He starts thrusting, hard and deep, his hips meeting mine in a rhythm that matches the jackhammer of my heart. We fuck like this until we both climax, me screaming his name and him biting my shoulder to muffle his primal roar.

Afterward, we order room service: steak, potatoes, and a bottle of red wine. The waiter leaves, and Aksel locks the door behind him. I'm left panting, feeling both satisfied and anxious as he pulls me into his lap. We share a glass of champagne, the bubbles cool and tingly around my tongue. I lean into his chest as he traces circles with his thumb around my earlobe, making me shiver.

He leans in to whisper, "You're mine, you know that?"

A familiar shiver runs down my spine, but I don't pull away. I can't help but feel both scared and turned on by his possessiveness. He kisses my neck, and I melt into him like hot chocolate on snow. Our bodies fit together perfectly, our hearts syncing up like a well-rehearsed dance.

We devour the steak with a hunger that matches our passion, each bite sending electricity through us. The potatoes are mashed, creamy and salty, adding a much-needed texture to balance out the strong flavors of the steak. Aksel feeds me a piece of beef and watches as I chew, like watching me eat is the most captivating thing he's ever seen. Weird,

I know, but no man is perfect.

Then he stands up abruptly and grabs the champagne bottle. He arranges pillows neatly at the back of the bed, puffing them up against the headboard, and carefully tilts me back so my tits are pointing skyward. He pours it over my chest, letting it drip down my cleavage and between my breasts, dripping onto my stomach. My breath hitches as the cool bubbles hit my warm skin.

"You want more?" He asks, his voice husky.

I nod eagerly, not wanting to deny him anything. He pulls away the bottle and kisses his way down my body, trailing his tongue along the path of the golden liquid. He flicks his tongue over my nipple, sending shockwaves straight to my core. I whimper when he pulls my panties down with his teeth and begins to suck on them, tugging gently.

He looks up at me with hooded eyes. "Still wet for me, Fallon-y?" He glances down at himself, his cock already hard again.

I swallow hard and nod. "Always."

He positions my legs around his hips and thrusts into me, moaning into my neck as he pumps harder and harder. I wrap my arms around him, nails digging into his back. His cock feels like it was made for me, a fraction too big so that he drags the length of my walls, my pussy suctioned to him, craving him even as he's inside me.

His lips move up to my ear, his hot breath sending chills down my neck. "You belong here, underneath me, taking my cock like a good girl."

The words fuel my desire. I suck in air as he picks up the pace, slamming into me again and again. Our bodies slap together in a rhythm that feels primal and forbidden. We groan in unison, our love for each other mixed with our hatred and lust.

And then it hits me—he's right. I do belong to him, even when I hate him. Even when the journey is difficult. I'm his, always have been, always will be. This is the dark side of love, and I can't escape it.

I bite my bottom lip, trying to stifle my cries as the pleasure builds up inside me. Aksel's hands grip my hips, holding me down as he takes control once more. I'm nothing but very happy putty in his hands, his body pounding into mine, our sweat mingling on our skin. I feel every inch of him inside me, filling me up and making me whole.

"Come again for me, baby girl," he whispers against my ear, the huskiness of his voice sending shivers down my spine. "Show me how much you want this."

I clench around him, helping him find that release he longs for. My walls tighten, milking him as he growls and loses himself in me. Our lips crash together in a messy, needy kiss that tastes of lust and emotions that reflect the tumultuous journey of our relationship up to this point.

As he shudders above me, the bed groaning beneath us, I whisper hoarsely, "I hate you... but I need you."

He pulls out of me with a grunt and rolls over, pulling me on top of him. His eyes search mine, full of emotion that I can't quite decipher.

I lean down to kiss him again, trying to hide my confusion, my lips soft against his jaw. We breathe together, our hearts racing like two criminals who've just committed a crime.

He guides my hips back and forth, fingernails digging into my thighs as he watches me ride him with an intensity that makes my stomach flutter. I feel so desired, so wanted... so needed.

His cock throbs inside me, filling me up perfectly as our bodies align in a rhythm that promises more pleasure than pain.

Sweat drips down my forehead as I lean forward to take one of his nipples between my teeth, pulling on it gently. He moans softly, the sound vibrating against my lips.

"Fuck, you're killing me," he whispers, arching into the sensation. "I can't get enough of you. But I'm starting to get a little sore," he laughs.

In response, I slide down and start sucking his cock, taking it deep into my throat until I taste his salty skin on my tongue as well as my own arousal. His hips jerk up off the bed in surprise and his fingers dig into my hair.

"Fuck, Fallon," he growls, thrusting his hips up to meet my mouth, his breathing ragged.

I look up at him through my lashes, seeing the desire burning in his eyes.

We fall back onto the mattress together, panting hard, our chests rising and falling in unison.

He trails kisses down my body, tasting every inch of skin he can reach, leaving a trail of fire in his wake. When he reaches my core, he parts my pussy lips with his fingers and licks me slowly, teasingly.

I've come so many times already I doubt I'll be able to do it again so quickly. But within minutes my back is arching off the mattress as I shout his name, my latest orgasm crashing over me in waves. His name is a prayer on my lips as he devours me, lapping up every drop of my release.

I collapse on top of him, our sweat-slicked bodies sticking together. He rolls over, pinning me under his weight, his smile wicked as he whispers, "This is only the beginning."

His hands grip my hips tightly as he thrusts into me, claiming me once more as his own. Our rhythm is desperate and hungry, a feral growl rumbling from his chest with every powerful stroke. I come apart under him, screaming his name into the silence of our bedroom.

He shudders violently, filling me with his warmth before collapsing next to me, his chest heaving.

After a while, we fall into a fitful sleep, tangled up in each other's arms.

We wake up to the sun streaming through the windows, our limbs entangled. We crawl into the shower together, the hot water washing over us, steam rising around us. It's a rainforest shower, high pressure, and it feels like heaven against my skin. Aksel's hands explore every inch of my body, tracing patterns on my back, my stomach, my thighs. I let out a moan as he soaps up my breasts, his touch making me want more.

He grabs my hips and pulls me against his erection, my pussy lips parting to accommodate him. It hurts for a moment, but then he's inside me again, the soft sing a marker of the previous night where we barely slept. We fuck under the water, our movements slick and steady. His hands wrap around my neck, pulling me closer until our lips meet in yet another devouring kiss.

I taste myself on his tongue and it only makes me want him more.

Afterward, we step out of the shower and dry off together with thick, fluffy oversized towels, our bodies cooling quickly in the breeze. He drapes a towel around my shoulders, his eyes dark pools of lust.

We make love one last time on the bed, his thrusts deep and hard, like he's trying to claim me. My nails dig into his back, leaving red lines in its wake, but he doesn't flinch. In the end, he comes inside me, our hearts pounding against each other's chests. We lie entwined, our breathing slowing down.

"Aksel," I whisper, my voice hoarse. "I want you to know that I'm not just using you for revenge."

His eyes glint, full of mischief. "I didn't think you were. Especially after that performance." He smirks. "And if it makes you feel better, neither am I," he growls back.

I bite his neck, hard enough to draw blood. He groans, his hands finding mine, pulling them to his chest. "Fuck," he breathes out.

We lie in naked, companionable silence for a while, and then I feel his foot shaking the mattress.

"Fallon," He whispers, his voice rough with emotion. "You're mine."

"And you're mine," I whisper back, a feral grin spreading across my face.

"I can't imagine my life, my future, without you in it." Aksel trails his fingers down my arm, his touch featherlight. "I don't want to lose you again."

His words make my heart ache. I turn to face him, cupping his cheek. "You won't. I'm not going anywhere."

He presses his forehead against mine. "Promise?"

"I promise." I seal it with a kiss.

When we part, his eyes are shining. "I want to marry you, Fallon. I want to have a life with you, a family. I want it all."

My breath hitches. I never thought I'd hear those words from him, at least not quite like that.

"You're the only one for me," he continues quietly. "You always have been."

Tears well up in my eyes. I kiss him again, fiercely, pouring all my love and devotion into it. "I feel the same way."

Joy lights up his face. He rolls on top of me, kissing me with renewed passion. I wrap my legs around his waist, pulling him closer.

Our lovemaking is slow and tender this time. Whispered 'I love you's are exchanged, promises for the future, to never be apart again.

When we climax together, I feel whole again. Complete in a way I haven't been in years.

Aksel rests his head over my heart, his arms holding me close. I stroke his hair, thinking of rings and white dresses and maybe even babies with his eyes.

"Happy?" He asks softly.

"Beyond happy," I reply, meaning it with all my heart. "You're my always, Aksel. My forever."

He lifts his head to smile at me, his eyes shining with love and joy. "As you are mine, Fallon. As you are mine."

Chapter 92

FALLON

The phone rings, startling me from my brooding. I glance at the caller ID and see that it's Grave.

Great. Just what I need. A judgmental tough guy who I can no longer count on. Someone planted by Aksel to spy on me.

Please, I take a deep breath and answer. "Grave. What do you want?"

"Fallon, wait. Please just listen." His voice is strained, laced with desperation.

I grip the phone tighter, my knuckles turning white. "You have two minutes. Talk."

"I'm sorry about what happened. I never meant to hurt you or be dishonest in any way. I was hired to protect you and as soon as we started working together, I knew our partnership was meant to be. I never spied on you and reported back to Aksel or anything like that. To be honest, I'd basically forgotten that he had me cross paths with you in the first place."

His words hit me like a punch to the gut, reopening wounds that have barely begun to heal. I swallow the ache in my throat and remain silent. I believe what he's saying, but the way Aksel placed him in my life just feels so deceptive. Still, I can see that both of their intentions were good. I'm not a child that needs to be coddled, or a damsel in distress racing upstairs in a horror movie. I'm a grown ass woman with a revenge business. Conflicted is an understatement.

"Fallon, please. Say something. I can't lose you."

Too little too late. He made his choice, and now he has to live with the consequences.

"You've said enough," I snap. "Time's up."

I'm about to hang up when he speaks again, his voice barely above a whisper.

"Fallon. You're the closest thing I have to family. I love you as a sister... I always have."

I freeze, caught between fury and anguish, love and hate. My fingers tremble around the phone as a single tear slips down my cheek. I know words like this basically never leave his mouth. He's devoid of emotion, a robot. I know he means it.

But after everything he's done, how dare he say that now?

"Don't." My voice shakes. "Just...don't."

The line goes dead. I fling the phone across the room and collapse onto the floor, surrendering to the storm of emotions ravaging my soul.

The next day

My father summons us to an emergency family meeting. We gather in his lavish study, anxiety etched into every frown and furrowed brow.

Glancing around, I can see everyone else is feeling just as clueless about this meeting as I am.

Colton Dempsey stands before the unlit fireplace, hands clasped behind his back. His face is pale and drawn, aged beyond his years overnight. "I have a confession to make," he says heavily. "The fortune we built—it was never clean money. It's been making me feel really hypocritical in light of Fallon venturing out with her own business. I haven't really told this story before, although I'm sure you've heard whispers. Now, with everything going on, it feels like the right time to be up front with you all."

Shock ripples through the room. Skeletons tumble out of closets as my father admits how our wealth came to be—through underhanded business practices, financial scams and dealing drugs to addicts.

I stare at the luxe Persian rug, bile rising in my throat. How could he have hidden all of this? How could we be so blind to think our family just somehow innocently—deservedly came into massive intergenerational wealth? I feel like an idiot for never having questioned it, only resenting it for the burden of familial expectations that accompany it.

"I'm so sorry," Colton says hoarsely. "The greed for more power and money consumed me. I should have put our family first, but I failed you all. There are several things I could have put a stop to. But instead, I turned a blind eye, transfixed by the financial incentives. And now, I'm afraid, there's a chance we're going to be investigated by federal agents. They've started closing in on some of our closest associates, people who know our skeletons. It's only a matter of time until someone slips or trades our secrets in a plea deal. We'll control the narrative as much as we can, but things are bound to come out." He pauses. "Ironically, Fallon and Link may be the only Dempseys with viable companies at the end of all this."

No one speaks for what seems like minutes.

Cheston is the first to move. He strides over and embraces our father in a fierce hug. "You're still our father," he says gruffly. "We'll get through this together."

The rest of us follow suit, a tangled mess of tears and recriminations. But underneath the hurt and betrayal lies the faintest spark of hope—that we can rebuild what was broken, and forge new beginnings from the ashes of the past.

After the emotional upheaval subsides, I confront my father. "You have to stop interfering in my business," I tell him bluntly. "Let me run things my way."

To my surprise, Colton simply nods. "I see that now. You've proven yourself," he says. A wistful smile touches his lips. "I couldn't be prouder of the woman you've become. And your business—I took a closer look at some of the course content and, well—it's very impressive. I see potential for global syndication."

Warmth blooms in my chest at the unexpected praise. Perhaps we've turned a corner after all.

He pauses for a moment, as if deciding whether to go on.

"I've always been hard on you, Fallon. You're my only daughter. And you're smart, capable, and you have a habit of making life more difficult for yourself than it needs to be. So I don't regret it, other than to say I realize I've been pushing you harder than ever. Too hard."

I'm beginning to think my dad's body has been taken over by a pod person, so I just nod, trying to keep my own body still.

"Just remember we're here for you if you need us," Dad adds. "But your business and personal decisions are your own. I'll stop questioning you about every single thing. You've earned that right."

I hug him, blinking back tears. "Thank you, Dad," I whisper.

After so many years, I finally have my father's blessing. Now nothing can hold me back from forging my own path to success—on my own terms.

I leave the study with a lighter heart than I've had in years. The future is filled with promise and possibility, a blank canvas I'm free to paint as I choose.

Link catches up to me in the hallway, a hesitant smile on his face. "I'm glad you and Dad worked things out," he says. "You deserve to be happy."

"We all do," I reply. Perhaps it's time to bury the hatchet with my brother as well. We have too much history, too many shared memories, to stay estranged forever.

Link shifts his weight, visibly nervous. "Fallon, there's something I have to tell you," he blurts out. "About the family business. I've discovered some...irregularities. Things beyond what dad shared. Things that don't add up."

My senses heighten at his words. "Go on."

"Not here," Link says, casting a furtive glance around. "Meet me at the old treehouse at midnight. I'll explain everything."

With that, he strides off.

"Seriously? The tree house? At midnight?" I call after him. It sounds like a bad murder mystery plot. Surely there can't be more scandal within our family. What other scandals could the Dempsey empire possibly hold?

"Just kidding!" he calls back. I roll my eyes. The cheeky little shit. Some things never change.

Chapter 93

FALLON

Mia slides into the booth across from me, smoothing her skirt under her thighs. Her hair is shorter, choppier—it suits the new steel in her eyes.

"You look good," I say.

"So do you." Her gaze rakes over me, scrutinizing every last detail. "Success agrees with you."

I arch a brow. "What makes you think I'm successful?"

"You wouldn't have suggested this meeting otherwise."

She's right. My empowerment startup just got acquired for an obscene amount of money. But I'm not here to brag. This meeting is about friendship and doing the right thing.

"How's the MBA?" I ask, though I already know. I've kept tabs on Mia, like I said I would. She's averaging straight As and already has several companies courting her for summer internships and full-time jobs upon graduation.

"Almost done." She stirs her latte, shoulders tense. "Fallon, I know we're not here to discuss my course catalog. Why are we here?" She quirks a brow.

"I wanted to see you." It's the truth, as much as the other reasons, spiking my heart rate. "We didn't end things right. I know we made up, but... things definitely haven't gone back to anything like they were before. And I miss you. Of course I miss you at work, but more than that, I miss my friend."

She slashes a hand through the air. "I don't want to rehash the past. We've both moved on. And I don't want to sound crude or ungrateful, but I don't miss working with you at all. And I have really been focused on finding some, let's say... more reliable friends. It turns out they do exist and I don't need to settle."

Her words are like a slap in the face. I know I wasn't the best friend possible right before she quit, but I certainly wasn't the worst. "Then why are you here? Why did you agree to come?" I demand.

Silence. She worries her lip between her teeth.

Finally she meets my gaze, clearly hesitant to share whatever she's about to. "To tell you I'm getting married... to a woman. She's my everything."

My eyes widen. "Well, congratulations!" I narrow my brow. "Wait, what happened to Liam, the Montgomery guy? I thought you two were pretty hot and heavy."

"Oh, you know," she shrugs. "He turned out to be a snake, just like everyone else who works for that company. I should never have trusted anyone who would work for a place who goes up against the Dempseys." She gives a wry grin. "But you live, you learn. I brushed myself off and got right back on the dating bandwagon, and that's when I found the one for me."

"So who is this girl? Do I know her?"

"I wouldn't think so. Her name is Kirsty. We met at a place where I've been temping, and we've been inseparable ever since. You'd like her. She's funny, smart, beautiful. Reminds me a lot of you, in fact." Mia beams as she describes her fiancée. It's quick, but I'm not one to talk, and sometimes when you know, you know.

I smile back. "Well, I'd love to meet her one day. And I'm so happy for you! I need to give you a hug!" I jump up from my seat, moving around to Mia's side of the table and I squeeze her tightly, genuinely happy for my friend. "Congratulations, really. You deserve to be with someone who makes you very happy."

Chapter 94

FALLON

The knife glints in my hands, blood dripping off the tip onto Harvey's pale skin. He whimpers, clutching at the deep gash across his ribs.

My stomach churns as I stare at the mess I've made. How did I get here again?

Harvey was just supposed to be another job, another scumbag to bring to justice. But now he's bleeding out on the floor of my basement, begging for mercy. I was meant to let him go, but I haven't been able to bring myself to do it. Every time I try, something comes up or I manufacture an excuse. A reason to keep this man here one more day. It's like I've gotten used to his company, like some weird basement pet that I occasionally take pleasure in torturing. Aksel seemed to assume I'd let him go already, and I didn't correct him.

"Please," Harvey gasps. "I'll do anything. I have money. I can make you rich."

I press my lips together. He's right, I could use the money. But at what cost? If I let him buy his way out of this, how am I any better than the corrupt bastards I'm trying to take down? This isn't a financial exercise. This is about revenge. This is for Claudia.

The knife trembles in my grip as I wrestle with indecision. Do I end this now and release Harvey to face the legal consequences of his crimes, or do I give in to the temptations of profit and power?

My knuckles turn white around the hilt. The boundaries between justice and revenge have never seemed so blurry. But one thing is clear: there's no going back from here.

Tonight, I'll decide what kind of monster I want to become.

A floorboard creaks behind me. I whirl around to find Grave leaning against the wall, arms folded over his chest. His expression is unreadable, his eyes hooded by shadows cast by the dim overhead light.

How long has he been standing there? Watching me torture a helpless man?

Heat floods my cheeks. I've never felt so exposed, so ashamed of what I've become. Grave was supposed to keep me grounded, and remind me of the difference between justice and vengeance. Instead, he's enabled my worst impulses. I wonder how he feels, silently watching me apply the torture techniques he taught me.

Anger bubbles in my chest, momentarily overpowering the guilt. "What are you doing here, Grave?" I snap.

"You haven't been returning my phone calls or texts, and you didn't answer the doorbell upstairs." Grave's voice is flat, emotionless. "I was worried."

"So you decided to intrude on my private business?"

"I think this is beyond private business, Fallon. It's a job, remember? Or have you lost touch with reality?"

"I'm delivering justice, Grave. That's what we're here to do, not argue semantics of whether this is for personal or professional enjoyment. Not to argue about who we're doing it for."

"This isn't justice, Fallon." His gaze drifts to Harvey, then back to me, full of disappointment. Harvey is pale, his breathing ragged. The pool of blood around him continues to grow. "It's about to be murder. If you don't let him go soon, he's going to bleed out right here. It's going to be a bitch to clean up, too," he says, eyeing the bloodied basement floor.

The words hit me like a slap. I stare at the knife in my hands, the blood already congealing along the blade, and I know he's right.

My fingers go numb. The knife clatters to the floor.

I stumble back against the wall and slide down until I'm huddled on the cold concrete, staring at what I've done. This man, restrained here for weeks in my condo basement. Deserving of revenge, but maybe not the quantity of torture I've inflicted during his stay. He'll be scarred for life in many places, a permanent memory of the pain and suffering he's inflicted on others. His financial information, on a thumb drive and ready to go to Claudia. His professional life is in ruins; his family, disowned. He'll return to his previous life as a nothing and a no one.

I did good, but at the same time, how did I let things go this far? And how can I undo this to the point where it feels right again?

Grave crouches beside me, resting a hand on my knee. The warmth of his touch steadies me, grounding me in the present. "It's not too late to do the right thing," he says gently.

I swallow hard. Summoning my courage, I lift my gaze to meet his. "Will you help me?"

A flicker of relief softens his eyes. He squeezes my knee. "Always."

Together, we bandage Harvey's wounds to staunch the bleeding. We clean the basement of any evidence, then haul him up to my car and drive into the night.

By the time the sun peeks over the horizon, Harvey is in an emergency room, and I'm back in my condo sleeping next to Aksel. The future is uncertain, but for now, his embrace is enough. I've walked away from the brink, and I won't go back. The revenge business is officially closed.

Chapter 95

AKSEL

Raine sets plates of eggs and toast in front of Fallon and me, her piercing gaze lingering on Fallon.

The TV blares, "Kent Farrington and Isabella Warner, found dead, sunk in the river."

My gut twists with a mix of triumph and dread. "Wow, our Grandmother really doesn't play," I say to Raine.

Raine nods and smirks. "She never has, and she never will."

Fallon pales, clutching her mug. She knows what our Grandmother is capable of, and the lengths she'll go to protect her family. A shiver visibly runs up Fallon's spine, her knuckles whitening around the mug as she trembles. "I'm never going to fit in here either, am I?"

"Of course you are," I say. I try to meet her gaze but she looks down, averting eye contact.

"No. Why would you assume your family is so much better than mine?" Her eyes flash as she blurts out what she's thinking. Raine and I exchange a look.

I reach over, covering her hand with mine. "It's over now. You're part of the family. Grandmother accepts you, accepts us."

"Yeah, I'll just remember not to get on her bad side!"

Raine and Fallon laugh. "Easier said than done, sometimes," says Raine. "Although I think she has a soft spot for you." She beams at Fallon. "I think you're only at risk of her wrath if you try to soil the King family name. Or if you try to pass her pumpkin pie recipe off as your own. That's grounds for homicide, for sure.

The three of us laugh.

Fallon frowns and looks like she wants to say something, but instead, she excuses herself and steps outside.

Ten minutes later, she hasn't returned, and I go searching. I find her in the gardens, sitting on a stone bench with her head bowed. Her shoulders shake with silent sobs.

My heart clenches. I walk over and sit beside her, close enough that our thighs touch. She doesn't pull away this time.

"I'm sorry," she whispers. "I shouldn't have snapped at you or got all awkward. I just got so jealous and envious that you have a grandmother who would move mountains to make things right for you. And I can't even get back at the guys who—"

"You have every right to be angry about your lot in life." I take her hand, relieved when she lets me. "What they did to you—".

"It's in the past." She cuts me off and looks up, her eyes shining with tears. "It still hurts, but I'll work through it. I've spent so much time dwelling on it, resenting them. It's been hard not to when they never received justice. I guess that's why I got so hellbent on exacting revenge on behalf of everyone else. People who stand a chance at actual retribution. People who the system might have failed, but I pledge not to." She pauses and finally meets my gaze. "What matters now is the future. Our future."

A surge of hope ignites in my chest. "You mean that? You really see the two of us having a future, making it in the long-term?"

"I do." A watery smile curves across her lips. "We make a good team, you and I. We survived this together...and we'll survive anything else that comes our way."

"Damn right we will." I pull her into my arms, pressing a fierce kiss to her adorably fiery hair. "I love you, Fallon. So goddamn much. We'll get through this, and whatever else life throws at us, together."

"Together," she echoes, tightening her arms around me.

The battle isn't over, not by a long shot. But with Fallon by my side, I know we'll win. We're survivors. Fighters.

And we have a long, vengeful memory.

Chapter 96

FALLON

My heartbeat drums in my ears as I lead Grave and Aksel down the crumbling alleyway behind O'Malley's Pub. Four figures slouch against the brick wall, bathed in shadows, their faces obscured by the dim light of a single flickering bulb.

But I'd recognize those silhouettes anywhere.

It didn't take much to lure them here, eager to get their hands on me once again. Thrilled that I'd respond to their sick little game of cat-and-mouse on our phones.

My stomach clenches, bile rising in my throat. I grip Aksel's hand, my knuckles turning white. He squeezes back, a silent reassurance. Grave stalks ahead, rage radiating off his massive frame in waves.

I stop before the men who ruined my life and whisper, "Them. They're the ones who raped me."

The figures startle, peering at us through narrowed eyes. "Well, well, if it isn't little Fallon Dempsey." The leader, Mike, pushes off the wall with a sneer. "We've been waiting for you." He glances at Grave and then Aksel. "We weren't expecting you to bring friends, but, you know what?" He shrugs. "The more, the merrier. You know what, fellows? We've been fucking this slut for years and let me tell you, it's something we look forward to every year."

My stomach roils at his words when all of a sudden Grave lunges, his massive fist connecting with Mike's jaw. There's a sickening crack and Mike crumples, out cold.

The other men surge forward, but Grave is faster, a flurry of kicks and punches leaving them broken on the ground.

My breath catches in my throat. They're getting what they deserve, and the violence excites me, although Grave is going a little harder than he probably needs to. I grip Aksel's arm, torn between stopping this and letting Grave continue.

Then Aksel whispers in my ear, "It's okay, Fallon. Let him finish this for you."

Grave straightens, chest heaving, his knuckles dripping red. The alley is eerily silent except for the men's faint groans. I gasp as he pulls a revolver from his pocket and attaches a silencer to the end, screwing it on tightly.

He stands over the first three men one by one, and shoots them at point blank range. And then he wipes off the gun with his gloved hand, puts it in Mike's bare right hand, and angles it toward his right temple, pulling the trigger using Mike's finger.

He turns to me, walks over, and rasps, "It's done."

I stare at the figures littering the ground, unmoving, dead. The knot in my chest loosens. They're gone—never again to hurt anyone.

Gone, like they never existed at all.

Justice, at long last, is mine.

Aksel gathers me close, one arm banded around my waist as I tremble against him. "Fallon. Talk to me."

I swallow hard, my gaze fixed on the carnage. "They're dead. "

"Yes." His voice is rough. "I'm sorry you had to see that. But Grave—we both want you to feel safe. Truly safe, for the first time since..." Since they ruined me.

I nod jerkily. "I know. It's just—a lot to process." My knees wobble, and Aksel scoops me into his arms, carrying me from the gruesome scene.

Cop sirens ring out against the chilly night air. "Come on, let's go," says Aksel, leading me back out of the dark alleyway and into our waiting vehicle. Grave flashes a peace sign as he saunters off in the opposite direction, hoodie on and cap pulled down low over his head.

Chapter 97

FALLON

The morning sun filters through the curtains, warming my skin. I open my eyes and stare at the ceiling, my mind drifting to the events of the past few months. The sale of my business. My bloodlust for vengeance that nearly destroyed me.

A comfortable stillness settles over me. The darkness I've nurtured for so long lifts, revealing a glimmer of light.

I turn to Aksel, his chest rising and falling with each breath, our limbs entangled. His love has been my personal anchor in the churning sea of my emotions. "It's time to embrace a new beginning," I whisper. "One filled with light and positivity." Aksel stirs, blinking open his eyes. A slow smile spreads across his face as he pulls me closer. "I couldn't agree more."

The seed of an idea takes root in my mind. A place of healing and renewal for those who have lost their way. A sanctuary for the soul. I prop myself up on one elbow. "I want to create a wellness sanctuary, Aksel. A place where people can find peace and healing."

Aksel's eyes light up. He kisses my forehead, my cheek, the corner of my mouth. "That's perfect for you. I can see it now—gardens and walking paths, yoga and meditation spaces. You'll be amazing at it. This project is meant for you." Warmth blooms in my chest at his unending support. The darkness that once consumed me fades into the light of new beginnings. Of second chances.

"Will you help me?" I ask softly. "I don't want to do this alone."

"Always," he murmurs. "I'm with you every step of the way."

The light threatens to overwhelm me. But this time, I don't fight it. I let it in.

A smile tugs at my lips as I rest my head on Aksel's chest. The end is in sight. A new beginning awaits. Hand in hand, we step into the light.

Aksel leads me through the garden, a riot of colors under the golden glow of sunset. My heart flutters with each step as I take in the scene around me.

Fairy lights draped between trees. Rose petals scattered across cobblestone paths. The distant sound of a violin playing a sweet, melancholy tune. We stop in front of a white wooden trellis covered in climbing roses in full bloom. Aksel faces me, his hands clasped behind his back, a nervous energy radiating off him. "Fallon." He swallows hard. "These last few months have been the happiest of my life. You brought light to my world when all seemed lost. You saw beyond the darkness that once consumed me and found a glimmer of hope."

He pulls a velvet ring box from his pocket, and flips it open to reveal a diamond solitaire ring nestled on white silk. My heart leaps at the sight. "Fallon, will you marry me again? This time, with your heart fully free and your dreams taking flight? With nobody pressuring me or you. With this being totally at our will and on our timeline..."

Joy and wonder rise in my chest, blotting out the ache of memories too painful to dwell on. I meet his gaze, tears blurring my vision. There's no question in my mind that this is the right answer. For me. For us. "Yes, Aksel. Yes, I will."

The smile that breaks across his face steals my breath. He slips the ring onto my finger, pulls me into his arms, and kisses me soundly as our families erupt into cheers around us. The celebration that follows is filled with laughter and joyful tears, but I have eyes only for Aksel. Our pasts may be filled with shadows, but our future is filled with light. Hand in hand, we step into our new beginning. We dance under the stars, surrounded by the love and support of our families. The fairy lights strung through the trees cast a golden glow over the garden, fireflies flickering in the bushes. Aksel pulls me close, one hand warm on my waist, the other clasping mine. We sway gently to the melody of crickets chirping and leaves rustling in the breeze.

"You're thinking about the sanctuary again, aren't you?" Aksel murmurs, brushing his lips over my temple.

A smile tugs at my lips. "Is it that obvious?" "I can see the wheels turning in that brilliant mind of yours."

His eyes shine with warmth and affection as he meets my gaze. "It's going to be amazing, Fallon. A place of healing and light for those who need it most."

"I want to help people the way you've helped me." Emotion clogs my throat, and I blink back tears. "To give them hope when all seems lost."

Aksel stops, cupping my face in his hands. "You have so much love and compassion in your heart, Fallon. This sanctuary will be a testament to the light you carry within you. It's always been there, too. It's just been waiting to be freed. We'll find a way to honor your darkness alongside it, of course." He brushes a soft kiss over my lips. "And I will be by your side every step of the way."

Joy blossoms in my chest, spreading through my veins like the golden glow of sunset. Here, in Aksel's arms, with our future stretching before us, I've finally found my happy ending.

Epilogue

FALLON

Aksel's hand fists in my hair, dragging my mouth to his own. His kiss is bruising, possessive, marking me as his. Heat ignites in my core, flames licking through my veins.

I moan into his mouth, my hands clutching at his shoulders. He growls, the sound reverberating in his chest where it's pressed against mine. His thigh thrusts between my legs and I grind down on it, desperate for friction.

"You're mine," he rasps, trailing hot kisses down my throat. I tilt my head back with a gasp as his teeth graze my pulse point. "Always have been, always will be."

"Yes," I hiss. My nails dig into his back and he groans. "Yours, Aksel. Only yours."

He lifts me then, my legs wrapping around his waist as he carries me to the bedroom. The door slams behind us, rattling in its frame.

Our clothes are shed in a flurry of impatient hands and clutching lips. When he's poised at my entrance, his gaze locks with mine, his eyes blazing gray fire.

"I love you, Fallon," he says, voice rough with emotion. "I always have."

Tears gather in my eyes and a sob hitches in my throat. He kisses them away, a tender press of lips. My heart swells, overflowing with love for this man.

"I love you too," I whisper. "So much."

With a powerful thrust of his hips, he sinks into me. We moan in unison, the feeling of completeness overwhelming both of us.

He begins to move, slow and deep. I meet each stroke, clinging to him as ecstasy builds. Our hearts beat as one, our souls intertwined. This will never get old.

Nothing will ever tear us apart again.

The next morning, I wake to sunlight streaming through the window and Aksel's arm draped over my waist. I smile, tracing idle patterns over his skin. He stirs, pulling me closer with a contented hum.

"Morning," he rasps, pressing a kiss to the back of my neck.

"Good morning." I roll over to face him, tangling our legs together. "How did you sleep?"

"Best sleep I've had in a long time." His lips quirk up. "Must've been the company."

I laugh, swatting his chest. "Charmer."

"Only for you, darling." He brushes a lock of hair from my face, gaze softening. "I meant what I said last night. I'm yours, forever, Fallon."

"And I'm yours," I whisper. "Always have been, always will be."

The intercom buzzes, startling us from our reverie. I sigh, extricating myself from Aksel's arms.

"I should get that. The contractors are starting renovations on the new wing today."

Aksel groans. "Can't they wait until a decent hour?"

I laugh, pressing a quick kiss to his lips before sliding out of bed. "Duty calls, I'm afraid."

He watches me dress with a pout. "At least promise me dinner tonight? I'm not quite ready to share you with the world again."

"It's a date." I smile, warmth blooming in my chest. "I'll make your favorite."

After a lengthy meeting with the contractors, I feel like progress has been made. So I head out and find Mia in the cafe where we used to grab coffee together frequently before she quit. She glances up from her tea and does a double take, eyes widening.

"Well, look at you! I take it things went well with Aksel?" She grins knowingly.

I blush. "That obvious?"

"It's written all over your face." Mia stands, enveloping me in a hug. "I'm really happy for you both. You deserve this."

I cling to her, blinking back tears. "Thank you. For everything."

Mia has been my rock these past few months, a steady presence amidst the chaos and heartbreak. She believed in me when I didn't believe in myself, and pushed me to follow my dreams. I don't know what I'd do without her.

"Of course." She pulls back, smiling softly. "What are friends for?"

"About that..." I take a deep breath, meeting her gaze. "I was hoping you'd consider being more than a friend. How would you like to be the Director of Operations for the sanctuary?"

Mia stares at me, stunned into silence. I rush to fill it, heart pounding.

"I want to make this official. You've been instrumental in getting the retreat up and running, and your business expertise has been invaluable. You were made for a leadership role like this." I bite my lip. "If you want it, that is." Her comments about enjoying not working with me anymore run through my head, although I have a feeling she was exaggerating.

"Are you serious?" Mia breathes. I nod, and she throws her arms around me again. "Yes! Of course, I'll do it. Thank you so much for this opportunity."

"You're going to be amazing." I grin, excitement bubbling up inside me.

With Mia officially on board, the future of the sanctuary looks brighter than ever.

"By the way," she says, suddenly shy. "I was hoping you might want to be my maid of honor?"

"Oh my gosh, I would *love* to!" I run around to her side of the table and squeeze her with excitement.

Several months later

Aksel wraps me in his arms, nuzzling my neck as we slow dance in the moonlight on the beach behind the sanctuary.

"Can you believe all this is really happening?" I whisper, still stunned by the ring on my finger.

"I knew from the moment I met you that you were the one." Aksel presses a soft kiss to my lips. "You've always been my future, Fallon. Now it's just official."

Warmth floods my chest at his words. "I love you so much."

"And I love you." His eyes shine with emotion. "More than anything in this world. You're my always, my forever."

My heart swells to bursting. After everything we've been through, all the heartbreak and pain, we've finally found our happy ending. Now we just need to get through the ultimate test of a relationship—wedding planning.

I retrieve the familiar shape of a postcard from my stack of mail and smile at the familiar handwriting. Another from Grave. I can't help but grin every time I receive one, both because it's nice he's thinking of me, but also because it confirms he's still alive and kicking.

Wellness retreats are definitely not his thing, so I can't blame him for having moved on from working with me for now. I'm glad we're staying in touch, and that he's taking a break to travel the world while he figures out what's next in store for him. It's probably the only nice thing he's ever done for himself. He sends me postcards from each of his destinations, and they're always cryptic, no doubt to keep the technology conspirators in the dark.

You never know what to expect with that guy, and I'll always love that about him.

Grave may have moved on to his next adventure, but he'll always remain an important part of my life. I know that no matter how far apart we are, our connection will endure. And whenever a new postcard arrives in my mailbox, scrawled with his untidy handwriting, it's a reminder of the man who helped make me who I am today. I'll always be grateful for that.

I attach Grave's latest postcard to my fridge with a magnet next to all the others, like someone might display their toddler's latest artwork, and pick up a brochure from the mail stack. It's emblazoned with a familiar logo and details of a personal empowerment workshop aimed at those who deserve better. I smile and nod to myself. I've left my business in capable hands. A group of ambitious, intelligent women driven to continue the cause. To eradicate each fuckboy one by one, and give other women the tools to do the same.

The dark revenge ops side of my business? I did away with that... on paper. What anyone else might do to keep it alive, I wouldn't know anything about that...

Ready for more? Preorder Bronson and Wren's story on Amazon.

And visit this page for a complimentary bonus scene.

Acknowledgements

To my biggest supporters.

To Anne and Alexia, for both being incredible cheerleaders throughout this process and supporting me through some very challenging times. You are both kind, compassionate and wonderful people and I'm honored to call you two of my closest friends.

To my grandma, M, who chooses to read my books even though the 'naughty parts are hard to miss'.

To my editing and beta teams (especially Jasmine!) who helped me make things make more sense—here's to logistically and anatomically possible spicy scenes ;)

To Fang, who managed to transform a sex wedge into a hybrid laptop desk/cat tower. You are me in cat form.

And to Rossy, my love. You made this more challenging to write. You made this easier to write. You made it a better book, just by being you. PS Please stop inspiring torture scenes xo.

Available for Preorder

- Marco: Hearts of the Underworld (MF mafia romance)

- Sea of Redemption (Blood & Sand series)

- Bronson & Wren's story — title TBC (standalone with interconnected characters and shared world with *F*CKBOYS*)

Standalones

- Ruthless Choices

Blood and Sand (Dark Reverse Harem Mafia Romance)

- Sea of Snakes(Book 1)

- Sea of Sinners(Book 2)

- Sea of Rage (Book 3)

- Sea of Pain(Book 4)

- Sinners, Rage & Pain: The Brixton Trilogy(Books 2, 3 and 4 combined)

- Sea of Demons(Book 5)

- Sea of Redemption (Book 6) – preorder

Billionaire's Takeover Collection

- Irreversible Decision

- Compelling Proposal

- Love Merger

- The Billionaire's Takeover Collection (all 3 of the above!)

Novellas

- Love in a Seedy Motel Room

Sign up for my newsletter herefor the latest on new releases, promos, giveaways and events!

Join me on social media:

Facebook: @heidistarkauthor

Instagram: @heiditstarkauthor

TikTok: @heidistark_author

Twitter: @heidistarkauthr

Websitehttps://heidistarkauthor.com

www.ingramcontent.com/pod-product-compliance
Lightning Source LLC
Chambersburg PA
CBHW061853310726
48972CB00004B/1005